Mary Jane Holmes

The homestead on the hillside

and other tales

Mary Jane Holmes

The homestead on the hillside
and other tales

ISBN/EAN: 9783743367807

Manufactured in Europe, USA, Canada, Australia, Japa

Cover: Foto ©Andreas Hilbeck / pixelio.de

Manufactured and distributed by brebook publishing software (www.brebook.com)

Mary Jane Holmes

The homestead on the hillside

THE

HOMESTEAD ON THE HILLSIDE

And Other Tales.

BY

MRS. MARY J. HOLMES,

AUTHOR OF "TEMPEST AND SUNSHINE," AND "THE ENGLISH ORPHANS,"

NEW YORK:

Carleton, Publisher, 413 Broadway.

M DCCC LXVII.

Entered according to Act of Congress, in the year one thousand eight hundred
and fifty-five,

BY MILLER, ORTON & MULLIGAN,

In the Clerk's Office of the District Court of the Northern District of New York.

TO

MY FRIENDS IN BROCKPORT,

This Volume is

RESPECTFULLY DEDICATED.

CONTENTS.

I.

THE HOMESTEAD ON THE HILLSIDE.

CHAPTER.   PAGE

I. Mrs. Hamilton,   11
II. Lenora and her Mother,   15
III. One Step Toward the Homestead,   19
IV. After the Burial,   25
V. Kate Kirby,   32
VI. Raising the Wind,   40
VII. The Step-mother,   45
VIII. Domestic Life at the Homestead,   57
IX. Lenora and Carrie,   71
X. Darkness,   75
XI. Margaret and her Father,   87
XII. "Carrying out Dear Mr. Hamilton's Plans,"   94
XIII. Retribution,   100
XIV. Finale,   113

II.

RICE CORNER.

I. Introductory,   115
II. The Belle of Rice Corner,   122
III. Monsieur Penoyer,   125
IV. Cousin Emma,   132

CHAPTER.   PAGE

   V. Richard Evelyn and Harley Ashmore, . . 136
  VI. Mike and Sally, ... 147
 VII. The Bride, ... 150

III.

THE GILBERTS; OR, RICE CORNER NUMBER TWO.

    I. The Gilberts, ... 157
   II. Nellie, ... 161
  III. The Haunted House, ... 166
  IV. Jealousy, ... 171
   V. New Relations, ... 174
  VI. Poor, poor Nellie, ... 179

IV.

THE THANKSGIVING PARTY AND ITS CONSEQUENCES.

     I. Night before Thanksgiving, . . . 181
    II. Thanksgiving Day, ... 184
   III. Ada Harcourt, ... 196
   IV. Lucy, ... 199
    V. Uncle Israel, ... 202
   VI. Explanation, ... 205
  VII. A Maneuver, ... 208
VIII. Cousin Berintha and Lucy's Party, . . 213
   IX. A Wedding at St. Luke's, . . . 223
    X. A Surprise, ... 227
   XI. Lizzie, ... 230

V.

THE OLD RED HOUSE AMONG THE MOUNTAINS.

CHAPTER.	PAGE
I. Uncle Amos and Aunt Polly,	237
II. Alice,	238
III. Little Items,	243
IV. Frank,	245
V. Woman's Nature,	249
VI. Squire Herndon and Ira,	251
VII. Alice's Mother,	254
VIII. The Wanderer's Return,	258
IX. Father and Child,	262
X. The Old Man's Death-bed,	264
XI. The Recognition,	266
XII. The Funeral,	268
XIII. "All's well that ends well,"	270

VI.

GLEN'S CREEK.

I. Reminiscences,	273
II. Deacon Wilder,	275
III. Cato and Dillah,	279
IV. The Gortons,	281
V. The New Home,	282
VI. Orianna,	284
VII. Marian,	286
VIII. Robert and Orianna,	290
IX. The Bridal,	296
X. Orianna's Faith,	301
XI. Preparations for a Journey,	305
XII. Ella,	309
XIII. The Death-bed,	314
XIV. The Denouement,	317

A

VII.

THE GABLE-ROOFED HOUSE AT SNOWDON.

CHAPTER.	PAGE
I. Josephine,	323
II. A Peep at the Gable-Roofed House at Snowdon,	333
III. Locust Grove,	336
IV. Delphine and M'Gregor,	342
V. Jimmy,	345
VI. Snowdon,	350
VII. The New House,	354
VIII. Mrs. M'Gregor,	361
IX. Changes,	371

The Homestead on the Hillside

CHAPTER I.

MRS. HAMILTON.

FOR many years the broad, rich acres, and old fash
ioned, massive building known as "The Homestead on
the Hillside," had passed successively from father to son,
until at last it belonged by right of inheritance to Ernest
Hamilton. Neither time nor expense had been spared in
beautifying and embellishing both house and grounds, and
at the time of which we are speaking, there was not, for
miles around, so lovely a spot as was the shady old
homestead.

It stood at some distance from the road, and on the
bright green lawn in front, were many majestic forest
trees, on which had fallen the lights and shadows of more
than a century; and under whose wide-spreading branches
oft, in the olden time, the Indian warrior had paused from
the chase until the noonday heat was passed. Leading
from the street to the house, was a wide, graveled walk
bordered with box, and peeping out from the wilderness
of vines and climbing roses, were the white walls of the
huge building, which was surrounded on all sides by a
double piazza.

Many and hallowed were the associations connected
with that old homestead. On the curiously carved seats
beneath the tall shade trees, were cut the names of some,

who there had lived, and loved, and passed away Through the little gate at the foot of the garden, and just across the brooklet, whose clear waters leaped and laughed in the glad sunshine, and then went dancing away in the woodland below, was a quiet spot, where gracefully the willow tree was bending, where the wild sweet brier was blooming, and where, too, lay sleeping those who once gathered round the hearth-stone and basked in the sunlight which ever seemed resting upon the Homestead on the Hillside.

But a darker day was coming; a night was approaching when a deep gloom would overshadow the homestead and the loved ones within its borders. The servants, ever superstitious, now whispered mysteriously that the spirits of the departed returned nightly to their old accustomed places, and that dusky hands from the graves of the slumbering dead were uplifted, as if to warn the master of the domain of the desolation which was to come. For more than a year the wife of Ernest Hamilton had been dying — slowly, surely dying — and though when the skies were brightest and the sunshine warmest she ever seemed better, each morning's light still revealed some fresh ravage the disease had made, until at last there was no hope, and the anxious group which watched her knew full well that ere long among them would be a vacant chair,, and in the family burying ground an added grave.

One evening Mrs. Hamilton seemed more than usually restless, and requested her daughters to leave her, that she might compose herself to sleep. Scarcely was she alone, when with cat-like tread there glided through the doorway the dark figure of a woman, who advanced toward the bedside, noiselessly as a serpent would steal to his ambush. She was apparently forty-five years of age, and dressed in deep mourning, which seemed to increase

the marble whiteness of her face. Her eyes, large, black, and glittering, fastened themselves upon the invalid with a gaze so intense that Mrs. Hamilton's hand involuntarily
ght the bell-rope, to summon some one else to her
oom.

But ere the bell was rung, a strangely sweet, musical voice fell on her ear, and arrested her movements. "Pardon me for intruding," said the stranger, "and suffer me to introduce myself. I am Mrs. Carter, who not long since removed to the village. I have heard of your illness, and wishing to render you any assistance in my power, I have ventured, unannounced, into your presence, hoping that I at least am not unwelcome.

Mrs. Hamilton had heard of a widow lady, who with an only daughter had' recently removed to the village, which lay at the foot of the long hill on which stood the old homestead. She had heard, too, that Mrs. Carter, though rather singular in some respects, was unusually benevolent, spending much time in visiting the sick and needy, and, as far as possible, ministering to their comfort.

Extending her hand, she said, "I know you by reputation, Mrs. Carter, and feel greatly pleased that you have thought to visit me. Pray be seated."

This last invitation was superfluous, for with the air of a person entirely at home, the lady had seated herself, and as the room was rather warm, she threw back her bonnet, disclosing to view a mass of rich brown hair, which made her look several years younger than she really was. Nothing could be more apparently kind and sincere than were her words of sympathy, nothing more soothing than the sound of her voice; and when she for a moment raised Mrs. Hamilton, while she adjusted her pillows, the sick woman declared that never before had any one done it so gently or so well.

Mrs. Carter was just resuming her seat, when, in the adjoining hall, there was the sound of a heavy tread, and had Mrs. Hamilton been at all suspicious of her visitor, she would have wondered at the flush which deepened on her cheek when the door opened, and Mr. Hamilton stood in their midst. On seeing a stranger, he turned to leave, but his wife immediately introduced him, and seating himself upon the sofa, he remarked, "I have seen you frequently in church, Mrs. Carter, but I believe I have never spoken with you before."

A peculiar expression flitted over her features at these words, an expression which Mr. Hamilton noticed, and which awoke remembrances of something unpleasant, though he could not tell what.

"Where have I seen her before?" thought he, as she bade them good night, promising to come again and stay a longer time. "Where have I seen her before?" and then involuntarily his thoughts went back to the time, years and years ago, when a wild young man in college, he had thoughtlessly trifled with the handsome daughter of his landlady. Even now he seemed to hear her last words, as he bade her farewell: "You may go, Ernest Hamilton, and forget me if you can, but Luella does not so easily forget; and remember, when least you expect it, we shall meet again."

Could this strange being, with honeyed words and winning ways, be that fiery, vindictive girl? Impossible! and satisfied with this conclusion, Mr. Hamilton resumed his evening paper.

CHAPTER II.

LENORA AND HER MOTHER.

FROM the windows of a small, white cottage, at the extremity of Glenwood village, Lenora Carter watched for her mother's return. "She stays long," thought she, "but it bodes success to her plan; though when did she undertake a thing and fail!"

The fall of the gate-latch was heard, and in a moment Mrs. Carter was with her daughter, whose first exclamation was, "What a little eternity you've been gone! Did you renew your early vows to the old man?"

"I've no vows to renew," answered Mrs. Carter, "but I've paved the way well, and got invited to call again."

"Oh, capital!" said Lenora. "It takes you, mother, to do up things, after all; but, really, was Mrs. Hamilton pleased with you?"

"Judging by the pressure of her hand when she bade me good-by, I should say she was," answered Mrs. Carter; and Lenora continued: "Did you see old Moneybags?"

"Lenora, child, you must not speak so disrespectfully of Mr. Hamilton," said Mrs. Carter.

"I beg your pardon," answered Lenora, while her mother continued: "I saw him, but do not think he recognized me; and perhaps it is as well that he should not, until I have made myself indispensable to him and his family."

"Which you will never do with the haughty Mag, I am sure," said Lenora; "but tell me, is the interior of the house as handsome as the exterior?"

"Far more so," was the reply; and Mrs. Carter pro

ceeded to enumerate the many costly articles of furniture she had seen.

She was interrupted by Lenora, who asked, "How long, think you, will the incumbrance live?"

"Lenora," said Mrs. Carter, "you shall not talk so. No one wishes Mrs. Hamilton to die; but if such an afflictive dispensation does occur, I trust we shall all be resigned."

"Oh, I keep forgetting that you are acting the part of a resigned widow; but I, thank fortune, have no part to act, and can say what I please."

"And spoil all our plans, too, by your foolish babbling," interposed Mrs. Carter.

"Let me alone for that," answered Lenora. "I haven't been trained by such a mother for nothing. But, seriously, how is Mrs. Hamilton's health?"

"She is very low, and cannot possibly live long," was the reply.

Here there was a pause in the conversation, during which we will take the opportunity of introducing more fully to our readers the estimable Mrs. Carter and her daughter. Mr. Hamilton was right when he associated the resigned widow with his old flame, Luella Blackburn, whom he had never seriously thought of marrying, though by way of pastime he had frequently teased, tormented, and flattered her. Luella was ambitious, artful, and designing. Wealth and position was the goal at which she aimed. Both of these she knew Ernest Hamilton possessed, and she had felt greatly pleased at his evident preference. When, therefore, at the end of his college course he left her with a few commonplace remarks, such as he would have spoken to any familiar acquaintance, her rage knew no bounds; and in the anger of the moment she resolved, sooner or later, to be revenged upon him.

Years, however, passed on, and a man whom she thought wealthy offered her his hand. She accepted it, and found, too late, that she was wedded to poverty. This aroused the evil of her nature to such an extent, that her husband's life became one of great unhappiness, and four years after Lenora's birth, he left her. Several years later she succeeded in procuring a divorce, although she still retained his name. Recently she had heard of his death, and about the same time, too, she heard that the wife of Ernest Hamilton was dying. Suddenly a wild scheme entered her mind. She would remove to the village of Glenwood, would ingratiate herself into the favor of Mrs. Hamilton, win her confidence and love, and then, when she was dead, the rest she fancied would be an easy matter, for she knew that Mr. Hamilton was weak, and easily flattered.

For several weeks they had been in Glenwood, impatiently waiting an opportunity for making the acquaintance of the Hamiltons. But as neither Margaret nor Carrie called, Lenora became discouraged, and one day exclaimed, "I should like to know what you are going to do. There is no probability of that proud Mag's calling on me. How I hate her, with her big black eyes and hateful ways!"

"Patience, patience," said Mrs. Carter, "I'll manage it; as Mrs. Hamilton is sick, it will be perfectly proper for me to go and see her;" and then was planned the visit which we have described.

"Oh, won't it be grand!" said Lenora, that night, as she sat sipping her tea, "Won't it be grand, if you do succeed, and won't I lord it over Miss Margaret! As for that little white-faced Carrie, she's too insipid for one to trouble herself about, and I dare say thinks you a very nice woman, for how can her Sabbath-schoo' teacher be otherwise;" and a satirical laugh echoed through the room. Suddenly springing up, Lenora glanced at herself in the mirror, and turning to her mother, said, "Did you hear when Walter is expected, and am I so very ugly looking?"

While Mrs. Carter is preparing an answer to the first question, we, for the sake of our readers, will answer the last one. Lenora was a little, dark-looking girl, about eighteen years of age. Her eyes were black, her face was black, and her hair was black, standing out from her head in short, thick curls, which gave to her features a strange, witch-like expression. From her mother she had inherited the same sweet, cooing voice, the same gliding, noiseless footsteps, which had led some of their acquaintance to accuse them of what, in the days of New England witchcraft, would have secured their passport to another world.

Lenora had spoken truthfully when she said that she had not been trained by such a mother for nothing, for whatever of evil appeared in her conduct was more the result of her mother's training than of a naturally bad disposition. At times, her mother petted and caressed her, and again, in a fit of ill humor, drove her from the room, taunting her with the strong resemblance which she bore to the man whom she had once called father! On such occasions, Lenora was never at a loss for words, and the scenes which sometimes occurred were too disgraceful for repetition. On one subject, however, they were united, and that was in their efforts to become inmates of the Homestead on the Hillside. In the accomplishment of this, Lenora had a threefold object: first, it would secure her a luxuriant home; second, she would be thrown in the way of Walter Hamilton, who was about finishing his college course; and last, though not least, it would be such a triumph over Margaret, who, she fancied, treated her with cold indifference.

Long after the hour of midnight was rung from the village clock, the widow and her daughter sat by their fireside, forming plans for the future, and when at last they retired to sleep, it was to dream of funeral processions, bridal favors, step-children, half-sisters, and double connections all around.

CHAPTER III.

ONE STEP TOWARD THE HOMESTEAD.

WEEKS passed on, and so necessary to the comfort of the invalid did the presence of Mrs. Carter become, that at last, by particular request, she took up her abode at the homestead, becoming Mrs. Hamilton's constant nurse and attendant. Lenora, for the time being, was sent to the house of a friend, who lived not far distant. When Margaret Hamilton learned of the arrangement, she opposed it with all her force.

"Send her away, mother," said she one evening; "please send her away, for I cannot endure her presence, with her oily words and silent footsteps. She reminds me of the serpent, who decoyed Eve into eating that apple, and I always feel an attack of the nightmare, whenever I know that her big, black eyes are fastened upon me."

"How differently people see," laughed Carrie, who was

sitting by. "Why, Mag, I always fancy *her* to be in a nightmare when your big eyes light upon her."

"It's because she knows she's guilty," answered Mag, her words and manner warming up with the subject. "Say, mother, won't you send her off? It seems as though a dark shadow falls upon us all the moment she enters the house."

"She is too invaluable a nurse to be discharged for a slight whim," answered Mrs. Hamilton. "Besides, she bears the best of reputations, and I don't see what possible harm can come of her being here."

Margaret sighed, for though she knew full well the "possible harm" which might come of it, she could not tell it to her pale, dying mother; and ere she had time for any answer, the black bombasin dress, white linen collar, and white, smooth face of Widow Carter moved silently into the room. There was a gleam of intense hatred in the dark eyes which for a moment flashed on Margaret's face, and then a soft hand gently stroked the glossy hair of the indignant girl, and in the most musical tones imaginable, a low voice murmured, "Maggie, dear, you look flushed and wearied. Are you quite well?"

"Perfectly so," answered Margaret; and then rising, she left the room, but not until she had heard her mother say, "Dear Mrs. Carter, I am so glad you've come!"

"Is everybody bewitched," thought Mag, as she repaired to her chamber, "father, mother, Carrie, and all? How I wish Walter was here. He always sees things as I do."

Margaret Hamilton was a high spirited, intelligent girl, about nineteen years of age. She was not beautiful, but had you asked for the finest looking girl in all Glenwood, Mag would surely have been pointed out. She was rather above the medium height, and in her whole bearing there was a quiet dignity, which many mistook for hauteur. Naturally frank, affectionate, and kind-hearted, she was, perhaps, a little strong in her prejudices, which, when once satisfactorily formed, could not easily be shaken.

For Mrs. Carter she had conceived a strong dislike, for she believed her to be an artful, hypocritical woman; and now, as she sat by the window in her room, her heart swelled with indignation toward one who had thus usurped her place by her mother's bedside, whom Carrie was learning to confide in, and of whom even the father said, "she is a most excellent woman."

"I will write to Walter," said she, "and tell him to come immediately."

Suiting the action to the word, she drew up her writing desk, and soon a finished letter was lying before her. Ere she had time to fold and direct it, a loud cry from her young brother Willie, summoned her for a few moments from the room, and on her return, she met in the doorway the black bombasin and linen collar.

"Madam," said she, "did you wish for anything?"

"Yes, dear," was the soft answer, which, however, in this case failed to turn away wrath. "Yes, dear, your mother said you knew where there were some fine bits of linen."

"And could not Carrie come for them?" asked Mag.

"Yes, dear, but she looks so delicate that I do not like to send her up these long stairs oftener than is necessary. Haven't you noticed how pale she is getting of late? I shouldn't be at all surprised——;" but before the sentence was finished, the linen was found, and the door closed upon Mrs. Carter.

A new idea had been awakened in Margaret's mind, and for the first time she thought how much her sister ro ally had changed. Carrie, who was four years younger than Margaret, had ever been delicate, and her parents had always feared that not long could they keep her; but though each winter her cough had returned with increased severity, though the veins on her white brow grew more distinct, and her large, blue eyes glowed with unwonted luster, still Margaret had never before dreamed of danger, never thought that soon her sister's voice would be missed, and that Carrie would be gone. But she thought of it now, and laying her head upon the table, wept for a time in silence.

At length, drying her tears, she folded her letter and took it to the post-office. As she was returning home, she was met by a servant, who exclaimed, "Run, Miss Margaret, run; your mother is dying, and Mrs. Carter sent me for you!"

Swift as the mountain chamois, Margaret sped up the long, steep hill, and in a few moments stood within her mother's sick-room. Supported in the arms of Mrs. Carter lay the dying woman, while her eyes, already overshadowed with the mists of coming death, wandered anxiously around the room, as if in quest of some one. The moment Margaret appeared, a satisfied smile broke over her wasted features, and beckoning her daughter to her bedside, she whispered, "Dear Maggie, you did not think I'd die so soon, when you went away."

A burst of tears was Maggie's only answer, as she passionately kissed the cold, white lips, which had never breathed aught to her save words of love and gentleness Far different, however, would have been her reply, had she known the reason of her mother's question. Not long after she had left the house for the office, Mrs. Hamilton had been taken worse, and the physician, who chanced to be present, pronounced her dying. Instantly the alarmed husband summoned together his household, but Mag was missing. No one had seen her; no one knew where she was, until Mrs. Carter, who had been some little time absent from the room, reëntered it, saying, "Margaret had started for the post-office with a letter, when I sent a servant to tell her of her mother's danger, but for some reason she kept on, though I dare say she will soon be back."

As we well know, the substance of this speech was true, though the impression which Mrs. Carter's words conveyed was entirely false. For the advancement of her own cause, she felt that it was necessary to weaken the high estimation in which Mr. Hamilton held his daughter, and she fancied that the mother's death-bed was as fitting a place where to commence operations as she could select.

As Margaret hung over her mother's pillow, the false woman, as if to confirm the assertion she had made, leaned forward and said, "Robin told you, I suppose? I sent him to do so."

Margaret nodded assent, while a deeper gloom fell upon the brow of Mr. Hamilton, who stood with folded arms, watching the advance of the great destroyer. It came at last, and though no perceptible change heralded its approach, there was one fearful spasm, one long drawn sigh, a striving of the eye for one more glimpse of the loved ones gathered near, and then Mrs. Hamilton was dead. On the bosom of Mrs. Carter her life was breathed away, and when all was over, that lady laid gently down her burden, carefully adjusted the tumbled covering, and then stepping to the window, looked out, while the stricken group deplored their loss.

Long and bitterly over their dead they wept, but not on one of that weeping band fell the bolt so crushingly as upon Willie, the youngest of the flock, the child four summers old, who had ever lived in the light of his mother's love. They had told him she would die, but he understood them not, for never before had he looked on death; and now, when to his childish words of love his mother made no answer, most piteously rang out the infantile cry, "Mother, oh, my mother, who'll be my mother now?"

Caressingly, a small, white hand was laid on Willie's yellow curls, but ere the words of love were spoken, Margaret took the little fellow in her arms, and whispered, through her tears, "I'll be your mother, darling."

Willie brushed the tear-drops from his sister's cheek, and laying his fair, round face upon her neck, said, "And who'll be Maggie's mother? Mrs. Carter?"

"Never! never!" answered Mag, while to the glance of hatred and defiance cast upon her, she returned one equally scornful and determined.

Soon from the village there came words of sympathy and offers of assistance; but Mrs. Carter could do everything, and in her blandest tones she declined the services of the neighbors, refusing even to admit them into the presence of Margaret and Carrie, who, she said, were so much exhausted as to be unable to bear the fresh burst of grief which the sight of an old friend would surely produce. So the neighbors went home, and, as the world will ever do, descanted upon the probable result of Mrs. Carter's labors at the homestead. Thus, ere Ernest Hamilton had been three days a widower, many in fancy had wedded him to Mrs Carter, saying that nowhere 'could he find so good a mother for his children.

'And truly she did seem to be indispensable in that house of mourning. 'Twas she who saw that everything was done, quietly and in order; 't was she who so neatly arranged the muslin shroud; 't was her arms that supported the half fainting Carrie when first her eye rested on her mother, coffined for the grave; 't was she who whispered words of comfort to the desolate husband; and she, too, it was, who, on the night when Walter was expected home, *kindly* sat up until past midnight to receive him!

She had read Mag's letter, and by being first to welcome the young man home, she hoped to remove from his mind any prejudice which he might feel for her, and by her bland smiles and gentle words to lure him into the belief that she was perfect, and Margaret uncharitable. Partially she succeeded, too, for when next morning Mag expressed a desire that Mrs. Carter would go home, he replied, "I think you judge her wrongfully; she seems to be a most amiable, kind-hearted woman."

"*Et tu, Brute!*" Mag could have said, but 't was neither the time nor the place, and linking her arm within her brother's, she led him into the adjoining room, where stood their mother's coffin.

CHAPTER IV.

AFTER THE BURIAL.

Across the bright waters of the silvery lake which lay not far from Glenwood village, over the grassy hillside, and down the long, green valley, had floated the notes of the tolling bell. In the Hamilton mansion, sympathizing friends had gathered, and through the crowded parlors a solemn hush had reigned, broken only by the voice of the white-haired man of God, who in trembling tones prayed for the bereaved ones. Over the costly coffin tear-wet faces had bent, and on the marble features of her who slept within it, had been pressed the passionate kisses of a long, a last farewell.

Through the shady garden and across the running brook, whose waters this day murmured more sadly than 't was their wont to do, the funeral train had passed; and in the dark, moist earth, by the side of many other still, pale sleepers, who offered no remonstrance when among them another came, they had buried the departed. From the windows of the homestead lights were gleaming, and in the common sitting-room sat Ernest Hamilton, and by his side his four motherless children. In the stuffed arm chair, sacred for the sake of one who had called it hers, reclined the black bombasin and linen collar of Widow Carter!

She had, as she said, fully intended to return home immediately after the burial, but there were so many little things to be seen to, so much to be done, which Margaret, of course, did not feel like doing, that she decided to stay until after supper, together with Lenora, who had come to the funeral. When supper was over, and there was no longer an excuse for lingering, she found, very greatly to her surprise and chagrin, no doubt, that the clouds which all day had looked dark and angry, were now pouring rain.

"What shall I do?" she exclaimed in great apparent distress; then stepping to the door of the sitting-room, she said, "Maggie, dear, can you lend me an umbrella? It is raining very hard, and I do not wish to go home without one; I will send it back to-morrow." ·

"Certainly," answered Margaret. "Umbrella and overshoes, too;" and rising, she left the room to procure them.

"But you surely are not going out in this storm, "said
Mr. Hamilton; while Carrie, who really liked Mrs. Carter, and felt that it would be more lonely when she was
gone, exclaimed eagerly, "Oh, don't leave us to-night,
Mrs. Carter. Don't."

"Yes, I think I must," was the answer, while Mr. Hamilton continued: "You had better stay; but if you insist
upon going, I will order the carriage, as you must not
walk."

"Rather than put you to all that trouble, I will remain," said Mrs. Carter; and when Mag returned with
two umbrellas and two pair of overshoes, she found the
widow comfortably seated in her mother's arm chair,
while on the stool at her side, sat Lenora looking not unlike
a little imp, with her wild, black face, and short, thick curls.

Walter Hamilton had not had much opportunity for
scanning the face of Mrs. Carter, but now, as she sat
there with the firelight flickering over her features, he
fancied that he could trace marks of the treacherous deceit of which Mag had warned him; and when the full
black eyes rested upon Margaret, he failed not to note
the glance of scorn which flashed from them, and which
changed to a look of affectionate regard the moment she
saw she was observed. "There is something wrong
about her," thought he, "and the next time I am alone
with Mag I'll ask what it is she fears from this woman."

That night, in the solitude of their room, mother and
child communed together as follows: "I do believe,
mother, you are twin sister to the old one himself. Why,
who would have thought, when first you made that
friendly visit, that in five weeks' time both of us would
be snugly ensconced in the best chamber of the homestead?"

"If you think we are in the best chamber, you are

greatly mistaken," replied Mrs. Carter. "Margaret Hamilton has power enough yet to keep us out of that. Didn't she look crest-fallen, though, when she found I was going to stay, notwithstanding her very disinterested offer of umbrellas and overshoes? but I'll pay it all back when I become——"

"Mistress of the house," added Lenora. "Why not speak out plainly? Or are you afraid the walls have ears, and that the devoted Mrs. Carter's speeches would not sound well, repeated? Oh, how sanctimonious you did look, to-day, when you were talking pious to Carrie! I actually had to force a sneeze, to keep from laughing outright, though she, little simpleton, swallowed it all, and I dare say wonders where you keep your wings! But really, mother, I hope you don't intend to pet her so always, for 't would be more than it's worth to see it."

"I guess I know how to manage," returned Mrs. Carter. "There's nothing will win a parent's affection so soon as to pet the children."

"And so I suppose you expect Mr. Hamilton to pet *this* beautiful child!" said Lenora, laughing loudly at the idea, and waltzing back and forth before the mirror.

"Lenora! *behave ;* I will not see you conduct so," said the widow; to which the young lady replied, "Shut your eyes, and then you can't!"

Meantime, an entirely different conversation was going on in another part of the house, where sat Walter Hamilton, with his arm thrown affectionately around Mag, who briefly told of what she feared would result from Mrs. Carter's intimacy at their house.

"Impossible!" said the young man, starting to his feet. "Impossible! our father has too much sense to marry again, any way, and much more, to marry one so greatly inferior to our own dear mother."

"I hope it may prove so," answered Mag; "but, with all due respect for our father, *you* know and I know that mother's was the stronger mind, the controlling spirit; and now that she is gone, father will be more easily deceived."

Margaret told the truth; for her mother had possessed a strong intelligent mind, and was greatly the superior of her father, who, as we have before remarked, was rather weak, and easily flattered. Always sincere himself in what he said, he could not believe that other people were aught than what they seemed to be, and thus oftentimes his confidence had been betrayed by those in whom he trusted. As yet, he had, of course, entertained no thought of ever making Mrs. Carter his wife; but her society was agreeable, her words and manner soothing, and when, on the day following the burial, she actually took her departure, bag, baggage, Lenora, and all, he felt how doubly lonely was the old homestead, and wondered why she could not stay. There was room enough, and then Margaret was too young to assume the duties of housekeeper. Other men, in similar circumstances, had hired housekeepers, and why could not he? He would speak to Mag about it that very night. But when evening came, Walter, Carrie, and Willie all were present, and he found no opportunity of seeing Margaret alone; neither did any occur until after Walter had returned to college, which he did the week following his mother's death.

That night the little parlor at the cottage where dwelt the Widow Carter, looked unusually snug and cozy. It was autumn, and as the evenings were rather cool, a cheerful wood fire was blazing on the hearth. Before it stood a tasteful little workstand, near which were seated Lenora and her mother, the one industriously knitting, and the other occasionally touching the strings of her guitar, which was suspended from her neck by a crimson ribbon. On the sideboard stood a fruit dish loaded with red and golden apples, and near it a basket filled with the rich purple grapes.

That day in the street Lenora had met Mr. Hamilton, who asked if her mother would be at home that evening, saying he intended to call for the purpose of settling the bill which he owed her for services rendered to his family in their late affliction.

"When I once get him here, I will keep him as long as possible," said Mrs. Carter; "and, Lenora, child, if he stays late, say till nine o'clock, you had better go quietly to bed."

"Or into the next room, and listen," thought Lenora.

Seven o'clock came, and on the graveled walk there was heard the sound of footsteps, and in a moment Ernest Hamilton stood in the room, shaking the warm hand of the widow, who was delighted to see him, but *so* sorry to find him looking pale and thin! Rejecting a seat in the comfortable rocking-chair, which Lenora pushed toward him, he proceeded at once to business, and taking from his purse fifteen dollars, passed them toward Mrs. Carter, asking if that would remunerate her for the three weeks' services in his family.

But Mrs. Carter thrust them aside, saying, "Sit down, Mr. Hamilton, sit down. I have a great deal to ask you about Maggie and dear Carrie's health."

"And sweet little Willie," chimed in Lenora.

Accordingly, Mr. Hamilton sat down, and so fast did Mrs. Carter talk, that the clock was pointing to half past eight ere he got another chance to offer his bills. Then, with the look of a much injured woman, Mrs. Carter declined the money, saying, "Is it possible, Mr. Hamilton, that you suppose my services can be bought! What I did for your wife, I would do for any one who needed me, though for but few could I entertain the same feelings I did for her. Short as was our acquaintance, she seemed to me like a beloved sister; and now that she is gone, I feel that we have lost an invaluable treasure——"

Here Mrs. Carter broke down entirely, and was obliged to raise her cambric handkerchief to her eyes, while Lenora walked to the window to conceal her emotions, whatever they might have been! When the agitation of the company had somewhat subsided, Mr. Hamilton again insisted, and again Mrs. Carter refused. At last, finding her perfectly inexorable, he proceeded to express his warmest thanks and deepest gratitude for what she had done, saying he should ever feel indebted to her for her great kindness; then, as the clock struck nine, he arose to go, in spite of Mrs. Carter's zealous efforts to detain him longer.

"Call again," said she, as she lighted him to the door; "call again, and we will talk over old times, when we were young, and lived in New Haven!"

Mr. Hamilton started, and looking her full in the face, exclaimed, "Luella Blackburn! It is as I at first suspected; but who would have thought it!"

"Yes,—I am Luella," said Mrs. Carter; "though greatly changed, I trust, from the Luella you once knew, and of whom even I have no very pleasant reminiscences; but call again, and I will tell you of many of your old classmates."

Mr. Hamilton would have gone almost anywhere for the sake of hearing from his classmates, many of whom he greatly esteemed; and as in this case the "anywhere" was only at Widow Carter's, the idea was not altogether distasteful to him, and when he bade her good night, he was under a promise to call again soon. All hopes, however, of procuring her for his housekeeper were given up, for if she resented his offer of payment for what she had already done, she surely would be doubly indignant at his last proposed plan. After becoming convinced of this fact, it is a little strange how suddenly he found that he did not need a housekeeper—that Margaret, who before could not do at all, could now do very well — as well as anybody. And Margaret did do well, both as house-keeper and mother of little Willie, who seemed to have transferred to her the affection he had borne for his mother.

At intervals during the autumn, Mrs. Carter called, al-ways giving a world of good advice, patting Carrie's pale cheek, kissing Willie, and then going away. But as none of her calls were ever returned, they gradually became less frequent, and as the winter advanced, ceased alto-gether; while Margaret, hearing nothing and seeing no-thing, began to forget her fears, and to laugh at them as having been groundless.

———◆———

CHAPTER V.

KATE KIRBY.

THE little brooklet, which danced so merrily by the homestead burial-place, and then flowed on in many graceful turns and evolutions, finally lost itself in a glossy mill-pond, whose waters, when the forest trees were stripped of their foliage, gleamed and twinkled in the smoky autumn light, or lay cold and still beneath the breath of winter. During this season of the year, from the upper windows of the homestead the mill-pond was discernible, together with a small red building which stood upon its banks.

For many years this house had been occupied by Mr. Kirby, who had been a schoolboy with Ernest Hamilton, and who, though naturally intelligent, had never aspired to any higher employment than that of being miller on the farm of his old friend. Three years before our story opens, Mr. Kirby had died, and a stranger had been employed to take his place. Mrs. Kirby, however, was so much attached to her woodland home and its forest scenery, that she still continued to occupy the low red house together with her daughter Kate, who sighed for no better or more elegant home, although rumor whispered that there was in store for her a far more costly dwelling, even the "Homestead on the Hillside."

Currently was it reported, that during Walter Hamilton's vacations, the winding footpath, which followed the course of the streamlet down to the mill-pond, was trodden more frequently than usual. The postmaster's wife, too, had hinted strongly of certain ominous letters from New Haven, which regularly came directed to Kate, when Walter was not at home; so, putting together these two facts, and adding to them the high estimation in which Mrs. Kirby and her daughter were known to be held by the Hamiltons, it was generally conceded that there could be no shadow of doubt concerning the state of affairs between the heir apparent of the old homestead and the daughter of the poor miller.

Kate was a universal favorite, and by nearly all was it thought, that in everything save money she was fully the equal of Walter Hamilton. To a face and form of the most perfect beauty, she added a degree of intelligence and sparkling wit, which, in all the rides, parties, and fêtes given by the young people of Glenwood, caused her society to be chosen in preference to those whose fathers counted their money by thousands.

A few there were who said that Kate's long intimacy with Margaret Hamilton had made her proud; but in the rude dwellings and crazy tenements which skirted the borders of Glenwood village, was many a blind old woman, and many a hoary-headed man, who, in their daily prayers, remembered the beautiful Kate, the "fair forest-flower," who came so oft among them with her sweet young face and gentle words. For Kate, both Margaret and Carrie Hamilton already felt a sisterly affection, while their father smiled graciously upon her, secretly hoping, however, that his son would make a more brilliant match, but resolving not to interfere, if at last his choice should fall upon her.

One afternoon, early in April, as Margaret sat in her chamber, busy upon a piece of needle-work, the door softly opened, and a mass of bright chestnut curls became visible; next appeared the laughing blue eyes; and finally the whole of Kate Kirby bounded into the room, saying, "Good afternoon, Maggie; are you very busy, and wish I hadn't come?"

"I am never too busy to see you," answered Margaret, at the same time pushing toward Kate the little ottoman, on which she always sat when in that room.

Kate took the proffered seat, and throwing aside her bonnet, began with, "Maggie, I want to tell you something, though I don't know as it is quite right to do so; still you may as well hear it from me as any one."

"Do pray tell," answered Mag, "I am dying with curiosity."

So Kate smoothed down her black silk apron, twisted one of her curls into a horridly ugly shape, and commenced

with, " What kind of a woman is that Mrs. Carter, down
in the village ? "

Instantly Margaret's suspicions were roused, and starting as if a serpent had stung her, she exclaimed, " Mrs.
Carter ! is it of her you will tell me ?   She is a most dangerous woman—a woman whom your mother would call
a 'snake in the grass.' "

" Precisely so," answered Kate. " That is just what
mother says of her, and yet nearly all the village are
ready to fall down and worship her."

" Let them, then," said Mag; " I have no objections,
provided they keep their molten calf to themselves. No
one wants her here.   But what is it about her? tell me."

Briefly then Kate told how Mr. Hamilton was, and for
a long time had been, in the habit of spending one evening every week with Mrs. Carter; and that people, not
without good cause, were already pointing her out as the
future mistress of the homestead.

" Never, never ! " cried Mag, vehemently. " Never
shall she come here. She our mother, indeed! It shall
not be, if I can prevent it."

After a little further conversation, Kate departed, leaving
Mag to meditate upon the best means by which to avert
the threatened evil. What Kate had told her was true.
Mr. Hamilton had so many questions to ask concerning his
old classmates, and Mrs. Carter had so much to tell, that,
though they had worked industriously all winter, they
were not through yet; neither would they be until Mrs.
Carter found herself again within the old homestead.

The night following Kate's visit, Mag determined to
speak with her father; but immediately after tea he went
out, saying he should not return until nine o'clock. With
a great effort Mag forced down the angry words which she
felt rising within her, and then seating herself at her work,

she resolved to await his return. Not a word on the sub
ject did she say to Carrie, who retired to her room at
half past eight, as was her usual custom. Alone, now,
Margaret waited. Nine, ten, eleven had been struck,
and then into the sitting-room came Mr. Hamilton, greatly
astonished at finding his daughter there.

"Why, Margaret," said he, "why are you sitting up
so late?"

"If it is late for me, it is late for you," answered Margaret, who, now that the trial had come, felt the awkwardness of the task she had undertaken.

"But I had business," answered Mr. Hamilton; and
Margaret, looking him steadily in the face, asked, "Is
not your business of a nature which equally concerns us
all?"

A momentary flush passed over his features, as he replied, "What do you mean? I do not comprehend."

Hurriedly, and in broken sentences, Margaret told him
what she meant, and then tremblingly she waited for his
answer. Frowning angrily, he spoke to his daughter the
first harsh words which had ever passed his lips toward
either of his children.

"Go to your room, and don't presume to interfere with
me again. I trust I am competent to tend to my own
matters!"

Almost convulsively Margaret's arms closed round her
father's neck, as she said, "Don't speak so to me, father.
You never did before — never would now, but for *her*.
Oh, father, promise me, by the memory of my angel
mother, never to see her again. She is a base, designing
woman."

Mr. Hamilton unwound his daughter's arms from his
neck, and speaking more gently, said, "What proof have

you of that assertion? Give me proof, and I promise to do your bidding."

But Mag had no such proof at hand, and she could only reiterate her suspicions, her belief, which, of course, failed to convince the biased man, who, rising, said, " Your mother confided and trusted in her, so why should not you ? "

The next moment Margaret was alone. For a long time she wept, and it was not until the eastern horizon began to grow gray in the morning twilight, that she laid her head upon her pillow, and forgot in sleep how unhappy she had been. Her words, however, were not without their effect, for when the night came round on which her father was accustomed to pay his weekly visit, he staid at home, spending the whole evening with his daughters, and appearing really gratified at Margaret's efforts to entertain him. But, alas! the chain of the widow was too firmly thrown around him for a daughter's hand alone to sever the fast bound links.

When the next Thursday evening came, Mag was confined to her room by a sick headache, from which she had been suffering all day. As night approached, she frequently asked if her father were below. At last, the front door opened, and she heard his step upon the piazza. Starting up, she hurried to the window, while at the same moment Mr. Hamilton paused, and raising his eyes, saw the white face of his daughter pressed against the window-pane, as she looked imploringly after him ; but there was not enough of power in a single look to deter him, and, wafting her a kiss, he turned away. Sadly Margaret watched him, until he disappeared down the long hill ; then, returning to her couch, she wept bitterly.

Meantime, Mrs. Carter, who had been greatly chagrined at the non-appearance of Mr. Hamilton the week before, was now confidently expecting him. He had not yet asked her to be his wife, and the delay somewhat annoyed both herself and Lenora.

"I declare, mother," said Lenora, "I should suppose you might contrive up something to bring matters to a focus. I think it's perfectly ridiculous to see two old crones, who ought to be trotting their grandchildren, cooing and simpering away at each other, and all for nothing, too."

"Can't you be easy a while longer?" asked Mrs. Carter; "hasn't he said everything he can say, except, 'will you marry me?'"

"A very important question, too," returned Lenora; "and I don't know what business you have to expect anything from him until it is asked."

· "Mr. Hamilton is proud," answered Mrs. Carter—"is afraid of doing anything which might possibly lower him. Now, if by any means I could make him believe that I had received an offer from some one fully if not more than his equal, I think it would settle the matter, and I've decided upon the following plan. I'll write a proposal myself, sign old Judge B——'s name to it, and next time Mr. Hamilton comes, let him surprise me in reading it. Then, as he is such a *dear*, long tried friend, it will be quite proper for me to confide in him, and ask his advice."

Lenora's eyes opened wider, as she exclaimed, "*My gracious!* who, but *you*, would ever have thought of that."

· Accordingly the letter was written, sealed, directed, broken open, laughed over, and laid away in the stand drawer.

"Mr. Hamilton, mother," said Lenora, as half an hour afterward, she ushered that gentleman into the room,

But so wholly absorbed was the black bombasin and linen collar in the contents of an open letter, which she held in her hand, that the words were twice repeated,—"Mr. Hamilton, mother"—ere she raised her eyes! Then coming forward with well-feigned confusion, she apologized for not having observed him before, saying she was sure he would excuse her if he knew the contents of her letter. Of course he wanted to know, and of course she didn't want to tell. He was too polite to urge her, and the conversation soon took another channel.

After a time Lenora left the room, and Mrs. Carter, again speaking of the letter, begged to make a confidant of Mr. Hamilton, and ask his advice. He heard the letter read through, and after a moment's silence, asked, "Do you like him, Mrs. Carter?"

"Why,—no,—I don't think I do," said she, "but then the widow's lot is *so* lonely."

"I know it is," sighed he, while through the keyhole of the opposite door came something which sounded very much like a stifled laugh! It was the hour of Ernest Hamilton's temptation, and but for the remembrance of the sad, white face which had gazed so sorrowfully at him from the window, he had fallen. But Maggie's presence seemed with him,—her voice whispered in his ear, "Don't do it, father, don't,"—and he calmly answered that it would be a good match. But he could not, no he could not advise her to marry him; so he qualified what he had said by asking her not to be in a hurry,—to wait awhile. The laugh through the keyhole was changed to a hiss, which Mrs. Carter said must be the wind, although there was not enough stirring to move the rose bushes which grew by the door step!

So much was Mr. Hamilton held in thrall by the widow, that on his way home he hardly knew whether to be glad

or sorry that he had not proposed. If Judge B——
would marry her she surely was good enough for him.
Anon, too, he recalled her hesitation about confessing
that the judge was indifferent to her. Jealousy crept in,
and completed what flattery and intrigue had commenced.
One week from that night Ernest Hamilton and Luella
Carter were engaged, but for appearance's sake, their
marriage was not to take place until the ensuing autumn.

CHAPTER VI.

RAISING THE WIND.

"WHERE are you going now?" asked Mrs. Carter of
her daughter, as she saw her preparing to go out one
afternoon, a few weeks after the engagement.

"Going to raise the wind," was the answer.

"Going to what?" exclaimed Mrs. Carter.

"To raise the wind! Are you deaf?" yelled Lenora.

"Raise the wind!" repeated Mrs. Carter; "what do
you mean?"

"Mean what I say," said Lenora; and closing the door
after her she left her mother to wonder "what fresh mischief the little torment was at."

But she was only going to make a *friendly* call on
Margaret and Carrie, the latter of whom she had heard
was sick.

"Is Miss Hamilton at home?" asked she of the servant girl, who answered her ring, and whom she had
never seen before.

Yes, ma'am; walk in the parlor. What name shall I give her if you please?"

"Miss Carter,—Lenora Carter;" and the servant girl departed, repeating to herself all the way up the stairs, "Miss Carther,—Lenora Carther!"

"Lenora Carter want to see me!" exclaimed Mag, who, together with Kate Kirby, was in her sister's room.

"Yes, ma'am; an' sure 'twas Miss Hampleton she was wishin' to see," said the Irish girl.

"Well, I shall not go down," answered Mag. "Tel' her, Rachel, that I am otherwise engaged."

"Oh, Maggie," said Carrie, "why not see her? I would if I were you."

"Rachel can ask her up here if you wish it," answered Mag, "but I shall leave the room."

"Faith, an' what shall I do?" asked Rachel, who was fresh from "swate Ireland" and felt puzzled to know why a "silk frock and smart bonnet" should not always be welcome.

"Ask her up," answered Kate. "I've never seen her nearer than across the church and have some curiosity —"

A moment after Rachel thrust her head in at the parlor door, saying, "If you please, ma'am, Miss Marget is engaged, and does not want to see you, but Miss Carrie says you may come up there."

"Very well," said Lenora; and tripping after the servant girl, she was soon in Carrie's room.

After retailing nearly all the gossip of which she was mistress, she suddenly turned to Carrie, and said, "Did you know that your father was going to be married?"

"My father going to be married!" said Carrie, opening her blue eyes in astonishment. "My father going to be married! To whom, pray?"

"To a lady from the east,—one whom he used to know

and flirt with when he was in college!" was Lenora's grave reply.

"What is her name?" asked Kate.

"Her name? Let me see,— Miss — Blackwell,— Black mer,— *Blackheart*. It sounds the most like Blackheart."

"What a queer name," said Kate, "but tell us what opportunity has Mr. Hamilton had of renewing his early acquaintance with the lady."

"Don't you know he's been east this winter?" asked Lenora.

"Yes, as far as Albany," answered Carrie.

"Well," continued Lenora, "'t was during his eastern trip that the matter was settled; but pray don't repeat it from me, except it be to Maggie, who, I dare say, will feel glad to be relieved of her heavy responsibilities;—but as I live, Carrie, you are crying! What is the matter?"

But Carrie made no answer, and for a time wept on in silence. She could not endure the thought that another would so soon take the place of her lost mother in the household and in the affections of her father. There was, besides, something exceedingly annoying in the manner of her who communicated the intelligence, and secretly Carrie felt glad that the dreaded, "Miss Blackheart" had, of course, no Lenora to bring with her!

"Do you know all this to be true?" asked Kate.

"Perfectly true," said Lenora. "We have friends living in the vicinity of the lady, and there can be no mistake, except indeed in the name, which I am not sure is right!"

Then hastily kissing Carrie, the little hussy went away, very well satisfied with her afternoon's call. As soon as she was out of hearing Margaret entered her sister's room, and on noticing Carrie's flushed cheek and red eyes, in-

quired the cause. Immediately Kate told her what Lenora had said, but instead of weeping as Carrie had done,
she betrayed no emotion whatever.

"Why, Maggie, ain't you sorry?" asked Carrie.

"No, I am glad," returned Mag. "I've seen all along
that sooner or later father would make himself ridiculous,
and I'd rather he'd marry forty women from the east,
than one woman not far from here whom I know."

All that afternoon Mag tripped with unwonted gayety
about the house. A weight was lifted from her heart,
for in her estimation, any one whom her father would
marry was preferable to Mrs. Carter.

*   *   *   *   *   *

Oh, how the widow scolded the daughter, and how the
daughter laughed at the widow, when she related the particulars of her call.

"Lenora, what could have possessed you to tell such a
lie?" said Mrs. Carter.

"Not so fast, mother mine," answered Lenora.
"'Twasn't a lie. Mr. Hamilton *is* engaged to a lady
from the east. He *did* flirt with her in his younger days;
and, pray, didn't he have to come east when he called to
inquire after his beloved classmates, and ended by getting
checkmated! Besides I think you ought to thank me
for turning the channel of gossip in another direction,
for now you will be saved from all impertinent questions
and remarks."

This mode of reasoning failed to convince the widow,
who felt quite willing that people should know of her
flattering prospects; and when, a few days after, Mrs.
Dr. Otis told her that Mrs. Kimball said that Polly Lar-
kins said, that her hired girl told her, that Mrs Kirby's

hired girl told her, that she overheard Miss Kate telling her mother, that Lenora Carter said that Mr. Hamilton was going to be married to her mother's intimate friend, Mrs. Carter would have denied the whole, and probably divulged her own secret, had not Lenora, who chanced to be present, declared, with the coolest effrontery, that 'twas all true—that her mother had promised to stand up with them; and so folks would find it to be if they did not die of curiosity before autumn!

Lenora, child, how can you talk so?" asked the dis tressed lady, as the door closed upon her visitor.

Lenora went off into fits of explosive laughter, bounding up and down like an India rubber ball, and at last condescended to say, "I know what I'm about. Do you want Mag Hamilton breaking up the match, as she surely would do, between this and autumn, if she knew it?"

"And what can she do?" asked Mrs. Carter.

"Why, returned Lenora, "can't she write to the place you came from, if, indeed, such a spot can be found, for I believe you sometimes book yourself from one town and sometimes from another? But depend upon it, you had better take my advice and keep still, and in the denouément which follows, *I* alone shall be blamed for a slight stretch of truth which you can easily excuse, as "one of *dear* Lenora's silly, childish freaks!"

Upon second thoughts Mrs. Carter concluded to follow her daughter's advice, and the next time Mr. Hamilton called, she laughingly told the story which Lenora had set afloat, saying, by way of excuse, that the dear girl did not like to hear her mother joked on the subject of matrimony, and had turned the attention of people another way.

Mr. Hamilton hardly relished this, and half wished, mayhap, as, indeed, gentlemen generally do in similar circumstances, that the little "objection" in the shape of Lenora, had never had existence, or at least had never called the widow mother!

* * *

CHAPTER VII.

THE STEP-MOTHER.

RAPIDLY the summer was passing away, and as autumn drew near, the wise gossips of Glenwood began to whisper that the lady from the east was in danger of being supplanted in her rights by the widow, whose house Mr. Hamilton was known to visit two or three times each week. But Lenora had always some plausible story on hand. "Mother and the lady had been *so* intimate — in fact more than once rocked in the same cradle — and 't was no wonder Mr. Hamilton came often to a place where he could hear so much about her."

So when business again took Mr. Hamilton to Albany, suspicion was wholly lulled, and Walter, on his return from college, was told by Mag that her fears concerning Mrs. Carter were groundless. During the spring, Carrie had been confined to her bed, but now she seemed much better, and after Walter had been at home awhile, he proposed that he and his sisters should take a traveling excursion, going first to Saratoga, thence to Lake Champlain and Montreal, and returning home by way of Canada and the Falls. This plan Mr. Hamilton warmly seconded, and when Carrie asked if he would not feel lonely, he answered, "Oh, no; Willie and I will do very well while you are gone."

"But who will stay with Willie evenings, when you are away?" asked Mag, looking her father steadily in the face.

Mr. Hamilton colored slightly, but after a moment, replied: "I shall spend my evenings at home."

"'Twill be what he hasn't done for many a week," thought Mag, as she again busied herself with her preparations.

The morning came, at last, on which our travelers were to leave. Kate Kirby had been invited to accompany them, but her mother would not consent. "It would give people too much chance for talk," she said; so Kate was obliged to content herself with going as far as the depot, and watching, until out of sight, the car which bore them away.

Upon the piazza stood the little group, awaiting the arrival of the carriage, which was to convey them to the station. Mr. Hamilton seemed unusually gloomy, and with folded arms paced up and down the long piazza, rarely speaking or noticing any one.

"Are you sorry we are going, father?" asked Carrie, going up to him. "If you are, I will gladly stay with you."

Mr. Hamilton paused, and pushing back the fair hair from his daughter's white brow, he kissed her tenderly, saying, "No, Carrie; I want you to go. The journey will do you good, for you are getting too much the look your poor mother used to wear."

Why thought he then of Carrie's mother? Was it because he knew that ere his child returned to him, another would be in that mother's place? Anon, Margaret came near, and motioning Carrie away, Mr. Hamilton took his other daughter's hand, and led her to the end of the piazza, where could easily be seen the little grave-yard, and tall white monument pointing toward the bright blue sky, where dwelt the one whose grave that costly marble marked.

Pointing out the spot to Margaret, he said, "Tell me truly, Maggie, did you love your father or your mother best?"

Mag looked wonderingly at him a moment, and then replied, "While mother lived, I loved her more than you, but now that she is dead, I think of and love you as both father and mother."

"And will you always love me thus?" asked he.

"Always," was Mag's reply, as she looked curiously in her father's face, and thinking that he had not said what he intended to when first he drew her there.

Just then the carriage drove up, and after a few good-bys and parting words, Ernest Hamilton's children were gone, and he was left alone.

"Why didn't I tell her, as I intended to?" thought he. "Is it because I fear her,— fear my own child? No, it cannot be,— and yet there is that in her eye which sometimes makes me quail, and which, if necessary, would keep at bay a dozen step-mothers. But neither she, nor either one of them, has ought to dread from Mrs. Carter, whose presence will, I think, be of great benefit to us all, and whose gentle manners, I trust, will tend to soften Mag!"

Meantime his children were discussing and wondering at the strange mood of their father. Walter, however, took no part in the conversation. He had lived longer than his sisters,— had seen more of human nature, and had his own suspicions with regard to what would take place during their absence; but he could not spoil all Margaret's happiness by telling her his thoughts, so he kept them to himself, secretly resolving to make the best of whatever might occur, and to advise Mag to do the same.

Now for a time we leave them, and take a look into the cottage of Widow Carter, where, one September morning, about three weeks after the departure of the Hamiltons, preparations were making for some great event. In the kitchen a servant girl was busily at work, while in the parlor Lenora was talking and the widow was listening.

"Oh, mother," said Lenora, "isn't it so nice that they went away just now? But won't Mag look daggers at us, when she comes home and finds us in quiet possession, and is told to call you *mother!*"

"I never expect her to do that," answered Mrs. Carter. "The most I can hope for is that she will call me Mrs. Hamilton."

"Now really, mother, if I were in Mag's place, I wouldn't please you enough to say Mrs. Hamilton; I'd always call you Mrs. Carter," said Lenora.

"How absurd," was the reply; and Lenora continued: "I know it's absurd, but I'd do it; though if she does, I, as the dutiful child of a most worthy parent, shall feel compelled to resent the insult by calling her father *Mr. Carter!*"

By this time Mrs. Carter was needed in the kitchen; so, leaving Lenora, who at once was the pest and torment of her mother's life, we will go into the village and see what effect the approaching nuptials were producing. It was now generally known that the "lady from the east" who had been "rocked in Mrs. Carter's cradle," was none other than Mrs. Carter herself, and many were the reproving looks which the people had cast toward Lenora for the trick she had put upon them. The little hussy only laughed at them good humoredly, telling them they were angry because she had cheated them out of five months' gossip, and that if her mother could have had her way, she would have sent the news to the Herald and had it inserted under the head of "Awful Catastrophe!" Thus Mrs. Carter was exonerated from all blame; but many a wise old lady shook her head, saying, "How strange that so fine a woman as Mrs. Carter should have such a reprobate of a daughter."

When this remark came to Lenora's ears, she cut numerous flourishes, which ended in the upsetting of a bowl of starch on her mother's new black silk; then dancing before the highly indignant lady, she said, "Perhaps if they knew what a scapegrace you represent my father to have been, and how you whipped me once to make me say I saw him strike you, when I never did, they would wonder 'at my being as good as I am."

Mrs. Carter was too furious to venture a verbal reply; so seizing the starch bowl, she hurled it with the remainder of the contents at the head of the little vixen, who, with an elastic bound, not entirely unlike a summerset, dodged the missile, which passed on and fell upon the hearth rug.

This is but one of a series of similar scenes, which occurred between the widow and her child before the happy day arrived, when, in the presence of a select few of the villagers, Luella Carter was transformed into Luella Hamilton. The ceremony was scarcely over, when Mr. Hamilton, who for a few days had been rather indisposed, complained of feeling sick. Immediately Lenora, with a sidelong glance at her mother, exclaimed, "What, sick of your bargain so quick? It's sooner, even, than *I* thought 't would be, and I'm sure I'm capable of judging."

"Dear Lenora," said Mrs. Carter, turning toward one

of her neighbors, "she has such a flow of spirits, that I am afraid Mr. Hamilton will find her troublesome.

"Don't be alarmed, mother; he'll never think of me when you are around," was Lenora's reply, in which Mrs. Carter saw more than one meaning.

That evening the bridal party repaired to the homestead, where, at Mr. Hamilton's request, Mrs. Kirby was waiting to receive them. Willie had been told by the servants that his mother was coming home that night, and, with the trusting faith of childhood, he had drawn a chair to the window from which he could see his mother's grave; and there for more than an hour he watched for the first indications of her coming, saying, occasionally, "Oh, I wish she'd come. Willie's so sorry here."

At last growing weary and discouraged, he turned away and said, "No ma 'll never come home again; Maggie said she wouldn't."

Upon the carriage road which wound from the street to the house, there was the sound of coming wheels, and Rachel, seizing Willie, bore him to the front door, exclaiming, "An' faith, Willie, don't you see her? That's your mother, honey, with the black gown."

But Willie saw only the wild eyes of Lenora, who caught him in her arms, overwhelming him with caresses. "Let me go, Leno," said he "I want to see my ma. Where is she?"

A smile of scorn curled Lenora's lips, as she released him, and leading him toward her mother, she said, "There she is; there's your ma. Now hold up your head and make a bow."

Willie's lip quivered, his eyes filled with tears, and hiding his face in his apron, he sobbed, "I want my own ma,—the one they shut up in a big black box. Where is she, Leno?

Mr. Hamilton took Willie on his knee, and tried to ex plain to him, how that now his own mother was dead, he had got a new one, who would love him and be kind to him. Then putting him down, he said, "Go, my son, and speak to her, won't you?"

Willie advanced rather cautiously toward the black silk figure, which reached out its hand, saying, "Dear Willie, you'll love me a little, won't you?"

"Yes, if you are good to me," was the answer, which made the new step-mother mentally exclaim, "A young rebel, I know," while Lenora, bending between the two, whispered emphatically, "She *shall* be good to you!"

And soon, in due order, the servants were presented to their new mistress. Some were disposed to like her, others eyed her askance, and old Polly Pepper, the black cook, who had been in the family ever since Mr. Hamilton's first marriage, returned her salutation rather gruffly, and then, stalking back to the kitchen, muttered to those who followed her, "I don't like her face no how; she looks just like the milk-snakes, when they stick their heads in at the door."

"But you knew how she looked before," said Lucy, the chambermaid.

"I know it," returned Polly; "but when she was here nussin', I never noticed *her*, more'n I would any on you; for who'd of thought that Mr. Hamilton would marry her, when he knows, or or'to know, that nusses ain't fust cut, no how; and you may depend on't, things ain't a goin' to be here as they used to be."

Here Rachel started up, and related the circumstance of Margaret's refusing to see "that little evil-eyed lookin' varmint, with curls almost like Polly's."

Lucy, too, suddenly remembered something which she had seen, or heard, or made up, so that Mrs. Carter had not been an hour in the coveted homestead ere there was mutiny against her afloat in the kitchen; "But," said Aunt Polly, "I 'vises you all to be civil till she sasses you fust!"

*   *   *   *   *   *

"My dear, what room can Lenora have for her own?" asked Mrs, Hamilton, as we must now call her, the morning following her marriage.

"Why, really, I don't know," answered the husband; "you must suit yourselves with regard to that."

"Yes; but I'd rather you'd select, and then no one can blame me," was the answer.

"Choose any room you please, except the one which Mag and Carrie now occupy, and rest assured you shall not be blamed," said Mr. Hamilton.

The night before, Lenora had appropriated to herself the best chamber, but the room was so large and so far distant from any one, and the windows and fireboard rattled so, that she felt afraid, and did not care to repeat her experiment.

"I 'clar for 't!" said Polly, when she heard of it, "Gone right into the best bed, where even Miss Margaret never goes! What are we all comin' to? Tell her, Luce, the story of the ghosts, and I'll be bound she'll make herself scarce in them rooms!"

"Tell her yourself," said Lucy; and when, after breakfast, Lenora, anxious to spy out everything, appeared in the kitchen, Aunt Polly called out, "Did you hear anything last night, Miss Lenora?"

"Why, yes—I heard the windows rattle," was the answer; and Aunt Polly, with an ominous shake of the head, continued: "There's more than windows rattle, I guess. Didn't you see nothin', all white and corpse-like, go a whizzin' and rappin' by your bed ? "

"Why, no," said Lenora; "what do you mean ? "

So Polly told her of the ghosts and goblins which nightly ranged the two chambers, over the front and back parlors. Lenora said nothing, but she secretly resolved not to venture again after dark into the haunted portion of the house. But where should she sleep? That was now the important question. Adjoining the sitting-room was a pleasant, cozy little place, which Margaret called her music-room. In it she kept her piano, her music-stand, books, and several fine plants, besides numerous other little conveniences. At the end of this room was a large closet, where, at different seasons of the year, Mag hung away the articles of clothing which she and her sister did not need.

Toward this place Lenora turned her eyes; for, besides being unusually pleasant, it was also very near her mother, whose sleeping-room joined, though it did not communicate with it. Accordingly, before noon the piano was removed to the parlor; the plants were placed, some on the piazza, and some in the sitting-room window, while Margaret and Carrie's dresses were removed to the closet of their room, which chanced to be a trifle too small to hold them all conveniently; so they were crowded one above the other, and left for "the girls to see to when they came home!"

In perfect horror Aunt Polly looked on, regretting for once the ghost story which she had told.

"Why don't you take the chamber jinin' the young ladies? that ain't haunted," said she, when they sent for her to help move the piano. "Miss Margaret won't thank you for scatterin' her things."

"You've nothing to do with Lenora," said Mrs. Hamilton; "you've only to attend to your own matters."

"Wonder then what I'm up here for a h'istin' this pianner," muttered Polly. "This ain't my matters, sartin'."

When Mr. Hamilton came in to dinner, he was shown the little room with its single bed, tiny bureau, silken lounge and easy chair, of which the last two were Mag's especial property.

"All very nice," said he, "but where is Mag's piano?"

"In the parlor," answered his wife. "People often ask for music, and it is more convenient to have it there, than to come across the hall and through the sitting-room."

Mr. Hamilton said nothing, but he secretly wished Mag's rights had not been invaded quite so soon. His wife must have guessed as much; for, laying her hand on his, she, with the utmost deference, offered to undo all she had done, if it did not please him.

"Certainly not — certainly not; it does please me," said he; while Polly, who stood on the cellar stairs listening, exclaimed, "What a fool a woman can make of a man!"

Three days after Mr. Hamilton's marriage, he received a letter from Walter, saying that they would be at home on the Thursday night following. Willie was in ecstasies, for though, as yet, he liked his new mother tolerably well, he still loved Maggie better; and the thought of seeing her again made him wild with delight. All day long on Thursday he sat in the doorway, listening for the shrill cry of the train which was to bring her home.

"Don't you love Maggie?" said he to Lenora, who chanced to pass him.

"Don't I love Maggie? No, I don't; neither does she love me," was the answer

Willie was puzzled to know why any one should not like Mag; but his confidence in her was not at all shaken, and when, soon after sunset, Lenora cried, "There, they've come," he rushed to the door, and was soon in the arms of his sister-mother. Pressing his lips to hers, he said, "Did you know I'd got a new mother? Mrs. Carter and Leno — they are in there," pointing toward the parlor.

Instantly Mag dropped him. It was the first intimation of her father's marriage which she had received, and reeling backward, she would have fallen, had not Walter supported her. Quickly rallying, she advanced toward her father, who came to meet her, and whose hand trembled in her grasp. After greeting each of his children, he turned to present them to *his wife*, wisely taking Carrie first. She was not prejudiced, like Mag, and returned her step-mother's salutation with something like affection, for which Lenora rewarded her by terming her a 'little simpleton.'

But Mag—she who had warned her father against that woman — she who on her knees had begged him not to marry her—she had no word of welcome, and when Mrs. Hamilton offered her hand, she affected not to see it, though, with the most frigid politeness, she said, "Good evening, madam; this is, indeed, a surprise!"

"And not a very pleasant one, either, I imagine," whispered Lenora to Carrie.

Walter came last, and though he took the lady's hand, there was something in his manner which plainly said, she was not wanted there. Tea was now announced, and Mag bit her lip when she saw her accustomed seat occupied by another.

Feigning to recollect herself, Mrs. Hamilton, in the

blandest tones, said, "Perhaps, dear Maggie, you would prefer this seat?"

"Of course not," said Mag; while Lenora thought to herself, "And if she does, I wonder what good it will do?"

That young lady, however, made no remarks, for Walter Hamilton's searching eyes were upon her and kept her silent. After tea, Walter said, "Come, Mag, I have not heard your piano in a long time. Give us some music."

Mag arose to comply with his wishes, but ere she had reached the door, Mrs. Hamilton, gently detained her, saying, "Maggie, dear, Lenora has always slept near me, and as I knew you would not object, if you were here, I took the liberty to remove your piano to the parlor, and to fit this up for Lenora's sleeping room. See—" and she threw open the door, disclosing the metamorphose, while Willie, who began to get an inkling of matters, and who always called the piazza "out doors," chimed in, "And they throw'd your little trees out doors, too!"

Mag stood for a moment, mute with astonishment; then, thinking she could not "do the subject justice," she turned silently away. A roguish smile from Walter met her eye, but she did not laugh, until, with Carrie, she repaired to her own room, and tried to put something in the closet. Then coming upon the pile of extra clothes, she exclaimed, "What in the world! Here's all our winter clothing, and, as I live, five dresses crammed upon one nail! We'll have to move to the barn, next!"

This was too much, and sitting down, Mag cried and laughed alternately.

CHAPTER VIII.

DOMESTIC LIFE AT THE HOMESTEAD.

For a few weeks after Margaret's return, matters at the homestead glided on smoothly enough, but at the end of that time Mrs. Hamilton began to reveal her real character. Carrie's journey had not been as beneficial as her father had hoped it would be, and as the days grew colder, she complained of extreme languor and a severe pain in her side, and at last kept her room entirely, notwithstanding the numerous hints from her step-mother, that it was no small trouble to carry so many dishes up and down stairs three times a day.

Mrs. Hamilton was naturally very stirring and active, and in spite of her remarkable skill in nursing, she felt exceedingly annoyed when any of her own family were ill. She fancied, too, that Carrie was feigning all her bad feelings, and that she would be much better if she exerted herself more. Accordingly, one afternoon when Mag was gone, she repaired to Carrie's room, giving vent to her opinion as follows: "Carrie," said she, (she now dropped the *dear*, when Mr. Hamilton was not by,) "Carrie, I shouldn't suppose you'd ever expect to get well, so long as you stay moped up here all day. You ought to come down stairs, and stir round more."

"Oh, I should be so glad if I could," answered Carrie.

"Could!" repeated Mrs. Hamilton; "you could if you would. Now, it's my opinion that you complain altogether too much, and fancy you are a great deal worse than you really are, when all you want is exercise. A short walk on the piazza, and a little fresh air, each morning, would soon cure you."

C*

"I know fresh air does me good," said Carrie; "but walking makes my side ache so hard, and makes me cough so, that Maggie thinks I'd better not."

Mag, quoted as authority, exasperated Mrs. Hamilton, who replied, rather sharply, "Fudge on Mag's old-maid-ish whims! I know that any one who eats as much as you do, can't be so very weak!"

"I don't eat half you send me," said poor Carrie, beginning to cry at her mother's unkind remarks; "Willie most always comes up here and eats with me."

"For mercy's sake, mother, let the child have what she wants to eat, for 'tisn't long she'll need it," said Lenora, suddenly appearing in the room.

"Lenora, go right down; you are not wanted here," said Mrs. Hamilton.

"Neither are you, I fancy," was Lenora's reply, as she coolly seated herself on the foot of Carrie's bed, while her mother continued: "Really, Carrie, you must try and come down to your meals, for you have no idea how much it hinders the work, to bring them up here. Polly isn't good for anything until she has conjured up something extra for your breakfast, and then they break so many dishes!"

"I'll try to come down to-morrow," said Carrie, meekly; and, as the door bell just then rang, Mrs. Hamilton departed, leaving her with Lenora, whose first exclamation was, "If I were in your place, Carrie, I wouldn't eat anything, and die quick."

"I don't want to die," said Carrie; and Lenora, clapping her hands together, replied, "Why, you poor little innocent, who supposed you did? Nobody wants to die, not even *I*, good as I am; but I should expect to, if I had the consumption.'

"Lenora, have I got the consumption?" asked Carrie

fixing her eyes with mournful earnestness upon her companion, who thoughtlessly replied : "To be sure you have. They say one lung is entirely gone, and the other nearly so."

Wearily the sick girl turned upon her side ; and, resting her dimpled cheek upon her hand, she said, softly, "Go away now, Lenora ; I want to be alone."

Lenora complied; and when Margaret returned from the village, she found her sister lying in the same position in which Lenora had left her, with her fair hair falling over her face, which it hid from view.

"Are you asleep, Carrie ? " said Mag; but Carrie made no answer, and there was something so still and motionless in her repose, that Mag went up to her, and pushing back from her face the long silken hair, saw that she had fainted.

The excitement of her step-mother's visit, added to the startling news which Lenora had told her, were too much for her weak nerves, and for a time she remained insensible. At length, rousing herself, she looked dreamily around, saying, "Was it a dream, Maggie—all a dream?"

"Was what a dream, love? " said Margaret, supporting her sister's head upon her bosom.

Suddenly Carrie remembered the whole, but she resolved not to tell of her step-mother's visit, though she earnestly desired to know if what Lenora had told her were true. Raising herself, so that she could see Margaret's face, she said, "Maggie, is there no hope for me ; and do the physicians say I must die ? "

"Why, what do you mean ? I never knew that they said so," answered Mag ; and then with breathless indignation she listened, while Carrie told her what Lenora had said. "I'll see that she doesn't get in here again," said Margaret. "I know she made more than half of that up; for, though the physicians say your lungs are very much diseased, they have never said that you could not recover."

The next morning, greatly to Mag's astonishment, Carrie insisted upon going down to breakfast.

"Why, you must not do it; you are not able," said Mag. But Carrie was determined; and, wrapping herself in her thick shawl, she slowly descended the stairs, though the cold air in the long hall made her shiver.

"Carrie, dear, you are better this morning, and there is quite a rosy flush on your cheek," said Mrs. Hamilton, rising to meet her. (*Mr.* Hamilton, be it remembered, was present.) But Carrie shrank instinctively from her step-mother's advances, and took her seat by the side of her father.

After breakfast, Mag remembered that she had an errand in the village, and Carrie, who felt too weary to return immediately to her room, said she would wait below until her sister returned. Mag had been gone but a few moments, when Mrs. Hamilton, opening the outer door, called to Lenora, saying, "Come and take a few turns on the piazza with Carrie. The air is bracing this morning, and will do her good."

Willie, who was present, cried out, "No — Carrie is sick; she can't walk—Maggie said she couldn't," and he grasped his sister's hand to hold her. With a not very gentle jerk, Mrs. Hamilton pulled him off, while Lenora, who came bobbing and bounding into the room, took Carrie's arm, saying, "Oh yes, I'll walk with you; shall we have a hop, skip, or jump?"

"Don't, don't!" said Carrie, holding back; "I can't walk fast, Lenora," and actuated by some sudden impulse of kindness, Lenora conformed her steps to those of the invalid. Twice they walked up and down the piazza, and were about turning for the third time, when Carrie, clasping her hand over her side, exclaimed, "No, no;.I can't go again."

Little Willie, who fancied that his sister was being hurt, sprang toward Lenora, saying, "Leno, you mustn't hurt Carrie. Let her go; she's sick."

And now to the scene of action came Dame Hamilton, and seizing her young step-son, she tore him away from Lenora, administering, at the same time, a bit of a motherly shake. Willie's blood was up, and in return he dealt her blow, for which she rewarded him by another shake, and by tying him to the table.

That Lenora was not all bad, was shown by the unselfish affection she ever manifested for Willie, although her untimely interference between him and her mother oftentimes made matters worse. Thus, on the occasion of which we have been speaking, Mrs. Hamilton had scarcely left the room ere Lenora released Willie from his confinement, thereby giving him the impression that his mother alone was to blame. Fortunately, however, Margaret's judgment was better, and though she felt justly indignant at the cruelty practiced upon poor Carrie, she could not uphold Willie in striking his mother. Calling him to her room, she talked to him until he was wholly softened, and offered, of his own accord, to go and say he was sorry, provided Maggie would accompany him as far as the door of the sitting-room, where his mother would probably be found. Accordingly, Mag descended the stairs with him, and meeting Lenora in the hall, said, "Is she in the sitting-room?"

"Is *she* in the sitting room?" repeated Lenora, "and pray who may *she* be?" then quick as thought she added, "Oh, yes, I know. She is in there telling HE!"

Lenora was right in her conjecture, for Mrs. Hamilton,

greatly enraged at Willie's presumption in striking her, and still more provoked at him for untying himself, as she supposed he had, was laying before her husband quite an aggravated case of assault and battery.

In the midst of her argument Willie entered the room, with tear-stained eyes, and without noticing the presence of his father, went directly to his mother, and burying his face in her lap, sobbed out, " Willie is sorry he struck you, and will never do so again, if you will forgive him."

In a much gentler tone than she would have assumed had not her husband been present, Mrs. Hamilton replied, " I can forgive you for striking me,. Willie, but what have you to say about untying yourself? "

" I didn't do it," said Willie, " Leno did that."

" Be careful what you say," returned Mrs. Hamilton. " I can't believe Lenora would do so."

Ere Willie had time to repeat his assertion, Lenora, who all the time had been standing by the door, appeared, saying, " you may believe him, for he has never been whipped to make him lie. I did do it, and I would do it again."

" Lenora," said Mr. Hamilton, rather sternly, " you should not interfere in that manner. You will spoil the child."

It was the first time he had presumed to reprove his step-daughter, and as there was nothing on earth which Mrs. Hamilton so much feared as Lenora's tongue, she dreaded the disclosures which farther remark from her husband might call forth. So, assuming an air of great distress, she said, " leave her to me, my dear. She is a strange girl, as I always told you, and no one can man. age her as well as myself." Then kissing Willie in token of forgiveness, she left the room, drawing Lenora after her and whispering fiercely in her ear, " how can you ever expect to succeed with the son, if you show off this way before the father."

With a mocking laugh, Lenora replied, "Pshaw! I gave that up the first time I ever saw him, for of course he thinks me a second edition of Mrs. Carter, minus any improvements. But, he's mistaken; I'm not half as bad as I seem. I'm only what you've made me."

Mrs. Hamilton turned away, thinking that if her daughter could so easily give up Walter Hamilton, *she* would not. She was resolved upon an alliance between him and Lenora. And who ever knew *her* to fail in what she undertook!

She had wrung from her husband the confession, that "he believed there was a sort of childish affection between Walter and Kate Kirby, though 'twas doubtful whether it ever amounted to anything." She had also learned that he was rather averse to the match, and though Lenora had not yet been named as a substitute for Kate, she strove, in many ways, to impress her husband with a sense of her daughter's superior abilities, at the same time taking pains to mortify Margaret by setting Lenora above her.

For this, however, Margaret cared but little, and it was only when her mother ill-treated Willie, which she frequently did, that her spirit was fully roused.

At Mrs. Hamilton's first marriage she had been presented with a handsome glass pitcher, which she of course greatly prized. One day it stood upon the stand in her room, where Willie was also playing with some spools, which Lenora had found and arranged for him. Malta, the pet kitten, was amusing herself by running after the spools, and when at last Willie, becoming tired, laid them on the stand, she sprang toward them, upsetting the pitcher, which was broken in a dozen pieces. On hearing the crash, Mrs. Hamilton hastened toward the room, where the sight of her favorite pitcher in fragments greatly enraged her. Thinking, of course, that Willie had done it, she rudely seized him by the arm, administered a cuff or so, and then dragged him toward the china closet.

As soon as Willie could regain his breath, he screamed, "Oh, ma, don't shut me up; I'll be good; I didn't do it, certain true; kittie knocked it off."

"None of your lies," said Mrs. Hamilton." It's likely kittie knocked it off!"

Lenora, who had seen the whole, and knew that what Willie said was true, was about coming to the rescue, when looking up, she saw Margaret, with dilated nostrils and eyes flashing fire, watching the proceedings of her step-mother.

"He's safe," thought Lenora; "I'll let Mag fire the first gun, and then I'll bring up the rear."

Margaret had never known Willie to tell a lie, and had no reason for thinking he had done so in this instance. Besides, the blows her mother gave him exasperated her, and she stepped forward, just as Mrs. Hamilton was about pushing him into the closet. So engrossed was that lady that she heard not Margaret's approach, until a firm hand was laid upon her shoulder, while Willie was violently wrested from her grasp, and ere she could recover from her astonishment, she herself was pushed into the closet, the door of which was closed and locked against her.

' Bravo, Margaret Hamilton," cried Lenora, "I'm with you now, if I never was before. It serves her right, for Willie told the truth. I was sitting by and saw it all. Keep her in there an hour, will you? It will pay her for the many times she has shut me up for nothing."

Mrs. Hamilton stamped and pushed against the door, while Lenora danced and sung at the top of her voice,

"My dear precious mother got wrathy one day
And seized little Will by the hair;
But when in the closet she'd stow him away,
She herself was pushed headlong in there."

At length the bolt, yielding to the continued pressure of Mrs. Hamilton's body, broke, and out came the termagant, foaming with rage. She dared not molest Margaret, of whose physical powers she had just received such mortifying proof, so she aimed a box at the ears of Lenora. But the lithe little thing dodged it, and with one bound cleared the table which sat in the center of the room, landing safely on the other side; and then, shaking her short, black curls at her mother, she said, "You didn't come it, that time, my darling."

Mr. Hamilton, who chanced to be absent for a few days, was, on his return, regaled with an exaggerated account of the proceeding, his wife ending her discourse by saying—"If you don't do something with your upstart daughter, I'll leave the house; yes, I will."

Mr. Hamilton was cowardly. He was afraid of his wife, and he was afraid of Mag. So he tried to compromise the matter, by promising the one that he surely would see to it, and by asking the other if she were not ashamed. But old Polly didn't let the matter pass so easily. She was greatly shocked at having "such shameful carryin's on in a decent man's house."

"'Clare for't," said she, "I'll give marster a piece of Polly Pepper's mind the fust time I get a lick at him."

In the course of a few days Mr. Hamilton had occasion to go for something into Aunt Polly's dominions. The old lady was ready for him. "Mr. Hampleton," said she, "I've been waitin' to see you this long spell."

"To see me, Polly?" said he; "what do you want?"

"What I wants is this," answered Polly, dropping into a chair. "I want to know what this house is a comin' to, with such bedivilment in it as there's been since madam came here with that little black-headed, ugly-favored, ill-begotten, Satan-possessed, shoulder-unj'inted young-one of her'n. It's been nothin' but a rowdedow the whole time, and you hain't grit enough to stop it. Madam boxes Willie, and undertakes to shet him up for a lie he never told; Miss Margaret interferes jest as she or'to, takes Willie away, and shets up madam; while that ill-marnered Lenora jumps and screeches loud enough to wake the dead. Madam busts the door down, and pitches into the varmint, who jumps spang over a four foot table, which Lord knows *I* never could have done in my spryest days."

"But how can I help all this?" asked Mr. Hamilton.

"Help it?" returned Polly, "You needn't have got into the fire in the fust place. I hain't lived fifty odd year for nothin', and though I hain't no larnin', I know too much to heave myself away on the fust nussin' wo man that comes along."

"Stop, Polly; you must not speak so of Mrs Hamilton," said Mr. Hamilton; while Polly continued: "And I wouldn't nuther, if she could hold a candle to the t'other one; but she can't. You'd no business to marry a second time, even if you didn't marry a nuss; neither has any man, who's got growd up gals, and a faithful critter like Polly in the kitchen. Step-mothers don't often do well; particularly them as is sot up by marryin'."

Here Mr. Hamilton, who did not like to hear so much truth, left the kitchen, while Aunt Polly said to herself, "I've gin it to him good, this time."

Lenora, who always happened to be near when she was

talked about, had overheard the whole, and repeated it to her mother. Accordingly, that very afternoon word came to the kitchen that Mrs. Hamilton wished to see Polly.

"Reckon she'll find this child ain't afeard on her," said Polly, as she wiped the flour from her face and repaired to Mrs. Hamilton's room.

"Polly," began that lady, with a very grave face, "Lenora tells me that you have been talking very disrespectfully to Mr. Hamilton."

"In the name of the Lord, can't he fight his own battles?" interrupted Polly. "I only tried to show him that he was henpecked, and he is."

"It isn't of him alone I would speak," resumed Mrs. Hamilton, with stately gravity; "you spoke insultingly of me, and as I make it a practice never to keep a servant after they get insolent, I have ——"

"For the dear Lord's sake," again interrupted Polly, "I 'spect we's the fust servants you ever had."

"Good!" said a voice from some quarter, and Mrs. Hamilton continued: "I have sent for you to give you twenty-four hours' warning to leave this house."

"I shan't budge an inch until marster says so," said Polly. "Wonder who's the best title deed here? Warn't I here long afore you come a nussin' t'other one?"

And Polly went back to the kitchen, secretly fearing that Mr. Hamilton, who she knew was wholly ruled by his wife, would say that she must go. And he did say so, though much against his will. Lenora ran with the decision to Aunt Polly, causing her to drop a loaf of new bread. But the old negress chased her from the cellar with the oven broom, and then stealing by a back staircase to Margaret's room, laid the case before her, acknowledging that she was sorry and asking her young mistress to intercede for her. Margaret stepped to the head of the stairs, and calling to her father, requested him to come for a moment to her room. This he was more ready to do, as he had no suspicion why he was sent for, but on seeing old Polly, he half resolved to turn back. Margaret, however, led him into the room, and then entreated him not to send away one who had served him so long, and so faithfully.

Polly, too, joined in with her tears and prayers, saying, "She was an old black fool any way, and let her tongue get the better on her, though she didn't mean to say more than was true, and reckoned she hadn't."

In his heart Mr. Hamilton wished to revoke what he had said, but dread of the explosive storm which he knew would surely follow, made him irresolute, until Carrie said, "Father, the first person of whom I have any definite recollection is Aunt Polly, and I shall be so lonesome if she goes away. For my sake let her stay, at least until I am dead."

This decided the matter. "She *shall* stay," said Mr. Hamilton, and Aunt Polly, highly elated, returned to the kitchen with the news. Lenora, who seemed to be everywhere at once, overheard it, and, bent on mischief, ran with it to her mother. In the meantime, Mr. Hamilton wished, yet dreaded, to go down, and finally, mentally cursing himself for his weakness, asked Margaret to accompany him. She was about to comply with his request, when Mrs. Hamilton came up the stairs, furious at her husband, whom she called "a craven coward, led by the nose by all who chose to lead him." Wishing to shut out her noise, Mag closed and bolted the door, and in the hall the modern Xantippe expended her wrath against her husband and his offspring, while poor Mr. Hamilton laid his face in Carrie's lap and wept. Margaret was try ing to devise some means by which to rid herself of her step-mother, when Lenora was heard to exclaim, "shall I pitch her over the stairs, Mag? I will if you say so."

Immediately Mrs. Hamilton's anger took another channel, and turning upon her daughter, she said, "What are you here for, you prating parrot! Didn't you tell me what Aunt Polly said, and haven't you acted in the capacity of reporter ever since?"

"To be sure I did," said Lenora, poising herself on one foot, and whirling around in circles; "but if you thought I did it because I blamed Aunt Polly, you are mistaken."

"What did you do it for, then?" said Mrs. Hamilton; and Lenora, giving the finishing touch to her circles by dropping upon the floor, answered, "I like to live in a hurricane — so I told you what I did. Now, if you think it will add at all to the excitement of the present occasion, I'll get an ax for you to split the door down."

"Oh, don't, Lenora," screamed Carrie, from within, to which Lenora responded, "Poor little simple chick bird, I wouldn't harm a hair of your soft head for anything. But there is a *man* in there, or one who passes for a man, that I think would look far more respectable if he'd come out and face the tornado. She's easy to manage when you know how. At least, Mag and I find her so."

Here Mr. Hamilton, ashamed of himself and emboldened, perhaps, by Lenora's words, slipped back the bolt of the door, and walking out, confronted his wife.

"Shall I order pistols and coffee for two?" asked Lenora, swinging herself entirely over the bannister, and dropping like a squirrel on the stair below.

"Is Polly going to stay in this house?" asked Mrs Hamilton.

"She is," was the reply.

"Then I leave to-night," said Mrs. Hamilton.

"Very well, you can go," returned the husband, grow
ing stronger in himself each moment.

Mrs. Hamilton turned away to her own room, where
she remained until supper time, when Lenora asked "if
she had got her chest packed, and where they should
direct their letters!" Neither Margaret nor her father
could refrain from laughter. Mrs. Hamilton, too, who
had no notion of leaving the comfortable homestead, and
who thought this as good a time to veer round as any
she would have, also joined in the laugh, saying, "What
a child you are, Lenora!"

Gradually the state of affairs at the homestead was
noised throughout the village, and numerous were the little tea parties where none dared speak above a whisper,
to tell what they had heard, and where each and every
one were bound to the most profound secrecy, for fear
the reports might not be true. At length, however, the
story of the china closet got out, causing Sally Martin to
spend one whole day in retailing the gossip from door to
door. Many, too, suddenly remembered certain suspicious things which they had seen in Mrs. Hamilton, who
was unanimously voted to be a bad woman, and who, of
course, began to be slighted.

The result of this was, to increase the sourness of her
disposition; and life at the homestead would have been
one continuous scene of turmoil, had not Margaret wisely
concluded to treat whatever her step-mother did with silent contempt. Lenora, too, always seemed ready to fill
up all vacant niches, until even Mag acknowledged that
the mother would be unendurable without the daughter.

CHAPTER IX.

LENORA AND CARRIE.

EVER since the day on which Lenora had startled Carrie by informing her of her danger, she had been carefully kept from the room, or allowed only to enter it when Margaret was present. One afternoon, however, early in February, Mag had occasion to go to the village. Lenora, who saw her depart, hastily gathered up her work, and repaired to Carrie's room, saying, as she entered it, "Now, Carrie, we'll have a good time; Mag has gone to see old deaf Peggy, who asks a thousand questions, and will keep her at least two hours, and I am going to entertain you to the best of my ability."

Carrie's cheek flushed, for she felt some misgivings with regard to the nature of Lenora's entertainment; but she knew there was no help for it, so she tried to smile, and said, "I am willing you should stay, Lenora, but you mustn't talk bad things to me, for I can't bear it."

"Bad things!" repeated Lenora, "Who ever heard me talk bad things? What do you mean?"

"I mean," said Carrie, "that you must not talk about your mother, as you sometimes do. It is wicked."

"Why, you dear little thing," answered Lenora, " don't you know that what would be wicked for you, isn't wicked for me?"

"No, I do not know so," answered Carrie; "but I know I wouldn't talk about my mother as you do about yours, for anything."

"Bless your heart," said Lenora, "have n't you sense enough to see that there is a great difference between Mrs. Hamilton 1st, and Mrs. Hamilton 2d? Now, I'm

not naturally bad, and if I had been the daughter of Mrs.
Hamilton 1st, instead of Widow Carter's young-one, why,
I should have been as good as you;—no, not as good as
you, for you don't know enough to be bad,—but as good
as Mag, who, in my opinion, has the right kind of goodness, for all I used to hate her so."

"Hate Margaret!" said Carrie, opening her eyes to
their utmost extent. "What did you hate Margaret
for?"

"Because I didn't know her, I suppose," returned Lenora; "for now I like her well enough—not quite as well
as I do you, perhaps; and yet, when I see you bear
mother's abuse so meekly, I positively hate you for a minute, and ache to box your ears; but when Mag squares
up to her, shuts her in the china closet, and all that, I
want to put my arms right round her neck."

"Why, don't you like your mother?" asked Carrie;
and Lenora replied: "Of course I do; but I know what
she is, and I know she is n't what she sometimes seems.
Why, she'd be anything to suit the circumstances. She
wanted your father, and she assumed the character most
likely to secure him; for, between you and me, he is n't
very smart."

"What did she marry him for, then?" asked Carrie.

"Marry *him!* I hope you don't for a moment suppose
she married *him!*"

"Why, Lenora, *ain't they married?* I thought they
were. Oh, dreadful!" and Carrie started to her feet,
while the perspiration stood thickly on her forehead.

Lenora screamed with delight, saying, "You certainly
have the softest brain I ever saw. Of course the minister
went through with the ceremony; but it was not your
father that mother wanted; it was his house—his money
—his horses—his servants, and his name. Now, may be,

in your simplicity, you have thought that mother came here out of kindness to the motherless children; but I tell you, she would be better satisfied if neither of you had ever been born. I suppose it is wicked in me to say so, but I think she makes me worse than I would otherwise be; for I am not naturally so bad, and I like people much better than I pretend to. Any way, I like you, and *love* little Willie, and always have, since the first time I saw him. Your mother lay in her coffin, and Willie stood by her, caressing her cold cheek, and saying, "Wake up, mamma, it's Willie; don't you know Willie?" I took him in my arms, and vowed to love and shield him from the coming evil; for I knew then, as well as I do now, that what has happened would happen. Mag wasn't there; she didn't see me. If he had, she might have liked me better; now she thinks there is no good in me; and if, when you die, I should feel like shedding tears, and perhaps I shall, it would be just like her to wonder 'what business *I* had to cry — it was none of my funeral!'"

"You do wrong to talk so, Lenora," said Carrie· "but tell me, did you never have any one to love except Willie?"

"Yes," said Lenora; "when I was a child, a little, innocent child, I had a grandmother—my father's mother— who taught me to pray, and told me of God."

"Where is she now?" asked Carrie.

"In heaven," was the answer. "I know she is there, because when she died, there was the same look on her face that there was on your mother's—the same that there will be on yours, when you are dead."

"Never mind," gasped Carrie, who did not care to be so frequently reminded of her mortality, while Lenora continued: "Perhaps you don't know that my father was as mother says, a bad man; though I always loved him dearly, and cried when he went away. We lived with grandmother, and sometimes now, in my dreams, I am a child again, kneeling by grandma's side, in our dear old eastern home, where the sunshine fell so warmly, where the summer birds sang in the old maple trees, and where the long shadows, which I called spirits, came and went over the bright green meadows. But there was a sadder day; a narrow coffin, a black hearse, and a tolling bell, which always wakes me from my sleep, and I find the dream all gone, and nothing left of the little child but the wicked Lenora Carter."

Here the dark girl buried her face in her hands and wept, while Carrie gently smoothed her tangled curls. After a while, as if ashamed of her emotion, Lenora dried· her tears, and Carrie said, "Tell me more of your early life. I like you when you act as you do now."

"There is nothing more to tell but wickedness," answered Lenora. "Grandma died, and I had no one to teach me what was right. About a year after her death, mother wanted to get a divorce from father; and one day she told me that a lawyer was coming to inquire about my father's treatment of her. 'Perhaps,' said she, 'he will ask if you ever saw him strike me, and you must say that you have, a great many times.' 'But I never did,' said I; and then she insisted upon my telling that falsehood, and I refused, until she whipped me, and made me promise to say whatever she wished me to. In this way I was trained to be what I am. Nobody loves me; nobody ever can love me; and sometimes when Mag speaks so kindly to you, and looks so affectionately upon you, I think, what would I not give for some one to love me; and then I go away to cry, and wish I had never been born."

Here Mrs. Hamilton called to her daughter, and, gathering up her work, Lenora left the room just as Margaret entered it, on her return from the village.

CHAPTER X.

DARKNESS.

As the spring opened and the days grew warmer, Carrie's health seemed much improved; and, though she did not leave her room, she was able to sit up nearly all day, busying herself with some light work. Ever hopeful, Margaret hugged to her bosom the delusion which whispered, "she will not die," while even the physician was deceived, and spoke encouragingly of her recovery.

For several months Margaret had thought of visiting her grandmother, who lived in Albany; and as Mr. Hamilton had occasion to visit that city, Carrie urged her to accompany him, saying she was perfectly able to be left alone, and she wished her sister would go, for the trip would do her good.

For some time past, Mrs. Hamilton had seemed exceedingly amiable and affectionate, although her husband appeared greatly depressed, and acted, as Lenora said, "just as though he had been stealing sheep."

" This depression Mag had tried in vain to fathom, and at last fancying that a change of place and scene might do him good, she consented to accompany him, on condition that Kate Kirby would stay with Carrie. At the mention of Kate's name, Mr. Hamilton's eyes instantly went over to his wife, whose face wore the same calm, stony expression, as she answered, " Yes, Maggie, Kate can come."

Accordingly, on the morning when the travelers would start, Kate came up to the homestead, receiving a thousand and one directions about what to do and when to do it, hearing not more than half the injunctions, and promising to comply with every one. Long before the door the carriage waited, while Margaret, lingering in Carrie's room, kissed again and again her sister's pure brow, and gazed into her deep blue eyes, as if she knew that it was the last time. Even when halfway down the stairs, she turned back again to say good-by, this time whispering, " I have half a mind not to go, for something tells me I shall never see you again."

" Oh, Mag," said Carrie, " don't be superstitious. I am a great deal better, and when you come home, you will find me in the parlor."

In the lower hall Mr. Hamilton caressed his little Willie, who begged that he, too, might go. " Don't leave me, Maggie, don't," said he, as Mag came up to say good-by.

Long years after the golden curls which Mag pushed back from Willie's forehead were covered by the dark, moist earth, did she remember her baby-brother's childish farewell, and oft in bitterness of heart she asked, " Why did I go—why leave my loved ones to die alone?"

Just a week after Mag's departure, news was received at the homestead that Walter was coming to Glenwood for a day or two, and on the afternoon of the same day, Kate had occasion to go home. As she was leaving the house, Mrs. Hamilton detained her, while she said, " Miss Kirby, we are all greatly obliged to you for your kindness in staying with Carrie, although your services really are not needed. I understand how matters stand between you and Walter, and as he is to be here to-morrow, you of course will feel some delicacy about remaining; consequently, I release you from all obligations to do so."

Of course there was no demurring to this. Kate's pride was touched; and though Carrie wept, and begged her not to go, she yielded only so far as to stay until the next morning, when, with a promise to call frequently, she left. Lonely and long seemed the hours to poor Carrie; for, though Walter came, he staid but two days, and spent a part of that time at the mill-pond cottage.

The evening after he went away, as Carrie lay, half dozing, thinking of Mag, and counting the weary days which must pass ere her return, she was startled by the sound of Lenora's voice, in the room opposite, the door of which was ajar. Lenora had been absent a few days, and Carrie was about calling to her, when some words spoken by her step-mother arrested her attention, and roused her curiosity. They were, "You think too little of yourself, Lenora. Now, I know there is nothing in the way of your winning Walter, if you choose."

"I should say there was everything in the way," answered Lenora. "In the first place, there is Kate Kirby; and who, after seeing her handsome face, would ever look at such a black, turned-up nose, bristle-headed thing as I am. But I perceive there is some weighty secret on your mind, so what is it? Have Walter and Kate quarreled, or have you told him some falsehood about her?"

"Neither," said Mrs. Hamilton. "What I have to say, concerns your father."

"My father!" interrupted Lenora; "my own father! Oh, is he living?"

"No, I hope not," was the answer; "it is Mr. Hamilton whom I mean."

Instantly Lenora's tone changed, and she replied, "If you please, you need not call that putty-headed man *my* father. He acts too much like a whipped spaniel to suit me, and I really think Carrie ought to be respected for knowing what little she does, while I wonder where Walter, Mag, and Willie got their good sense. But what is it? What have you made Mr. Hamilton do? something ridiculous, of course."

"I've made him make his will," was the answer; while Lenora continued: "Well, what then? What good will that do me?"

"It may do you a great deal of good," said Mrs. Hamilton; "that is, if Walter likes the homestead as I think he does. But I tell you, it was hard work, and I did n't know, one while, but I should have to give it up. However, I succeeded, and he has willed the homestead to Walter, provided he marries you. If not, Walter has nothing, and the homestead comes to *me* and my heirs forever!"

"Heartless old fool!" exclaimed Lenora, while Carrie, too, groaned in sympathy. "And do you suppose he intends to let it go so! Of course not; he'll make another when you don't know it."

"I'll watch him too closely for that," said Mrs. Hamilton; and after a moment Lenora asked, "what made you so anxious for a will? Have you received warning of his sudden demise!"

"How foolish," said Mrs. Hamilton. "Isn't it the easiest thing in the world for me to let Walter know what's in the will, and I fancy that'll bring him to terms, for he likes money, no mistake about that."

"Mr. Hamilton is a bigger fool, and you a worse woman, than I supposed," said Lenora." Do you think I am mean enough to marry Walter under such circumstances? Indeed, I'm not. But how is Carrie? I must go and see her."

She was about leaving the room, when she turned back, saying in a whisper, "mother, mother, her door is wide open, as well as this one, and she must have heard every word!"

"Oh, horror!" exclaimed Mrs. Hamilton; "go in and ascertain the fact, if possible."

It took but one-glance to convince Lenora that Carrie was in possession of the secret. Her cheeks were flushed, her eyes wet with tears; and when Lenora stooped to kiss her, she said, "I know it all, I heard it all."

"Then I hope you feel better," said Mrs. Hamilton, coming forward. "Listeners never hear any good of themselves."

"Particularly if it's Widow Carter who is listened to," suggested Lenora.

Mrs. Hamilton did not reply to this, but continued speaking to Carrie. "If you have learned anything new, you can keep it to yourself. No one has interfered with you, or intends to. Your father has a right to do what he chooses with his own, and I shall see that he exercises that right, too."

So saying, she left the room, while Carrie, again bursting into tears, wept until perfectly exhausted. The next morning she was attacked with bleeding at the lungs, which, in a short time, reduced her so low that the physician spoke doubtfully of her recovery, should the hemorrhage again return. In the course of two or three days she was again attacked; and now, when there was no longer hope of life, her thoughts turned with earnest longings toward her absent father and sister, and once, as the physician was preparing to leave her, she said, "Doctor, tell me truly, can I live twenty-four hours?"

"I think you may," was the answer.

"Then I shall see them, for if you telegraph to-night,

they can come in the morning train. Go yourself and see it done, will you?"

The physician promised that he would, and then left her room. In the hall he met Mrs. Hamilton, who, with the utmost anxiety depicted upon her countenance, said, "Dear Carrie is leaving us, isn't she? I have telegraphed for her father, who will be here in the morning. 'Twas right to do so, was it not?"

"Quite right," answered the physician. "I promised to see to it myself, and was just going to do so."

"Poor child," returned Mrs. Hamilton, "she feels anxious, I suppose. But I have saved you the trouble."

The reader will not, perhaps, be greatly surprised to learn that what Mrs. Hamilton had said was false. She suspected that one reason why Carrie so greatly desired to see her father, was to tell him what she had heard, and beg of him to undo what he had done; and as she feared the effect which the sight and words of his dying child might have upon him, she resolved, if possible, to keep him away until Carrie's voice was hushed in death. Overhearing what had been said by the doctor, she resorted to the stratagem of which we have just spoken. The next morning, however, she ordered a telegram to be dispatched, knowing, full well, that her husband could not reach home until the day following.

Meantime, as the hour for the morning train drew near, Carrie, resting upon pillows, and whiter than the linen which covered them, strained her ears to catch the first sound of the locomotive. At last, far off through an opening among the hills, was heard a rumbling noise, which increased each moment in loudness, until the puffing engine shot out into the long, green valley, and then rolled rapidly up to the depot.

Little Willie had seemed unwell for a few days, but

since his sister's illness he had staid by her almost constantly, gazing half curiously, half timidly into her face,
and asking if she were going to the home where his
mamma lived. She had told him that Margaret was
coming, and when the shrill whistle of the eastern train
sounded through the room, he ran to the window,
whither Lenora had preceded him, and there together
they watched for the coming of the omnibus. A sinister
smile curled the lips of Mrs. Hamilton, who was present,
and who, of course, affected to feel interested.

At last Willie, clapping his hands, exclaimed, "There
'tis! They're coming. That's Maggie's big trunk!"
Then, noticing the glow which his announcement called
up to Carrie's cheek, he said, "she'll make you well,
Carrie, Maggie will. Oh, I'm so glad, and so is Leno."

Nearer and nearer came the omnibus, brighter and
deeper grew the flush on Carrie's face, while little Willie danced up and down with joy.

"It isn't coming here," said Mrs. Hamilton, "it has
gone by," and Carrie's feverish heat was succeeded by an
icy chill.

"Haven't they come, Lenora?" she said.

Lenora shook her head, and Willie, running to his sister, wound his arms around her neck, and for several
minutes the two lone, motherless children wept.

"If Maggie knew how my head ached, she'd come,"
said Willie ; but Carrie thought not of *her* aching head,
nor of the faintness of death which was fast coming on.
One idea alone engrossed her. Her brother;—how would
he be saved from the threatened evil, and her father's
name from dishonor?

At last, Mrs. Hamilton left the room, and Carrie,
speaking to Lenora and one of the villagers who was
present, asked if they, too, would not leave her alone for

a time with Willie. They complied with her request, and then asking her brother to bring her pencil and paper, she hurriedly wrote a few lines to her father, telling him of what she had heard, and entreating him, for her sake, and the sake of the mother with whom she would be when those words met his eye, not to do Walter so great a wrong. "I shall give this to Willie's care," she wrote, in conclusion, "and he will keep it carefully until you come. And now, I bid you a long farewell, my precious father,—my noble Mag,—my darling Walter."

The note was finished, and calling Willie to her, she said, "I am going to die. When Maggie returns I shall be dead and still, like our own dear mother."

"Oh Carrie, Carrie," sobbed the child, "don't leave me till Maggie comes."

There was a footstep on the stairs, and Carrie, without replying to her brother, said quickly, "Take this paper, Willie, and give it to father when he comes; let no one see it,—Lenora, mother, nor any one."

Willie promised compliance, and had but just time to conceal the note in his bosom ere Mrs. Hamilton entered the room, accompanied by the physician, to whom she loudly expressed her regrets that her husband had not come, saying, that she had that morning telegraphed again, although he could not now reach home until the morrow.

"To-morrow I shall never see," said Carrie, faintly. And she spoke truly, too, for even then death was freezing her life-blood with the touch of his icy hand. To the last she seemed conscious of the tiny arms which so fondly encircled her neck; and when the soul had drifted far out on the dark channel of death, the childish words of "Carrie, Carrie, speak once more," roused her, and folding her brother more closely to her bosom, she mur mured, "Willie, darling Willie, our mother is waiting for us both."

Mrs. Hamilton, who stood near, now bent down, and laying her hand on the pale, damp brow, said gently, "Carrie, dear, have you no word of love for this mother?"

There was a visible shudder, an attempt to speak, a low moan, in which the word "Walter" seemed struggling to be spoken; and then death, as if impatient of delay, bore away the spirit, leaving only the form which in life had been most beautiful. Softly Lenora closed over the blue eyes the long, fringed lids, and pushed back from the forehead the sunny tresses which clustered so thickly around it; then, kissing the white lips and leaving on the face of the dead traces of her tears, she lead Willie from the room, soothing him in her arms until he fell asleep.

Elsewhere we have said that for a few days Willie had not seemed well; but so absorbed were all in Carrie's more alarming symptoms, that no one had heeded him, although his cheeks were flushed with fever, and his head was throbbing with pain. He was in the habit of sleeping in his parents' room, and that night his loud breathings and uneasy turnings disturbed and annoyed his mother, who at last called out in harsh tones, "Willie, Willie, for mercy's sake stop that horrid noise! I shall never get sleep this way. I know there's no need of breathing like hat!"

"It chokes me so," sobbed little Willie, "but I'll try."

Then pressing his hands tightly over his mouth, he tried the experiment of holding his breath as long as possible. Hearing no sound from his mother, he thought her asleep, but not venturing to breathe naturally until assured of the fact, he whispered, "Ma, ma, are you asleep?"

. "Asleep! no,—and never shall be, as I see! What do you want?"

"Oh, I want to breathe," said Willie.

"Well, breathe then; who hinders you?" was the reply; and ere the offensive sound again greeted her ear, Mrs. Hamilton was too far gone in slumber to be disturbed.

For two hours Willie lay awake, tossing from side to side, scorched with fever and longing for water to quench his burning thirst. By this time Mrs. Hamilton was again awake; but to his earnest entreaties for water—"just one little drop of water, ma,"—she answered, "William Hamilton, if you don't be still, I'll move your crib into the room where Carrie is, and leave you there alone!"

Unlike many children, Willie had no fears of the cold, white figure which lay so still and motionless upon the parlor sofa. To him it was Carrie, his sister; and many times that day, had he stolen in alone, and laying back the thin muslin which shaded her face, he had looked long upon her;—had laid his hand on her icy cheek, wondering if she knew how cold she was, and if the way which she had gone was so long and dark that he could never find it. To him there was naught to fear in that room of death, and to his mother's threat he answered, eagerly, "Oh, ma, give me some water, just a little bit of water, and you may carry me in there. I ain't afraid, and my breathing wont wake Carrie up;" but before he had finished speaking, his mother was again dozing.

"Won't anybody bring me some water,—Maggie, Carrie,—Leno,—nobody?" murmured poor Willie, as he wet his pillow with tears.

At last he could bear it no longer. He knew where the water-bucket stood, and stepping from his bed, he groped his way down the long stairs to the basement

The spring moon was low in the western horizon, and shining through the curtained window, dimly lighted up the room. The pail was soon reached, and then in his eagerness to drink, he put his lips to the side. Lower, lower, lower it came, until he discovered, alas! that the pail was empty.

"What shall I do? what shall I do?" said he, as he crouched upon the cold hearth-stone.

A new idea entered his mind. The well stood near the outer door; and, quickly pushing back the bolt, he went out, all flushed and feverish as he was, into the chill night air. There was ice upon the curb-stone, but he did not mind it, although his little toes, as they trod upon it, looked red by the pale moonlight. Quickly a cup of the coveted water was drained; then, with careful forethought, he filled it again, and taking it back to his room, crept shivering to bed. Nature was exhausted; and whether he fainted or fell asleep is not known, for never again to consciousness in this world awoke the little boy.

The morning sunlight came softly in at the window, touching his golden curls with a still more golden hue. Sadly over him Lenora bent, saying, "Willie, Willie! wake up, Willie. Don't you know me?"

Greatly Mrs. Hamilton marveled whence came the cup of water which stood there, as if reproaching her for her cruelty. But the delirious words of the dreamer soon told her all. "Maggie, Maggie," he said, "rub my feet; they feel like Carrie's face. The curb-stone was cold, but the water was so good. Give me more, more; mother won't care, for I got it myself, and tried not to breathe, so she could sleep;—and Carrie, too, is dead—dead."

Lenora fiercely grasped her mother's arm, and said,

"How could you refuse him water, and sleep while he got it himself?"

But Mrs. Hamilton needed not that her daughter should accuse her. Willie had been her favorite, and the tears which she dropped upon his pillow were genuine. The physician who was called, pronounced his disease to be scarlet fever, saying that its violence was greatly increased by a severe cold which he had taken.

"You have killed him, mother; you have killed him!" said Lenora.

Twenty-four hours had passed since, with straining ear, Carrie had listened for the morning train, and again down the valley floated the smoke of the engine, and over the blue hills echoed the loud scream of the locomotive; but no sound could awaken the fair young sleeper, though Willie started, and throwing up his hands, one of which, the right one, was firmly clenched, murmured, "Maggie, Maggie."

Ten minutes more, and Margaret was there, weeping in agony over the inanimate form of her sister, and almost shrieking as she saw Willie's wild eye, and heard his incoherent words. Terrible to Mr. Hamilton was this coming home. Like one who walks in sleep, he went from room to room, kissing the burning brow of one child, and then, while the hot breath was yet warm upon his lips, pressing them to the cold face of the other.

All day Margaret sat by her dying brother, praying that he might be spared until Walter came. Her prayer was answered; for at nightfall Walter was with them. Half an hour after his return, Willie died; but ere his right hand dropped lifeless by his side, he held it up to view, saying, "Father,—give it to nobody but father."

After a moment, Margaret, taking within hers the fast

stiffening hand, gently unclosed the fingers, and found
the crumpled piece of paper on which Carrie had written
to her father.

CHAPTER XI.

MARGARET AND HER FATHER.

'Twas midnight — midnight after the burial. In the
library of the old homestead sat its owner, his arms resting upon the table, and his face reclining upon his arms.
Sadly was he reviewing the dreary past, since first among
them death had been, bearing away his wife, the wife of
his first, only love. Now, by her grave there was an
other, on which the pale moonbeams and the chill night-
dews were falling, but they could not disturb the rest of
the two, who, side by side, in the same coffin lay sleeping,
and for whom the father's tears were falling fast, and the
father's heart was bleeding.

"Desolate, desolate—all is desolate," said the stricken
man. "Would that I, too, were asleep with my lost
ones!"

There was a rustling sound near him, a footfall, and an
arm was thrown lovingly around his neck. Margaret's
tears were on his cheek, and Margaret's voice whispered
in his ear, "Dear father, we must love each other better,
now."

Margaret had not retired, and on passing through
the hall, had discovered the light gleaming through the
crevice of the library door. Knowing that her father
must be there, she had come in to comfort him. Long
the father and child wept together, and then Margaret,

drying her tears, said, "It is right — all right; mother has two, and you have two; and though the dead will never return to us, we, in God's good time, will return to them?"

"Yes, soon, very soon, shall I go," said Mr. Hamilton. "I am weary, weary, Margaret; my life is one scene of bitterness. Oh, why, why was I left to do it?"

Margaret knew well to what he referred, but she made no answer; and after he had become somewhat composed, thinking this a good opportunity for broaching the subject which had so troubled Carrie's dying moments, she drew from her bosom the soiled piece of paper, and placing it in his hands, watched him while he read. The moan of anguish which came from his lips as he finished, made her repent of her act, and, springing to his side, she exclaimed, "Forgive me, father; I ought not to have done it now. You have enough to bear."

"It is right, my child," said Mr. Hamilton; "for, after the wound had slightly healed, I might have wavered. Not that I love Walter less; but, fool that I am, I fear her who has made me the cowardly wretch you see!"

"Rouse yourself, then," answered Margaret. "Shake off her chain, and be free."

"I cannot, I cannot," said he. "But this I will do. I will make another will. I always intended to do so, and Walter shall not be wronged." Then rising, he hurriedly paced the room, saying, "Walter shall not be wronged; no, no—Walter shall not be wronged."

After a time he resumed his former seat, and taking his daughter's hand in his, he told her of all he had suffered, of the power which his wife held over him, and which he was too weak to shake off. This last he did not say, but Margaret knew it, and it prevented her from giving him other consolation than that of assuring him of her own unchanged, undying love.

The morning twilight was streaming through the closed hutters ere the conference ended; and then Mr. Hamilton, kissing his daughter, dismissed her from the room but as she was leaving him, he called her back, saying, "Don't tell Walter; he would despise me; but he shan't be wronged—no, he shan't be wronged."

Six weeks from that night, Margaret stood, with her brother, watching her father as the light from his eyes went out, and the tones of his voice ceased forever. Grief for the loss of his children, and remorse for the blight which he had brought upon his household, had undermined his constitution, never strong; and when a prevailing fever settled upon him, it found an easy prey. In ten days' time, Margaret and Walter alone were left of the happy band, who, two years before, had gathered around the fireside of the old homestead.

Loudly Mrs. Hamilton deplored her loss, shutting herself up in her room, and refusing to see any one, saying that she could not be comforted, and it was of no use trying! Lenora, however, managed to find an opportunity of whispering to her that it would hardly be advisable to commit suicide, since she had got the homestead left, and everything else for which she had married Mr. Hamilton.

"Lenora, how can you thus trifle with my feelings? "Don't you see that my trouble is killing me?" said the greatly distressed lady.

"I don't apprehend any such catastrophe as that," answered Lenora. "You found the weeds of Widow Carter easy enough to wear, and those of Widow Hamilton won't hurt you any worse, I imagine."

"Lenora," groaned Mrs. Hamilton, "may you never

know what it is to be the unhappy mother of such a child !"

" Amen !" was Lenora's fervent response, as she glided from the room.

For three days the body of Mr. Hamilton lay upon the marble center-table in the darkened parlor. Up and down the long stair-cases, and through the silent rooms, the servants moved noiselessly. Down in the basement Aunt Polly forgot her wonted skill in cooking, and in a broken rocking-chair swayed to and fro, brushing the big tears from her dusky face, and lamenting the loss of one who seemed to her "just like a brother, only a little nigher."

In the chamber above, where, six weeks before, Carrie had died, sat Margaret,—not weeping; she could not do that;—her grief was too great, and the fountain of her tears seemed scorched and dried; but, with white, com pressed lips, and hands tightly clasped, she thought of the past and of the cheerless future. Occasionally through the doorway there came a small, dark figure; a pair of slender arms were thrown around her neck, and a voice murmured in her ear, " Poor, poor Maggie." The next moment the figure would be gone, and in the hall below Lenora would be heard singing snatches of some song, either to provoke her mother, or to make the astonished servants believe that she was really heartless and hard-ened.

What Walter suffered could not be expressed. Hour after hour, from the sun's rising till its going down, he sat by his father's coflin, unmindful of the many who came in to look at the dead, and then gazing pitifully upon the face of the living, walked away, whispering mysteriously of insanity. Near *him* Lenora dared not come, though through the open door she watched him, and oftentimes he met the glance of her wild, black eyes, fixed upon him with a mournful interest; then, as if moved by some spirit of evil, she would turn away, and seeking her mother's room, would mock at that lady's grief, advising her not to make too much of an effort.

At last there came a change. In the yard there was the sound of many feet, and in the house the hum of many voices, all low and subdued. Again in the village of Glenwood was heard the sound of the tolling bell; again through the garden and over the running water brook moved the long procession to the grave-yard; and soon Ernest Hamilton lay quietly sleeping by the side of his wife and children.

For some time after the funeral, nothing was said concerning the will, and Margaret had almost forgotten the existence of one, when one day as she was passing the library door, her mother appeared, and asked her to enter. She did so, and found there her brother, whose face, besides the marks of recent sorrow which it wore, now seemed anxious and expectant.

"Maggie, dear," said the oily-tongued woman, "I have sent for you to hear read your beloved father's last will and testament."

A deep flush mounted to Margaret's face, as she repeated, somewhat inquiringly, "Father's last will and testament?"

"Yes, dear," answered her mother, "his last will and testament. He made it several weeks ago, even before poor Carrie died; and as Walter is now the eldest and only son, I think it quite proper that he should read it."

So saying, she passed toward Walter a sealed package, which he nervously opened; while Margaret, going to his side, looked over his shoulder, as he read.

It is impossible to describe the look of mingled surprise, anger, and mortification which Mrs. Hamilton's face assumed, as she heard the will which her husband had made four weeks before his death, and in which Walter shared equally with his sister. Her first impulse was to destroy it; and springing forward, she attempted to snatch it from Walter's hand, but was prevented by Margaret, who caught her arm and forcibly held her back.

Angrily confronting her step-daughter, Mrs. Hamilton demanded, "What does this mean?" to which Mag replied, "It means, madam, that for once you are foiled. You coaxed my father into making a will, the thought of which ought to make you blush. Carrie overheard you telling Lenora, and when she found that she must die, she wrote it on a piece of paper, and consigned it to Willie's care!"

Several times Mrs. Hamilton essayed to speak, but the words died away in her throat, until, at last, summoning all her boldness, she said, in a hoarse whisper, "But the homestead is mine — mine forever, and we'll see how delightful I can make your home!"

"I'll save you that trouble, madam," said Walter, rising and advancing toward the door. "Neither my sister nor myself will remain beneath the same roof which shelters you. To-morrow we leave, knowing well that vengeance belongeth to One higher than we."

All the remainder of that day Walter and Margaret spent in devising some plan for the future, deciding at last that Margaret should, on the morrow, go for a time to Mrs. Kirby's, while Walter returned to the city. The next morning, however, Walter did not appear in the breakfast parlor, and when Margaret, alarmed at his absence, repaired to his room, she found him unable to rise. The fever with which his father had died, and which was still prevailing in the village, had fastened upon him, and for many days was his life despaired of. The ablest phy sicians were called, but few of them gave any hope to the pale, weeping sister, who, with untiring love, kept her vigils by her brother's bedside.

When he was first taken ill, he had manifested great uneasiness at his step-mother's presence, and when at last he became delirious, he no longer concealed his feelings, and if she entered the room, he would shriek, "Take her away from me! Take her away! Chain her in the cellar; — anywhere out of my sight."

Again he would speak of Kate, and entreat that she might come to him. "I have nothing left but her and Margaret," he would say; "and why does she stay away?"
. Three different times had Margaret sent to her young friend, urging her to come, and still she tarried, while Margaret marveled greatly at the delay. She did not know that the girl whom she had told to go, had received different directions from Mrs. Hamilton, and that each day beneath her mother's roof Kate Kirby wept and prayed that Walter might not die.

One night he seemed to be dying, and gathered in the room were many sympathizing friends and neighbors. Without, 't was pitchy dark. The rain fell in torrents, and the wind, which had increased in violence since the setting of the sun, howled mournfully about the windows, as if waiting to bear the soul company in its upward flight. Many times had Walter attempted to speak. At last he succeeded, and the word which fell from his lips, was "Kate!"

Lenora, who had that day accidentally learned of her mother's commands with regard to Miss Kirby, now glided noiselessly from the room, and in a moment was alone in the fearful storm, which she did not heed. Lightly bounding over the swollen brook, she ran on until the mill-pond cottage was reached. It was midnight, and its inmates were asleep, but they awoke at the sound of Lenora's voice.

"Walter is dying," said she to Kate, "and would see you once more. Come quickly."

Hastily dressing herself, Kate went forth with the strange girl, who spoke not a word until Walter's room was reached. Feebly the sick man wound his arms around Kate's neck, exclaiming, "My own, my beautiful Kate, I knew you would come. I am better now,—I shall live!" and as if there was indeed something life-giving in her very presence and the sound of her voice, Walter from that hour grew better; and in three week's time he, together with Margaret, left his childhood's home, once so dear, but now darkened by the presence of her who watched their departure with joy, exulting in the thought that she was mistress of all she surveyed.

Walter, who was studying law in the city about twenty miles distant, resolved to return thither immediately, and after some consultation with his sister it was determined that both she and Kate should accompany him. Accordingly, a few mornings after they left the homestead, there was a quiet bridal at the mill-pond cottage; after which, Walter Hamilton bore away to his city home his sister and his bride, the beautiful Kate.

CHAPTER XII.

"CARRYING OUT DEAR MR. HAMILTON'S PLANS."

ONE morning about ten days after the departure of Walter, the good people of Glenwood were greatly surprised at the unusual confusion which seemed to pervade the homestead. The blinds were taken off, windows taken out, carpets taken up, and where so lately physicians, clergymen and death had officiated, were now seen carpenters, masons and other workmen. Many were the surmises as to the cause of all this; and one old lady, more curious than the rest, determined upon a friendly call, to ascertain, if possible, what was going on.

She found Mrs. Hamilton with her sleeves rolled up and her hair tucked under a black cap, consulting with a carpenter about enlarging her bedroom and adding to it a bathing room. Being received but coldly by the mistress of the house, she descended to the basement, where she was told by Aunt Polly that "the blinds were going to be repainted, an addition built, the house turned wrong side out, and Cain raised generally."

"It's a burning shame," said Aunt Polly, warmed up by her subject and the hot oven into which she was thrusting loaves of bread and pies. "It's a burning shame,— a tearin' down and a goin' on this way, and marster not cold in his grave. Miss Lenora, with all her badness, says it's disgraceful, but he might ha' know'd it. *I* did. I know'd it the fust time she came here a nussin'. I don't see what got into him to have her. Polly Pepper, without any larnin', never would ha' done such a thing," continued she, as the door closed upon her visitor, who was anxious to carry the gossip back to the village.

It was even as Aunt Polly had said. Mrs. Hamilton, who possessed a strong propensity for pulling down and building up, and who would have made an excellent carpenter, had long had an earnest desire for improving the homestead; and now that there was no one to prevent her, she went to work with a right good will, saying to Lenora, who remonstrated with her upon the impropriety of her conduct, that "she was merely carrying out dear Mr

Hamilton's plans," who had proposed making these chan ges before his death.

"Dear Mr. Hamilton!" repeated Lenora, "very dear has he become to you, all at once. I think if you had always manifested a little more affection for him and his, they might not have been where they now are."

"Seems to me you take a different text from what you did some months ago," said Mrs. Hamilton; "but perhaps you don't remember the time?"

"I remember it well," answered Lenora, "and quite likely, with your training, I should do the same again. We were poor, and I wished for a more elegant home. I fancied that Margaret Hamilton was proud and had slighted me, and I longed for revenge; but when I knew her, I liked her better, and when I saw that she was not to be trampled down by you or me, my hatred of her turned to admiration. The silly man, who has paid the penalty of his weakness, I always despised; but when I saw how fast the gray hairs thickened on his head, and how care-worn and bowed down he grew, I pitied him, for I knew that his heart was breaking. Willie I truly, unselfishly loved; and I am charitable enough to think that even *you* loved *him*, but it was through your neglect that he died, and for his death you will answer. Carrie was gentle and trusting, but weak, like her father. I do not think you killed her, for she was dying when we came here, but you put the crowning act of wickedness to your life, when you compelled a man, shattered in body and intellect, to write a will which disinherited his only son; but on that point you are baffled. To be sure, you've got the homestead, and for decency's sake I think I'd wait awhile longer, ere I commenced tearing down and building up."

Lenora's words had no effect, whatever, upon her mother who still kept on with her plans, treating with silent contempt the remarks of the neighbors, or wishing, perhaps, that they would attend to their own business, just as she was attending to hers! Day after day the work went on. Scaffoldings were raised—paper and plastering torn off—boards were seasoning in the sun — shingles lying upon the ground — ladders raised against the wall; and all this while the two new graves showed not a single blade of grass, and the earth upon them looked black and fresh as it did when first it was placed there.

When, at last, the blinds were hung, the house cleaned, and the carpets nailed down, Mrs. Hamilton, who had designed doing it all the time, called together the servants, whom she had always disliked on account of their preference for Margaret, and told them to look for new places, as their services were no longer needed there.

"You can make out your bills," said she, at the same time intimating that they hadn't one of them more than earned their board, if indeed they had that! Polly Pepper wasn't of a material to stand coolly by and hear such language from one whom she considered far beneath her. "Hadn't she as good a right there as anybody? Yes, indeed, she had! Wasn't she there a full thirty year before any of your low-lived trash came round a nussin?"

"Polly," interposed Mrs. Hamilton, "leave the room, instantly, you ungrateful thing'!"

"Ungrateful for what?" returned old Polly. "Haven't I worked and slaved like an old nigger, as I am? and now you call me ungrateful, and say I bain't half arnt my bread. I'll sue you for slander, yes I will;" and the enraged Polly left the room, muttering to herself, "half arnt my board! Indeed! I'll bet I've made a hundred thousan' pies, to say nothin' of the puddings. *I* not arn my board!"

When once again safe in what for so many years had been her own peculiar province, she sat down to meditate,

"I'd as good go without any fuss," thought she, "but my curse on the madam who sends me away!"

In the midst of her reverie, Lenora entered the kitchen, and to her the old lady detailed her grievances, ending with, "'Pears like she don't know nothin' at all about etiquette, nor nothin' else."

"Etiquette!" repeated Lenora. "You are mistaken, Polly; mother would sit on a point of etiquette till she wore the back breadth of her dress out. But it isn't that which she lacks — it's decency. But, Polly," said she, changing the subject, "where do you intend to go, and how?"

. "To my brother Sam's," said Polly. "He lives three miles in the country, and I've sent Robin to the village for a horse and wagon to carry my things."

Here Mrs. Hamilton entered the kitchen, followed by a strapping Irish girl, nearly six feet in height. Her hair, flaming red, was twisted round a huge back comb; her faded calico dress came far above her ancles; her brawny arms were folded one over the other; and there was in her appearance something altogether disagreeable and defiant. Mrs. Hamilton introduced her as Ruth, her new cook, saying she hoped she would know enough to keep her place better than her predecessor had done.

Aunt Polly surveyed her rival from head to foot, and then glancing aside to Lenora, muttered, "Low-lived, depend on't."

Robin now drove up with the wagon, and Mrs. Hamilton and Lenora left the room, while Polly went to prepare herself for her ride. Her sleeping apartment was in the basement and communicated with the kitchen. This was observed by the new cook, who had a strong dislike of negroes, and who feared that she might be expected to occupy the same bed.

" An' faith," said she, " is it where the like of ye have burrowed that I am to turn in ? "

" I don't understand no such low-flung stuff," answered Polly, " but if you mean are you to have this bedroom, I suppose you are."

Here Polly had occasion to go up stairs for something, and on her return, she found that Ruth, during her absence, had set fire to a large linen rag, which she held on a shovel and was carrying about the bedroom, as if to purify it from every atom of negro atmosphere which might remain.   Polly was quick-wittted, and instantly comprehending the truth, she struck the shovel from the hands of Ruth, exclaiming, " You spalpeen, is it because my skin ain't a dingy yaller and all freckled like yourn ? Lord, look at your carrot-topped cocoanut, and then tell me if wool ain't a heap the most genteel."

In a moment a portion of the boasted wool was lying on the floor, or being shaken from the thick, red fingers of the cook, while Irish blood was flowing freely from the nose, which Polly, in her vengeful wrath, had wrung. Further hostilities were prevented by Robin, who screamed that he couldn't wait any longer, and shaking her fist fiercely at the red-head, Polly departed.

That day Lucy and Rachel also left, and their places were supplied by two raw hands, one of whom, before the close of the second day, tumbled up stairs with the large soup tureen, breaking it in fragments and scalding the foot of Mrs. Hamilton, who was in the rear, and who, having waited an hour for dinner, had descended to the kitchen to know why it was not forthcoming, saying that Polly had never been so behind the time.

The other one, on being asked if she understood chamber work, had replied, " Indade, and it's been my business all my life."   She was accordingly sent to make the beds and empty the slop.   Thinking it an easy way to dispose of the latter, she had thrown it from the window, deluging the head and shoulders of her mistress, who was bending down to examine a rose-bush which had been recently set out.   Lenora was in ecstasies, and when at noon her mother received a sprinkling of red-hot soup, she gravely asked her "which she relished most, cold or warm baths!"

CHAPTER XIII.

RETRIBUTION.

Two years have passsed away, and again we open the scene at the homestead, which had not proved an altogether pleasant home to Mrs. Hamilton.   There was around her everything to make her happy, but she was far from being so.   One by one her servants, with whom she was very unpopular, had left her, until there now remained but one.   The villagers, too, shunned her, and she was wholly dependent for society upon Lenora, who, as usual, provoked and tormented her.

One day, Hester, the servant, came up from the basement, saying there was a poor old man below, who asked for money.

"Send him away; I've nothing for him," said Mrs. Hamilton, whose avaricious hand, larger far than her heart, grasped at and retained everything.

"But, if you please, ma'am, he seems very poor," said Hester.

"Let him go to work, then.   'Twon't hurt him more than 't will me," was the reply.

Lenora, whose eyes and ears were always open, no sooner heard that there was a beggar in the kitchen, than she ran down to see him. He was a miserable looking object, and still there was something in his appearance which denoted him to be above the common order of beggars. His eyes were large and intensely black, and his hair, short, thick, and curly, reminded Lenora of her own. The moment she appeared, a peculiar expression passed for a moment over his face, and he half started up; then resuming his seat, he fixed his glittering eyes upon the young lady, and seemed watching her closely.

At last she began questioning him, but his answers were so unsatisfactory that she gave it up, and, thinking it the easiest way to be rid of him, she took from her pocket a shilling and handed it to him, saying, "It's all I can give you, unless it is a dinner. Are you hungry?"

Hester, who had returned to the kitchen, was busy in a distant part of the room, and she did not notice the paleness which overspread Lenora's face, at the words which the beggar uttered, when she presented the money to him. She caught, however, the low murmur of their voices, as they spoke together for a moment, and as Lenora accompanied him to the door, she distinctly heard the words, "In the garden."

"And may be that's some of your kin; you look like him," said she to Lenora, after the stranger was gone.

"That's my business, not yours," answered Lenora, as she left the kitchen and repaired to her mother's room.

"Lenora, what ails you?" said Mrs Hamilton to her daughter at the tea-table, that night, when, after putting salt in one cup of tea, and upsetting a second, she commenced spreading her biscuit with cheese instead of butter. "What ails you? What are you thinking about?

You don't seem to know any more what you are doing, than the dead."

Lenora made no direct reply to this, but soon after she said, "Mother, how long has father been dead,—my own father I mean?"

"Two or three years, I don't exactly know which," returned her mother, and Lenora continued: "How did he look? I hardly remember him."

"You have asked me that fifty times," answered her mother, "and fifty times I have told you that he looked like you, only worse, if possible."

"Let me see, where did you say he died?" said Lenora.

"In New Orleans, with yellow fever, or black measles, or small pox, or something," Mrs. Hamilton replied; "but, mercy's sake! can't you choose a better subject to talk about? What made you think of him? He's been haunt ing me all day, and I feel kind of nervous and want to look over my shoulder whenever I am alone."

Lenora made no further remark until after tea, when she announced her intention of going to the village.

"Come back early, for I don't feel like staying alone," said her mother.

The sun had set when Lenora left the village, and by the time she reached home, it was wholly dark. As she entered the garden, the outline of a figure, sitting on a bench at its farther extremity, made her stop for a moment, but thinking to herself, "I expected it, and why should I be afraid?" she walked on fearlessly, until the person, roused by the sound of her footsteps, started up, and turning toward her, said, half aloud, "Lenora, is it you?"

Quickly she sprang forward, and soon one hand of the beggar was clasped in hers, while the other rested upon her head, as he said, "Lenora, my child, my daughter, ~~you do~~ not hate me?"

"Hate you, father?" she answered, "never, never."

"But," he continued, "has not she,— my,—— no, not my wife,—thank heaven not my wife now,—but your mother, has not she taught you to despise and hate me?"

"No," answered Lenora, bitterly. "She has taught me enough of evil, but my memories of you were too sweet, too pleasant, for me to despise you, though I do not think you always did right, more than mother."

The stranger groaned, and murmured, "It's true, all true;" while Lenora continued: "But where have you been all these years, and how came we to hear of your death?"

"I have been in St. Louis most of the time, and the report of my death resulted from the fact that a man bearing my name, and who was also from Connecticut, died of yellow fever in New Orleans about two years and a half ago. A friend of mine, observing a notice of his death, and supposing it to refer to me, forwarded the paper to your mother, who, though then free from me, undoubtedly felt glad, for she never loved me, but married me because she thought I had money."

"But how have you lived?" asked Lenora.

"Lived!" he repeated, "I have not lived. I have merely existed. Gambling and drinking, drinking and gambling, have been the business of my life, and have reduced me to the miserable wretch whom you see."

"Oh, father, father," cried Lenora, "reform. It is not too late, and you can yet be saved. Do it for my sake, for, in spite of all your faults, I love you, and you are my father."

The first words of affection which had greeted his ear for many long years made the wretched man weep, as he answered, "Lenora, I have sworn to reform, and I will keep my vow. During one of my drunken revels in St. Louis, a dream of home came over me, and when I became sober, I started for Connecticut. There I heard where and what your mother was. I had no wish ever to meet her again, for though I greatly erred in my conduct toward her, I think she was always the most to blame. You I remembered with love, and I longed to see you once more, to hear again the word 'father,' and know that I was not forgotten. I came as far as the city, and there fell into temptation. For the last two months I have been there, gambling and drinking, until I lost all, even the clothes which I wore, and was compelled to assume these rags. I am now without home or money, and have no place to lay my head."

"I can give you money," said Lenora. "Meet me here to-morrow night, and you shall have all you want. But what do you purpose doing? Where will you stay?"

"In the village, for the sake of being near you," said he, at the same time bidding his daughter return to the house, as the night air was damp and chilly.

Within a week from that time, a middle-aged man, calling himself John Robinson, appeared in the village, hiring himself out as a porter at one of the hotels. There was a very striking resemblance between him and Lenora Carter, which was noticed by the villagers, and mentioned to Mrs. Hamilton, who, however, could never obtain a full view of the stranger's face, for without any apparent design, he always avoided meeting her He had not been long in town, before it was whispered about that between him and Lenora Carter a strange intimacy existed, and rumors soon reached Mrs. Hamilton that her daughter was in the habit of frequently stealing out, after sunset, to meet the old porter, and that once, when watched, she had been seen to put her arms around his neck.   Highly indignant, Mrs. Hamilton questioned Lenora on the subject, and was astonished beyond measure when she replied, "It is all true.   I have met Mr. Robinson often, and I have put my arms around his neck, and shall probably do it again."

"Oh, my child, my child," groaned Mrs. Hamilton, really distressed at her daughter's conduct.   "How can you do so?   You will bring my gray hairs with sorrow to the grave."

"Not if you pull out as many of them as you now do, and use Twiggs' Preparation besides," said Lenora.

Mrs. Hamilton did not answer, but covering her face with her hands, wept, really wept, thinking for the first time, perhaps, that as she had sowed so was she reaping. For some time past, her health had been failing, and as the summer days grew warmer and more oppressive, she felt a degree of lassitude and physical weakness which she had never before experienced; and one day unable longer to sit up, she took her bed, where she lay for many days.

Now that her mother was really sick, Lenora seemed suddenly changed, and with unwearied care watched over her as kindly and faithfully as if no words, save those of affection, had ever passed between them.   Warmer and more sultry grew the days, and more fiercely raged the fever in Mrs. Hamilton's veins, until at last the crisis was reached and passed, and she was in a fair way for recovry, when she was attacked by chills, which again reduced her to a state of helplessness.   One day, about this time, a ragged little boy, whose business seemed to be lounging around the hotel, brought to Lenora a soiled and crumpled note, on which was traced with an unsteady hand, "Dear Lenora, I am sick, all alone in the little attic; come to me, quick; come."

Lenora was in a state of great perplexity. Her mother when awake, needed all her care; and as she seldom slept during the day, there seemed but little chance of getting away. The night before, however, she had been unusually restless and wakeful, and about noon she seemed drowsy, and finally fell into a deep sleep.

"Now is my time," thought Lenora; and calling Hester, she bade her watch by her mother until she returned, saying, "If she wakes, tell her I have gone to the village, and will soon be back."

Hester promised compliance, and was for a time faithful to her trust; but suddenly recollecting something which she wished to tell the girl who lived at the next neighbor's, she stole away, leaving her mistress alone. For five minutes Mrs. Hamilton slept on, and then with a start awoke from a troubled dream, in which she had seemed dying of thirst, while little Willie, standing by a hogshead of water, refused her a drop. A part of her dream was true, for she was suffering from the most intolerable thirst, and called loudly for Lenora; but Lenora was not there. Hester next was called, but she, too, was gone. Then, seizing the bell which stood upon the table, she rung it with all her force, and still there came no one to her relief.

Again Willie stood by her, offering her a goblet overflowing with water; but when she attempted to take it, Willie changed into Lenora, who laughed mockingly at her distress, telling her there was water in the well and ice on the curb-stone. Once more the phantom faded away, and the old porter was there, wading through a limpid stream and offering her to drink a cup of molten lead.

"Merciful heaven!" shrieked the sick woman, as she writhed from side to side on her bed, which seemed changed to burning coals; "will no one bring me water, water, water!"

An interval of calmness succeeded, during which she revolved in her mind the possibility of going herself to the kitchen, where she knew the water-pail was standing. No sooner had she decided upon this, than the room appeared full of little demons, who laughed, and chattered, and shouted in her ears, "Go—do it! Willie did, when the night was dark and chilly; but now it is warm—nice and warm—try it, do!"

Tremblingly Mrs. Hamilton stepped upon the floor, and finding herself too weak to walk, crouched down, and crept slowly down the stairs to the kitchen door, where she stopped to rest. Across the room by the window stood the pail, and as her eye fell upon it, the mirth of the little winged demons appeared, in her disordered fancy, to increase; and when the spot was reached, the tumbler seized and thrust into the pail, they darted hither and thither, shouting gleefully, "Lower, lower down; just as Willie did. You'll find it; oh, you'll find it!"

With a bitter cry, Mrs. Hamilton dashed the tumbler upon the floor, for the bucket was empty!

"Willie, Willie, you are avenged," she said; but the goblins answered, "Not yet; no, not yet."

There was no pump in the well, and Mrs. Hamilton knew she had not strength to raise the bucket by means of the windlass. Her exertions had increased her thirst tenfold, and now, for one cup of cooling water she would have given all her possessions. Across the yard, at the distance of twenty rods, there was a gushing spring, and thither in her despair she determined to go. Accordingly, she went forth into the fierce noontide blaze, and, with almost superhuman efforts, crawled to the place. But what! was it a film upon her eyes? Had blindness come upon her, or was the spring really dried up by the fervid summer heat?

"Willie's avenged! Willie's avenged!" yelled the imps, as the wretched woman fainted and fell backward upon the bank, where she lay with her white, thin face upturned, and blistering beneath the August sun!

*   *   *   *   *   *

Along the dusty highway came a handsome traveling carriage, in which, besides the driver, were seated two individuals, the one a young and elegantly dressed lady, and the other a gentleman, who appeared to be on the most intimate terms with his companion; for whenever he would direct her attention to any passing object, he laid his hand on hers, frequently retaining it, and calling her "Maggie."

The carriage was nearly opposite the homestead, when the lady exclaimed, "Oh, Richard, I must stop at my old home, once more. Only see how beautiful it is looking!"

In a moment the carriage was standing before the gate, and the gentleman, who was Margaret Hamilton's hus-band—a Mr. Elwyn, from the city—assisted his young wife to alight, and then followed her to the house. No answer was given to their loud ring, and as the doors and windows were all open, Margaret proposed that they should enter. They did so; and, going first into Mrs. Hamilton's sick-room, the sight of the little table full of vials, and the tumbled, empty bed, excited their wonder and curiosity, and induced them to go on. At last, de-scending to the kitchen, they saw the fragments of the tumbler lying upon the floor.

"Strange, isn't it?" said Margaret to her husband, who was standing in the outer door, and who had at that moment discovered Mrs. Hamilton lying near the spring.

Instantly they were at her side, and Margaret involuntarily shuddered as she recognized her step-mother, and guessed why she was there. Taking her in his arms, Mr. Elwyn bore her back to the house, and Margaret, filling a pitcher with water, bathed her face, moistened her lips, and applied other restoratives, until she revived enough to say, "More water, Willie. Give me more water!"

Eagerly she drained the goblet which Margaret held to her lips, and was about drinking the second, when her eyes for the first time sought Margaret's face. With a cry between a groan and a scream, she lay back upon her pillows, saying, "Margaret Hamilton, how came you here? What have you to do with me, and why do you give me water? Didn't I refuse it to Willie, when he begged so earnestly for it in the night time? But I've been paid—a thousand times paid—left by my own child to die alone!"

Margaret was about asking for Lenora, when the young lady herself appeared. She seemed for a moment greatly surprised at the sight of Margaret, and then bounding to ner side, greeted her with much affection; while Mrs. Hamilton jealously looked on, muttering to herself, "Loves everybody better than she does me, her own mother who has done so much for her."

Lenora made no reply to this, although she manifested much concern when Margaret told her in what state they had found her mother.

"I went for a few moments to visit a sick friend," said she, "but told Hester to stay with mother until I returned; and I wonder much that she should leave her."

"Lenora," said Mrs. Hamilton, "Lenora, was that sick friend the old porter?"

Lenora answered in the affirmative; and then her mother, turning to Margaret, said, "You don't know what a pest and torment this child has always been to me, and now when I am dying, she deserts me for a low-lived fellow, old enough to be her father."

Lenora's eyes flashed scornfully upon her mother, but she made no answer, and as Mr. Elwyn was in haste to proceed on his journey, Margaret arose to go. Lenora urged them to remain longer, but they declined; and as she accompanied them to the door, Margaret said, "Lenora, if your mother should die, and it would afford you any satisfaction to have me come, I will do so, for I suppose you have no near friends."

Lenora hesitated a moment, and then whispering to Margaret of the relationship existing between herself and the old porter, she said, "He is sick and poor, but he is my own father, and I love him dearly."

The tears came to Margaret's eyes, for she thought of her own father, called home while his brown hair was scarcely touched with the frosts of time. Wistfully Lenora watched the carriage as it disappeared from sight, and then half reluctantly entered the sick-room, where, for the remainder of the afternoon, she endured her mother's reproaches for having left her alone, and where once, when her patience was wholly exhausted, she said, "It served you right, for now you know how little Willie felt."

The next day Mrs. Hamilton was much worse, and Lenora, who had watched and who understood her symptoms, felt confident that she would die, and loudly her conscience upbraided her for her undutiful conduct. She longed, too, to tell her that her father was still living and one evening, when, for an hour or two, her mother seemed better, she arose, and bending over her pillow, said, "Mother, did it ever occur to you that father might not be dead?"

"Not be dead, Lenora! What do you mean?" asked Mrs. Hamilton, starting up from her pillow.

Cautiously then Lenora commenced her story by referring her mother back to the old beggar, who some months before had been in the kitchen. Then she spoke of the old porter, and the resemblance which was said to exist between him and herself; and finally, as she saw her mother could bear it, she told the whole story of her father's life. Slowly the sick woman's eyes closed, and Lenora saw that her eyelids were wet with tears, but as she made no reply, Lenora, ere long, whispered, "Would you like to see him, mother?"

"No, no; not now," was the answer.

For a time there was silence, and then Lenora, again speaking, said, "Mother, I have often been very wicked and disrespectful to you, and if you should die, I should feel much happier knowing that you forgave me. Will you do it, mother, say?"

Mrs. Hamilton comprehended only the words, "if you should die," so she said, "Die, die! who says that I must die? I shan't—I can't; for what could I tell her about her children, and how could I live endless ages without water. I tried it once, and I can't do it. No, I can't. I won't!"

In this way she talked all night; and though in the morning she was more rational, she turned away from the clergyman, who at Lenora's request had been sent for, saying, "It's of no use, no use; I know all you would say, but it's too late, too late!"

Thus she continued for three days, and at the close of

the third, it became evident to all that she was dying, and Hester was immediately sent to the hotel, with a request that the old porter would come quickly. Half an hour after, Lenora bent over her mother's pillow, and whispered in her ear, "Mother, can you hear me?"

A pressure of the hand was the reply, and Lenora continued: "You have not said that you forgave me, and now before you die, will you not tell me so?"

There was another pressure of the hand, and Lenora again spoke: "Mother, would you like to see him—my father? He is in the next room."

This roused the dying woman, and starting up, she exclaimed, "See John Carter! No, child, no. He'd only curse me. Let him wait until I am dead, and then I shall not hear it."

In ten minutes more, Lenora was sadly gazing upon the fixed, stony features of the dead. A gray-haired man was at her side, and his lip quivered, as he placed his hand upon the white, wrinkled brow of her who had once been his wife. "She is fearfully changed," were his only words, as he turned away from the bed of death.

True to her promise, Margaret came to attend her step-mother's funeral. Walter accompanied her, and shuddered as he looked on the face of one who had so darkened his home, and embittered his life. Kate was not there, and when, after the burial, Lenora asked Margaret for her, she was told of a little "Carrie Lenora," who, with pardonable pride, Walter thought was the only baby of any consequence in the world. Margaret was going on with a glowing description of the babe's many beauties, when she was interrupted by Lenora who laid her face in her lap and burst into tears.

"Why, Lenora, what is the matter?" asked Margaret.

As soon as Lenora became calm, she answered, "*that*

name, Maggie. You have given my name to Walter Hamilton's child, and if you had hated me, you would never have done it."

"Hated you!" repeated Margaret, "we do not hate you; now that we understand you, we like you very much, and one of Kate's last injunctions to Walter was, that he should again offer you a home with him."

Once more Lenora was weeping. She had not shed a tear when they carried from sight her mother, but words of kindness touched her heart, and the fountain was opened. At last, drying her eyes, she said, "I prefer to go with father. Walter will, of course, come back to the homestead, while father and I shall return to our old home in Connecticut, where, by being kind to him, I hope to atone, in a measure, for my great unkindness to mother."

* * *

CHAPTER XIV.

FINALE.

THROUGH the open casement of a small, white cottage in the village of P——, the rays of the September moon are stealing, disclosing to view a gray-haired man, whose placid face still shows marks of long years of dissipation. Affectionately he caresses the black, curly head, which is resting on his knee, and softly he says, "Lenora, my daughter, there are, I trust, years of happiness in store for us both."

"I hope it may be so," was the answer, "but there is no promise of many days to any save those who honor their father and mother. This last I have never done, though many, many times have I repented of it, and I begin to be assured that we may be happy yet."

*   *   *   *   *   *

Away to the westward, over many miles of woodland, valley, and hill, the same September moon shines upon the white walls of the homestead, where sits the owner, Walter Hamilton, gazing first upon his wife, and then upon the tiny treasure which lies sleeping upon her lap.

"We are very happy, Katy darling," he says, and the affection which looks from her large, blue eyes, as she lifts them to his face, is a sufficient answer.

Margaret, too, is there, and though but an hour ago her tears were falling upon the grass grown graves, where slept her father and mother, the gentle Carrie and golden-haired Willie, they are all gone now, and she responds to her brother's words, "Yes, Walter, we are very happy."

*   *   *   *   *   *

In the basement below the candle is burned to its socket, and as the last ray flickers up, illuminating for a moment the room, and then leaving it in darkness, Aunt Polly Pepper starts from her evening nap, and as if continuing her dream, mutters, "Yes, this is pleasant, and something like living."

*   *   *   *   *   *

And so with the moonlight and starlight falling upon the old homestead, and the sunlight of love falling upon the hearts of its inmates, we bid them adieu.

Rice Corner.

CHAPTER I.

RICE CORNER.

Yes, Rice Corner! Do you think it a queer name? Well, Rice Corner was a queer place, and deserved a queer name. Now whether it is celebrated for anything in particular, I really can't, at this moment, think, unless, indeed, it is famed for having been my birth-place! Whether this of itself is sufficient to immortalize a place, future generations may, perhaps, tell, but I have some misgivings whether the present will. This idea may be the result of my having recently received sundry knocks over the knuckles in the shape of criticisms.

But I know one thing,—on the bark of that old chestnut tree which stands near Rice Corner school-house, my name is cut higher than some of my more bulky cotemporary quill—or rather steel—pen-wielders ever dared to climb. To be sure, I tore my dress, scratched my face, and committed numerous other *little rompish miss*-demeanors, which procured for me a motherly scolding. That, however, was of minor consideration, when compared with having my name up—in the chestnut tree, at least, if it couldn't be up in the world. But pardon my egotism, and I will proceed with my story about Rice Corner.

Does any one wish to know whereabouts on this rolling

sphere Rice Corner is situated?   I don't believe you can
find it on the map, unless your eyes are bluer and bigger
than mine, which last they can't very well be.   But I can
tell you to a dot where Rice Corner should be.   Just
take your atlas,—not the last one published, but Olney's,
that's the one *I* studied,—and right in one of those little
towns in Worcester county is Rice Corner, snugly nestled
among the gray rocks and blue hills of New England.

Yes, Rice Corner was a great place, and so you would
have thought could you have seen it in all its phases,
with its brown, red, green, yellow, and white houses, each
of which had the usual quantity of rose bushes, lilacs,
hollyhocks, and sunflowers.   You should have seen my
home, my New England home, where once, not many
years ago, a happy group of children played.   Alas! alas!
some of those who gave the sunlight to.that spot, have
left us now forever, and on the bright shores of the eternal river they wait and watch our coming.   I do not expect a stranger to love our old homestead as I loved it, for
in each heart is a fresh, green spot—the memory of its
own early home—where the sunshine was brighter, the
well waters cooler, and the song-bird's carol sweeter than
elsewhere they are found.

I trust I shall be forgiven, if, in this chapter, I pause
awhile to speak of my home,—aye, and of myself, too,
when, a light-hearted child, I bounded through the meadows and orchards which lay around the old brown house
on my father's farm.   'Twas a large, square, two-storied
building, that old brown farm-house, containing rooms,
cupboards, and closets innumerable, and what was better
than all, a large, airy garret, where, on all rainy days,
and days when it looked as if it would rain, Bill, Joe,
Lizzie and I, assembled to hold our noisy revels.   Never,
since the days of our great-grandmothers, did little spin-

ning wheel buzz round faster than did the one which, in the darkest corner of that garret, had been safely stowed away, where they *guessed* "the young-ones would n't find it."

"Would n't find it!" I should like to know what there was in that old garret that we did n't find, and appropriate, too! Even the old oaken chest which contained our grandmother's once fashionable attire, was not sacred from the touch of our lawless hands. Into its deep recesses we plunged, and brought out such curiosities,—the queerest looking, high crowned, broad frilled caps, narrow gored shirts, and what was funnier than all, a strange looking thing which we thought must be a side saddle,—any way, it fitted Joe's rocking horse admirably, although we wondered why so much whalebone was necessary!

One day, in the midst of our gambols, in walked the identical owner of the chest, and seeing the side-saddle, she said, somewhat angrily, "Why, children, where upon airth did you find my old stays?" We never wondered again what made grandma's back keep its place so much better than ours, and Bill had serious thoughts of trying the effect of the stays upon himself.

In the rear of our house and sloping toward the setting sun, was a long, winding lane, leading far down into a wide-spreading tract of flowery woods, shady hillside, and grassy pasture land, each in their turn highly suggestive of brown nuts, delicious strawberries, and venomous snakes. These last were generally more the creatures of imagination than of reality, for in all my wanderings over those fields, and they were many, I never but once trod upon a green snake, and only once was I chased by a white ringed black snake; so I think I am safe in saying

that the snakes were not so numerous as were the nuts
and berries, which grew there in great profusion.

A little to the right of the woods, where, in winter,
Bill, Joe, Lizzie, and I dragged our sleds and boards for
the purpose of riding down hill, was a merry, frolicking
stream of water, over which, in times long gone, a saw-
mill had been erected; but owing to the inefficiency of its
former owner, or something else, the mill had fallen into
disuse, and gradually gone to decay. The water of the
brook, relieved from the necessity of turning the splut-
tering wheel, now went gaily dancing down, down into
the depths of the dim old woods, and far away, I never
knew exactly where; but having heard rumors of a jump-
ing off place, I had a vague impression that at that spot
the waters of the mill-dam put up.

Near the saw mill, and partially hidden by the scraggy
pine trees and thick bushes which drooped over its entrance, was a long, dark passage, leading underground;
not so large, probably, as Mammoth Cave, but in my estimation rivaling it in interest. This was an old mine,
where, years before, men had dug for gold. Strange
stories were told of those who, with blazing torches,
and blazing noses, most likely, there toiled for the yellow
dust. The "Ancient Henry" himself, it was said, sometimes left his affairs at home, and joined the nightly revels in that mine, where cards and wine played a conspicuous part. Be that as it may, the old mine was surrounded by a halo of fear, which we youngsters never
cared to penetrate.

On a fine afternoon an older sister would occasionally
wander that way, together with a young M. D., whose
principal patient seemed to be at our house, for his little
black pony very frequently found shelter in our stable by
the side of " old sorrel." From the north garret window

I would watch them, wondering how they dared venture so near the old mine, and wishing, mayhap, that the time would come when I, with some daring doctor, would risk everything.　The time *has come*, but alas! instead of being a doctor, he is only a lawyer, who never even saw the old mine in Rice Corner.

Though I never ventured close to the old mine, there was, not far from it, one pleasant spot where I loved dearly to go.　It was on the hillside, where, 'neath the shadow of a gracefully twining grape-vine, lay a large, flat rock.　Thither would I often repair, and sit for hours listening to the hum of the running water brook, or the song of the summer birds, who, like me, seemed to love that place.　Often would I gaze far off at the distant, misty horizon, wondering if I should ever know what was beyond it.　Wild fancies then filled my childish brain.　Strange voices whispered to me thoughts and ideas, which, if written down and carried out, would, I am sure, have placed my name higher than it was carved on the old chestnut tree.

> "But they came and went like shadows,
> Those blessed dreams of youth."

I was a strange child, I know.　Everybody told me so, and *I* knew it well enough without being told.　The wise old men of Rice Corner and their still wiser old wives, looked at me askance, as 'neath the thorn-apple tree I built my play-house and baked my little loaves of mud bread.　But when, forgetful of others, I talked aloud to myriads of little folks, unseen 'tis true, but still real to me, they shook their gray heads ominously, and whispering to my mother said, "Mark our words, that girl will one day be crazy.　In ten years more she will be an inmate of the mad-house!"

And then I wondered what a mad-house was, and if the people there all acted as our school teacher did when Bill and the big girls said he was mad! The ten years have passed, and I'm not in a mad-house yet, unless, indeed, it is one of my own getting up!

One thing more about Rice Corner, and then, honor bright, I'll finish the preface and go on with the story. I must tell you about the old school-house, and the road which led to it. This last wound around a long hill, and was skirted on either side with tall trees, flowering dogwood, blackberry bushes, and frost grape-vines. Halfway down the hill, and under one of the tallest walnut trees, was a little hollow, where dwelt the goblin with which nurses, housemaids, hired men, and older sisters were wont to frighten refractory children into quietness. It was the grave of an old negro. Alas! that to his last resting place the curse should follow him! Had it been a white person who rested there, not half so fearful would have been the spot; now, however, it was "the old nigger hole" — a place to run by, if by accident you were caught out after dark — a place to be threatened with, if you cried in the night and wanted the candle lighted—a landmark where to stop, when going part way home with the little girl who had been to visit you, and who, on leaving you, ran no less swiftly than you yourself did, half fearing that the dusky form in the hollow would rise and try his skill at running. Verily, my heart has beat faster at the thoughts of that dead negro, than it ever has since at the sight of a hundred live specimens, " way down south on the old plantation."

The old school-house, too, had its advantages and its disadvantages; of the latter, one was that there, both summer and winter, but more especially during the last mentioned season, all the rude boys in the place thought tney had a perfect right to congregate and annoy the girls in every possible way. But, never mind, not a few wry faces we made at them, and not a few "blockheads" we pinned to their backs! Oh! I've had rare times in that old house, and have seen there rare sights, too, to say nothing of the fights which occasionally occurred. In these last, brother Joe generally took the lead of one party, while Jim Brown commanded the other. Dire was the confusion which reigned at such times. Books were hurled from side to side. Then followed in quick succession shovel, tongs, poker, water cup, water pail, water and all; and to cap the climax, Jim Brown once seized the large iron pan, which stood upon the stove, half filled with hot water, and hurled it in the midst of the enemy. Luckily nobody was killed, and but few wounded.

Years in their rapid flight have rolled away since then, and he, my brother, is sleeping alone on the wild shore of California.

> For scarcely had the sad tones died,
>   Which echoed the farewell,
> When o'er the western prairies
>   There came a funeral knell;
> It said that he who went from us,
>   While yet upon his brow
> The dew of youth was glistening,
>   Had passed to heaven now.

James Brown, too, is resting in the church-yard, near his own home, and 'neath his own native sky.

CHAPTER II.

THE BELLE OF RICE CORNER.

YES, Rice Corner had a belle, but it was not I. Oh, no, nobody ever mistook *me* for a belle, or much of anything else, in fact; *I* was simply "Mary Jane," or, if that was not consise enough, "Crazy Jane," set the matter all right. The belle of which I speak was a bona fide one— fine complexion, handsome features, beautiful eyes, curling hair and all. And yet, in her composition there was something wanting, something very essential, too; for she lacked soul, and would at any time have sold her best friend for a flattering compliment.

Still Carrie Howard was generally a favorite. The old people liked her because her sparkling eye and merry laugh brought back to them a gleam of youth; the young people liked her, because to dislike her would seem like envy; and I, who was nothing, liked her because she was pretty, and I greatly admired beauty, though I am not certain that I should not have liked a handsome rose-bud quite as well as I did Carrie Howard's beautiful face, for beautiful she was.

Her mother, good, plain Mrs. Howard, was entirely un- like her daughter. She was simply "Mrs. Capt. How- ard," or, in other words, "Aunt Eunice," whose benevo- lent smile and kindly beaming eye carried contentment wherever she went. Really, I don't know how Rice Cor- ner could have existed one day without the presence of Aunt Eunice. Was there a cut foot or hand in the neigh borhood, hers was the salve which healed it, almost as soon as applied. Was there a pale, fretful baby, Aunt Eunice's large bundle of catnip was sure to soothe it · and did a sick person need watchers, Aunt Eunice was the one who, three nights out of the seven, trod softly and quietly about the sick-room, anticipating each want before you yourself knew what it was, and smoothing your tumbled pillow so gently that you almost felt it a luxury to be sick, for the sake of being nursed by Aunt Eunice. The very dogs and cats winked more composedly when she appeared; and even the chickens learned her voice almost as soon as they did the cluck of their "maternal ancestor."

But we must stop, or we shall make Aunt Eunice out to be the belle, instead of Carrie, who, instead of imitating her mother in her acts of kindness, sat all day in the large old parlor, thumping away on a rickety piano, or trying to transfer to broadcloth a poor little kittie, whose face was sufficiently indicative of surprise at finding its limbs so frightfully distorted.

When Carrie was fifteen years of age, her father, concluding that she knew all which could possibly be learned in the little brown house, where Joe and Jim once fought so fiercely, sent her for three years to Albany. It was currently reported that the uncle with whom she boarded, received his pay in butter, cheese, potatoes, apples, and other commodities, which were the product of Capt. Howard's farm. Whether this was true or not, I am not prepared to say, but I suppose it was, for it was told by those who had no ostensible business, except to attend to other people's affairs, and I am sure they ought to have known all about it, and probably did.

I cannot help thinking that Captain Howard made a mistake in sending Carrie away; for when at the end of three years she had "finished her education," and returned home, she was not half so good a scholar as some of those who had pored patiently over their books in the old brown house. Even *I* could beat her in spelling, for soon after she came home the boys teased for a spelling-school. I rather think they were quite as anxious for a chance to go home with the girls as they were to have their knowledge of Webster tested. Be that as it may, Carrie was there, and was, of course, chosen first; but *I,* "little crazy Jane," spelled the whole school down! I thought Carrie was not quite so handsome as she might be, when with an angry frown she dropped into her seat, hissed by a big, cross-eyed, red-haired boy, in the corner, because she *happened* to spell pumpkin, "*p-u-n pun k-i-n kin, punkin.*" I do not think she ever quite forgave me for the pert, loud way in which I spelled the word correctly, for she never gave me any more calicoes or silks, and instead of calling me "Mollie," as she had before done, she now addressed me as "Miss Mary."

Carrie possessed one accomplishment which the other girls did not. She could play the piano most skillfully, although as yet she had no instrument. Three weeks, however, after her return, a rich man, who lived in the village which was known as "Over the River," failed, and all his furniture was sold at auction. Many were the surmises of my grandmother, on the morning of the sale, as to what "Cap'n Howard could be going to buy at the *vandue* and put in the big lumber wagon," which he drove past our house.

As the day drew to a close, I was posted at the window to telegraph as soon as "Cap'n Howard's" white horses appeared over the hill. They came at last, but the long box in his wagon told no secret. Father, however, explained all, by saying that he had bid off Mr. Talbott's old piano for seventy dollars! Grandma shook her head mournfully at the degeneracy of the age, while sister Anna spoke sneeringly of Mr. Talbott's cracked piano.

Next day, arrayed in my Sunday red merino and white apron—a present from some cousin out west—I went to see Carrie; and truly, the music she drew from that old piano charmed me more than the finest performances since have done. Carrie and her piano were now the theme of every tongue, and many wondered how Captain Howard could afford to pay for three years' music lessons; but this was a mystery yet to be solved.

CHAPTER III.

MONSIEUR PENOYER.

WHEN Carrie had been at home about three months, all Rice Corner one day flew to the doors and windows to look at a stranger, a gentleman with fierce mustaches, who seemed not at all certain of his latitude, and evidently wanted to know where he was going. At least, if *he* didn't, they who watched him did.

Grandma, whose longevity had not impaired her guessing faculties, first suggested that "most likely it was Car'-line Howard's beau." This was altogether too probable to be doubted, and as grandmother had long contempla-ted a visit to Aunt Eunice, she now determined to go that very afternoon, as she " could judge for herself what kind of a match Car'line had made." Mother tried to dissuade her from going that day, but the old lady was incorrigible, and directly after dinner, dressed in her bom-basin, black silk apron, work bag, knitting and all, she de-parted for Captain Howard's.

They wouldn't confess it, but I knew well enough that Juliet and Anna were impatient for her return, and when the shadows of twilight began to fall, I was twice sent into the road to see if she was coming. The last time I was successful, and in a few moments grandmother was among us; but whatever she knew she kept to herself until the lamps were lighted in the sitting-room, and she, in her stuffed rocking-chair, was toeing off the stocking only that morning commenced. Then, at a hint from Anna, she cast toward Lizzie and me a rueful glance, saying, "There are too many *pitchers* here!" I knew then just as well as I did five minutes after, that Lizzie and I must go to bed. There was no help for it, and we complied with a tolerably good grace. Lizzie proposed that we should listen, but somehow I couldn't do that, and up to this time I don't exactly know what grandmother told them.

The next day, however, I heard enough to know that his name was Penoyer; that grandma did n't like him; that he had as much hair on his face as on his head; that Aunt Eunice would oppose the match, and that he would stay over Sunday. With this last I was delighted, for I should see him at church. I saw him before that, however; for it was unaccountable what a fancy Carrie suddenly took for traversing the woods and riding on horseback, for which purpose grandfather's side-saddle (not the one with which Joe saddled his pony!) was borrowed, and then, with her long curls and blue riding skirt floating in the wind, Carrie galloped over hills and through valleys, accompanied by Penoyer, who was a fierce looking fellow, with black eyes, black hair, black whiskers, and black face.

I couldn't help fancying that the negro who lay beneath the walnut tree, had resembled him, and I cried for fear Carrie might marry so ugly a man, thinking it would not be altogether unlike, " Beauty and the Beast." Sally, our housemaid, said that "most likely he'd prove to be some poor, mean scamp. Any way, seein' it was plantin' time, he'd better be *to hum* tendin' to his own business, if he had any."

Sally was a shrewd, sharp-sighted girl, and already had her preference in favor of Michael Welsh, father's hired man. Walking, riding on horseback, and wasting time generally, Sally held in great abhorrence. "All she wished to say to Mike on week days, she could tell him milking time." On Sundays, however, it was different, and regularly each Sunday night found Mike and Sally snugly ensconced in the "great room," while under the windows occasionally might have been seen three or four curly heads, eager to hear something about which to tease Sally during the week.

But to return to Monsieur Penoyer, as Carrie called him. His stay was prolonged beyond the Sabbath, and on Tuesday I was sent to Capt. Howard's on an errand. I found Aunt Eunice in the kitchen, her round, rosy face, always suggestive of seed cake and plum pudding, flushed with exertion, her sleeves tucked up and her arms buried in a large wooden bowl of dough, which she said was going to be made into loaves of 'lection cake, as Carrie was to have a party to-morrow, and I had come just in time to carry invitations to my sisters.

Carrie was in the parlor, and attracted by the sound of music, I drew near the door, when Aunt Eunice kindly bade me enter. I did so, and was presented to Monsieur Penoyer. At first, I was shy of him, for I remembered that Sally had said, "he don't know nothin'," and this in my estimation was the worst crime of which he could be guilty. Gradually, my timidity gave way, and when, at Carrie's

request, he played and sang for me, I was perfectly delighted, although I understood not a word he said.

When he finished, Carrie told him I was a little poet,
and then repeated some foolish lines I had once written
about her eyes. It was a very handsome set of teeth
which he showed, as he said, "*Magnifique! Tres bien!*
She be another grand *Dr. Watts!*"

I knew not who Dr. Watts was, but on one point my
mind was made up—Monsieur Penoyer knew a great deal!
Ere I left, Carrie commissioned me to invite my sisters to
her party on the morrow, and as I was leaving the room,
M. Penoyer said, "Ma chere Carrie, why vous no invite
la petite girl!"

Accordingly I was invited, with no earthly prospect,
however, of mother's letting me go. And she didn't
either; so next day, after Juliet and Anna were gone, I
went out behind the smoke-house and cried until I got
sleepy, and a headache too; then, wishing to make mother
think I had *run away*, I crept carefully up stairs to Bill's
room, where I slept until Sally's sharp eyes ferreted me
out, saying, "they were all scared to death about me, and
had looked for me high and low," up in the garret and
down in the well, I supposed. Concluding they were
plagued enough, I condescended to go down stairs, and have
my head bathed in camphor and my feet parboiled in hot
water; then I went to bed and dreamed of white teeth,
curling mustaches and "*Parlez vous Francais.*"

Of what occurred at the party I will tell you as it was
told to me. All the *elite* of Rice Corner were there, of
course, and as each new arrival entered the parlor, M.
Penoyer eyed them coolly through an opera glass. Sister
Anna returned his inspection with the worst face she could
well make up, for which I half blamed her and half didn't,

as I felt sure I should have done the same under like circumstances.

When all the invited guests had arrived, except myself,
(alas, no one asked why I tarried,) there ensued an awkward silence, broken only by the parrot-like chatter of M.
Penoyer, who seemed determined to talk nothing but
French, although Carrie understood him but little better
than did the rest.   At last he was posted up to the piano.

"Mon Dieu, it be von horrid tone," said he; then off
he dashed into a galloping waltz, keeping time with his
head, mouth, and eyes, which threatened to leave their
sockets and pounce upon the instrument.   Rattlety-bang
went the piano—like lightning went Monsieur's fingers,
first here, then there, right or wrong, hit or miss, and oftener miss than hit—now alighting among the keys pro-
miscuously, then with a tremendous thump making all
bound again,— and finishing up with a flourish, which
snapped two strings and made all the rest groan in sympathy, as did the astonished listeners.   For a time all was
still, and then a little modest girl, Lily Gordon, her face
blushing crimson, said, "I beg your pardon, Monsieur,
but haven't you taught music!"

The veins in his forehead swelled, as, darting a wrathful
look at poor Lily, he exclaimed, "Le Diable! vat vous
take me for? Von dem musique teacher, eh?"

Poor Lily tried to stammer her apologies, while Carrie
sought to soothe the enraged Frenchman, by saying, that
"Miss Gordon was merely complimenting his skill in
music."

At this point, the carriage which carried persons to
and from the depot drove up, and from it alighted a very
small, genteel looking lady, who rapped at the door and
asked, "if Capt. Howard lived there."

In a moment Carrie was half stifling her with kisses, ex-

9

claiming, "Dear Agnes, this is a pleasant surprise. I did not expect you so soon."

The lady called Agnes, was introduced as Miss Hovey a school-mate of Carrie's. She seemed very much disposed · to make herself at home, for, throwing her hat in one place and her shawl in another, she seated herself at the piano, hastily running over a few notes; then with a gesture of impatience, she said, " O, horrid! a few more such sounds would give me the vapors for a month; why don't you have it tuned ? "

Ere Carrie could reply, Agnes' eyes lighted upon Penoyer, who, either with or without design, had drawn himself as closely into a corner as he well could. Springing up, she brought her little hands together with energy, exclaiming, "Now, heaven defend me, what fresh game brought you here ? " Then casting on Carrie an angry glance, she said, in a low tone, "What does it mean? Why didn't you tell me ? "

Carrie drew nearer, and said coaxingly, "I didn't expect you so soon; but, never mind, he leaves to-morrow. For my sake treat him decently."

The pressure which Agnes gave Carrie's hand seemed to say, "For your sake, I will, but for no other." Then turning to Penoyer, who had risen to his feet, she said respectfully, "I hardly expected to meet you here, sir."

Her tone and manner had changed. Penoyer knew it, and, with the coolest effrontery imaginable, he came forward, bowing and scraping, and saying, " Comment vous portez vous, Mademoiselle. Je suis perfaitement delighted to see you," at the same time offering her his hand.

All saw with what hauteur she declined it, but only one, and that was Anna, heard her as she said, " Keep off, Penoyer; don't make a donkey of yourself." It was strange, Anna said, "how far into his boots Penoyer tried to draw himself," while at each fresh flash of Agnes' keen, black eyes, he winced, either from fear or sympathy.

The restraint which had surrounded the little company gave way beneath the lively sallies and sparkling wit of Agnes, who, instead of seeming amazed at the country girls, was apparently as much at ease as though she had been entertaining a drawing room full of polished city belles. When at last the party broke up, each and every one was in love with the little Albany lady, although all noticed that Carrie seemed troubled, watching Agnes narrowly; and whenever she saw her tete-a-tete with either of her companions, she would instantly draw near, and seem greatly relieved on finding that Penoyer was not the subject of conversation.

"I told you so," was grandmother's reply, when informed of all this. "I told you so. I knew Car'line warn't goin' to make out no great."

Juliet and Anna thought so too, but this did not prevent them from running to the windows next morning to see Penoyer as he passed on his way to the cars. I, who with Lizzie was tugging away at a big board with which we thought to make a "see-saw," was honored with a graceful wave of Monsieur's hands, and the words, "Au revoir, ma chere Marie."

That day Phoebe, Aunt Eunice's hired girl, came to our house. Immediately Juliet and Anna assailed her with a multitude of questions. The amount of knowledge obtained was, that "Miss Hovey was a lady, and no mistake, for she had sights of silks and jewelry, and she that morning went with Phoebe to see her milk, although she didn't dare venture inside the yard. "But," added Phoebe, "for all she was up so early she did not come out to breakfast until that gentleman was gone."

This was fresh proof that Penoyer was not "comme il

faut," and Anna expressed her determination to find out all about him ere Agnes went home. *I* remembered " *Dt. Watts* " and the invitation to the party, and secretly hoped she would find out nothing bad.

------ ♦ ------

CHAPTER IV.

COUSIN EMMA.

AGNES had been in town about two weeks, when my home was one morning thrown into a state of unusual excitement by the arrival of a letter from Boston, containing the intelligence that Cousin Emma Rushton, who had been an invalid for more than a year, was about to try the effect of country life and country air.

This piece of news operated differently upon different members of our family. Juliet exclaimed, "Good, good; Carrie Howard won't hold her head quite so high, now, for we shall have a city lady, too." Anna was delighted, because she would thus have an opportunity of acquiring city manners and city fashions. Sally said, snappishly, " There's enough to wait on now, without having a stuck-up city flirt, faintin' at the sight of a worm, and screachin' if a fly comes toward her." Mother had some misgivings on the subject. She was perfectly willing Emma should come, but she doubted our ability to entertain her, knowing that the change would be great from a fashionable city home to a country farm-house. Grandmother, who loved to talk of "my daughter in the city," was pleased, and to console mother, said, " Never you mind, Fanny;

leave her to me; you find victuals and drink, and I'll do
the entertaining."

Among so many opinions it was hard for me to arrive
at a conclusion. On the whole, however, I was glad, until told that during Cousin Emma's stay our garret gambols must be given up, and that I must not laugh loud, or
scarcely speak above a whisper, for she was sick, and it
would hurt her head. Then I wished Cousin Emma and
Cousin Emma's head would stay where they belonged.

The letter was received on Monday, but Emma would
not come until Thursday; so there was ample time for
"fixing up." The parlor-chamber was repapered, the
carpet taken up and shaken, red and white curtains hung
at the windows, a fresh ball of Castile soap bought for
the washstand, and on Thursday morning our pretty
flower beds were shorn of their finest ornaments, with
which to make bouquets for the parlor and parlor-chamber. Besides that, Sally had filled the pantry with cakes,
pies, gingerbread, and Dutch cheese, to the last of which
I fancied Emma's city taste would not take kindly. Then
there was in the cellar a barrel of fresh beer; so everything was done which could be expected.

When I went home for my dinner that day, I teased
hard to be allowed to stay out of school for one afternoon,
but mother said "No," although she suffered me to wear
my pink gingham, with sundry injunctions "not to burst
the hooks and eyes all off before night." This, by the way,
was my besetting sin; I never could climb a tree, no matter what the size might be, without invariably coming
down minus at least six hooks and eyes; but I seriously
thought I should get over it when I got older and joined
the church.

That afternoon seemed of interminable length, but at
last I saw father's carriage coming, and quick as thought

I threw my grammar out of the window; after which I demurely asked "to go out and get a book which I had dropped." Permission was granted, and I was out just in time to courtesy straight down, as father, pointing to me, said, "There, that's our little crazy Mollie," and then I got a glimpse of a remarkably sweet face, which made the tears come in my eyes, it was so pale.

Perhaps I wronged our school teacher; I think I did, for she has since died; but really I fancied she kept us longer that night on purpose. At least, it was nearly five before we were dismissed. Then, with my bonnet in hand, I ran for home, falling down once, and bursting off the lower hook! I entered the house with a bound, but was quieted by grandmother, who said Emma was lying down, and I mustn't disturb her.

After waiting some time for her to. make her appearance, I stole softly up the stairs and looked in where she was. She saw me, and instantly rising, said, with a smile that went to my heart: "And this must be Mary, the little crazy girl; come and kiss your Cousin Emma."

Twining my arms around her neck, I think I must have cried, for she repeatedly asked me what was the matter, and as I could think of no better answer, I at last told her, "I didn't like to have folks call me *crazy*. I couldn't help acting like *Sal Furbush*, the old crazy woman, who threatened to toss us up in the umbrella."

"Forgive me, darling," said Emma, coaxingly, "I will not do it again;" then stooping down, she looked intently into my eyes, soliloquizing, "Yes, it is wrong to tell her so."

In a few moments I concluded Emma was the most beau tiful creature in the world; I would not even except Carrie Howard. Emma's features were perfectly regular, and her complexion white and pure as alabaster. Her hair, which was a rich auburn, lay around her forehead in thick waves, but her great beauty consisted in her lustrous blue eyes, which were very large and dark. When she was pleased they laughed, and when she was sad they were sad, too. Her dress was a white muslin wrapper, confined at the waist by a light blue ribbon, while one of the same hue encircled her neck, and was fastened by a small gold pin, which, with the exception of the costly diamond ring on her finger, was the only ornament she wore.

When supper was ready, I proudly led her to the dining-room, casting a look of triumph at Juliet and Anna, and feeling, it may be, a *trifle* above grandmother, who said, "Don't be troublesome, child."

How grateful I was when Emma answered for me, "She doesn't trouble me in the least; I am very fond of children."

Indeed, she seemed to be very fond of everybody and everything — all except Sally's Dutch cheese, which, as I expected, she hardly relished. In less than three days she was beloved by all the household; Billy whispering to me confidentially that "never before had he seen any one except *mother*, whom he would like to marry."

Saturday afternoon Carrie and Agnes called on Emma, and as I saw them together I fancied I had never looked on three more charming faces. They appeared mutually pleased with each other, too, although for some reason there seemed to be more affinity between Emma and Agnes. Carrie appeared thoughtful and absent-minded which made Anna joke her about her "lover, Penoyer." As she was about leaving the room, she made no reply, but after she was gone, Agnes looked searchingly at Anna and said, "Is it possible, Miss Anna, that you are so mistaken ? "

"How—why?" asked Anna.   "Is Penoyer a bad man? What is his occupation ?"

" His occupation is well enough," returned Agnes.   "I would not think less of him for that, were he right in other respects.   However, he was Carrie's and my own music teacher."

"Impossible," said Anna, but at that moment Carrie reëntered the room, and, together with Agnes, soon took her leave.

" Penoyer a music teacher, after all his anger at Lily Gordon, for suggesting such an idea!"   This was now the theme of Juliet and Anna, although they wondered what there was so *bad* about him—something, evidently, from Agnes' manner, and for many days they puzzled their brains in vain to solve the mystery.

CHAPTER V.

RICHARD EVELYN AND HARLEY ASHMORE.

Emma had not long been with us, ere her fame reached the little village " over the river," and drew from thence many calls, both from gentlemen and ladies.   Among these was a Mr. Richard Evelyn and his sister, both of whom had the honor of standing on the topmost round of the aristocratic ladder in the village.   Mr. Evelyn, who was nearly thirty years of age, was a wealthy lawyer, and what is a little remarkable for that craft, (I speak from experience,) to an unusual degree of intelligence and polish of manners, he added many social and *religious* qualities.   Many kind-hearted mothers, who had on their hands

good-for-nothing daughters, wondered how he managed
to live without a wife, but he seemed to think it the easiest thing in nature, for, since the death of his parents, his
sister Susan had acted in the capacity of his housekeeper.

I have an idea that grandmother, whose disposition
was slightly spiced with a love for match-making, bethought herself how admirably Mr. Evelyn and Emma
were suited for each other; for, after his calls became frequent, I heard her many times slily hint of the possibil·
ity of our being able to keep Emma in town always. *She,*
probably, did not think so; for, each time after being
teased, she repaired to her room and read, for the twentieth time, some ominous looking letters which she had
received since being with us.

It was now three weeks since she came, and each day
she had gained in health and strength. Twice had she
walked to the woods, accompanied by Mr. Evelyn, once
to the school-house, while every day she swung under the .
old maple. About this time Agnes began to think of returning home, so Juliet and Anna determined on a party
in honor of her and Emma. It was a bright summer afternoon; and, for a wonder, I was suffered to remain
from school, although I received numerous charges to
keep my tongue still, and was again reminded of that excellent old proverb, (the composition of some old maid, I
know,) "*children* should be seen and not heard;" so,
seated in a corner, my hand pressed closely over my
mouth, the better to guard against contingencies, I looked
on and thought, with ineffable satisfaction, how much
handsomer Cousin Emma was than any one else, although
I could not help acknowledging that Carrie never looked
more beautiful than she did that afternoon, in a neatly·
fitting white muslin, with a few rose-buds nestling in her
long, glossy curls.

Matters were going on swimmingly, and I had three times ventured a remark, when Anna, who was sitting near the window, exclaimed, "Look here, girls, did you ever see a finer looking gentleman?" at the same time calling their attention to a stranger in the street. Emma looked, too, and the bright flush which suffused her cheek made me associate the gentleman with the letters she had received, and I was not surprised when he entered our yard and knocked at our door. Juliet arose to answer his summons, but Emma prevented her, saying, "Suffer me to go, will you?"

She was gone some time, and when she returned was accompanied by the stranger, whom she introduced as Mr. Ashmore. I surveyed him with childish curiosity, and drew two very satisfactory breaths when I saw that he was wholly unlike Monsieur Penoyer. He was a very fine looking man, but I did not exactly like the expression of his face. It was hardly open enough to suit me, and I noticed that he never looked you directly in the eye. In five minutes I had come to the conclusion that he was not half so good a man as Mr. Evelyn. I was in great danger, however, of changing my mind, when I saw how fondly his dark eye rested on Emma, and how delighted he seemed to be at her improved health; and when he, without any apparent exertion, kept the whole company entertained, I was charmed, and did not blame Emma for liking him. Anna's doctor was nothing to him, and I even fancied that he would dare to go *all alone* to the old mine!

Suddenly he faced about, and espying me in the corner, he said, "Here is a little lady I've not seen. Will some one introduce me?"

With the utmost gravity, Anna said, "It is my sister. little crazy Jane."

I glanced quickly at him to see how he would receive the intelligence, and when, looking inquiringly first at me and then at Emma, he said, "Is it really so? what a pity!" the die was cast—I never liked him again. That night in my little low bed, long after Lizzie was asleep, I wept bitterly, wondering what made Anna so unkind, and why people called me crazy. I knew I looked like other children, and I thought I acted like them, too; unless, indeed, I climbed more trees, tore more dresses, and burst off more hooks.

But to return to the party. After a time I thought that Mr. Ashmore's eyes went over admiringly to Carrie more frequently than was necessary, and for once I regretted that she was so pretty. Ere long, Mr. Ashmore, too, went over, and immediately there ensued between himself and Carrie a lively conversation, in which she adroitly managed to let him know that she had been three years at school in Albany. The next thing that I saw was that he took from her curls a rose-bud and appropriated it to his button hole. I glanced at Emma to see how she was affected, but her face was perfectly calm, and wore the old sweet smile. When the young ladies were about leaving, I was greatly shocked to see Mr. Ashmore offer to accompany Carrie and Agnes home.

After they were gone, grandmother said, "Emma, if I's you, I'd put a stop to that chap's flirtin' so with Car'line Howard."

Emma laughed gaily, as she replied, "Oh, grandma, I can trust Harley; I have been sick so long that he has the privilege of walking or riding with anybody he pleases."

Grandmother shook her head, saying, "It wasn't so with her and our poor grandfather;" then I fell into a fit of musing as to whether grandma was ever young, and if she ever fixed her hair before the glass, as Anna did when she expected the doctor! In the midst of my reverie, Mr. Ashmore returned, and for the remainder of the evening devoted himself so entirely to Emma that I forgave him for going home with Carrie. Next day, however, he found the walk to Capt. Howard's a very convenient one, staying a long time, too. The next day it was the same, and the next, and the next, until I fancied that even Emma began to be anxious.

Grandma was highly indignant, and Sally declared, "that, as true as she lived and breathed, if Mike should serve her so, he'd catch it." About this time, Agnes went home. The evening before she left, she spent at our house with Emma, of whom she seemed to be very fond. Carrie and Ashmore were, as usual, out riding or walking, and the conversation naturally turned upon them. At last, Anna, whose curiosity was still on the alert, to know something of Penoyer, asked Agnes of him. I will repeat, in substance, what Agnes said.

It seems that for many years Penoyer had been a teacher of music in Albany. Agnes was one of his pupils, and while teaching her music he thought proper to fall overwhelmingly in love with her. This, for a time, she did not notice; but when his attentions became so pointed as to become a subject of remark, she very coolly tried to make him understand his position. He persevered, however, until he became exceedingly impudent and annoying.

About this time there came well authenticated stories of his being not only a professed gambler, but also very dissipated in his habits. To this last charge Agnes could testify, as his breath had frequently betrayed him. He was accordingly dismissed. Still he perseveringly pursued her, always managing, if possible, to get near her in all public places, and troubling her in various ways.

At last Agnes heard that he was showing among her acquaintances two notes bearing her signature. The contents of these notes he covered with his hand, exposing to view only her name. She had twice written, requesting him to purchase some new piece of music, and it was these messages which he was now showing, insinuating that Agnes thought favorably of him, but was opposed by her father. The consequence of this was, that the next time Agnes' brother met Penoyer in the street, he gave him a sound caning, ordering him, under pain of a worse flogging, never again to mention his sister's name. This he was probably more willing to do, as he had already conceived a great liking for Carrie, who was silly enough to be pleased with and suffer his attentions.

"I wonder, though, that Carrie allowed him to visit her," said Agnes, "but then I believe she is under some obligations to him, and dare not refuse when he asked permission to come."

If Agnes knew what these obligations were, she did not tell, and grandmother, who, during the narration had knit with unwonted speed, making her needles rattle again, said, "It's plain to me that Car'line let him come to make folks think she had got a city beau."

"Quite likely," returned Agnes; "Carrie is a sad flirt, but I think, at least, that she should not interfere with other people's rights."

Here my eye followed hers to Emma, who, I thought, was looking a little paler. Just then Carrie and Ashmore came in, and the latter throwing himself upon the sofa by the side of Emma, took her hand caressingly, saying, "How are you to-night, my dear?"

"Quite well," was her quiet reply, and soon after, under pretense of moving from the window, she took a seat across the room. That night Mr. Ashmore accompanied

Carrie and Agnes home, and it was at a much later hour than usual, that old Rover first growled and then whined as he recognized our visitor.

The next morning Emma was suffering from a severe headache, which prevented her from appearing at breakfast. Mr. Ashmore seemed somewhat disturbed, and made many anxious inquiries about her. At dinner time she was well enough to come, and the extreme kindness of Mr. Ashmore's manner called a deep glow to her cheek. After dinner, however, he departed for a walk, taking his accustomed road toward Capt. Howard's.

When I returned from school he was still absent, and as Emma was quite well, she asked me to accompany her to my favorite resort, the old rock beneath the grape-vine. We were soon there, and for a long time we sat watching the shadows as they came and went upon the bright green grass, and listening to the music of the brook, which seemed to me to sing more sadly than it was wont to do.

Suddenly our ears were arrested by the sound of voices, which we knew belonged to Mr. Ashmore and Carrie. They were standing near us, just behind a clump of alders, and Carrie, in reply to something Mr. Ashmore had said, answered, " Oh, you can't be in earnest, for you have only known me ten days, and besides that, what have you done with your pale, sick lady ? "

Instantly I started up, clinching my fist in imitation of brother Billy when he was angry, but Cousin Emma's arm was thrown convulsively around me, as drawing me closely to her side, she whispered, " keep quiet."

I did keep quiet, and listened while Mr. Ashmore replied, "I entertain for Miss Rushton the highest esteem, for I know she possesses many excellent qualities. Once I thought I loved her, (how tightly Emma held me,) but she has been sick a long time, and somehow I cannot

marry an invalid. Whether she ever gets well is doubtful, and even if she does, after having seen you, she can
be nothing to me. And yet I like her, and when I am
alone with her I almost fancy I love her, but one look at
your sparkling, healthy face drives her from my mind —"

The rest of what he said I could not hear, neither did I
understand Carrie's answer, but his next words were distinct, " My dear Carrie forever."

I know the brook stopped running, or at least I did not
hear it. The sun went down; the birds went to rest;
Mr. Ashmore and Carrie went home; and still I sat there
by the side of Emma, who had lain her head in my lap,
and was so still and motionless that the dread fear came
over me that she might be dead. I attempted to lift her
up, saying, " Cousin Emma, speak to me, won't you ? "
but she made me no answer, and another ten minutes went
by. By this time the stars had come out and were looking quietly down upon us. The waters of the mill-dam
chanted mournfully, and in my disordered imagination,
fantastic images danced before the entrance of the old
mine. Half crying with fear, I again laid my hand on
Emma's head. Her hair was wet with the heavy night
dews, and my eyes were wet with something else, as I
said, " Oh, Emma, speak to me, for I am afraid and want
to go home."

This roused her, and lifting up her head I caught a
glimpse of a face of so startling whiteness, that throwing
my arms around her neck, I cried, " Oh, Emma, dear Emma, don't look so. I love you a great deal better than I
do Carrie Howard, and so I am sure does Mr. Evelyn."

I don't know how I chanced to think of Mr. Evelyn,
but he recurred to me naturally enough. All thoughts
of him, however, were soon driven from my mind, by the

sound of Emma's voice, as she said, "Mollie, darling, can you keep a secret?"

I didn't think I could, as I never had been entrusted with one, so I advised her to give it to Anna, who was very fond of them. But she said, "I am sure you can do it, Mollie. Promise me that you will not tell them at home what you have seen or heard."

I promised, and then in my joy at owning a secret, I forgot the little figures which waltzed back and forth before the old mine, I forgot the woods through which we passed, nor was the silence broken until we reached the lane Then I said, "What shall we tell the folks when they ask where we have been?"

"Leave that to me," answered Emma.

As we drew near the house, we met grandmother, Juliet, Anna and Sally, all armed and equipped for a general hunt. We were immediately assailed with a score of questions as to what had kept us so long. I looked to Emma for the answer, at the same time keeping my hand tightly over my mouth for fear I should tell.

"We found more things of interest than we expected," said Emma, consequently tarried longer than we should otherwise have done."

"Why, how hoarse you be," said grandmother, while Sally continued, "Starlight is a mighty queer time to see things in."

"Some things look better by starlight," answered Emma; "but we staid longer than we ought to, for I have got a severe headache and must go immediately to bed."

"Have some tea first," said grandmother, "and some strawberries and cream," repeated Sally; but Emma declined both and went at once to her room.

Mr. Ashmore did not come home until late that night, for I was awake and heard him stumbling up stairs in the dark. I remember, too, of having experienced the very benevolent wish that he would break his neck! As I expected, Emma did not make her appearance at the breakfast table, but about ten she came down to the parlor and asked to see Mr. Ashmore alone. Of what occurred during that interval I never knew, except that at its close cousin looked very white, and Mr. Ashmore very black, notwithstanding which he soon took his accustomed walk to Capt. Howard's. He was gone about three hours, and on his return announced his intention of going to Boston in the afternoon train. No one opposed him, for all were glad to have him go.

Just before he left, grandmother, who knew all was not right, said to him,—"Young man, I wish you well; but mind what I say, you'll get your pay yet for the capers you've cut here."

"I beg your pardon, madam," he returned, with much more emphasis on *madam* than was at all necessary, "I beg your pardon, but I think she has cut the capers, at least she dismissed me of her own accord."

I thought of what I had heard, but 'twas a secret, so I kept it safely, although I almost bit my tongue off in my zealous efforts. After Ashmore was gone, Emma, who had taken a violent cold the evening before, took her bed, and was slightly ill for nearly a week. Almost every day Mr. Evelyn called to see how she was, always bringing her a fresh bouquet of flowers. On Thursday, Carrie called, bringing Emma some ice cream which Aunt Eunice had made. She did not ask to see her, but before she left she asked Anna if she did not wish to buy her old piano.

"What will you do without it?" asked Anna.

"Oh," said Carrie, "I cannot use two. I have got a new one."

10

The stocking dropped from grandmother's hand as she exclaimed—"What is the world a comin' to! Got two pianners! Where'd you get 'em?"

"My new one was a present, and came from Boston," answered Carrie, with the utmost sang froid.

"You don't say Ashmore sent it to you!—how much did it cost?" asked grandma.

"Mr. Ashmore wrote that it cost three hundred and fifty dollars," was Carrie's reply.

Grandmother was perfectly horror stricken; but desirous of making Carrie feel as comfortable as possible, she said, "Sposin' somebody should tell him about Penoyer?"

For an instant Carrie turned pale, as she said quickly, "What does any one know about him to tell?"

"A great deal—more than you think they do—yes, a great deal," was grandma's answer.

After that, Carrie came *very* frequently to see us, always bringing something nice for Emma *or grandma!*

Meanwhile Mr. Evelyn's visits continued, and when at last Emma could see him, I was sure that she received him more kindly than she ever had before. "That'll go yet," was grandma's prediction. But her scheming was cut short by a letter from Emma's father, requesting her immediate return. Mr. Evelyn, who found he had business which required his presence in Worcester, was to accompany her thus far. It was a sad day when she left us, for she was a universal favorite. Sally cried, I cried, and Bill either cried or made believe, for he very industriously wiped his eyes and nasal organ on his shirt sleeves; besides that, things went on wrong side up generally. Grandma was cross—Sally was cross—and the school teacher was cross; the bucket fell into the well, and the cows got into the corn. I got called up at school and set with some hateful boys, one of whom amused himself by pricking me with a pin, and when, in self-defense, I gave him a good pinch, he actually yelled out—"She keeps a pinchin' me!"   On the whole, 'twas a dreadful day, and when at night I threw myself exhausted upon my little bed, I cried myself to sleep, thinking of Cousin Emma and wishing she would come back.

CHAPTER VI.

MIKE AND SALLY.

I HAVE spoken of Sally, but have said nothing of Mike, whom, of all my father's hired men, I liked the best.   He it was who made the best cornstalk fiddles, and whittled out the shrillest whistles with which to drive grandma "ravin' distracted."   He, too, it was who, on cold winter mornings, carried Lizzie to school in his arms, making me forget how my fingers ached, by telling some exploit of *his* school days.

I do not wonder that Sally liked him, and I always had an idea how that liking would end, but did not think it would be so soon.   Consequently, I suspected nothing when Sally's white dress was bleached on the grass in the clothes' yard, for nearly a week.   One day Billy came to me with a face full of wonder, saying he had just overheard Mike tell one of the men that he and Sally were going to be married in a few weeks.

I knew now what all that bleaching was for, and why Sally bought so much cotton lace of pedlars.   I was in ecstacies, too, for I had never seen any one married, but regretted the circumstance, whatever it might have been.

which prevented me from being present at mother's mar·
riage. Like many other children, I had been deceived
into the belief that the marriage ceremony consisted
mainly in leaping the broomstick, and, by myself, I had
frequently tried the experiment, delighted to find that I
could jump it at almost any distance from the ground;
but I had some misgivings as to Sally's ability to clear
the stick, for she was rather clumsy; however, I should
see the fun, for they were to be married at our house.

A week before the time appointed, mother was taken
very ill, which made it necessary that the wedding should
be postponed, or take place somewhere else. To the first,
Mike would not hear, and as good old Parson S——,
whose sermons were never more than two hours long,
came regularly every Sunday night to preach in the school-
house, Mike proposed that they be married there. Sally
did not like this exactly, but grandmother, who now
ruled the household, said it was just the thing, and accordingly it took place there.

The house was filled full, and those who could not obtain seats took their station near the windows. Our party
was early, but I was three times compelled to relinquish
my seat in favor of more distinguished persons, and I began to think that if any one was obliged to go home for
want of room, it would be me; but I resolutely determined
not to go. I'd climb the chestnut tree first! At last I
was squeezed on a high desk between two old ladies,
wearing two old black bonnets, their breath sufficiently
tinctured with tobacco smoke to be very disagreeable to
me, whose olfactories chanced to be rather aristocratic
than otherwise.

To my horror, Father S—— concluded to give us the
sermon before he did the bride. He was afraid some of
his audience would leave. Accordingly there ensued a

prayer half an hour long, after which eight verses of a long metre psalm were sung to the tune of Windham. By this time I gave a slight sign to the two old ladies that I would like to move, but they merely shook their two black bonnets at me, telling me, in fierce whispers, that "I must n't stir in meetin'." Must n't stir! I wonder how I could stir, squeezed in as I was, unless they chose to let me. So I sat bolt upright, looking straight ahead at a point where the tips of my red shoes were visible, for my feet were sticking straight out.

All at once, my attention was drawn to a spider on the wall, who was laying a net for a fly, and in watching his maneuvers I forgot the lapse of time, until Father S—— had passed his sixthly and seventhly, and was driving furiously away at the eighthly. By this time the spider had caught the fly, whose cries sounded to me like the waters of the saw-mill; the tips of my red shoes looked like the red berries which grew near the mine; the two old ladies at my side were transformed into two tall black walnut trees, while I seemed to be sliding down hill.

At this juncture, one of the old ladies moved away from me a foot at least, (she could have done so before, had she chosen to,) and I was precipitated off from the bench, striking my head on the sharp corner of a seat below. It was a dreadful blow which I received, making the blood gush from my nostrils. My loud screams brought matters to a focus, and the sermon to an end. My grandmother and one of the old ladies took me and the water pail out doors, where I was literally deluged; at the same time they called me "Poor girl! Poor Mollie! Little dear, &c."

But while they were attending to my bumped head, Mike and Sally were married, and I did n't see it after all! 'Twas too bad!

CHAPTER VII.

THE BRIDE.

AFTER Sally's marriage, there occurred at our house an interval of quiet, enlivened occasionally by letters from Cousin Emma, whose health was not as much improved by her visit to the country as she had at first hoped it would be; consequently, she proposed spending the winter south. Meantime, from Boston letters came frequently to Carrie Howard, and as the autumn advanced, things within and about her father's house foretold some unusual event. Two dress-makers were hired from the village, and it was stated, on good authority, that among Carrie's wardrobe was a white satin and an elegantly embroidered merino traveling dress.

Numerous were the surmises of Juliet and Anna as to who and how many would be invited to the wedding. All misgivings concerning themselves were happily brought to an end a week before the time, for there came to our house handsome cards of invitation for Juliet and Anna, and—I could scarcely believe my eyes—there was one for me too. For this I was indebted to Aunt Eunice, who had heard of and commiserated my misfortunes at Sally's wedding.

I was sorry that my invitation came so soon, for I had but little hope that the time would ever come. It did, however, and so did Mr. Ashmore and Agnes. As soon as dinner was over, I commenced my toilet, although the wedding was not to take place until eight that evening; but then I believed, as I do now, in being ready in season. Oh, how slowly the hours passed, and at last in perfect despair I watched my opportunity to set the clock forward when no one saw me. For this purpose I put the footstool in a chair, and mounting, was about to move the long hand, when—

But I always was the most unfortunate of mortals, so 'twas no wonder that at this point the chair slipped, the stool slipped, and I slipped. I caught at the clock to save myself; consequently both clock and I came to the floor with a terrible crash. My first thought was for the hooks and eyes, which, undoubtedly, were scattered with the fragments of the clock, but fortunately every hook was in its place, and only one eye was straightened. I draw a vail over the scolding which I got, and the numerous threats that I should stay at home.

As the clock was broken we had no means for judging of the time, and thus we were among the first who arrived at Capt. Howard's. This gave Juliet and Anna an opportunity of telling Agnes of my mishap. She laughed heartily, and then immediately changing the subject, she inquired after Cousin Emma, and when we had heard from her. After replying to these questions, Anna asked Agnes about Penoyer, and when she had seen him.

"Don't mention it," said Agnes, "but I have a suspicion that he stopped yesterday at the depot when I did. I may have been mistaken, for I was looking after my baggage and only caught a glimpse of him. If it were he, his presence bodes no good."

"Have you told Carrie?" asked Juliet.

"No, I have not. She seems so nervous whenever he is mentioned," was Agnes' reply.

I thought of the *obligations* once referred to by Agnes, and felt that I should breathe more freely when Carrie really was married. Other guests now began to arrive, and we who had fixed long enough before the looking glass, repaired to the parlor below. Bill, who saw Sally married,

had convinced me that the story of the broomstick was a
falsehood, so I was prepared for its absence, but I wondered then, not more than I do now, why grown up people should n't be whipped for telling untruths to children,
as well as children for telling untruths to grown up
people.

The parlor was now rapidly filling, and I was in great
danger of being thrust into the corner, where I could see
nothing, when Aunt Eunice very benevolently drew me
near her, saying, I should see, if no one else did. At last
Mr. Ashmore and Carrie came. Anna can tell you exactly what she wore, but I cannot. I only know that
she looked most beautifully, though I have a vague recollection of fancying that in the making of her dress,
the sleeves were forgotten entirely, and the neck very
nearly so.

The marriage ceremony commenced, and I listened
breathlessly, but this did not prevent me from hearing
some one enter the house by the kitchen door. Aunt
Eunice heard it, too, and when the minister began to say
something about Mrs. Ashmore, she arose and went out.
Something had just commenced, I think they called them
congratulations, when the crowd around the door began
to huddle together in order to make room for some person to enter. I looked up and saw Penoyer, his glittering teeth now partially disclosed, looking a very little
fiendish, I thought. Carrie saw him, too, and instantly
turned as white as the satin dress she wore, while Agnes,
who seemed to have some suspicion of his errand, exclaimed,
"impudent scoundrel!" at the same time advancing
forward, she laid her hand upon his arm.

He shook it off lightly, saying, "Pardonnez moi, ma
chere; I've no come to trouble you." Then turning to

Ashmore he said, pointing to Carrie, " She be your wife, I take it ? "

" Yes, sir," replied Ashmore haughtily. " Have you any objections ? If so they have come too late."

" Not von, not in the least, no sar," said the French-man, bowing nearly to the floor. " It give me one grand plaisir ; so now you will please settle von lectle bill I have against her ; " at the same time he drew from his pocket a sheet of half-worn paper.

Carrie, who was leaning heavily against Mr. Ashmore, instantly sprang forward and endeavored to snatch the paper, saying half imploringly, " Don't, Penoyer, you know my father will pay it."

But Penoyer passed it to Mr. Ashmore, while Capt. Howard, coming forward, said, " Pay what ? What is all this about ! "

" Only a trifle," said Penoyer ; " just a bill for giving your daughter musique lessons three years in Albany."

" *You* give my daughter music lessons ? " demanded Capt. Howard.

" Oui, Monsieur, I do that same thing," answered Penoyer.

" Oh, Carrie, Carrie," said Capt. Howard, in his sur-prise, forgetting the time and place, " why did you tell me that your knowledge of music you acquired yourself, with the assistance of your cousin, and a little help from her music teacher, and why, when this man was here a few months ago, did you not tell me he was your music teacher and had not been paid."

Bursting into tears, Carrie answered, " Forgive me, father, but he said he had no bill against me ; he made no charge."

" But she gave me von big, large mitten," said the Frenchman, " when she see this man, who has more l'argent; but no difference, no difference, sar, this gentleman," bowing toward Ashmore, "parfaitement delighted to pay it."

Whether he were delighted or not, he did pay it, for drawing from his pocket his purse, while his large black eyes emitted gleams of fire, he counted out the required amount, one hundred and twenty-five dollars; then confronting Penoyer, he said, fiercely, "Give me a receipt for this, instantly, after which I will take it upon me to show you the door."

"Certainement, certainement, all I want is my l'argent," said Penoyer.

The money was paid, the receipt given, and then, as Penoyer hesitated a moment, Ashmore said, "Are you waiting to be helped out, sir?"

"No, Monsieur, si vous plait, I have tree letters from Madame, which will give you one grande satisfaction to read." Then tossing toward Ashmore the letters, with a malicious smile he left the house.

Poor Carrie! When sure that he was gone, she fainted away and was carried from the room. At supper, however, she made her appearance, and after that was over, the guests, unopposed, left en masse.

What effect Penoyer's disclosures had on Ashmore we never exactly knew, but when, a few days before the young couple left home, they called at our house, we all fancied that Carrie was looking more thoughtful than usual, while a cloud seemed to be resting on Ashmore's brow. The week following their marriage they left for New York, where they were going to reside. During the winter Carrie wrote home frequently, giving accounts of the many gay and fashionable parties which she attended, and once in a letter to Anne she wrote, "The flattering attentions which I receive have more than once made Ashmore jealous."

Two years from the time they were married, Mrs. Ashmore was brought back to her home, a pale faded invalid, worn out by constant dissipation and the care of a sickly baby, so poor and blue that even I couldn't bear to touch it. Three days after their arrival Mr. Evelyn brought to us his bride, Cousin Emma, blooming with health and beauty. I could scarcely believe that the exceedingly beautiful Mrs. Evelyn was the same white faced girl, who, two years before, had sat with me beneath the old grape-vine.

The day after she came, I went with her to visit Carrie, who, the physicians said, was in a decline. I had not seen her before since her return, and on entering the sick-room, I was as much surprised at her haggard face, sunken eyes, and sallow skin, as was Mr. Ashmore at the appearance of Emma. "Is it possible," said he, coming forward, "Is it possible, Emma—Mrs. Evelyn, that you have entirely recovered?"

I remembered what he had once said about "invalid wives," and I feared that the comparison he was evidently making would not be very favorable toward Carrie. We afterwards learned, however, that he was the kindest of husbands, frequently walking half the night with his crying baby, and at other times trying to soothe his nervous wife, who was sometimes very irritable.

Before we left, Carrie drew Emma closely to her and said, "They tell me I probably shall never get well, and now, while I have time, I wish to ask your forgiveness for the great wrong I once did you."

"How? When?" asked Emma, quickly, and Carrie continued: "When first I saw him who is my husband, I determined to leave no means untried to secure him for myself; I knew you were engaged, but I fancied that your ill health annoyed him, and I played my part well. You know how I succeeded, but I am sure you forgive me, for you love Mr. Evelyn quite as well, perhaps better."

"Yes, far better," was Emma's reply, as she kissed Carrie's wan cheek; then bidding her good-by, she promised to call frequently during her stay in town. She kept her word, and was often accompanied by Mr. Evelyn, who strove faithfully and successfully, too, to lead into the path of peace, her whose days were well nigh ended.

'Twas on one of those bright days in the Indian summer time, that Carrie at last slept the sleep that knows no awakening. The evening after the burial, I went in at Capt. Howard's, and all the animosity I had cherished for Mr. Ashmore vanished, when I saw the large tear-drops, as they fell on the face of his motherless babe, whose wailing cries he endeavored in vain to hush. When the first snow flakes came, they fell on a little mound, where by the side of her mother Mr. Ashmore had laid his baby, Emma.

> Now, side by side they are sleeping,
>   In the grave's dark, dreamless bed,
> While the willow boughs seem weeping,
>   As they bend above the dead.

And now, dear reader, after telling you that, yielding to the importunities of Emma's parents, Mr. Evelyn, at last moved to the city, where, if I mistake not, he is still living, my story is finished. But do not, I pray you, think that these few pages contain all that I know of the olden time;

> Oh no, far down in memory's well,
>   Exhaustless stores remain,
> From which, perchance, some future day,
>   I'll weave a tale again.

The Gilberts;

OR,

RICE CORNER NUMBER TWO.

CHAPTER I.

THE GILBERTS.

THE spring following Carrie Howard's death, Rice Corner was thrown into a commotion by the astounding fact
that Capt. Howard was going out west, and had sold his
farm to a gentleman from the city, whose wife "kept six
servants, wore silk all the time, never went inside of the
kitchen, never saw a churn, breakfasted at ten, dined at
three, and had supper the next day!"

Such was the story which Mercy Jenkins detailed to
us, early one Monday morning, and then, eager to communicate so desirable a piece of news to others of her acquaintance, she started off, stopping for a moment as she
passed the wash-room, to see if Sally's clothes "wan't
kinder dingy and yaller." As soon as she was gone, the
astonishment of our household broke forth, grandma wondering why Capt. Howard wanted to go to the ends of
the earth, as she designated Chicago, their place of destination, and what she should do without Aunt Eunice,
who, having been born on grandma's wedding day, was
very dear to her, and then *her age was so easy to keep!*

But the best of friends must part, and when at Mrs. How-ard's last tea-drinking with us, I saw how badly they all felt, and how many tears were shed, I firmly resolved never to like anybody but my own folks, unless, indeed, I made an exception in favor of *Tom Jenkins*, who so often drew me to school on his sled, and who made such comi-cal looking jack-o'-lanterns out of the big yellow pumpkins.

In reply to the numerous questions concerning Mr. Gil-bert, the purchaser of their farm, Mrs. Howard could only reply, that he was very wealthy and had got tired of liv-ing in the city; adding, further, that he wore a "mon-strous pair of musquitoes," had an evil looking eye, four children, smoked cigars, and was a lawyer by profession. This last was all grandma wanted to know about him,— "that told the whole story," for there never was but *one* decent lawyer, and that was Mr. Evelyn, Cousin Emma's husband. Dear old lady!—when, a few years ago, she heard that I, her favorite grandchild, was to marry one of the craft, she made another exception in *his* favor, say-ing that "if he wasn't all straight, Mary would soon make him so!"

Within a short time after Aunt Eunice's visit, she left Rice Corner, and on the same day wagon load after wag-on load of Mr. Gilbert's furniture passed our house, until Sally declared "there was enough to keep a tavern, and she didn't see nothin' where they's goin' to put it," at the same time announcing her intention of "running down there after dinner, to see what was going on."

It will be remembered that Sally was now a married woman—"Mrs. Michael Welsh;" consequently, mother, who lived with her, instead of her living with mother, did not presume to interfere with her much, though she hinted pretty strongly that she "always liked to see people mind their own affairs." But Sally was incorrigible. The dinner dishes were washed with a whew, I was coaxed into sweeping the back room — which I did, leaving the dirt under the broom behind the door — while Mrs. Welsh, donning a pink calico, blue shawl, and bonnet trimmed with dark green, started off on her prying excursion, stopping by the roadside where Mike was making fence, and keeping him, as grandma said, "full half an hour by the clock from his work."

Not long after Sally's departure, a handsome carriage, drawn by two fine bay horses, passed our house; and, as the windows were down, we could plainly discern a pale, delicate-looking lady, wrapped in shawls, a tall, stylish-looking girl, another one about my own age, and two beautiful little boys.

"That 's the Gilberts, I know," said Anna. "Oh, I 'm so glad Sally's gone, for now we shall have the full particulars;" and again we waited as impatiently for Sally's return as we had once done before for grandma.

At last, to our great relief, the green ribbons and blue shawl were descried in the distance, and ere long Sally was with us, ejaculating, "Oh, my — mercy me!" etc., thus giving us an inkling of what was to follow. "Of all the sights that ever I have seen," said she, folding up the blue shawl, and smoothing down the pink calico. "There's carpeting enough to cover every crack and crevice — all pure *Bristles*, too!"

Here I tittered, whereupon Sally angrily retorted, that "she guessed she knew how to talk proper, if she had n't studied grarmar."

"Never mind," said Anna, "go on; Brussels carpeting and what else?"

"Mercy knows what else," answered Sally. "I can't begin to guess the names of half the things. There's mahogany, and rosewood, and marble fixin's,—and in Miss

Gilbert's room there's lace curtains and silk *damson* ones—"

A look from Anna restrained me this time, and Sally continued.

" Mercy Jenkins is there, helpin', and she says Mr. Gilbert told 'em his wife never et a piece of salt pork in her life, and knew no more how bread was made than a child two years old."

" What a simple critter she must be," said grandma, while Anna asked if she saw Mrs. Gilbert, and if that tall girl was her daughter.

" Yes, I seen her," answered Sally, " and I guess she's weakly, for the minit she got into the house she lay down on the sofa, which Mr. Gilbert says cost seventy-five dollars. That tall, proud-lookin' thing they call Miss Adaline, but I'll warrant you don't catch me puttin' on the Miss. *I* called her Adaline, and you had orto seen how her big eyes looked at me. Says she, at last, 'Are you one of pa's new servants ?'

" 'Servants !' says I, 'no, indeed; I'm Mrs. Michael Welsh, one of your nighest neighbors.'

" Then I told her that there were two nice girls lived in the house with me, and she'd better get acquainted with 'em, right away; and then with the hatefulest of all hateful laughs, she asked if 'they wore glass beads and went barefoot.'"

I fancied that neither Juliet nor Anna were greatly pleased at being introduced by Sally, the housemaid, to the elegant Adaline Gilbert, who had come to the country with anything but a favorable impression of its inhabitants. The second daughter, the one about my own age, Sally said they called Nellie; " and a nice, clever creature she is, too — not a bit stuck up like t'other one. Why, I do believe she'd walked every big beam in the barn before she'd been there half an hour, and the last I saw of her, she was coaxing a cow to lie still while she got upon her back!"

How my heart warmed toward the romping Nellie, and how I wondered if, after that beam-walking exploit, her hooks and eyes were all in their places! The two little boys, Sally said, were twins, Edward and Egbert, or, as they were familiarly called, Burt and Eddie. This was nearly all she had learned, if we except the fact that the family ate with silver forks, and drank wine after dinner. This last, mother pronounced heterodox, while I, who dearly loved the juice of the grape, and sometimes left finger marks on the top shelf, whither I had climbed for a sip from grandma's decanter, secretly hoped I should some day dine with Nellie Gilbert, and drink all the wine I wanted, thinking how many times I'd rinse my mouth so mother should n't smell my breath!

In the course of a few weeks the affairs of the Gilbert family were pretty generally canvassed in Rice Corner, Mercy Jenkins giving it as her opinion that "Miss Gil bert was much the likeliest of the two, and that Mr. Gil bert was cross, overbearing, and big feeling."

CHAPTER II.

NELLIE.

As yet I had only seen Nellie in the distance, and was about despairing of making her acquaintance, when accident threw her in my way. Directly opposite our house, and just accross a long green meadow, was a piece of

11

woods which belonged to Mr. Gilbert, and there, one afternoon early in May, I saw Nellie. I had seen her there
before, but never dared approach her; and now I divided
my time between watching her and a dense black cloud
which had appeared in the west, and was fast approach
ing the zenith. I was just thinking how nice it would be
if the rain should drive her to our house for shelter, when
patter, patter came the large drops in my face; thicker
and faster they fell, until it seemed like a perfect deluge;
and through the almost blinding sheet of rain I descried
Nellie coming toward me at a furious rate. With the
agility of a fawn she bounded over the gate, and with the
exclamation of, "Ain't I wetter than a *drownded* rat?"
we were perfectly well acquainted.

It took but a short time to divest her of her dripping
garments, and array her in some of mine, which Sally said
"fitted her to a T," though I fancied she looked sadly out
of place in my linen pantalets and long-sleeved dress. She
was a great lover of fun and frolic, and in less than half
an hour had "ridden to Boston" on Joe's rocking-horse,
turned the little wheel faster than even *I* dared to turn
it, tried on grandma's stays, and then, as a crowning feat,
tried the rather dangerous experiment of riding down the
garret stairs on a board! The clatter brought up grandma, and I felt some doubts about her relishing a kind of
play which savored so much of what she called "a racket,"·
but the soft brown eyes which looked at her so pleadingly,
were too full of love, gentleness, and mischief to be resisted, and permission for "one more ride" was given,
"provided she'd promise not to break her neck."

Oh, what fun we had that afternoon! What a big rent
she tore in my gingham frock, and what a "dear, delightful old haunted castle of a thing" she pronounced our
house to be. Darling, darling Nellie! I shut my eyes

and she comes before me again, the same bright, beautiful creature she was when I saw her first, as she was when I saw her for the last, last time.

It rained until dark, and Nellie, who confidently expected to stay all night, had whispered to me her intention of "tying our toes together," when there came a tremendous rap upon the door, and, without waiting to be bidden, in walked Mr. Gilbert, puffing and swelling, and making himself perfectly at home, in a kind of off-hand manner, which had in it so much of condescension that I was disgusted, and, when sure Nellie would not see me, I made at him a wry face, thereby feeling greatly relieved!

After managing to let mother know how expensive his family was, how much he paid yearly for wines and cigars, and how much Adaline's education and piano had cost, he arose to go, saying to his daughter, "Come, Puss, take off those,—ahem!—those habiliments, and let's be off!"

Nellie obeyed, and just before she was ready to start, she asked, "When I would come and spend the day with her?"

I looked at mother, mother looked at Mr. Gilbert, Mr. Gilbert looked at me, and after surveying me from head to foot, said, spitting between every other word, "Ye-es, ye-es, we've come to live in the country, and I suppose, (here he spit three successive times,) and I suppose we may as well be on friendly terms as any other; so madam, (turning to mother,) I am willing to have your little daughter visit us occasionally." Then adding that "he would extend the same invitation to her, were it not that his wife was an invalid and saw no company," he departed.

One morning, several days afterward, a servant brought

to our house a neat little note from Mrs. Gilbert, asking mother to let me spend the day with Nellie. After some consultation between mother and grandma, it was decided that I might go, and in less than an hour I was dressed and on the road, my hair braided so tightly in my neck that the little red bumps of flesh set up here and there, like currants on a brown earthen platter.

Nellie did not wait to receive me formally, but came running down the road, telling me that Robin had made a swing in the barn, and that we would play there most all day, as her mother was sick, and Adaline, who occupied two-thirds of the house, would n't let us come near . her. This Adaline was to me a very formidable personage. Hitherto I had only caught glimpses of her, as with long skirts and waving plumes she sometimes dashed past our house on horseback, and it was with great trepidation that I now followed Nellie into the parlor, where she told me her sister was.

"Adaline, this is my little friend," said she ; and Adaline replied, "How do you do, *little friend ?*"

My cheeks tingled, and for the first time, raising my eyes, I found myself face to face with the haughty belle. She was very tall and queen-like in her figure, and though she could hardly be called handsome, there was about her an air of elegance and refinement which partially compensated for the absence of beauty. That she was proud, one could see from the glance of her large black eyes and the curl of her lip. Coolly surveying me for a moment, as she would any other curious specimen, she resumed her book, never speaking to me again, except to ask, when she saw me gazing wonderingly around the splendidly furnished room, "if I supposed I could remember every article of furniture, and give a faithful report."

I thought I was insulted when she called me "little

friend," and now, feeling sure of it, I tartly replied, that "if I couldn't, she, perhaps, might lend me paper and pencil, with which to write them down."

"Original, truly," said she, again poring over her book.

Nellie, who had left me for a moment, now returned, bidding me come and see her mother, and passing through the long hall, I was soon in Mrs. Gilbert's room, which was as tastefully, though perhaps not quite so richly, furnished as the parlor. Mrs. Gilbert was lying upon a sofa, and the moment I looked upon her, the love which I had so freely given the daughter, was shared with the mother, in whose pale, sweet face, and soft, brown eyes, I saw a strong resemblance to Nellie. She was attired in a rose-colored morning-gown, which flowed open in front, disclosing to view a larger quantity of rich French embroidery than I had ever before seen.

Many times during the day, and many times since, have I wondered what made her marry, and if she really loved, the bearish looking man who occasionally stalked into the room, smoking cigars and talking very loudly, when he knew how her head was throbbing with pain. I had eaten but little breakfast that morning, and verily I thought I should famish before their dinner hour arrived; and when at last it came, and I saw the table glittering with silver, I felt many misgivings as to my ability to acquit myself creditably. But by dint of watching Nellie, doing just what she did, and refusing just what she refused, I managed to get through with it tolerably well. For once, too, in my life, I drank all the wine I wanted; the result of which was, that long before sun set I went home, crying and vomiting with the sick headache, which Sally said "served me right;" at the same time hinting her belief that I was slightly intoxicated!

CHAPTER III.

THE HAUNTED HOUSE.

Down our long, green lane, and at the farther extrem ity of the narrow foot-path which led to the "old mine," was another path or wagon road, which wound along among the fern bushes, under the chestnut trees, across the hemlock swamp, and up to a grassy ridge which overlooked a small pond, said, *of course*, to have no bottom. Fully crediting this story, and knowing, moreover, that *China* was opposite to us, I had often taken down my atlas and hunted through that ancient empire, in hopes of finding a corresponding sheet of water. Failing to do so, I had made one with my pencil, writing against it, "Cranberry Pond," that being the name of its American brother.

Just above the pond on the grassy ridge, stood an old, dilapidated building, which had long borne the name of the "haunted house." I never knew whether this title was given it on account of its proximity to the "old mine," or because it stood near the very spot where, years and years ago, the "bloody Indians" pushed those cart loads of burning hemp against the doors "of the only remaining house in Quaboag"—for which see Goodrich's Child's History, page ——, somewhere toward the commencement. I only know that 't was called the "haunted house," and that, for a long time, no one would live there, on account of the rapping, dancing, and cutting up generally, which was said to prevail there, particularly in the west room, the one overhung by creepers and grape-vines.

Three or four years before our story opens, a widow

lady, Mrs. Hudson, with her only daughter, Mabel, appeared in our neighborhood, hiring the " haunted house,"
and, in spite of the neighbors' predictions to the contrary,
living there quietly and peaceably, unharmed by ghost or
goblin. At first, Mrs. Hudson was looked upon with distrust, and even a league with a certain old fellow was
hinted at; but as she seemed to be well disposed, kind,
and affable toward all, this feeling gradually wore away,
and now she was universally liked, while Mabel, her
daughter, was a general favorite. For two years past,
Mabel had worked in the Fiskdale factory a portion of
the time, going to school the remainder of the year. She
was fitting herself for a teacher, and as the school in our
district was small, the trustees had this summer kindly
offered it to her. This arrangement delighted me; for,
next to Nellie Gilbert, I loved Mabel Hudson best of
anybody; and I fancied, too, that they looked alike, but
of course it was all fancy.

Mrs. Hudson was a tailoress, and the day following my
visit to Mr. Gilbert's I was sent by mother to take her
some work. I found her in the little porch, her white
cap-border falling over her placid face, and her wide
checked apron coming nearly to the bottom of her dress.
Mabel was there, too, and as she arose to receive me,
something about her reminded me of Adaline Gilbert. I
could not tell what it was, for Mabel was very beautiful,
and beside her Adaline would be plain; still, there was a
resemblance, either in voice or manner, and this it was,
perhaps, which made me so soon mention the Gilberts,
and my visit to them the day previous.

Instantly Mrs. Hudson and Mabel exchanged glances,
and I thought the face of the former grew a shade paler·
still, I may have been mistaken, for, in her usual tone of
voice, she began to ask me numberless questions concern-

ing the family, which seemed singular, as she was not re-markable for curiosity. But it suited me. I loved to talk then not less than I do now, and in a few minutes I had told all I knew, and more, too, most likely.

At last, Mrs. Hudson asked about Mr. Gilbert, and how I liked *him.*

"Not a bit," said I. "He's the hatefulest, crossest, big-feelingest man I ever saw, and Adaline is just like him!"

Had I been a little older I might, perhaps, have won-dered at the crimson flush which my hasty words brought to Mrs. Hudson's cheek, but I did not notice it then, and thinking she was, of course, highly entertained, I contin-ued to talk about Mr. Gilbert and Adaline, in the last of whom Mabel seemed the most interested. Of Nellie I spoke with the utmost affection, and when Mrs. Hudson expressed a wish to see her, I promised, if possible, to bring her there; then, as I had already outstaid the time for which permission had been given, I tied on my sun-bonnet and started for home, revolving the ways and means by which I should keep my promise.

This proved to be a very easy matter; for, within a few days, Nellie came to return my visit, and as mother had other company, she the more readily gave us permis-sion to go where we pleased. Nellie had a perfect pas-sion for ghost and witch stories, saying, though, that "she never liked to have them explained—she'd rather they'd be left in solemn mystery;" so when I told her of the "old mine" and the "haunted house," she immediately expressed a desire to see them. Hiding our bonnets un-der our aprons, the better to conceal our intentions from sister Lizzie, who, we fancied, had serious thoughts of *tagging,* we sent her up stairs in quest of something which we knew was not there, and then away we scampered down the green lane and across the pasture, dropping once into some alders as Lizzie's yellow hair became visible on the fence at the foot of the lane. Our consciences smote us a little, but we kept still until she returned to the house; then, continuing our way, we soon came in sight of the mine, which Nellie determined to explore.

It was in vain that I tried to dissuade her from the attempt. She was resolved, and stationing myself at a safe distance, I waited while she scrambled over stones, sticks, logs, and bushes, until she finally disappeared in the cave. Ere long, however, she returned with soiled pantalets, torn apron, and scratched face, saying that "the mine was nothing in the world but a hole in the ground, and a mighty little one at that." After this, I didn't know but I would sometime venture in, but for fear of what *might* happen, I concluded to choose a time when I had'nt run away from Liz!

When I presented Nellie to Mrs. Hudson, she took both her hands in hers, and, greatly to my surprise, kissed her on both cheeks. Then she walked hastily into the next room, but not until I saw something fall from her eyes, which I am sure were tears.

"Funny, isn't it?" said Nellie, looking wonderingly at me. "I don't know whether to laugh, or what."

Mabel now came in, and though she manifested no particular emotion, she was exceedingly kind to Nellie, asking her many questions, and sometimes smoothing her brown curls. When Mrs. Hudson again appeared, she was very calm, but I noticed that her eyes constantly rested upon Nellie, who, with Mabel's gray kitten in her lap, was seated upon the door-step, the very image of childish innocence and beauty. Mrs. Hudson urged us to stay to tea, but I declined, knowing that there was company at home, with three kinds of cake, besides cookies, for supper. So bidding her good-by, and promising to come again, we started homeward, where we found the ladies discussing their green tea and making large inroads upon the three kinds of cake.

One of them, a Mrs. Thompson, was gifted with the art of fortune-telling, by means of tea-grounds, and when Nellie and I took our seats at the table, she kindly offered to see what was in store for us. She had frequently told my fortune, each time managing to fish up a freckle-faced boy, so nearly resembling her grandson, my particular aversion, that I did n't care to hear it again. But with Nellie 't was all new, and after a great whirling of tea grounds and staining of mother's best table-cloth, she passed her cup to Mrs. Thompson, confidently whispering to me that she *guessed* she'd tell her something about Willie Raymond, who lived in the city, and who gave her the little cornelian ring which she wore. With the utmost gravity Mrs. Thompson read off the past and present, and then peering far into the future, she suddenly exclaimed, " Oh my ! there's a gulf, or something, before you, and you are going to tumble into it headlong; don't ask me anything more."

I never did and never shall believe in fortune-telling, much less in Granny Thompson's " turned up cups," but years after, I thought of her prediction with regard to Nellie Poor poor Nellie!

CHAPTER IV.

JEALOUSY.

On the first Monday in June our school commenced, and long before breakfast Lizzie and I were dressed, and had turned inside out the little cupboard over the fire-place, where our books were kept during vacation. Breakfast being over, we deposited in our dinner-basket the whole of a custard pie, and were about starting off, when mother said "we should n't go a step until half past eight," adding further, that "we must put that pie back, for 'twas one she'd saved for their own dinner."

Lizzie pouted, while I cried, and taking my bonnet, I repaired to the "great rock," where the sassafras, black-berries, and black snakes grew. Here I sat for a long time, thinking if I ever did grow up and get married, (I was sure of the latter,) I'd have all the custard pie I could eat, for once! In the midst of my reverie a footstep sounded near, and looking up I saw before me Nellie Gil-bert, with her satchel of books on her arm, and her sun-bonnet hanging down her back, after the fashion in which I usually wore mine. In reply to my look of inquiry, she said her father had concluded to let her go to the district school, though he didn't expect her to learn anything but "slang terms and ill manners."

By this time it was half past eight, and, together with Lizzie, we repaired to the school-house, where we found assembled a dozen girls and as many boys, among whom was Tom Jenkins. Tom was a great admirer of beauty, and hence I could never account for the preference he had hitherto shown for me, whom my brothers called "bung-eyed" and Sally "raw-boned." He, however, didn't think so. My eyes, he said, were none too large, and many a night had he carried home my books for me, and many a morning had he brought me nuts and raisins, to say nothing of the time when I found in my desk a little note, which said ——, but everybody who's been to school, knows what it said!

Taking it all round, we were as good as engaged; so you can judge what my feelings were when, before the night of Nellie's first day at school, I saw Tom Jenkins giving her an orange, which I had every reason to think was originally intended for me! I knew very well that Nellie's brown curls and eyes had done the mischief; and though I did not love her the less, I blamed him the more for his fickleness, for only a week before he had praised my eyes, calling them a "beautiful indigo blue," and all that. I was highly incensed, and when on our way from school he tried to speak good-humoredly, I said, "I'd thank you to let me alone! I don't like you, and never did!"

He looked sorry for a minute, but soon forgot it all in talking to Nellie, who, after he had left us, said "he was a cleverish kind of boy, though he couldn't begin with William Raymond." After that I was very cool toward Tom, who attached himself more and more to Nellie, saying "she had the handsomest eyes he ever saw;" and, indeed, I think it chiefly owing to those soft, brown, dreamy eyes, that I am not now "Mrs. Tom Jenkins, of Jenkinsville," a place way out west, whither Tom and his mother have migrated!

One day Nellie was later to school than usual, giving as a reason that their folks had company — a Mr. Sherwood and his mother, from Hartford; and adding, that "if I'd never tell anybody as long as I lived and breathed, she'd tell me something."

Of course I promised, and then Nellie told me how she

guessed that Mr. Sherwood, who was rich and handsome, liked Adaline. "Any way, Adaline likes him," said she; "and oh, she's so nice and good when he's around. I ain't 'Nell, you hateful thing' then, but I'm 'Sister Nellie.' They are going to ride this morning, and perhaps they'll go by here.—There they are, now!" and looking toward the road, I saw Mr. Sherwood and Adaline Gilbert on horseback, riding leisurely past the school-house. She was nodding to Nellie, but he was looking intently at Mabel, who was sitting near the window. I know he asked Adaline something about her, for I distinctly heard a part of her reply — "a poor factory-girl," and Adaline's head tossed scornfully, as if that were a sufficient reason why Mabel should be despised.

Mr. Sherwood evidently did not think so, for the next day he walked by alone,—and the next day he did the same, this time bringing with him a book, and seating himself in the shadow of a chestnut tree not far from the school-house. The moment school was out, he arose and came forward, inquiring for Nellie, who, of course, introduced him to Mabel. The three then walked on together, while Tom Jenkins staid in the rear with me, wondering what I wanted to act so for; "couldn't a *feller* like more than one girl if he wanted to ?"

"Yes, I s'posed a *feller* could, though I didn't know, nor care!"

Tom made no reply, but whittled away upon a bit of shingle, which finally assumed the shape of a heart, and which I afterward found in his desk with the letter "N" written upon it, and then scratched out. When at last we reached our house, Mr. Sherwood asked Nellie "where that old mine and saw-mill were, of which she had told him so much."

"Right on Miss Hudson's way home," said Nellie,

"Let's walk along with her;" and the next moment Mr. Sherwood, Mabel, and Nellie were in the long, green lane which led down to the saw-mill.

Oh, how Adaline stormed when she heard of it, and how sneeringly she spoke to Mr. Sherwood of the "factory girl," insinuating that the bloom on her cheek was *paint*, and the lily on her brow *powder!* But he probably did not believe it, for almost every day he passed the school-house, generally managing to speak with Mabel; and once he went all the way home with her, staying ever so long, too, for I watched until 'twas pitch dark, and he hadn't got back yet!

In a day or two he went home, and I thought no more about him, until Tom, who had been to the post-office, brought Mabel a letter, which made her turn red and white alternately, until at last she cried. She was very absent-minded the remainder of that day, letting us do as we pleased, and never in my life did I have a better time "carrying on" than I did that afternoon when Mabel received her first letter from Mr. Sherwood.

CHAPTER V.

NEW RELATIONS.

ABOUT six weeks after the close of Mabel's school, we were one day startled with the intelligence that she was going to be married, and to Mr. Sherwood, too. He had become tired of the fashionable ladies of his acquaintance, and when he saw how pure and artless Mabel was, he im-

mediately became interested in her; and at last overcom-
ing all feelings of pride, he had offered her his hand, and
had been accepted. At first we could hardly credit the
story; but when Mrs. Hudson herself confirmed it, we
'gave it up, and again I wondered if I should be invited.
All the nicest and best chestnuts which I could find, to
say nothing of the apples and butternuts, I carried to her,
not without my reward either, for when invitations came
to us, I was included with the rest. Our family were the
only invited guests, and I felt no fears, this time, of being
hidden by the crowd.

Just before the ceremony commenced, there was the
sound of a heavy footstep upon the outer porch, a loud
knock at the door, and then into the room came Mr. Gilbert! He seemed slightly agitated, but not one-half so
much as Mrs. Hudson, who exclaimed, "William, *my son*,
why are you here?"

"I came to witness my sister's bridal," was the
answer; and turning toward the clergyman, he said,
somewhat authoritatively, "Do not delay for me, sir
Go on."

There was a movement in the next room, and then the
bridal party entered, both starting with surprise as they
saw Mr. Gilbert. Very beautiful did Mabel look, as she
stood up to take upon herself the marriage vow, not a
syllable of which did one of us hear. We were thinking
of Mr. Gilbert, and the strange words, "my son" and "my
sister."

When it was over, and Mabel was Mrs. Sherwood, Mr.
Gilbert approached Mrs. Hudson, saying, "Come, mother,
let me lead you to the bride."

With an impatient gesture she waved him off, and going alone to her daughter, threw her arms around her
neck, sobbing convulsively. There was an awkward si-

lence, and then Mr. Gilbert, thinking he was called upon for an explanation, arose, and addressing himself mostly to Mr. Sherwood, said, "I suppose what has transpired here to night seems rather strange, and will undoubtedly furnish the neighborhood with gossip for more than a week, but they are welcome to canvass whatever I do. I can't help it if I was born with an unusual degree of pride; neither can I help feeling mortified, as I many times did, at my family, particularly after she," glancing at his mother, "married the man whose name she bears."

Here Mrs. Hudson lifted up her head, and coming to Mr. Gilbert's side, stood proudly erect, while he continued: "She would tell you he was a good man, but I hated him, and swore never to enter the house while he lived. I went away, took care of myself, grew rich, married into one of the first families in Hartford, and,— and —"

Here he paused, and his mother, continuing the sentence, added, "and grew ashamed of your own mother, who many a time went without the comforts of life that you might be educated. You were always a proud, wayward boy, William, but never did I think you would do as you have done. You have treated me with utter neglect, never allowing your wife to see me, and when I once proposed visiting you in Hartford, you asked your brother, now dead, to dissuade me from it, if possible, for you could not introduce me to your acquaintances as your mother. Never do you speak of me to your children, who, if they know they have a grandmother, little dream that she lives within a mile of their father's dwelling. One of them I have seen, and my heart yearned toward her as it did toward you when first I took you in my arms, my first-born baby; and yet, William, I thank heaven there is in her sweet face no trace of her father's features. This may sound harsh, unmotherly, but greatly have I been

sinned against, and now, just as a brighter day is dawning upon me, why have you come here! Say, William,
why?"

By the time Mrs. Hudson had finished, nearly all in the
room were weeping. Mr. Gilbert, however, seemed perfectly indifferent, and with the most provoking coolness
replied, "I came to see my fair sister married—to con-
gratulate her upon an alliance which will bring us upon a
more equal footing."

"You greatly mistake *me*, sir, "said Mr. Sherwood,
turning haughtily toward Mr. Gilbert, at the same time
drawing Mabel nearer to him; "you greatly mistake me,
if, after what I have heard, you think I would wish for
your acquaintance. If my wife, when poor and obscure,
was not worthy of your attention, *you* certainly are not
now worthy of hers, and it is my request that our intercourse should end here."

Mr. Gilbert muttered something about "extenuating
circumstances," and "the whole not being told," but no
one paid him any attention; and at last, snatching up his
hat, he precipitately left the house, I sending after him a
hearty good riddance, and mentally hoping he would
measure his length in the ditch which he must pass on his
way across hemlock swamp.

The next morning Mr. and Mrs. Sherwood departed on
their bridal tour, intending, on their return, to take their
mother with them to the city. Several times during their
absence I saw Mr. Gilbert, either going to or returning
from the "haunted house," and I readily guessed he was
trying to talk his mother over, for nothing could be more
mortifying than to be *cut* by the Sherwoods, who were
among the first in Hartford. Afterward, greatly to my
satisfaction, I heard that though, mother-like, Mrs. Hudson had forgiven her son, Mr. Sherwood ever treated him

with a cool haughtiness, which effectually kept him at a distance.

Once, indeed, at Mabel's earnest request, Mrs. Gilbert and Nellie were invited to visit her, and as the former was too feeble to accomplish the journey, Nellie went alone, staying a long time, and torturing her sister on her return with a glowing account of the elegantly furnished house, of which Adaline had once hoped to be the proud mistress.

For several years after Mabel's departure from Rice Corner, nothing especial occurred in the Gilbert family, except the marriage of Adaline with a rich bachelor, who must have been many years older than her father, for he colored his whiskers, wore false teeth and a wig, besides having, as Nellie declared, a wooden leg! For the truth of this last I will not vouch, as Nellie's assertion was only founded upon the fact of her having once looked through the keyhole of his door, and espied standing by his bed something which looked like a cork leg, but which might have been a boot! What Adaline saw in him to like, I could never guess. I suppose, however, that she only ooked at his rich gilding, which covered a multitude of defects.

Immediately after the wedding, the happy pair started for a two years' tour in Europe, where the youthful bride so enraged her bald-headed lord by flirting with a mus-tached Frenchman, that in a fit of anger the old man picked up his goods, chattels, and wife, and returned to New York within three months of his leaving it!

CHAPTER VI.

POOR, POOR NELLIE.

AND now, in the closing chapter of this brief sketch of the Gilberts, I come to the saddest part, the fate of poor Nellie, the dearest playmate my childhood ever knew; she whom the lapse of years ripened into a graceful, beautiful girl, loved by everybody, even by Tom Jenkins, whose boyish affection had grown with his growth and strengthened with his strength.

And now Nellie was the affianced bride of William Raymond, who had replaced the little cornelian with the engagement ring. At last the rumor reached Tom Jenkins, awaking him from the sweetest dream he had ever known. He could not ask Nellie if it were true, so he came to me; and when I saw how he grew pale and trembled, I felt that Nellie was not altogether blameless. But he breathed no word of censure against her; and when, a year or two afterward, I saw her given to William Raymond, I knew that the love of two hearts was hers; the one to cherish and watch over her, the other to love and worship, silently, secretly, as a miser worships his hidden treasure.

*　　*　　*　　*　　*　　*

.

The bridal was over. The farewells were over, and Nellie had gone,—gone from the home whose sunlight she had made, and which she had left forever. Sadly the pale, sick mother wept, and mourned her absence, listening in vain for the light foot-fall and soft, ringing voice she would never hear again.

Three weeks had passed away, and then, far and near, the papers teemed with accounts of the horrible Norwalk catastrophe, which desolated many a home, and wrung from many a heart its choicest treasure. Side by side they found them—Nellie and her husband—the light of her brown eyes quenched forever, and the pulses of his heart still in death!

I was present when they told the poor invalid of her loss, and even now I seem to hear the bitter, wailing cry which broke from her white lips, as she begged them " to unsay what they had said; and tell her Nellie was not dead—that she would come back again."

It could not be. Nellie would never return; and in six week's time the broken-hearted mother was at rest with her child.

The Thanksgiving Party,

AND

ITS CONSEQUENCES.

CHAPTER I.

NIGHT BEFORE THANKSGIVING.

"Oh, I do hope it will be pleasant to-morrow," said Lizzie Dayton, as on the night before Thanksgiving she stood at the parlor window, watching a dense mass of clouds, behind which the sun had lately gone to his nightly rest.

"I hope so, too, said Lucy, coming forward, and joining her sister; but then it isn't likely it will be. There has been a big circle around the moon these three nights, and, besides that, I never knew it fail to storm when I was particularly anxious that it should be pleasant;" and the indignant beauty pouted very becomingly at the insult so frequently offered by that most capricious of all things, the weather.

"Thee shouldn't talk so, Lucy," said Grandma Dayton, who was of Quaker descent, at the same time holding up between herself and the window the long stocking which she was knitting. "Doesn't thee know that when thee is finding fault with the weather, thee finds fault with Him who made the weather?"

"I do wish, grandma, answered Lucy, "that I could

ever say anything which did not furnish you with a text from which to preach me a sermon."

Grandma did not reply directly to this rather uncivil speech, but she continued : "I don't see how the weather will hurt thee, if it's the party thee is thinking of, for Mr. Graham's is only ten rods or so from here."

"I'm not afraid I can't go," answered Lucy ; "but you know as well as I, that if the wind blows enough to put out a candle, father is so old-maidish as to think Lizzie and I must wear thick stockings and dresses, and I shouldn't wonder if he insisted on flannel wrappers!"

"Well," answered grandma, "I think myself it will be very imprudent for Lizzie, in her present state of health, to expose her neck and arms. Thy poor marm died with consumption when she wasn't much older than thee is. Let me see,—she was twenty-three the day she died, and thee was twenty-two in Sep——"

"For heaven's sake, grandmother," interrupted Lucy, " don't continually remind me of my age, and tell me how much younger mother was when she was married. *I* can't help it if I am twenty-two, and not married or engaged either. But I *will* be both, before I am a year older."

So saying, she quitted the apartment, and repaired to her own room.

Ere we follow her thither, we will introduce both her and her sister to our readers. Lucy and Lizzie were the only children of Mr. Dayton, a wealthy, intelligent, and naturally social man, the early death of whose idolized, beautiful wife had thrown a deep gloom over his spirits, which time could never entirely dispel. It was now seventeen years since, a lonely, desolate widower, at the dusky twilight hour he had drawn closely to his bosom his motherless children, and thought that but for them he would gladly have lain down by her whose home was now in heaven. His acquaintances spoke lightly of his grief, saying he would soon get over it and marry again. They were mistaken, for he remained single, his widowed mother supplying to his daughters the place of their lost parent.

In one thing was Mr. Dayton rather peculiar. Owing to the death of his wife, he had always been in the habit of dictating to his daughters in various small matters, such as dress, and so forth, about which fathers seldom trouble themselves. And even now he seemed to forget that they were children no longer, and often interfered in their plans in a way exceedingly annoying to Lucy, the eldest of the girls, who was now twenty-two, and was as proud, selfish, and self-willed as she was handsome and accomplished. Old maids she held in great abhorrence, and her great object in life was to secure a wealthy and distinguished husband. Hitherto she had been unsuccessful, for the right one had not yet appeared. Now, however, a new star was dawning on her horizon, in the person of Hugh St. Leon, of New Orleans. His fame had preceded him, and half the village of S—— were ready to do homage to the proud millionaire, who would make his first appearance at the thanksgiving party. This, then, was the reason why Lucy felt so anxious to be becomingly dressed, for she had resolved upon a conquest, and she felt sure of success. She knew she was beautiful. Her companions told her so, her mirror told her so, and her sweet sister Lizzie told her so, more than twenty times a day.

Lizzie was four years younger than her sister, and wholly unlike her, both in personal appearance and disposition. She had from childhood evinced a predisposition to the disease which had consigned her mother to an early grave. On her fair, soft cheek the rose of health had never bloomed, and in the light which shone from her clear hazel eye, her fond father read, but too clearly, "passing away,—passing away."

If there was in Lucy Dayton's selfish nature any redeeming quality, it was that she possessed for her frail young sister a love amounting almost to adoration. Years before, she had trembled as she thought how soon the time might come when for her sister's merry voice she would listen in vain; but as month after month and year after year went by, and still among them Lizzie staid, Lucy forgot her fears, and dreamed not that ere long *one* chair would be vacant,—that Lizzie would be gone.

Although so much younger than her sister, Lizzie, for more than a year, had been betrothed to Harry Graham, whom she had known from childhood. Now, between herself and him the broad Atlantic rolled, nor would he return until the coming autumn, when, with her father's consent, Lizzie would be all his own.

> Alas! alas! ere autumn came
>   How many hearts were weeping,
> For her, who 'neath the willow's shade,
>   Lay sweetly, calmly sleeping.

CHAPTER II.

THANKSGIVING DAY.

SLOWLY the feeble light of a stormy morning broke over the village of S——. Lucy's fears had been verified, for Thanksgiving's dawn was ushered in by a fierce driving storm. Thickly from the blackened clouds the feathery flakes had fallen, until the earth, far and near, was covered by an unbroken mass of white, untrodden snow.

Lucy had been awake for a long time, listening to the sad song of the wind, which swept howling by the casement. At length, with an impatient frown at the snow, which covered the window-pane, she turned on her pillow, and tried again to sleep. Her slumbers, however, were soon disturbed by her sister, who arose, and putting aside the curtain, looked out upon the storm, saying, half aloud, "Oh, I *am* sorry, for Lucy will be disappointed."

"*I* disappointed!" repeated Lucy; "now, Lizzie, why not own it, and say *you* are as much provoked at the weather as I am, and wish this horrid storm had staid in the icy caves of Greenland?"

"Because," answered Lizzie, "I really care but little about the party. You know Harry will not be there, and besides that, the old, ugly pain has come back to my side this morning;" and even as she spoke, a low, hacking cough fell on Lucy's ear like the echo of a distant knell.

Lucy raised herself up, and leaning on her elbow looked earnestly at her sister, and fancied, ('twas not all fancy,) that her cheeks had grown thinner and her brow whiter within a few weeks. Lizzie proceeded with her toilet, although she was twice obliged to stop on account of "the ugly pain," as she called it.

"Hurry, sister," said Lucy, "and you will feel better when you get to the warm parlor."

Lizzie thought so, too, and she accelerated her movements as much as possible. Just as she was leaving the room, Lucy detained her a moment by passing her arm caressingly around her. Lizzie well knew that some favor was wanted, and she said, "Well, what is it, Lucy? What do you wish me to give you?"

"Nothing, nothing," answered Lucy, "but do not say anything to father about the pain in your side, for fear he will keep *you* at home, and, worse than all, make me stay, too."

Lizzie gave the required promise, and then descended to the breakfast parlor, where she found her grandmother, and was soon joined by her sister and father. After the usual salutation of the morning, the latter said, "There is every prospect of our being alone to-day, for the snow is at least a foot and a half deep, and is drifting every moment."

"But, father," said Lucy, "that will not prevent Lizzie and me from going to the party to-night."

"You mean, if I choose to let you go, of course," answered Mr. Dayton.

"Why," quickly returned Lucy, "you cannot think of keeping us at home. It is only distant a few rods, and we will wrap up well."

"I have no objections to your going," replied Mr. Dayton, "provided you dress suitably for such a night."

"Oh, father," said Lucy, "you cannot be capricious enough to wish us to be bundled up in bags."

"I care but little *what* dress you wear," answered Mr. Dayton, "if it has what I consider necessary appendages, viz: *sleeves* and *waist*."

The tears glittered in Lucy's bright eyes, as she said, "Our party dresses are at Miss Carson's, and she is to send them home this morning."

"Wear them, then," answered Mr. Dayton, "provided they possess the qualities I spoke of, for without those you cannot go out on such a night as this will be."

Lucy knew that her dress was minus the sleeves, and that her father would consider the waist a mere apology for one, so she burst into tears and said, rather angrily, "I had rather stay at home than go rigged out as you would like to have me."

"Very well; you can stay at home," was Mr. Dayton's quiet reply.

In a few moments he left the room, and then Lucy's wrath burst forth unrestrainedly. She called her father all sorts of names, such as "an old granny,—an old fidget," and finished up her list with what she thought the most odious appellation of all, "an old maid."

In the midst of her tirade the door bell rang. It was the boy from Miss Carson's, and he brought the party dresses. Lucy's thoughts now took another channel, and while admiring her beautiful embroidered muslin and rich white satin skirt, she forgot that she could not wear it. Grandma was certainly unfortunate in her choice of words, this morning, for when Lucy for the twentieth time asked if her dress were not a perfect beauty, the old Quakeress answered, "why it looks very decent, but it can do thee no good, for thy pa has said thee cannot wear it; besides, the holy writ reads, 'Let your adorning ——' "

Here Lucy stopped her ears, exclaiming, "I do believe, grandma, you were manufactured from a chapter in the bible, for you throw your *holy writ* into my face on all occasions."

The good lady adjusted her spectacles, and replied, "How thee talks! I never thought of throwing my bible at thee, Lucy!"

Grandma had understood her literally.

Nothing more was said of the party, until dinner time, although there was a determined look in Lucy's flashing eye, which puzzled Lizzie not a little. Owing to the storm, Mr. Dayton's country cousins did not, as was their usual custom, come into town to dine with him, and for this Lucy was thankful, for she thought nothing could be more disagreeable than to be compelled to sit all day and ask Cousin Peter how much his fatting hogs weighed; or his wife, Elizabeth Betsey, how many teeth the baby had got; or, worse than all the rest, if the *old maid*, Cousin Berintha, were present, to be obliged to be asked at least three times, whether it's twenty-four or twenty-five she'd be next September, and on saying it was only twenty-three, have her word disputed and the family bible brought in question. Even then Miss Berintha would demur, until she had taken the bible to the window, and squinted to see if the *year* had not been scratched out and rewritten! Then closing the book with a profound sigh, she would say, "I never, now! it beats all how much older you look!"

All these annoyances Lucy was spared on this day, for neither Cousin Peter, Elizabeth Betsey, or Miss Berintha made their appearance. At the dinner table, Mr. Dayton remarked, quietly, to his daughters, "I believe you have given up attending the party!"

"Oh, no, father," said Lucy, "we are going, Lizzie and I."

"And what about your dress?" sasked Mr. Dayton.

Lucy bit her lip as she replied, "Why, of course, we must dress to suit you, or stay at home.'

Lizzie looked quickly at her sister, as if asking how long since she had come to this conclusion; but Lucy's face was calm and unruffled, betraying no secrets, although her tongue did when, after dinner, she found herself alone with Lizzie in their dressing-room. A long conversation followed, in which Lucy seemed trying to persuade Lizzie to do something wrong. Possessed of the stronger mind, Lucy's influence over her sister was great, and sometimes a bad one, but never before had she pro- posed an open act of disobedience toward their father, and Lizzie constantly replied, " No, no, Lucy, I can't do it ; besides, I really think I ought not to go, for that pain in my side is no better."

" Nonsense, Lizzie," said Lucy. " If you are going to be as whimsical as Miss Berintha, you had better begir at once to dose yourself with burdock or catnip tea." Then, again recurring to the dress, she continued, " Fa- ther did not say we must not wear them after we got there. I shall take mine, any way, and I wish you would do the same ; and then, if he ever knows it, he will not be as much displeased when he finds that *you*, too, are guilty."

After a time, Lizzie was persuaded, but her happiness for that day was destroyed, and when at tea time her fa- ther asked if she felt quite well, she could scarcely keep from bursting into tears. Lucy, however, came to her relief, and said she was feeling *blue* because Harry would not be present ! Just before the hour for the party, Lucy descended to the parlor, where her father was reading, in order, as she said, to let him see whether her dress were *fussy* enough to suit him. He approved her taste, and after asking if Lizzie, too, were dressed in the same man- ner, resumed his paper. Ere long, the covered sleigh stood at the door, and in a few moments Lucy and Lizzie were in Anna Graham's dressing-room, undergoing the process of a second toilet.

Nothing could be more beautiful than was Lucy Day- ton, after party dress, bracelets, curls, and flowers had all been adjusted. She probably thought so, too, for a smile of satisfaction curled her lip as she saw the radiant vision reflected by the mirror.   Her bright eye flashed, and her heart swelled with pride as she thought, "Yes, there's no help for it, I shall win him, sure;" then turning to Anna Graham, she asked, "Is that Mr. St. Leon to be here to-night?"

"Yes, you know he is," answered Anna, "and I pity him, for I see you are all equipped for an attack; but," continued she, glancing at Lizzie, "were not little Lizzie's heart so hedged up by brother Hal, I should say your chance was small."

Lucy looked at her sister, and a chill struck her heart as she observed a spasm of pain which for an instant contracted Lizzie's fair, sweet face.   Anna noticed it, too, and springing toward her, said, "What is it, Lizzie? are you ill?"

"No," answered Lizzie, laying her hand on her side; "nothing but a sharp pain. It will soon be better;" but while she spoke, her teeth almost chattered with the cold.

Oh, Lizzie, Lizzie!

For a short time, now, we will leave the young ladies in Miss Graham's dressing-room, and transport our readers to another part of the village.

CHAPTER III.

ADA HARCOURT.

In a small and neat, but scantily furnished chamber, a poor widow was preparing her only child, Ada, for the party. The plain, white muslin dress of two years old had been washed and ironed so carefully, that Ada said it looked just as well as new; but then everything looked well on Ada Harcourt, who was highly gifted, both with intellect and beauty. After her dress was arranged, she went to the table for her old white gloves, the cleaning of which had cost her much trouble, for her mother did not seem to be at all interested in them, so Ada did as well as she could. As she was about to put them on, her mother returned from a drawer, into the recesses of which she had been diving, and from which she brought a paper, carefully folded.

"Here, Ada," said she, "you need not wear those gloves; see here—" and she held up a pair of handsome mitts a fine linen handkerchief, and a neat little gold pin.

"Oh, mother, mother!" said Ada, joyfully, "where did you get them?"

"*I* know," answered Mrs. Harcourt, "and that is enough."

After a moment's thought, Ada knew, too. The little hoard of money her mother had laid by for a warm winter shawl, had been spent for her. From Ada's lustrous blue eyes the tears were dropping, as, twining her arm around her mother's neck, she said, "*Naughty, naughty mother!*" but there was a knock at the door. The sleigh which Anna Graham had promised to send for Ada, had come; so dashing away her tears, and adjusting her new mitts and pin, she was soon warmly wrapped up, and on her way to Mr. Graham's.

* * * * * *

"In the name of the people, *who* is that?" said Lucy Dayton, as Anna Graham entered the dressing-room, accompanied by a bundle of something securely shielded from the cold.

The removal of the hood soon showed Lucy who it was, and, with an exclamation of surprise, she turned inquiringly to a young lady who was standing near. To her look, the young lady replied, " A freak of Anna's I suppose. She thinks a great deal of those Harcourts."

An impatient " pshaw ! " burst from Lucy lips, accompanied with the words, " I wonder who she thinks wants to associate with that plebeian ! "

The words, the look, and the tone caught Ada's eye and ear, and instantly blighted her happiness. In the joy and surprise of receiving an invitation to the party, it had never occurred to her that she might be slighted there, and she was not prepared for Lucy's unkind remark. For an instant the tears moistened her long silken eyelashes, and a deeper glow mantled her usually bright cheek; but this only increased her beauty, which tended to increase Lucy's vexation. Lucy knew that in her own circle there was none to dispute her claim; but she knew, too, that in a low-roofed house, in the outskirts of the town, there dwelt a poor sewing woman, whose only daughter was famed for her wondrous beauty. Lucy had frequently seen Ada in the streets, but never before had she met her, and she now determined to treat her with the utmost disdain.

Not so was Lizzie affected by the presence of " the plebeian." Mrs. Harcourt had done plain sewing for her father, and Lizzie had frequently called there for the work. In this way an acquaintance had been commenced between herself and Ada, which had ripened into friendship. Lizzie, too, had heard the remark of her sister, and, anxious to atone, as far as possible, for the unkindness, she went up to Ada, expressed her pleasure at seeing her there, and then, as the young ladies were about descending to the parlors, she offered her arm, saying, " I will accompany you down, but I have no doubt scores of beaux will quickly take you off my hands."

The parlors were nearly filled when our party reached them, and Ada, half tremblingly, clung to Lizzie's arm, while, with queen-like grace and dignity, Lucy Dayton moved through the crowded drawing-rooms. Her quick-eye had scanned each gentleman, but her search was fruitless. *He* was not there, and during the next half hour she listened rather impatiently to the tide of flattery poured into her ear by some one of her admirers. Suddenly there was a stir at the door, and Mr. St. Leon was announced. He was a tall, fine looking man, probably about twenty-five years of age. The expression of his face was remarkably pleasing, and such as would lead an entire stranger to trust him, sure that his confidence would not be misplaced. His manners were highly polished, and in his dignified, self-possessed bearing, there was something which some called pride, but in all the wide world there was not a more generous heart than that of Hugh St. Leon.

Lucy for a moment watched him narrowly, and then her feelings became perfectly calm, for she felt sure that now, for the first time, she looked upon her future husband! Ere long, Anna Graham approached, accompanied by the gentleman, whom she introduced, and then turning, left them alone. Lucy would have given almost anything to have known whether St. Leon had requested an introduction, but no means of information were at hand, so she bent all her energies to be as agreeable as possible to the handsome stranger at her side, who each moment seemed more and more pleased with her.

Meantime, in another part of the room Lizzie and Ada were the center of attraction. The same kindness which prompted Anna Graham to invite Ada, was careful to see that she did not feel neglected. For this purpose, Anna's brother, Charlie, a youth of sixteen, had been instructed to pay her particular attention. This he was not unwilling to do, for he knew no reason why she should not be treated politely, even if she were a sewing woman's daughter. Others of the company, observing how attentive Charlie and Lizzie were to the beautiful girl, felt disposed to treat her graciously, so that to her the evening was passing very happily.

When St. Leon entered the room, the hum of voices prevented Ada from hearing his name; neither was she aware of his presence until he had been full fifteen minutes conversing with Lucy. Then her attention was directed toward him by Lizzie. For a moment, Ada gazed as if spell-bound; then a dizziness crept over her, and she nervously grasped the little plain gold ring which encircled the third finger of her left hand!

Turning to Lizzie, who, fortunately, had not noticed her agitation, she said, "What did you say his name was?"

"St. Leon, from New Orleans," replied Lizzie.

"Then I'm not mistaken," Ada said, inaudibly.

At that moment Anna Graham approached, and whispered something to Ada, who gave a startled look, saying, "Oh, no, Miss Anna; you would not have me make myself ridiculous."

"Certainly not," answered Anna; "neither will you do so, for some of your songs you sing most beautifully. Do come; I wish to surprise my friends."

Ada consented rather unwillingly, and Anna led her toward the music-room, followed by a dozen or more, all of whom wondered what a sewing woman's daughter knew about music. On their way to the piano, they passed near St. Leon and Lucy, the former of whom started as his eye fell upon Ada.

"I did not think there was another such face in the world," said he, apparently to himself; then turning to Lucy, he asked who that beautiful girl was.

"Which one?" asked Lucy; "there are many beauties here to-night."

"I mean the one with the white muslin, and dark auburn curls," said St. Leon.

Lucy's brow darkened, but she answered, "That? oh, that is Ada Harcourt. Her mother is a poor sewing woman. I never met Ada before, and cannot conceive how she came to be here; but then the Grahams are peculiar in their notions, and I suppose it was a whim of Anna's."

Without knowing it, St. Leon had advanced some steps toward the door through which Ada had disappeared. Lucy followed him, vexed beyond measure, that the despised Ada Harcourt should even have attracted his attention.

"Is she as accomplished as handsome?" asked he.

"Why, of course not," answered Lucy, with a forced laugh. "Poverty, ignorance, and vulgarity go together, usually, I believe."

St. Leon gave her a rapid, searching glance, in which disappointment was mingled, but before he could reply, there was the sound of music. It was a sweet, bird-like voice which floated through the rooms, and the song it sang was a favorite one of St. Leon's, who was passionately fond of music.

"Let us go nearer," said he to Lucy, who, nothing loth, accompanied him, for she, too, was anxious to know who it was that thus chained each listener into silence.

St. Leon at length got a sight of the singer, and said, with evident pleasure, " Why, it's Miss Harcourt!"

" Miss Harcourt!   Ada Harcourt!" exclaimed Lucy, " Impossible! Why, her mother daily toils for the bread they eat!"

But if St. Leon heard her, he answered not. His senses were locked in those strains of music which re-called memories of something, he scarcely knew what, and Lucy found herself standing alone, her heart swelling with anger toward Ada, who from that time was her hated rival. The music ceased, but scores of voices were loud in their call for another song; and again Ada sang, but this time there were in the tones of her voice a thrill-ing power, for which those who listened could not ac-count. To Ada, the atmosphere about her seemed charmed, for though she never for a moment raised her eyes, she well knew who it was that leaned upon the pi-ano, and looked intently upon her. Again the song was finished, and then, at St. Leon's request, he was intro-duced to the singer, who returned his salutation with per-fect self-possession, although her heart beat quickly, as she hoped, yet half feared, that he would recognize her. But he did not, and as they passed together into the next room, he wondered much why the hand which lay upon his arm trembled so violently, while Ada said to herself, " 'Tis not strange he does n't know me by this name." Whether St. Leon knew her or not, there seemed about her some strong attraction, which kept him at her side the remainder of the evening, greatly to Lucy Dayton's mortification and displeasure.

" I 'll be revenged on her yet," she muttered. " The upstart! I wonder where she learned to play."

This last sentence was said aloud; and Lizzie, who was standing near, replied, " Her father was once wealthy, and Ada had the best of teachers.   Since she has lived in S——, she has occasionally practiced on Anna's piano."

"I think I'd keep a piano for paupers to play on, " was Lucy's contemptuous reply, uttered with no small degree of bitterness, for at that moment St. Leon approached her with the object of her dislike leaning upon his arm.

Ada introduced Lizzie to St. Leon, who offered her his other arm, and the three kept together until Lizzie, uttering a low, sharp cry of pain, leaned heavily as if for support against St. Leon.   In an instant Lucy was at her side; but to all her anxious inquiries Lizzie could only reply, as she clasped her thin, white hand over her side, "The pain,— the pain,— take me home."

"Our sleigh has not yet come," said Lucy.   "Oh, what shall we do?"

"Mine is here, and at your command, Miss Dayton," said St. Leon.

Lucy thanked him, and then proceeded to prepare Lizzie, who, chilled through and through by the exposure of her chest and arms, had borne the racking pain in her side as long as possible, and now lay upon the sofa as helpless as an infant.   When all was ready St. Leon lifted her in his arms, and bearing her to the sleigh, stepped lightly in with her, and took his seat.

"It is hardly necessary for you to accompany us home," said Lucy, overjoyed beyond measure, though, to find that he was going.

"Allow me to be the judge," answered St. Leon; and other than that, not a word was spoken until they reached Mr. Dayton's door.   Then, carefully carrying Lizzie into the house, he was about to leave, when Lucy detained him to thank him for his kindness, adding that she hoped to see him again.

"Certainly, I shall call to-morrow," was his reply, as

he sprang down the steps, and entering his sleigh, was driven back to Mr. Graham's.

He found the company about dispersing, and meeting Ada in the hall, asked to accompany her home. Ada's pride for a moment hesitated, and then she answered in the affirmative. When St. Leon had seated her in his sleigh, he turned back, on pretext of looking for something, but in reality to ask Anna Graham where Ada lived, as he did not wish to question her on the subject.

When they were nearly home, St. Leon said, " Miss Harcourt, have you always lived in S——? "

"We have lived here but two years," answered Ada; and St. Leon continued: "I cannot rid myself of the impression that somewhere I have met you before."

"Indeed," said Ada, "when, and where?"

But his reply was prevented by the sleigh's stopping at Mrs. Harcourt's door. As St. Leon bade Ada good night, he whispered, "I shall see you again."

Ada made no answer, but going into the house where her mother was waiting for her, she exclaimed, "Oh, mother, mother, I've seen him! — he was there! — he brought me home!"

"Seen whom?" asked Mrs. Harcourt, alarmed at her daughter's agitation.

"Why, Hugh St. Leon!" replied Ada.

"St. Leon in town!" repeated Mrs. Harcourt, her eye lighting up with joy.

'Twas only for a moment, however, for the remembrance of what she was when she knew St. Leon, and what she now was, recurred to her, and she said calmly, "I thought you had forgotten that childish fancy.

"Forgotten!" said Ada bitterly; and then as she recalled the unkind remark of Lucy Dayton, she burst into a passionate fit of weeping.

After a time, Mrs. Harcourt succeeded in soothing her, and then drew from her all the particulars of the party, St. Leon and all. When Ada had finished, her mother kissed her fair cheek, saying, "I fancy St. Leon thinks as much of little Ada now as he did six years ago;" but Ada could not think so, though that night, in dreams, she was again happy in her old home in the distant city, while at her side was St. Leon, who even then was dreaming of a childish face which had haunted him six long years.

CHAPTER IV.

LUCY.

WE left Lizzie lying upon the sofa, where St. Leon had laid her. After he was gone, Lucy proposed calling their father and sending for a physician, but Lizzie objected, saying she should be better when she got warm. During the remainder of that night, Lucy sat by her sister's bedside, while each cry of pain which came from Lizzie's lips fell heavily upon her heart, for conscience accused her of being the cause of all this suffering. At length the weary night watches were finished, but the morning light showed more distinctly Lizzie's white brow and burning cheeks. She had taken a severe cold, which had settled upon her lungs, and now she was paying the penalty of her first act of disobedience.

Mr. Dayton had sent for the old family physician, who understood Lizzie's constitution perfectly. He shook his head as he said, "How came she by such a cold? Did she go the party?"

"Yes, sir," replied Mr. Dayton.

"And not half dressed, I'll warrant," said the gruff old doctor.

Lucy turned pale as her father answered, quickly and truthfully, as he thought, "No, sir, she was properly dressed."

Lizzie heard it, and though speaking was painful, she said, "Forgive me, father, forgive me; I disobeyed you. I wore the dress you said I must not wear!"

An exclamation of surprise escaped Mr. Dayton, who, glancing at Lucy, read in her guilty face what Lizzie generously would not betray.

"Oh, Lucy, Lucy," said he, "how could you do so?"

Lucy could only reply through her tears. She was sincerely sorry that by her means Lizzie had been brought into danger; but when the doctor said that by careful management she might soon be better, all feelings of regret vanished, and she again began to think of St. Leon and his promise to call. A look at herself in the mirror showed her that she was looking pale and jaded, and she half hoped he would not come. However, as the day wore on, she grew nervous as she thought he possibly might be spending his time with the hated Ada. But he was not, and at about four o'clock there was a ring at the door. From an upper window Lucy saw St. Leon, and when Bridget came up for her, she asked if the parlor was well darkened.

"An' sure it's darker nor a pocket," said Bridget," "an' he couldn't see a haporth was ye twice as sorry lookin'."

So bathing her face in cologne, in order to force a glow, Lucy descended to the parlor, which she found to be as dark as Bridget had said it was. St. Leon received her very kindly, for the devotion she had the night before shown for her sister, had partially counterbalanced the spitefulness he had observed in her manner when speaking of Ada at the party. Notwithstanding Bridget's precautions, he saw, too, that she was pale and spiritless, but he attributed it to her anxiety for her sister, and this raised her in his estimation. Lucy divined his thoughts, and in her efforts to appear amiable and agreeable, a half hour passed quickly away. At the end of that time she unfortunately asked, in a very sneering tone, "how long since he had seen the sewing girl?"

"If you mean Miss Harcourt," said St. Leon, coolly, "I've not seen her since I left her last night at her mother's door."

"You must have been in danger of upsetting if you attempted to turn round in Mrs. Harcourt's *spacious* yard," was Lucy's next remark.

"I did not attempt it," said St. Leon. "I carried Miss Ada in my arms from the street to the door."

The tone and manner were changed. Lucy knew it, and it exasperated her to say something more, but she was prevented by St. Leon's rising to go. As Lucy accompanied him to the door, she asked "how long he intended to remain in S——."

"I leave this evening, in the cars for New Haven," said he.

"This evening?" repeated Lucy in a disappointed tone, "and will you not return?"

"Yes, if the business on which I go is successful," answered St. Leon.

"A *lady* in question, perchance," remarked Lucy playfully.

"You interpret the truth accurately," said St. Leon, and with a cold, polite bow, he was gone.

"Why was he going to New Haven?" This was the thought which now tortured Lucy. He had confessed that a lady was concerned in his going, but who was she, and what was she to him? Any way, there was a comfort in knowing that Ada Harcourt had nothing to do with it!

Mistaken Lucy! Ada Harcourt had everything to do with it!

CHAPTER V.

UNCLE ISRAEL.

THE lamps were lighted in the cars, and on through the valley of the Connecticut, the New Haven train was speeding its way. In one corner of the car sat St. Leon, closely wrapped in cloak and thoughts, the latter of which occasionally suggested to him the possibility that his was a *Tomfool's* errand; "but then," thought he, "no one will know it if I fail, and if I do not, it is worth the trouble."

When the train reached Hartford, a number of passengers entered, all bound for New Haven. Among them was a comical-looking, middle aged man, whom St. Leon instantly recognized as a person whom he had known when in college, in New Haven, and whom the students familiarly called "Uncle Israel." The recognition was mutual, for Uncle Israel prided himself on never forgetting a person he had once seen. In a few moments St. Leon was overwhelming him with scores of questions, but Uncle Israel was a genuine Yankee, and never felt happier than when engaged in giving or guessing information.

At length St. Leon asked, "Does Ada Linwood fulfill the promise of beauty which she gave as a child?"

"Ada who?" said Uncle Israel.

"Linwood," repeated St. Leon, arguing from the jog in Uncle Israel's memory that all was not right. "Do you mean the daughter of Harcourt Linwood, he that was said to be so rich?"

"The same," returned St. Leon. "Where are they?"

Uncle Israel settled himself with the air of a man who has a long story on hand, and intends to tell it at his leisure. Filling his mouth with an enormous quid of tobacco, he commenced: "Better than four years ago Linwood smashed up, smack and clean; lost everything he had, and the rest had to be sold at vandue. But what was worse than all, seein' he was a fine feller in the main, and I guess didn't mean to fail, he took sick, and in about a month died."

"And what became of his widow and orphan?" asked St. Leon, eagerly.

"Why, it wasn't nateral," said Uncle Israel, "that they should keep the same company they did before, and they's too plaguy stuck up to keep any other; so they moved out of town and supported themselves by takin' in sewin' or ironin', I forgot which."

"But where are they now?" asked St. Leon.

Uncle Israel looked at him for a moment, and then replied, "The Lord knows, I suppose, but Israel don't."

"Did they suffer at all?" asked St. Leon.

"Not as long as I stuck to them, but they sarved me real mean," answered Uncle Israel.

"In what way?"

"Why, you see," said Uncle Israel, "I don't know why, but somehow I never thought of matrimony till I got a glimpse of Ada at her father's vandue. To be sure, I'd seen her before, but then she was mighty big feelin', and I couldn't ha' touched her with a hoe-handle, but now 't was different. I bought their house. I was rich and they was poor."

Involuntarily St. Leon clenched his fist, as Uncle Israel continued: "I seen to getting them a place in the coun. try, and then tended to 'em generally for more than six months, when I one day hinted to Mrs. Linwood that I would like to be her son-in-law. Christopher! how quick her back was up, and she gave me to understand that I was lookin' too high! 'Twas no go with Ada, and after a while I proposed to the mother. Then you ought to seen her! She didn't exactly turn me out o'door, but she coolly told me I wasn't wanted there. But I stuck to her, and kept kind o' offerin' myself, till at last they cut stick and cleared out, and I couldn't find them, high nor low. I hunted for more than a year, and at last found them in Hartford. Thinkin' may be, they had come to, I proposed again, and kept hangin' on till they gave me the slip again; and now I don't know where they be, but I guess they've changed their name."

At this point, the cars stopped, until the upward train should pass them, and St. Leon, rising, bade his companion good evening, saying "he had changed his mind, and should return to Hartford on the other train."

CHAPTER VI.

EXPLANATION.

Six years prior to the commencement of our story, New Haven boasted not a better or wealthier citizen than Harcourt Linwood, of whose subsequent failure and death we have heard from Uncle Israel. The great beauty of his only child, Ada, then a girl of nearly thirteen, was the subject of frequent comment among the circle in which he moved. No pains were spared with her education, and many were the conjectures as to what she would be when time had matured her mind and beauty.

Hugh St. Leon, of New Orleans, then nineteen years of age, and a student at Yale, had frequently met Ada at the house of his sister, Mrs. Durant, whose eldest daughter, Jenny, was about her own age. The uncommon beauty of the child greatly interested the young southerner, and once, in speaking of his future prospects to his sister, he playfully remarked, "Suppose I wait for Ada Linwood."

"You cannot do better," was the reply, and the conversation terminated.

The next evening there was to be a child's party at the house of Mrs Durant, and as Hugh was leaving the house, Jenny bounded after him, saying, "Oh, Uncle Hugh, you'll come to-morrow night, won't you? No matter if you are a grown up man, in the junior class, trying to raise some whiskers! You will be a sort of restraint, and keep us from getting too rude. Besides, we are going to have tableaux, and I want you to act the part of bride groom in one of the scenes."

"Who is to be the bride?" asked Hugh.

"Ada Linwood.   Now I know you'll come, won't you?"

"I'll see," was Hugh's answer, as he walked away.

Jenny well knew that "I'll see" meant "yes," and tying on her bonnet, she hastened off to tell Ada that Uncle Hugh would be present, and would act the part of bridegroom in the scene where she was to be bride.

"What! that big man?" said Ada. "How funny!"

Before seven the next evening Mrs. Durant's parlors were filled, for the guests were not old enough or fashionable enough to delay making their appearance until morning.   Hugh was the last to arrive, for which Jenny scolded him soundly, saying they were all ready for tableaux. "But come, now," said she, " and let me introduce you to the bride."

In ten minutes more the curtain rose, and Hugh St. Leon appeared with Ada on his arm, standing before a gentleman in clerical robes, who seemed performing the marriage ceremony.   Placing a ring on Ada's *third* finger, St. Leon, when the whole was finished, took advantage of his new relationship, and kissed the lips of the bride.   Amid a storm of applause the curtain dropped, and as he led the blushing Ada away, he bent down, and pointing to the ring, whispered, " Wear it until some future day, when, by replacing it, I shall make you really my little wife."

The words were few and lightly spoken, but they touched the heart of the young Ada, awakening within her thoughts and feelings of which she never before had dreamed. Frequently, after that, she met St. Leon, who sometimes teased her about being his wife; but when he saw how painfully embarrassed she seemed on such occasions, he desisted.

The next year he was graduated, and the same day on which he received the highest honors of his class was long remembered with heartfelt sorrow, for ere the city clocks tolled the hour of midnight, he stood with his orphan niece, Jenny, weeping over the inanimate form of his sister, Mrs. Durant, who had died suddenly in a fit of apoplexy. Mr. Durant had been dead some years, and as Jenny had now no relatives in New Haven, she accompanied her uncle to his southern home. Long and passionately she wept on Ada's bosom, as she bade her farewell, promising never to forget her, but to write her three pages of foolscap every week. To do Jenny justice, we must say that this promise was faithfully kept for a whole month, and then, with thousands of its sisterhood, it disappeared into the vale of broken promises and resolutions.

She still wrote occasionally, and at the end of each epistle there was always a long postscript from Hugh, which Ada prized almost as much as she did Jenny's whole letter; and when at last matters changed, the letter becoming Hugh's and the postscript Jenny's, she made no objection, even if she felt any. At the time of her father's failure and death, a long unanswered letter was lying in her port-folio, which was entirely forgotten until weeks after, when, in the home which Uncle Israel so *disinterestedly* helped them to procure, she and her mother were sewing for the food which they ate. Then a dozen times was an answer commenced, blotted with tears, and finally destroyed, until Ada, burrying her face in her mother's lap, sobbed out, "Oh, mother, I cannot do it. I cannot write to tell them how poor we are, for I remember that Jenny was proud, and laughed at the school-girls whose fathers were not rich."

So the letter was never answered, and as St. Leon about that time started on a tour through Europe, he knew nothing of their change of circumstances. On his way home, he had in Paris met with Harry Graham, who had been his classmate, and who now won from him a promise that on his return to America he would visit his parents, in S———. He did so, and there, as we have seen, met with Ada Harcourt, whose face, voice, and manner reminded him so strangely of the Ada he had known years before, and whom he had never forgotten.

As the reader will have supposed, the sewing woman, whose daughter Lucy Dayton so heartily despised, was none other than Mrs. Linwood, of New Haven, who had taken her husband's first name in order to avoid the persecutions of Uncle Israel. The day following the party, St. Leon spent in making inquiries concerning Mrs Harcourt, and the information thus obtained determined him to start at once for New Haven, in order to ascertain if his suspicions were correct.

The result of his journey we already know. Still he resolved not to make himself known, immediately, but to wait until he satisfied himself that Ada was as good as beautiful. And then?

A few more chapters will tell us what then ·

CHAPTER VII.

A MANEUVER.

THE grey twilight of a cold December afternoon was creeping over the village of S———, when Ada Harcourt left her seat by the window, where, the live-long day, she had sat stitching till her heart was sick and her eyes were dim. On the faded calico lounge near the fire, lay Mrs. Harcourt, who for several days had been unable to work, on account of a severe cold which seemed to have settled in her face and eyes.

"There," said Ada, as she brushed from her gingham apron the bits of thread and shreds of cotton, "There, it is done at last, and now before it is quite dark I will take it home."

"No, not to-night, child," said Mrs Harcourt; "to-morrow will do just as well."

"But, mother, answered Ada," you know Mrs. Dayton always pays as soon as the work is delivered, and what I have finished will come to two dollars and a half, which will last a long time, and we shall not be obliged to take any from the sum laid by to pay our rent; besides, you have had nothing nourishing for a long time; so let me go, and on my way home I will buy you something nice for supper."

Mrs. Harcourt said no more, but the tears fell from her aching eyes as she thought how hard her daughter was obliged to labor, now that she was unable to assist her. In a moment Ada was in the street. The little alley in which she lived was soon traversed, and she was about turning into Main street, when rapid footsteps approached her, and St. Leon appeared at her side, saying, "Good evening, Miss Harcourt; allow me to relieve you of that bundle."

And before she could prevent it, he took from her hands the package, while he continued, "May I ask how far you are walking to-night?"

Ada hesitated a moment, but quickly forcing down her pride, she answered, "Only as far as Mr. Dayton's. I am carrying home some work."

"Indeed!" said he, "then I can have your company all the way, for I am going to inquire after Lizzie."

They soon reached their destination, and their ring at
14

the door was not, as usual, answered by Bridget, but by Lucy herself, whose sweet smile, as she greeted St. Leon, changed into an angry scowl when she recognized his companion.

"Ada Harcourt!" said she, and Ada, blushing scarlet, began: "I have brought ——," but she was interrupted by St. Leon, who handed Lucy the bundle, saying, "Here is your work, Miss Dayton, and I hope it will suit you, for we took a great deal of pains with it."

Lucy tried to smile as she took the work, and then opening the parlor door she with one hand motioned St. Leon to enter, while with the other she held the hall door ajar, as if for Ada to depart. A tear trembled on Ada's long eyelashes, as she timidly asked, "Can I see your grandmother?"

"Mrs. Dayton, I presume you mean," said Lucy, haughtily.

Ada bowed, and Lucy continued: "She is not at home just at present."

"Perhaps, then, you can pay me for the work," said Ada.

The scowl on Lucy's face grew darker, as she replied, "I have nothing to do with grandma's hired help. Come to-morrow and she will be here. (How horridly cold this open door makes the hall!")

Ada thought of the empty cupboard at home, and of her pale, sick mother. Love for her conquered all other feelings, and in a choking voice she said, "Oh, Miss Dayton, if you will pay it you will confer a great favor on me, for mother is sick, and we need it so much!"

There was a movement in the parlor. St. Leon was approaching, and with an impatient gesture, Lucy opened the opposite door, saying to Ada, "Come in here."

The tone was so angry that, under any other circum

stances, Ada would have gone away. Now, however, she entered, and Lucy, taking out her purse, said, "How much is the sum about which you make so much fuss?"

"Two dollars and a half," answered Ada.

"Two dollars and a half," repeated Lucy; and then, as a tear fell from Ada's eye, she added, contemptuously, "It is a small amount to cry about."

Ada made no reply, and was about leaving the room, when Lucy detained her, by saying, "Pray, did you *ask* Mr. St. Leon to accompany you here and bring your bundle?"

"Miss Dayton, you know better,—you know I did not," answered Ada, as the fire of insulted pride flashed from her dark blue eyes, which became almost black, while her cheek grew pale as marble.

Instantly Lucy's manner changed, and in a softened tone she said, "I am glad to know that you did not; and now, as a friend, I warn you against receiving any marks of favor from St. Leon."

"What do you mean?" asked Ada, and Lucy continued: "You have sense enough to know, that when a man of St. Leon's standing shows any preference for a girl in your circumstances, it can be from no good design."

"You judge him wrongfully—you do not know him," said Ada; and Lucy answered, "Pray, where did you learn so much about him?"

Ada only answered by rising to go.

"Here, this way," said Lucy, and leading her through an outer passage to the back door, she added, "I do it to save your good name. St. Leon is undoubtedly waiting for you, and I would not trust my own sister with him, were she a poor sewing girl!"

The door was shut in Ada's face, and Lucy returned to the parlor, where she found her father entertaining her visitor. Seating herself on a crimson ottoman, she prepared to do the agreeable, when St. Leon rising, said, "Excuse my short call, for I must be going. Where have you left Miss Harcourt?"

"I left her at the door," answered Lucy, "and she is probably half way to 'Dirt Alley' by this time, so do not be in haste."

But he was in haste, for when he looked on the fast gathering darkness without, and thought of the by streets and lonely alleys through which Ada must pass on her way home, he felt uneasy, and bidding Miss Dayton goodnight, he hurried away.

Meantime, Ada had procured the articles she wished for, and proceeded home, with a heart which would have been light as a bird, had not the remembrance of Lucy's insulting language rung in her ears. Mrs. Harcourt saw that all was not right, but she forbore making any inquiries until supper was over. Then Ada, bringing a stool to her mother's side, and laying her head on her lap, told everything which had transpired between herself, St. Leon, and Lucy.

Scarcely was her story finished, when there was a rap at the door, and St. Leon himself entered the room. He had failed in overtaking Ada, and anxious to know of her safe return, had determined to call. The recognition between himself and Mrs. Harcourt was mutual, but for reasons of their own, neither chose to make it apparent, and Ada introduced him to her mother as she would have done any stranger. St. Leon possessed in an unusual degree the art of making himself agreeable, and in the animated conversation which ensued, Mrs. Harcourt forgot that she was poor,—forgot her aching eyes; while Ada forgot everything save that St. Leon was present, and that she was again listening to his voice, which charmed her now even more than in the olden time.

During the evening, St. Leon managed, in various ways, to draw Ada out on all the prominent topics of the day, and he felt pleased to find, that amid all her poverty she did not neglect the cultivation of her mind. A part of each day was devoted to study, which Mrs. Harcourt, who was a fine scholar, superintended.

It was fast merging toward the hour when phantoms walk abroad, ere St. Leon remembered that he must go. As he was leaving, he said to Ada, "I have a niece, Jenny about your age, whom I think you would like very much.

Oh how Ada longed to ask for her old playmate, but a look from her mother kept her silent, and in a moment St. Leon was gone.

CHAPTER VIII.

COUSIN BERINTHA AND LUCY'S PARTY.

Cousin Berintha, whom Lucy Dayton so much disliked and dreaded, was a cousin of Mr. Dayton, and was a prim, matter-of-fact maiden of fifty, or thereabouts. That she was still in a state of single blessedness, was partially her own fault, for at twenty she was engaged to the son of a wealthy farmer who lived near her father. But, alas! ere the wedding day arrived, there came to the neighborhood a young lady from Boston, in whose presence the beauty of the country girl grew dim, as do the stars in the rays of the morning sun.

Berintha had a plain face, but a strong heart, and when

she saw that Amy Holbrook was preferred, with steady hand and unflinching nerve, she wrote to her recreant lover that he was free.   And now Amy, to whom the false knight turned, took it into her capricious head that she could not marry a farmer,—she had always fancied a physician; and if young B—— would win her, he must first secure the title of M. D.   He complied with her request, and one week from the day on which he received his diploma, Berintha read, with a slightly blanched cheek, the notice of his marriage with the Boston beauty.   Three years from that day she read the announcement of Amy's death, and in two years more she refused the doctor's offer to give her a home by his lonely fireside, and a place in his widowed heart.   All this had the effect of making Berintha rather cross, but she seldom manifested her spite toward any one except Lucy, whom she seemed to take peculiar delight in teasing, and whose treatment of herself was not such as would warrant much kindness in return.

Lizzie she had always loved, and when Harry Graham went away, it was on Berintha's lap that the young girl sobbed out her grief, wondering, when with her tears Berintha's were mingled, how one apparently so cold and passionless could sympathize with her.   To no one had Berintha ever confided the story of her early love.   Mr. Dayton was a school-boy then, and as but little was said of it at the time, it faded entirely from memory; and when Lucy called her a " crabbed old maid," she knew not of the disappointment which had clouded every joy, and embittered a whole lifetime.

At the first intelligence of Lizzie's illness, Berintha came, and though her prescriptions of every kind of herb tea in the known world were rather numerous, and her doses of the same were rather large, and though her stiff cap, sharp nose, and curious little eyes, which saw every thing, were exceedingly annoying to Lucy, she proved herself an invaluable nurse, warming up old Dr. Benton's heart into a glow of admiration of her wonderful skill! Hour after hour she sat by Lizzie, bathing her burning brow, or smoothing her tumbled pillow. Night after night she kept her tireless watch, treading softly around the sick-room, and lowering her loud, harsh voice to a whisper, lest she should disturb the uneasy slumbers of the sick girl, who, under her skillful nursing, gradually grew better.

"Was there ever such a dear, good cousin," said Lizzie, one day, when a nervous headache had been coaxed away by what Berintha called her "mesmeric passes;" and "Was there ever such a horrid bore," said Lucy, on the same day, when Cousin Berintha "thought she saw a *white* hair in Lucy's raven curls!" adding, by way of consolation, "It wouldn't be anything strange, for I began to grow gray before I was as old as you."

"And that accounts for your head being just the color of wool," angrily retorted Lucy, little dreaming of the bitter tears and sleepless nights which had early blanched her cousin's hair to its present whiteness.

For several winters Lucy had been in the habit of giving a large party, and as she had heard that St. Leon was soon going south, she felt anxious to have it take place ere he left town. But what should she do with Berintha, who showed no indications of leaving, though Lizzie was much better.

"I declare," said she to herself, "that woman is enough to worry the life out of me. I'll speak to Liz about it this very day."

Accordingly, that afternoon, when alone with her sister, she said, "Lizzie, is it absolutely necessary that Berintha should stay here any longer, to tuck you up, and feed you sage tea through a straw?"

Lizzie looked inquiringly at her sister, who continued, "To tell you the truth, I'm tired of having her around, and must manage some way to get rid of her before next week, for I mean to have a party Thursday night."

Lizzie's eyes now opened in astonishment, as she exclaimed, "A party! oh, Lucy, wait until I get well."

"You'll be able by that time to come down stairs in your crimson morning-gown, which becomes you so well," answered Lucy.

"But father's away," rejoined Lizzie; to which Lucy replied, "So much the better, for now I shan't be obliged to ask any old things. I told him I meant to have it while he was gone, for you know he hates parties. But what shall I do with Berintha?"

"Why, what possible harm can she do?" asked Lizzie. "She would enjoy it very much, I know; for in spite of her oddities, she likes society."

"Well, suppose she does; nobody wants her round, prating about white hairs and mercy knows what. Come, you tell her you don't need her services any longer— that's a good girl."

There was a look of mischief in Lizzie's eye, and a merry smile on her lip, as she said, "Why, don't you know that father has invited her to spend the winter, and she has accepted the invitation?"

"Invited her to spend the winter!" repeated Lucy, while the tears glittered in her bright eyes. "What does he mean?"

"Why," answered Lizzie, "it is very lonely at Cousin John's, and his wife makes more of a servant of Berintha than she does a companion, so father, out of pity, asked her to stay with us, and she showed her good taste by accepting."

"I'll hang myself in the woodshed before spring — see if I don't!" and burying her face in her hands, Lucy wept aloud, while Lizzie, lying back upon her pillow, laughed immoderately at her sister's distress.

"There's a good deal to laugh at, I think," said Lucy, more angrily than she usually addressed her sister. "If you have any pity, do devise some means of getting rid of her, for a time, at least."

"Well, then," answered Lizzie, "she wants to go home for a few days, in order to make some necessary preparations for staying with us, and perhaps you can coax her to go now, though I for one would like to have her stay. Everybody knows she is your cousin, and no one will think less of you for having her here."

"But I won't do it," said Lucy, "and that settles it. Your plan is a good one, and I'll get her off — see if I don't!"

The next day, which was Saturday, Lucy was unusually kind to her cousin, giving her a collar, offering to fix her cap, and doing numerous other little things, which greatly astonished Berintha. At last, when dinner was over, she said, "Come, cousin, what do you say to a sleigh ride this afternoon? I haven't been down to Elizabeth Betsey's in a good while, so suppose we go to-day."

Berintha was taken by surprise, but after a moment she said just what Lucy hoped she would say, viz: that she was wanting to go home for a few days, and if Lizzie were only well enough, she would go now.

"Oh she is a great deal better," said Lucy, "and you can leave her as well as not. Dr. Benton says I am almost as good a nurse as you, and I will take good care of her,--besides, I really think you need rest; so go, if you wish to, and next Saturday I will come round after you."

Accordingly, Berintha, who suspected nothing, was coaxed into going home, and when at three o'clock the sleigh was said to be ready, she kissed Lizzie good-by, and taking her seat by the side of Lucy, was driven rapidly toward her brother's house.

*   *   *   *   *   *

"There! haven't I managed it capitally!" exclaimed Lucy, as she reëntered her sister's room, after her ride; "but the bother of it is, I've promised to go round next Saturday, and bring not only Berintha, but Elizabeth Betsey and her twins! Won't it be horrible! However, the party'll be over, so I don't care."

Cousin Berintha being gone, there was no longer any reason why the party should be kept a secret, and before nightfall every servant in the house was discussing it, Bridget saying, "Faith, an' I thought it was mighty good she was gettin' with that woman."

Mrs. Dayton was highly indignant at the trick which she plainly saw had been put upon Berintha, but Lucy only replied, "that she wished it were as easy a matter to get rid of grandma!"

On Monday cards of invitation to the number of one hundred and fifty were issued, and when Lizzie, in looking them over, asked why Ada Harcourt was left out, Lucy replied, that "she guessed she wasn't going to insult her guests by inviting a sewing girl with them. Anna Graham could do so, but nobody was going to imitate her."

"Invite her, then, for my sake, and in my name," pleaded Lizzie, but Lucy only replied, "I shall do no such thing;" and thus the matter was settled.

Amid the hurry and preparation for the party, days

glided rapidly away, and Thursday morning came, bright, beautiful, and balmy, almost, as an autumnal day.

"Isn't this delightful!" said Lucy, as she stepped out upon the piazza, and felt the warm southern breeze upon her cheek. "It's a wonder, though," she continued, "that madam nature didn't conjure up an awful storm for my benefit, as she usually does!"

Before night, she had occasion to change her mind concerning the day.

Dinner was over, and she in Lizzie's room was combing out her long curls, and trying the effect of wearing them entirely behind her ears. Suddenly there was the sound of sleigh bells, which came nearer, until they stopped before the door. Lucy flew to the window, and in tones of intense anger and surprise, exclaimed, "Now, heaven defend us! here is Cousin John's old lumber sleigh and rackabone horse, with Berintha and a hair trunk, a red trunk, two bandboxes, a carpet-bag, a box full of herbs, and a pillow-case full of stockings. What does it all mean?"

She soon found out what it all meant, for Berintha entered the room in high spirits. Kissing Lizzie, she next advanced toward Lucy, saying, "You did n't expect me, I know; but this morning was so warm and thawing, that John said he knew the sleighing would all be gone by Saturday, so I concluded to come to-day."

Lucy was too angry to reply, and rushing from the room, she closed the door after her, with a force which fairly made the windows rattle. Berintha looked inquiringly at Lizzie, who felt inadequate to an explanation; so Berintha knew nothing of the matter until she descended to the kitchen, and there learned the whole. Now, if Lucy had treated her cousin politely and good-naturedly, she would have saved herself much annoyance, but on the contrary, she told her that she was neither expected nor wanted there; that parties were never intended for "such old things;" and that now she was there, she hoped she would stay in her own room, unless she should happen to be wanted to wait on the table!

This speech, of course, exasperated Berintha, but she made no reply, although there was on her face a look of quiet determination, which Lucy mistook for tacit acquiescence in her proposal.

Five—six—seven—eight—struck the little brass clock, and no one had come except old Dr. Benton, who, being a widower and an intimate friend of the family, was invited, as Lucy said, for the purpose of beauing grandma! Lizzie, in crimson double-gown, and soft, warm shawl, was reclining on the sofa in the parlor, the old doctor muttering about carelessness, heated rooms, late hours, &c. Grandma, in rich black silk and plain Quaker cap, was hovering near her favorite child, asking continually if she were too hot, or too cold, or too tired, while Lucy, in white muslin dress and flowing curls, flitted hither and thither, fretting at the servants, or ordering grandma, and occasionally tapping her sister's pale cheek, to see if she could not coax some color into it.

"You'll live to see it whiter still," said the doctor, who was indignant at finding his patient down stairs.

And where all this time was Berintha? The doctor asked this question, and Lucy asked this question, while Lizzie replied, that "she was in her room."

"And I hope to goodness she'll stay there," said Lucy.

Dr. Benton's gray eyes fastened upon the amiable young lady, who, by way of explanation, proceeded to relate her maneuvers for keeping "the old maid" from the party.

We believe we have omitted to say that Lucy had

some well founded hopes of being one day, together with her sister, heiress of Dr. Benton's property, which was considerable. He was a widower, and had no relatives. He was also very intimate with Mr. Dayton's family, always evincing a great partiality for Lucy and Lizzie, and had more than once hinted at the probable disposal of his wealth. Of course, Lucy, in his presence, was all amiability, and though he was usually very far sighted, he but partially understood her real character. Something, however, in her remarks concerning Berintha, displeased him. Lucy saw it, but before she had time for any thought on the subject, the door-bell rang, and a dozen or more of guests entered.

The parlors now began to fill rapidly. Ere long, St. Leon came, and after paying his compliments to Lucy, he took his station between her and the sofa, on which Lizzie sat. So delighted was Lucy to have him thus near, that she forgot Berintha, until that lady herself appeared in the room, bowing to those she knew, and seating herself on the sofa, very near St. Leon. The angry blood rushed in torrents to Lucy's face, and St. Leon, who saw something was wrong, endeavored to divert her mind by asking her various questions.

At last he said, " I do not see Miss Harcourt. Where is she ? "

" She is not expected," answered Lucy, carelessly.

"Ah ! " said St. Leon ; and Berintha, touching his arm, rejoined, " Of course you could not think Ada Harcourt would be invited *here !* "

" Indeed ! Why not ? " asked St. Leon, and Berintha continued : "To be sure, Ada is handsome, and Ada is accomplished, but then Ada is *poor*, and consequently can't come ! "

" But I see no reason why poverty should debar her

from good society," said St. Leon; and Berintha, with an exultant glance at Lucy, who, if possible, would have paralyzed her tongue, replied, "Why, if Ada were present, she might rival somebody in somebody's good opinion. Wasn't that what you said, Cousin Lucy? Please correct me, if I get wrong."

Lucy frowned angrily, but made no reply, for Berintha had quoted her very words. After a moment's pause, she proceeded: "Yes, Ada is poor; so though she can come to the front door with a gentleman, she cannot go out that way, but must be led to a side door or back door; which was it, Cousin Lucy?"

"I don't know what you are talking about," answered Lucy; and Berintha, in evident surprise, exclaimed, "Why, don't you remember when Ada came here with a gentle man,—let me see, who was it?—well, no matter who 'twas,—she came with a gentleman,—he was ushered into the parlor, while you took her into a side room, then into a side passage, and out at the side door, kindly telling her to beware of the gentleman in the parlor, who could want nothing good of sewing girls!"

"You are very entertaining to-night," said Lucy; to which Berintha replied, "You did not think I could be so agreeable, did you, when you asked me to keep out of sight this evening, and said that such old fudges as grandma and I would appear much better in our rooms, taking snuff, and nodding at each other over our knitting work?"

Lucy looked so distressed that Lizzie pitied her, and touching Berintha, she said, "Please don't talk any more."

At that moment supper was announced, and after it was over, St. Leon departed, notwithstanding Lucy's urgent request that he would remain longer. As the street door closed after him, she felt that she would gladly have seen every other guest depart, also. A moody fit came on, and the party would have been voted a failure, had it not been for the timely interference of Dr. Benton and Berintha. Together they sought out any who seemed neglected, entertaining them to the best of their ability, and leaving with every one the impression that they were the best natured couple in the world. At eleven o'clock, Lizzie, wearied out, repaired to her chamber. Her departure was the signal for others, and before one o'clock the last good-night was said, the doors locked, the silver gathered up, the tired servants dismissed, and Lucy, in her sister's room, was giving vent to her wrath against Berintha, the party, St. Leon, and all.

Scolding, however, could do her no good, and ere long, throwing herself undressed upon a lounge, she fell asleep, and dreamed that grandma was married to the doctor, that Berintha had become her step-mother, and, worse than all, that Ada Harcourt was Mrs. St. Leon.

CHAPTER IX.

A WEDDING AT ST. LUKE'S.

THE day but one following the party, as Lucy was doing some shopping down street, she stepped for a moment into her dress-maker's, Miss Carson's, where she found three or four of her companions, all eagerly discussing what seemed to be quite an interesting topic. As Lucy entered, one of them, turning toward her, said, "Oh, isn't it strange? Or have'nt you heard?"

"Heard what?" asked Lucy; and her companion replied, "Why, Ada Harcourt is going to be married. Miss Carson is making her the most beautiful traveling dress, with silk hat to match——"

"Besides three or four elegant silk dresses," chimed in another.

"And the most charming morning-gown you ever saw — apple green, and dark green, striped — and lined with pink silk," rejoined a third.

By this time Lucy had sunk into the nearest chair. The truth had flashed upon her, as it probably has upon you; but as she did not wish to betray her real emotions, she forced a little bitter laugh, and said, "St. Leon, I suppose, is the bridegroom."

"Yes; who told you?" asked her companion.

"Oh, I've seen it all along," answered Lucy, carelessly. "He called with her once at our house!"

"But you did n't invite her to your party," said mischievous Bessie Lee, who loved dearly to tease Lucy Dayton. "You did n't invite her to your party, and so he left early, and I dare say went straight to Mrs. Harcourt's and proposed, if he had n't done so before. Now, don't you wish you'd been more polite to Ada? They say he's got a cousin south, as rich and handsome as he is, and if you'd only behaved as you should, who knows what might have happened!"

Lucy deigned Bessie no reply, and turning to another young lady, asked, "When is the wedding to be?"

"Next Thursday morning, in the church," was the answer; and Bessie Lee again interposed, saying, "Come, Lucy, I don't believe you have ever returned Ada's call, and as I am going to see her, and inquire all about that Cousin Frank, suppose you accompany me, and learn the particulars of the wedding."

"Thank you," said Lucy; "I don't care enough about it to take that trouble;" and soon rising, she left the shop.

If Lucy manifested so much indifference, we wot of some bright eyes and eager ears, which are willing to know the particulars, so we will give them, as follows: When St. Leon left Mr. Dayton's, it was ten o'clock, but notwithstanding the lateness of the hour, he started for the small brown house on "Dirt Alley," where dwelt the sewing woman and her daughter, who were both busy on some work which they wished to finish that night. Ada had stopped for a moment to replenish the fire, when a knock at the door startled her. Opening it, she saw St. Leon, and in much surprise said, "Why, I supposed you were at the party."

"So I have been," said he; "but I grew weary, and left for a more congenial atmosphere;" then advancing toward Mrs. Harcourt, he took her hand, saying, "Mrs. Linwood, allow me to address you by your right name this evening."

We draw a vail over the explanation which followed — over the fifty-nine questions asked by Ada concerning Jenny — and over the *one* question asked by St. Leon, the answer to which resulted in the purchase of all those dresses at Miss Carson's, and the well-founded rumor, that on Thursday morning a wedding would take place at St. Luke's church.

Poor Lucy! how disconsolate she felt! St. Leon was passing from her grasp, and there was no help. On her way home, she three times heard of the wedding, and of Ada's real name and former position in life, and each time her wrath waxed warmer and warmer. Fortunate was it for Berintha and grandma that neither made her appearance until tea time, for Lucy was in just the state when

15

an explosive storm would surely have followed any remark addressed to her!

The next day was the Sabbath, and as Lucy entered
the church, the first object which met her eye was St.
Leon, seated in the sewing woman's pew, and Ada *tolerably* though not *very* near him! "How disgusting!"
she hissed between her teeth, as she entered her own
richly cushioned seat, and opened her velvet-bound prayer
book. Precious little of the sermon heard she that day,
for, turn which way she would, she still saw in fancy the
sweet young face of her rival; and it took but a slight
stretch of imagination to bring to view a costly house in
the far off "sunny south," a troop of servants, a handsome, noble husband, and the hated Ada the happy mistress of them all! Before church was out, Lucy was really sick, and when at home in her room, she did not refuse the bowl of herb tea which Berintha kindly brought
her, saying "it had cured her when she felt just so."

* * * * * *

The morning of the wedding came, and though Lucy
had determined not to be present, yet as the hour approached she felt how utterly impossible it would be for
her to stay away; and when at half past eight the doors
were opened, she was among the first who entered the
church, which in a short time was filled. Nine rang
from the old clock in the belfry, and then up the broad
aisle came the bridal party, consisting of Mr. and Mrs.
Graham, Charlie and Anna, Mrs. Harcourt, or Mrs. Linwood, as we must now call her, St. Leon, and Ada.

"Was there ever a more beautiful bride?" whispered
Bessie Lee; but Lucy made no answer, and as soon as

the ceremony was concluded she hurried home, feeling almost in need of some more catnip tea!

In the eleven o'clock train St. Leon with his bride and her mother started for New Haven, where they spent a delightful week, and then returned to S——. A few days were passed at the house of Mr. Graham, and then they departed for their southern home. As we shall not again have occasion to speak of them in this story, we will here say that the following summer they came north, together with Jenny and Cousin Frank, the latter of whom was so much pleased with the rosy cheeks, laughing eyes, and playful manners of Bessie Lee, that when he returned home, he coaxed her to accompany him; and again was there a wedding in St. Luke's, and again did Miss Carson make the bridal outfit, wishing that all New Orleans gentlemen would come to S—— for their wives.

———◆———

CHAPTER X.

A SURPRISE.

"Reuben," said Grandma Dayton to her son, one evening after she had listened to the reading of a political article for which she did not care one fig, "Reuben, does thee suppose Dr. Benton makes a charge every time he calls?"

"I don't know," said Mr. Dayton; "what made you ask that question?"

"Because," answered grandma,—and her knitting needles rattled loud enough to be heard in the next room— 'because, I think he calls mighty often, considering that

Lizzie neither gets better nor worse; and I think, too, that he and Berintha have a good many private talks!"

The paper dropped from Mr. Dayton's hand, and " what can you mean ? " dropped from his lips.

" Why," resumed grandma, " every time he comes, he manages to see Berintha alone; and hain't thee noticed that she has colored her hair lately, and left off caps ? "

" Yes; and she looks fifteen years younger for it; but what of that ? "

Grandma, whose remarks had all been preparatory to the mighty secret she was about to divulge, coughed, and then informed her son that Berintha was going to be married, and wished to have the wedding there.

" Berintha and the doctor! Good!" exclaimed Mr. Dayton. " To be sure, I'll give her a wedding, and a wedding dress, too."

Here grandma left the room, and after reporting her success to Berintha, she sought her grand-daughters, and communicated to them the expected event. When Lucy learned of her cousin's intended marriage, she was nearly as much surprised and provoked as she had been when first she heard of Ada's.

Turning to Lizzie, she said, " It's too bad! for of course we shall have to give up all hopes of the doctor's money."

" And perhaps thee'll be the only old maid in the family, after all," suggested grandma, who knew Lucy's weak point, and sometimes loved to touch it.

" And if I am," retorted Lucy, angrily, " I hope I shall have sense enough to mind my own business, and not interfere with that of my grandchildren ! "

Grandma made no answer, but secretly she felt some conscientious scruples with regard to Lucy's grandchildren ! As for Berintha, she seemed entirely changed, and flitted about the house in a manner which caused Lucy to call her " an old fool, trying to ape sixteen." With a change of feelings, her personal appearance also changed, and when she one day returned from the dentist's with an entire set of new teeth, and came down to tea in a dark, fashionably made merino, the metamorphose was complete, and grandma declared that she looked better than she ever had before in her life. The doctor, too, was improved, and though he did not color his hair, he ordered six new shirts, a new coat, a new horse, and a pair of gold spectacles!

After a due lapse of time, the appointed day came, and with it, at an early hour, came Cousin John and Elizabeth Betsey, bringing with them the few *herbs* which Berintha, at the time of her removal, had overlooked. These Bridget demurely proposed should be given to Miss Lucy, " who of late was much given to drinking catnip." Perfectly indignant, Lucy threw the herbs, bag and all, into the fire, thereby filling the house with an odor which made the asthmatic old doctor wheeze and blow wonderfully, during the evening.

A few of the villagers were invited, and when all was ready, Mr. Dayton brought down in his arms his white-faced Lizzie, who imperceptibly had grown paler and weaker every day, while those who looked at her as she reclined upon the sofa, sighed, and thought of a different occasion when they probably would assemble there. For once Lucy was very amiable, and with the utmost politeness and good nature, waited upon the guests. There was a softened light in her eye, and a heightened bloom on her cheek, occasioned by a story which Berintha, two hours before, had told her, of a heart all crushed in its youth, and aching on through long years of loneliness, but which was about to be made happy by a union with the only object it had ever loved! Do you start and wonder?

Have you not guessed that Dr. Benton, who, that night, for the second time breathed the marriage vow, was the same who, years before, won the girlish love of Berintha Dayton, and then turned from her to the more beautiful Amy Holbrook, finding, too late, that all is not gold that glitters? It is even so, and could you have seen how tightly he clasped the hand of his new wife, and how fondly his eye rested upon her, you would have said that, however long his affections might have wandered, they had at last returned to her, his first, best love.

***

CHAPTER XI.

LIZZIE.

Gathered 'round a narrow coffin,
  Stand a mourning, funeral train,
While for her, redeemed thus early,
  Tears are falling now like rain.

Hopes are crushed and hearts are bleeding;
  Drear the fireside now, and lone;
She, the best loved and the dearest,
  Far away to heaven hath flown.

Long, long, will they miss thee, Lizzie,
  Long, long days for thee they'll weep;
And through many nights of sorrow
  Memory will her vigils keep.

In the chapter just finished, we casually mentioned that Lizzie, instead of growing stronger, had drooped day by day, until to all, save the fond hearts which watched her, she seemed surely passing away. But they to whom her presence was as sunlight to the flowers, shut their eyes to

the dreadful truth, refusing to believe that she was leaving them. Oftentimes, during the long winter nights,
would Mr. Dayton steal softly to her chamber, and kneeling by her bedside, gaze in mute anguish upon the wasted
face of his darling. And when from her transparent
brow and marble cheek he wiped the deadly night-sweats,
a chill, colder far than the chill of death, crept over his
heart, and burying his face in his hands he would cry,
"Oh, Father, let this cup pass from me!"

As spring approached, she seemed better, and the father's heart grew stronger, and Lucy's step was lighter, and
grandma's words more cheerful, as hope whispered, "she
will live." But when the snow was melted from off the
hillside, and over the earth the warm spring sun was shining, when the buds began to swell and the trees to put
forth their young leaves, there came over her a change so
fearful, that with one bitter cry of sorrow, hope fled forever; and again, in the lonely night season, the weeping
father knelt and asked for strength to bear it when his
best loved child was gone.

"Poor Harry!" said Lizzie one day to Anna, who was
sitting by her, "Poor Harry, if I could see him again;
but I never shall."

"Perhaps you will," answered Anna. "I wrote to
him three weeks ago, telling him to come quickly."

"Then he will," said Lizzie; "but if I should be dead
when he comes, tell him how I loved him to the last, and
that the thought of leaving him was the sharpest pang I
suffered."

There were tears in Anna's eyes as she kissed the cheek
of the sick girl, and promised to do her bidding. After
a moment's pause, Lizzie added, "I am afraid Harry is
not a christian, and you must promise not to leave him

until he has a well-founded hope that again in heaven 1 shall see him."

Anna promised all, and then as Lizzie seemed exhausted, she left her and returned home. One week from that day she stood once more in Lizzie's sick-room, listening, for the last time, to the tones of the dying girl, as she bade her friends adieu. Convulsed with grief, Lucy knelt by the bedside, pressing to her lips one little clammy hand, and accusing herself of destroying her sister's life. In the farthest corner of the room sat Mr. Dayton. He could not stand by and see stealing over his daughter's face the dark shadow which falls but once on all. He could not look upon her, when o'er her soft, brown eyes the white lids closed forever. Like a naked branch in the autumn wind, his whole frame shook with agony, and though each fibre of grandma's heart was throbbing with anguish, yet, for the sake of her son, she strove to be calm, and soothed him as she would a little child. Berintha, too, was there, and while her tears were dropping fast, she supported Lizzie in her arms, pushing back from her pale brow the soft curls, which, damp with the moisture of death, lay in thick rings upon her forehead.

"Has Harry come?" said Lizzie.

The answer was in the negative, and a moan of disappointment came from her lips.

Again she spoke: "Give him my bible,—and my curls;—when I am dead let Lucy arrange them,—she knows how,—then cut them off, and the best, the longest, the brightest is for Harry, the others for you all. And tell—tell—tell him to meet—me in heaven—where I'm—going—going."

A stifled shriek from Lucy, as she fell back, fainting, told that with the last word, "*going*," Lizzie had gone to heaven!

An hour after the tolling bell arrested the attention of many, and of the few who asked for whom it tolled, nearly all involuntarily sighed and said, "Poor Harry! Died before he came home!"

*　　*　　*　　*　　*　　*

It was the night before the burial, and in the back parlor stood a narrow coffin containing all that was mortal of Lizzie Dayton. In the front parlor Bridget and another domestic kept watch over the body of their young mistress. Twelve o'clock rang from the belfry of St. Luke's church, and then the midnight silence was broken by the shrill scream of the locomotive, as the eastern train thundered into the depot. But the senses of the Irish girls were too profoundly locked in sleep to heed that common sound; neither did they hear the outer door, which by accident had been left unlocked, swing softly open, nor saw they the tall figure which passed by them into the next room,—the room where stood the coffin.

Suddenly through the house there echoed a cry, so long, so loud, so despairing, that every sleeper started from their rest, and hurried with nervous haste to the parlor, where they saw Harry Graham, bending in wild agony over the body of his darling Lizzie, who never before had turned a deaf ear to his impassioned words of endearment. He had received his sister's letter, and started immediately for home, but owing to some delay, did not reach there in time to see her alive. Anxious to know the worst, he had not stopped at his father's house, but seeing a light in Mr. Dayton's parlors, hastened thither. Finding the door unlocked, he entered, and on seeing the two servant girls asleep, his heart beat quickly with apprehension. Still he was unprepared for the shock which awaited him, when on the coffin and her who slept within it his eye first rested. He did not faint, nor even weep, but when his friends came about him with words of sympathy, he only answered, "Lizzie, Lizzie, she is dead!"

During the remainder of that sad night, he sat by the coffin pressing his hand upon the icy forehead until its coldness seemed to benumb his faculties, for when in the morning his parents and sister came, he scarcely noticed them; and still the world, misjudging ever, looked upon his calm face and tearless eye, and said that all too lightly had he loved the gentle girl, whose last thoughts and words had been of him. Ah, they knew not the utter wreck the death of that young girl had made, of the bitter grief, deeper and more painful because no tear-drop fell to moisten its feverish agony. They buried her, and then back from the grave came the two heart-broken men, the father and Harry Graham, each going to his own desolate home, the one to commune with the God who had given and taken away, and the other to question the dealings of that providence which had taken from him his all.

Days passed, and nothing proved of any avail to win Harry from the deep despair which seemed to have settled upon him. At length, Anna bethought her of the soft, silken curl which had been reserved for him. Quickly she found it, and taking with her the bible, repaired to her brother's room. Twining her arms around his neck, she told him of the death-scene, of which he before had refused to hear. She finished her story by suddenly holding to view the long, bright ringlet, which once adorned the fair head now resting in the grave. Her plan was successful, for bursting into tears, Harry wept nearly two

hours. From that time, he seemed better, and was frequently found bathed in tears, and bending over Lizzie's
bible, which now was his daily companion.

Lucy, too, seemed greatly changed. She had loved her
sister as devotedly as one of her nature could love, and for
her death she mourned sincerely. Lizzie's words of love
and gentle persuasion had not been without their effect,
and when Mr. Dayton saw how kind, how affectionate and
considerate of other people's feelings his daughter had become, he felt that Lizzie had not died in vain.

* * * * * *

Seven times have the spring violets blossomed, seven
times the flowers of summer bloomed, seven times have the
autumnal stores been gathered in, and seven times have the
winds of winter sighed over the New England hills, since
Lizzie was laid to rest. In her home there have been few
changes. Mr. Dayton's hair is whiter than it was of old,
and the furrows on his brow deeper and more marked.
Grandma, quiet and gentle as ever, knits on, day after
day, ever and anon speaking of "our dear little Lizzie,
who died years ago."

Lucy is still unmarried, and satisfied, too, that it should
be so. A patient, self-sacrificing christian, she strives to
make up to her father for the loss of one over whose
memory she daily weeps, and to whose death she accuses
herself of being accessory. Dr. Benton and his rather
fashionable wife live in their great house, ride in their
handsome carriage, give large dinner parties, play chess
after supper, and then the old doctor nods over his evening paper, while Berintha nods over a piece of embroidery, intended to represent a little dog chasing a butterfly

and which would as readily be taken for that as for any thing else, and for anything else as that.

Two years ago a pale young missionary departed to carry the news of salvation to the heathen land. Some one suggested that he should take with him a wife, but he shook his head mournfully, saying, "I have one wife in heaven." The night before he left home, he might have been seen, long after midnight, seated upon a grassy grave, where the flowers of summer were growing. Around the stone which marks the spot, rose bushes have clustered so thickly as to hide from view the words there written, but push them aside and you will read, "Our darling Lizzie."

The Old Red House

AMONG THE MOUNTAINS.

------◆◆◆------

CHAPTER I.

UNCLE AMOS AND AUNT POLLY.

MANY years ago, before I was born, or you either, perchance, gentle reader, there lived, far away among the tall
mountains of New England, a sturdy farmer, Uncle Amos
Carey, and his good wife Polly. This worthy couple,
who seemed to be every body's uncle and aunt, were
known for many miles around, and their " old red house
among the mountains" was long the rendezvous for all
the young mountaineers, who, with their rosy cheeked
lasses, congregated there on all " great days," and on many
days which were not great.

There was some strong attraction about that low, red
building. Perhaps it was because the waters of the well
which stood in the rear were colder, or the grass in the
little yard was greener, and the elm trees and lilac bushes
taller there than elsewhere. Or it might have been because Aunt Polly was deeply skilled in the mysteries of
fortune-telling, by means of teacups and tea-grounds.

Many a time might the good dame have been seen, surrounded by half a dozen girls, all listening eagerly, while
Aunt Polly, with a dolefully grave expression about her

long nose, peered into some teacup, in the bottom of which lay a mass of tea-leaves in helter-skelter form. Slowly and solemnly would she unfold the shining future to some bright-eyed maiden, whose heart beat faster as the thoughts of a rich husband, fine house, and more dresses than she knew what to do with, were presented to her imagination. At other times, the end of Aunt Polly's nose would perceptibly flatten, and her voice would become fearfully low, as, with an ominous shake of her head, she dove into the teacup of some luckless wight, who was known to have pilfered her grapes and plundered her water-melon patch! On such occasions, dreadful was the fortune given to the unfortunate offender. A broken heart, broken leg, and most likely a broken neck, were awarded to him for his delinquencies.

Notwithstanding these occasional ill fortunes, Aunt Polly was a great favorite with the young folks, who, as we have said, were frequent visitors at "the old red house among the mountains."

<hr>

CHAPTER II.

ALICE.

UNCLE Amos had one child, a daughter, named Alice. At a period longer ago than I can remember, Alice was fifteen years of age, and was as wild and shy a creature as the timid deer, which sometimes bounded past her mountain home, trembling at the rustle of every leaf and the buzz of every bee. There was much doubt whether Alice were the veritable child of Uncle Amos and Aunt Polly, or not.

Rumor said that nearly fifteen years before, a fearful snow storm, such as the "oldest inhabitant" had never before known, swept over the mountains, blocking up the roads, and rendering them impassable for several days. On the first night of the storm, about dusk, a slight female form was seen toiling slowly up the mountain road, which led to Uncle Amos' house. A man who was hurrying home met her, and anxious to know who she was, looked under her bonnet. Her face, as he afterwards described it, was very white and crazy-like, and very beautiful. Another person, a woman, had been with her knitting work to one of the neighbors, and was also returning home. Suddenly turning a corner in the road, she came face to face with the weary traveler, who seemed anxious to pass unnoticed. But the woman was inquisitive, and desirous of knowing who the stranger could be; so she asked her name, and where she was going. A glance of anger shot from the large black eye of the strange woman, but farther than that she deigned no reply; and as she passed on, the questioner observed that she carried in her arms something which might or might not be an infant.

The next day the storm raged so violently that neither man, woman, nor child were seen outside their own yards For three days the storm continued with unabated fury and several more days passed before the process of "break ing roads" was gone through with, sufficiently to admit of a passage from one house to another. At the end of that time, one night, just after sunset, a whole sled load of folks drew up in front of Uncle Amos' dwelling They could not wait any longer before visiting Aunt Polly, whose smiling face appeared at the door, and called out, "Welcome to you all. I's expecting you, and have got a lot of mince pies and doughnuts made."

So the dames and lasses bounded off from the ox-sled,

and running hastily into the house, were soon relieving themselves of their warm wrappings. There was so much talking and laughing among them, that the cloaks, shawls, and hoods were all put away before one of them exclaimed, "Mercy sakes! Here's a cradle! Is your cat sick, Aunt Polly? But no,—as true as I live, it's a little bit of a baby! Where in this world did you get it, Aunt Polly?"

But if Aunt Polly knew where she got it, she kept the knowledge to herself, and bravely withstood the questioning and cross-questioning of her fair guests.

"Ask me no questions, and I will tell you no lies," said she. "It is my child, and haven't I as good a right to have a daughter as anybody?"

"Yes, thee has," said Dolly Dutton, a fair, chubby little Quakeress; "and well is it for the poor thing that it can call thee mother."

By this time the baby had been unceremoniously hustled out of its snug cradle by some of the young girls, who were all loud in their admiration of its beauty.

"What do you call it, Aunt Polly?" asked one.

"Alice," was Aunt Polly's quiet reply.

At that moment the baby slowly unclosed its large eyes, and fixed them on the face of the young girl who held her, with a strange, earnest gaze. Up sprung the girl as if stung by a serpent. "Gracious goodness!" exclaimed she, "will somebody please take her. She's got the 'evil eye' I do believe, and looks for all the world like old Squire Herndon."

Aunt Polly hastily stooped down to take the child, but she did not stoop soon enough or low enough to hide from Dolly Dutton's keen eye the deep flush which mantled her cheek at the mention of Squire Herndon. From that time Dolly's mind was made up respecting Alice. She knew something which most of her neighbors did not know, but as she chose to keep it a secret, so too will I, for a time, at least.

Merrily sang the round tea-kettle in the bright fire which blazed on Aunt Polly's clean hearth, and loudly hissed the strong green tea in the old black earthen tea-pot, while the long pine table, with its snowy cloth, groaned beneath its weight of edibles. The spirits of the company rose higher in proportion as the good cheer grew lower. Numerous were the jokes cracked at the expense of the little Alice, who, with her large, wild eyes, lay in her cradle bed, wholly unconscious of the wonder and gossip she was exciting.

"It's of no use, Richard, for thee to quiz Aunt Polly concerning Alice, for she ain't going to tell, and most likely has a good reason for her silence," said Dolly Dutton to Mr. Richard Hallidon, who had the honor of being schoolmaster in the little village which lay snugly nestled at the foot of the mountain.

"Neither would I give the worth of a quill pen to know," said Richard, "but I will stipulate with Aunt Polly that as soon as Alice is old enough, she shall come to my school."

To this proposition Aunt Polly readily assented, and after much laughing and joking, and the disappearance of a large tin pan full of red apples, and a gallon or so of egg nog, the little party left for home.

Ere the heavy tread of the oxen and the creaking of the cumbrous sled had died away in the distance, Uncle Amos was snugly ensconced in bed, and in the course of five minutes he was sending forth sundry loud noises which sounded like snoring; but as the good man warmly contended that he never snored, (has the reader ever seen a man who would confess he did snore?) we will suppose the sounds to have been something else. Aunt Polly sat by the, fire with the child of her adoption lying on her lap. Bending down, she closely scrutinized each feature of the small, white face, and as the infant opened its full, dark eyes, and fixed them inquiringly upon her, she murmured, " Yes, she does look like Squire Herndon ; strange I never thought of it before. But deary me," she continued, "who ever did see such awful eyes ? They fairly make me fidgety. There, shut them up," said she, at the same time pressing down the lids over the eyes, which seemed to look so knowingly at her.

The offending eyes being shut, the old lady continued her musing. "Yes," thought she, "Alice has the Herndon look. I wonder what the old squire would say if he knew all. I've half a mind to tell him, just to see what kind of a hurricane he would get up." Then followed a long reverie, in the midst of which stood a large, handsome castle, of which Alice was the proud nominal mistress, and Aunt Polly the real one.

By the time this castle was fully completed and furnished, Aunt Polly was fast nodding assent to every improvement. Fainter and fainter grew the fire on the hearth, clearer and clearer ticked the old long clock in the corner, louder and louder grew the breathings of Uncle Amos, while lower and lower nodded Aunt Polly's spectacles, till at last they dropped from the long, sharp nose, and rested quietly on the floor. How long this state of things would have continued, is not known, for matters were soon brought to a crisis by Uncle Amos who gave a snore so loud and long that it woke the baby, Alice, whose uneasy turnings soon roused her sleeping nurse.

"Bless my stars ! " said Aunt Polly, rubbing her eyes "where's my spectacles ? I must have nad a nap." A few moments more, and silence again settled round the house, and its occupants were wandering through the misty vales of dreamland.

———◆———

CHAPTER III.

LITTLE ITEMS.

WE pass rapidly over the first ten years of Alice's life, only pausing to say that she throve well under the kind care of Uncle Amos and Aunt Polly, whom she looked upon as her parents, for she knew no others. As she increased in stature and years, her personal appearance was remarked and commented upon by the matrons of the mountains, as well as those of the village at the foot of the mountain.

One would say, "She and old Herndon looked as much alike as two peas," while another would answer, "Yes, only Alice has got such strange, scornful eyes. They look at you as though they could read all your thoughts." And now I suppose some reader will say, "How did Alice look, and what was it about her eyes?" So here follows a description of Alice as she was at ten years of age.

Naturally healthy, the strength of her constitution was greatly increased by the mountain air and exercise to which she was daily accustomed. Still, in form she was delicate, and Aunt Polly often expressed her fears that the poor child would never attain her height, which was five feet ten inches! Alice's features were tolerably regular, and her complexion was as white and pure as the falling snow. Indeed, there was something almost startling in the marble whiteness of her face, contrasting, as it did, with the blackness of her hair, which hung in short, tangled curls about her neck, forehead, and eyes. Those eyes we will speak of, ere long. We are not yet through with Alice's hair, which cost her poor mother a world of trouble. Do what she might, it would curl. Soak it in suds as long as she chose, and as soon as it dried, it curled more than ever! What a pest it was! Aunt Polly couldn't spend her time in curling hair, and as Alice did not know how, there seemed but one alternative — cut it off; but this Alice would not suffer, so one hour every Sunday morning was devoted to combing and curling the really handsome hair, which during the week hung in wild disorder about her face, becoming each day more and more tangled and matted, until it was not strange that Alice thought she should surely die if it were combed more than once a week.

Now for those eyes. After all, there was nothing so very goblin-like about them. They were merely very large, very black, and very bright, and seemed, indeed, to look into the recesses of one's soul, and pry out his inmost thoughts. There was a world of pride and scorn beneath the long silken eyelashes, which seemed so seldom to be closed, for as one of the villagers said, "Alice's eyes were always looking, looking at you." On occasions when Aunt Polly was engaged in her favorite occupation of fortune-telling, Alice's eyes would flash forth her utter contempt of the whole matter, and many a young maiden, shamed by the scorn of the little wild girl, as she was called, would conclude not to have "her fortune told."

It was seldom, however, that Alice honored her mother's company by her presence. She seemed to prefer the woods, the birds, and flowers for her companions. Sometimes she would steal away into the little bed-room which joined her mother's sitting-room, and there, unobserved, she would watch, through a hole in the door, the counte- nances and proceedings of the company around her mother's tea-table. Often would some of the guests be startled by the fixed gaze of those large, black eyes, which seemed to look with such haughty pity on the farce which always followed one of Aunt Polly's tea drinkings.

CHAPTER IV.

FRANK.

ONE bright summer afternoon when there was no school, Alice wandered out alone into the woods, pluck- ing here and there a wild flower, which she placed in the matted curls of her hair. At last, coming to a little open- ing in the trees, where a rude seat had been constructed, she sat down, and commenced singing, in clear, musical tones, the old familiar song, "Bonnie Doon."

She was just finishing the first stanza, when she was startled by the sound of another voice, chiming in with hers. Springing up, she looked round for the intruder.

"Just cast those big eyes straight ahead, and you'll see me!" called out some one in a loud, merry tone.

Immediately Alice saw directly before her a roguish looking, handsome boy, apparently twelve or thirteen years of age. There was something in his air and dress which told that he was above the common order of moun- taineers. Alice suddenly recollected having heard that a widow lady, with one son, had recently moved into a pretty white cottage which stood about half a mile from her father's, and she readily concluded that the lad before her was Frank Seymour, whose beauty she had heard one of her school companions extol so highly. Her first impulse was to run, but the boy prevented her, by saying, "I'm Frank Seymour. I've just moved my mother up among these mountains. Now, who and what are you? You are a queer looking specimen, any way!"

Rude as this speech was, it pleased Alice, and she answered, "I am Alice Carey, and I don't care if I am queer looking."

"Alice Carey, are you? That's a pretty name," said Frank, cracking his fingers. "Alice Carey,—oh, I know, you are that old witch's daughter that lives in the red house. I've heard of you. They say you are as wild as a wild-cat,—and yet I like you."

Alice stood for an instant as if spell-bound. Her mother had been called an old witch, and herself a wild-cat, in such a comical way, too, that for a time anger and mirth strove for the mastery. The former conquered, and ere Frank was aware of her intention, he received a blow in his face which sent him reeling against an old tree. When he recovered a standing posture, he observed Alice far away in the distance, speeding it over logs and stumps, briers and bushes, and he instantly started in pursuit. The chase was long, for Alice ran swiftly, but gradually her pursuer gained upon her. At length she came to a tall tree, whose limbs grew near the ground. With a cat-like spring she caught the lower branch, and by the time Frank reached the tree, she was far up, near its top, cozily sitting on one of its boughs. In her hand she held a large worms' nest, which she had broken from the tree.

"Hallo, there, Master Frank!" said she. "Just as sure as you climb this tree I'll shake these worms in your face!"

If there was any living thing Frank feared, it was a worm, so he was obliged to give up his projected ascent.

"What a little spit-fire she is! I'll fetch her down, though," said he. At the same time gathering up a handful of stones, he called out, "Miss Alice Carey, if you don't come down, instanter, I'll stone you down."

"Hit me if you can," was the defiant answer.

Whizz went a stone through the air, but it missed its mark, and fell harmlessly to the ground. We must tell the truth, however, and say that Frank was very careful not to hit the white, unearthly face, which gleamed amid the dense foliage of the tree.

"Come, Alice," said he, coaxingly, "what's the use of being perched up there like a raccoon or hyena. Come down, and let us make up friends, for really I do like you."

"You called my mother an old witch," said Alice.

"I know I did," answered Frank, "but I'm sorry for it. I heard she told fortunes, and I couldn't think of any better name. But pray come down, and I won't call her so again."

Alice was finally persuaded, and rapidly descending the tree, she soon stood on the green turf beside Frank, who now eyed her from head to foot.

"I say, Alice," continued he, "just throw away that odious worms' nest, and act like somebody."

"I shall do no such thing, Master Frank," said Alice. "I know now that you are afraid of worms, and if you come one inch nearer me, I'll throw some on you!"

So Frank kept at a respectful distance, but he exerted himself to conquer Alice's evident dislike of him, and in five minutes' time he succeeded, for it was not in her nature to withstand the handsome face, laughing eye, and more than all, the droll humor of Frank.

The worms' nest was gradually forgotten, and when Frank, pulling a book from his pocket, said, "See here, look at my new history," it was dropped, while Alice drew so near to Frank that, ere the book was looked through, his hand was resting on her shoulder, and one of her snarled black curls lay amid his rich brown hair.

Before they parted that afternoon, they were sworn friends, and Frank had won from Alice an invitation to visit her mother the next day. "You may as well invite me," said he, "for I shall come, any way."

That night Alice related her adventure to her mother, and spoke of Frank in terms so extravagant, that the next day, when he made his appearance, he met with a hearty welcome from Aunt Polly, who was perfectly delighted with the bright, handsome boy. After tea, he said, "Come, Mrs. Carey, you must tell my fortune, and mind, now, tell me a good one."

"Frank, Frank!" said Alice, quickly.

"Well, what's wanted of Frank, Frank?" asked the young gentleman.

"I thought you despised the whole affair. I shan't like you if you don't," answered Alice.

"And so I do," said Frank; "but pity sakes, can't a *man* have a little fun?"

"You're a funny man," thought Alice, but she said nothing, and her mother proceeded to read Frank's fortune from the bottom of the cup. A handsome wife, who was rich and a lady, too, was promised him. Frank waited to hear no more; springing up, he struck the big blue cup from the hand of the astonished Aunt Polly, who exclaimed, "What ails the boy!"

"What ails me?" repeated Frank; "nobody wants a rich lady for a wife. Why didn't you promise me Alice? I like her best of anybody, and she's handsome, too, if she'd only comb out that squirrel's nest of hers. I say, Alice," continued he, "why don't you take better care of your hair? Come to my mother's, and she'll teach you how to curl it beautifully. Will you let her come to-morrow, Mrs. Carey?" said he, turning to Aunt Polly. "If you will, I will come for her, and will bring you two teacups to pay for the one I broke. I'm sorry I did that, but I couldn't help it."

Aunt Polly gave her consent to the visit, and the next day Frank joyfully introduced Alice to his mother. From that time she was a frequent visitor at the house of Mrs. Seymour, who was an accomplished woman, and took great pleasure in improving the manners and education of little Alice. Frank studied at home with his mother, and he begged so hard that his new friend might share his advantages, that Mrs. Seymour finally proposed to Aunt Polly to take Alice from school and let her study with Frank. To this plan Aunt Polly assented, and during the next six months Alice's improvement was as rapid as her happiness was unbounded.

CHAPTER V.

WOMAN'S NATURE.

WHEN the spring came, there was a change of teachers in the village school. Richard Hallidon, who for twelve years had swayed the birchen rod, was dismissed, and as a more talented and accomplished individual was hired in his stead, Mrs. Seymour concluded to send Frank there to school. Alice was his daily companion, and the intimacy between them was a subject of much ridicule for their companions.

Frank liked the fun of being teased about Alice, but she always declared that her preference for him, if she had any, arose from the fact that he was much better behaved than the other boys. Her affection was at last put to the test, in the following novel manner:

As she and some of her companions were one night returning from school, they came suddenly upon a group of boys, who were calling out, "That's it, Frank. Now make her draw. Who-a, haw, get up, Tabby."

Coming near, they discovered a kitten with a cord tied round its neck. To this cord was attached Frank's dinner basket and books. "He was tired of carrying them," he said, "and he meant to make kitty draw them."

"Frank Seymour!" said Alice, indignantly, "let that cat go, this instant."

Frank stood irresolute. There was something in the expression of Alice's eye which made him uncomfortable. He thought of the worms' nest, but one of the boys called out, "Shame, Frank; don't be afraid of her."

So Frank again attempted to make kitty draw the basket. In a twinkling, Alice pitched upon him. The boys gathered round and shouted, "A fight! a fight! Now for some fun! Give it to him, Alice! That's right, hit him another dig!"

The contest was a hot one, and on Frank's part a bloody one, for Alice seized his nose and wrung it until the blood gushed out! He, however, was the strongest, and was fast gaining the advantage. One of the girls perceived this, and turning to her brother, said, "Bob, help Alice don't you see she's getting the worst of it?"

Thus importuned, Bob fell upon Frank and belabored him so unmercifully that Frank cried for quarter. "Shall I let him alone, Alice?" said Bob. "I will do just as you say."

Alice's only answer was a fierce thrust at Bob's hair, hands full of which were soon floating on the air, like thistles in the autumn time.

"I declare, Alice," said Bob's sister, "I always knew you liked Frank, but I did not think you'd fight so like a tiger for him."

If this speech caused Alice any emotion, it was imperceptible, unless it were evinced by the increased brilliancy of her eyes, which emitted such lightning flashes, that during their walk home Frank very modestly suggested to her the propriety of keeping her eyes shut, while going through the woods, lest the dried leaves and shrubs should take fire! It is needless to say that thenceforth Frank and Alice were suffered to fight their own battles, undisturbed by Bob or any of his companions.

CHAPTER VI.

SQUIRE HERNDON AND IRA.

EVERY village, however small, has its aristocrat, and so had the little village at the foot of the mountain. At the upper end of the principal street stood a large, handsome building, whose high white walls, long green shutters, granite steps, and huge brass knocker, seemed to look down somewhat proudly upon their more humble neighbors. To the casual visitor or passing traveler, this dwelling was pointed out as belonging to Squire Herndon.

Squire Herndon was a man on whose head the frosts of sixty winters had fallen so heavily that they had bleached his once brown locks to a snowy whiteness. He was one who seemed to have outlived all natural affections. Long years had passed since he had laid the gentle wife of his youth to rest beneath the green willow, whose branches are now bent so low as almost to hide from view the low, grassy mound. By the side of that grave was another, the grave of Squire Herndon's only daughter. She was fair and beautiful, but the destroyer came, and one bright morning in autumn, just as the hoar frost was beginning to touch the foliage with a brighter hue, she passed away, and the old man's home was again desolate. Some of the villagers said of him in his affliction, "It's surely a judgment from heaven, to pay him for being so proud, and may be it will do him good;" but Squire Herndon was one whose morose nature adversity rendered still more sour.

He had yet one child left, Ira, his first-born and only son. On him his hopes were henceforth centered. Ira should marry some wealthy heiress, and thus the family name would not become extinct. Squire Herndon belonged to an English family, which was probably descended from one of those "three brothers who came over from England" long time ago! He was proud of his ancestors, proud of his wealth, his house, servants, and grounds, and had been proud of his daughter, but she was gone; and now he was proud of Ira, whom he tried to make generally disagreeable to the villagers.

But this he could not do, for Ira possessed too many of the social qualities of his mother to be very proud and arrogant. At length the time came when he entered

college at Amherst. During his collegiate course, he became acquainted with a beautiful and accomplished girl,
named Mary Calvert. That acquaintance soon ripened
into love, and Squire Herndon was one day startled by a
letter from Ira, saying that he was about to offer himself
to a Miss Calvert, with whom he knew his father would
be pleased.

This so enraged Squire Herndon, that, without stopping
to read more, he threw the letter aside, and for the next
half hour paced his apartment, stamping, puffing, and
foaming like a caged lion. At last it occurred to him that
he had not read all his son's letter, so catching it up, he
read it through, and found added as a postscript, the following clause: "I forgot to tell you that Mary's father is
very wealthy, and she is his only child."

This announcement changed the old squire at once;
his feelings underwent an entire revolution, and he now
regretted that Ira had not written that he *had* proposed
and was accepted. "But," thought the squire, "of
course she'll accept him; she cannot refuse such a boy as
Ira."

And yet she did! With many tears she confessed her
love, but said that far away over the seas was one to
whom she had been betrothed almost from childhood; he
was kind and noble, and until she saw Ira Herndon, she
had thought she loved him. Said she, "I have given him
so many assurances that I would be his, that I cannot recall them. I love you, Ira, far better, but I esteem Mr.
S., and respect myself so much that I cannot break my
word." No argument of Ira's could induce her to
change her resolution, and a few days before he was
graduated, he saw his Mary, with a face white as marble,
pronounce the vows which bound her to another.

CHAPTER VII.

ALICE'S MOTHER.

THREE years after the closing incidents of the last chapter, Ira was practicing law near the eastern boundary of the state of New York. From his office windows he frequently noticed a beautiful young girl of not more than sixteen summers, who passed and repassed every day to and from school. Her plain calico frock, coarse linen apron, and cambric sun-bonnet, showed that she was not a child of wealth, and yet there was something about her face and appearance strangely fascinating to the young lawyer.

He at length became acquainted with her, and found that her name was Lucy Edwards, that she was the adopted child of the family with whom she lived, and also the half sister of the famous Aunt Polly, among the mountains. Ira fancied that she resembled Mary Calvert, who was now lost to him forever, and ere he was aware of it, he was forming plans for the future, in all of which the young Lucy played a conspicuous part. Before the summer was over, he had asked her to be his wife. She gave her consent willingly, for she was ambitious, and had long sighed for something better than the humble home in which her childhood had been passed.

When next Ira visited his father, he was accompanied by Lucy, who was intending to spend several days with her sister. On parting with her at the hotel, he told her that the day following he would seek an interview with his father, to whom he would acknowledge their engagement, and ask him to sanction their union. Of that interview between father and son, we will speak but little. Suffice it to say, that Squire Herndon, in his rage, almost cursed his son for presuming to think of a poor, humble girl, whose sister disgraced her sex by telling fortunes, and finished his abuse by swearing to disinherit Ira the moment he should hear of his marrying Lucy Edwards. Ira knew his father too well to think of softening him by argument, so he rushed from his presence, and was soon on his way to the red house among the mountains, where Lucy was anxiously watching for him.

As soon as she saw him coming up the mountain path, she ran eagerly to meet him. At one glance she saw that something was wrong, and urged him to tell her the worst. In as few words as possible, he related to her what had passed between himself and his father. When he finished speaking, Lucy burst into tears, and said mournfully, "And so you will leave me, Ira? I might have known it would be so."

Ira was touched, and laying his hand on Lucy's dark locks, he vowed that she should be his, even at the cost of his father's curse. When they reached the gate, Lucy said, "I forgot to tell you that Polly has company—the Quakeress, Dolly Dutton—but you need not mind her."

After entering the house, Aunt Polly gradually led Ira to speak of the interview between himself and his father. By the time he had finished, Mrs. Carey's wrath was waxing warmer and warmer.

"Ira Herndon," she exclaimed, "you are cowardly if you do not show your independence by marrying whom you please."

"I intend to marry Lucy at some future time," answered Ira.

"Fudge on some future time!" was Aunt Polly's scornful answer; "why not marry her now? You'll never have a better time. We'll all keep it a secret, so your old father will not cut you off. Amos will go for

Parson Landon, who will not blab; and here to-night we will have the knot tied. What say you?"

Ira hesitated. He did not care about being married so hurriedly, and could he have considered until the morrow, he probably would have withstood all temptation; but as it was, he was overruled, and finally gave his consent that the ceremony should take place that night. Parson Landon was accordingly sent for, and ere Ira had time to think what he was doing, he was the husband of Lucy Edwards, Mr. and Mrs. Carey and Dolly Dutton alone witnessing the ceremony. When it was completed, Aunt Polly said, "Now we must all keep this a secret, for if it comes to Squire Herndon's ear, he'll sartingly cut 'm off."

The minister and Dolly readily promised silence, but Ira said "he cared not a farthing whether his father knew it or not, and thought seriously of telling him all."

This announcement was received by Aunt Polly with such a burst of indignation, and by Lucy with such a gush of tears, that Ira was glad to promise that he, too, would say nothing on the subject; but the painful thought entered his mind, that possibly Lucy had married him more from a love of wealth than from love to him.

In a few days he returned to the village where they resided, leaving Lucy with her sister for a time. At length he decided to remove to the village of C., in the western part of New York, where Lucy soon joined him. Here Alice was born. When she was about six months old, her father received a very lucrative offer, the acceptance of which required that he should go to India. For himself, he did not hesitate, but his wife and child needed his protection. To take the infant Alice to that hot clime, was to insure her death, and he had no wish that Lucy should remain behind.

In this extremity, Lucy thought of Aunt Polly, and proposed that Alice should be left with her. After much consultation, Aunt Polly was written to, and, as she consented to take the child, Lucy started with Alice to place her under Mrs. Carey's care. When within a mile of the village, she directed the stage driver to let her alight; she did not wish to pass through the village, but, striking into a circuitous path, she soon reached Uncle Amos' house unobserved, save by the man and woman whom we mentioned in our second chapter.

Aunt Polly regularly received remittances from Mr. Herndon for the support of his child, of whom he always spoke with much affection. Lucy, weak and frivolous in her nature, felt constrained to manifest some love for her offspring, but it was evident to Aunt Polly that she was heartily glad to be relieved of the care of little Alice.

When Alice was five years of age, there came a letter bearing an ominous seal of black. With a trembling hand Aunt Polly opened it, and, as she had feared, learned that her young and beautiful sister, at the early age of twenty-two, was sleeping the sleep of death, far off, 'neath the tropical skies of India. That night the motherless Alice looked wonderingly into the face of Aunt Polly, whose tears fell thick and fast, as she clasped the awe-stricken child to her bosom, and said, "You are mine forever, now." Alice remembered this in after years, and wept over the death of a mother whom she never knew.

17

CHAPTER VIII.

THE WANDERER'S RETURN.

FIFTEEN years had flown on rapid wing since Alice became an inmate of the old red house among the mountains. As yet she had no suspicion that she was other than the child of Uncle Amos and Aunt Polly. Under their guardianship, and the watchful supervision of Mrs. Seymour, she had grown into a tall, beautiful girl of fifteen. The childish predilection which she had early shown for Frank, had now ripened into a stronger feeling, and, although she would scarcely acknowledge it, even to herself, there was not, in all the wide world, an individual who possessed so much influence over the shrinking, timid mountain girl, as did Frank, who was now verging on to eighteen.

Some changes have taken place since we last looked upon the boy and girl, but we will again introduce them to our readers, at the respective ages of eighteen and fifteen. It was a mild September afternoon. The long line of mountain tops was enveloped by a blue, hazy mist, while the dense green of the towering forest trees was interspersed here and there by leaflets of a brighter hue, betokening the gradual but sure approach of nature's sad decay.

In the little vine-wreathed portico of Uncle Amos' house, are seated our old friends, Frank and Alice. He has changed much since we last saw him, and were it not for the same roguish twinkle of his hazel eyes, we should hardly recognize the mischievous school-boy, Frank, in the tall, handsome youth before us. During the last year he has been in college, but his vacations have all been spent at home, and as his mother half reprovingly said, "three-fourths of his time was devoted to Alice."

The afternoon of which we are speaking had been spent by them alone, for Aunt Polly was visiting in the village. Frank was just wishing she would delay her coming until nine o'clock, when she was seen hurrying toward the house at an astonishingly rapid rate for her, for she was rather asthmatic.

As soon as she had reached home, and found breath to speak, she said, "Alice, did you know your—did you know Squire Herndon's son Ira had come home from the Indies?"

"Yes, I heard so to-day," said Alice quietly, "and I'm glad, too, for 'twill cheer up his father, who is sick, and seems very lonely and unhappy."

"He ought to be lonely," said Frank. "In my opinion he is a hard old customer; and yet I always speak to the old gentleman when I meet him, for he is very respectful to me. But is n't it queer, mother will never let me say a word against the old squire. I sometimes tease her by saying that she evidently intends, sometime, to become Mrs. Herndon. If she does, you and I, Alice, will be Herndons too."

Alice was about to reply, when Aunt Polly prevented her by saying, "I can tell you, Mr. Seymour, that Alice will be a Herndon before your mother is."

Alice looked wonderingly at Aunt Polly, while Frank said, "Which will she marry, the old squire, or the returned Indian! Let me fix it. Alice marry the squire —my mother marry his son, and then Alice will be my grandmother?"

He was rattling on, when Aunt Polly stopped him, and going up to Alice, she wound her arms about her, and in trembling tones said, "Alice, my child, my darling, you must forgive me for having deceived you so. You are not my child !"

"Not your child !" said Alice, wildly.

"Not your child !" echoed Frank, starting up, "Whose child is she, then ? Speak; tell us quickly !"

"Her father is Ira Herndon, and her mother was my half sister, Lucy," answered Aunt Polly.

Heavily the yielding form of Alice sank into the arms of Frank, who bore the fainting girl into the house, and placed her upon the lounge. Then turning to Aunt Polly, he said, "Is what you have told us true ? and does Mr. Herndon own his daughter ?"

"It's all true as the gospel," answered Mrs. Carey, and Mr. Herndon is coming this night to see her."

Frank pressed one kiss on Alice's white lips, and then hurried away. Bitter thoughts were crowding upon him and choking his utterance. Why was he so affected? Was he sorry that Alice belonged to the proud race of Herndons,—that wealth and family distinction were suddenly placed before her ? Yes, he was sorry, for now was he fearful that his treasure would be snatched from him. He understood the haughty pride of Squire Herndon, and he feared that his son, too, might be like him, and refuse his Alice to one so obscure as Frank fancied himself to be.

On reaching home, he rushed into the little parlor in which his mother was sitting, and throwing himself upon the sofa, exclaimed passionately, "Mother, I do not wish to return to college. It is of no use for me to try to bo anything, now."

"Why, Frank," said his mother, in much alarm, "what has happened to disturb you ?"

"Enough has happened," answered Frank, "Alice is

rich,—an heiress; and, worse than all, she is old Squire Herndon's grand-daughter!"

"Squire Herndon's grand-daughter!" repeated Mrs. Seymour, "How can that be?"

"Why, she is Mr. Ira Herndon's daughter, and he has come to claim her," said Frank.

White as marble grew the cheek and forehead of Mrs. Seymour, and her voice was thick and indistinct, as she said, "Ira Herndon come home,—and Alice's father too?"

Frank darted to her side, exclaiming, "Why, mother, what is the matter? You are as cold and white as Alice was when they told her. Are you, too, Ira Herndon's daughter?"

"No, no," said Mrs. Seymour, "but I know Mr. Herndon well. Do not ask me more now. Be satisfied when I tell you that if he is the same man he used to be, you need have no fears for Alice. Now leave me; I would be alone."

Frank obeyed, wondering much what had come over his mother. Does the reader wonder, too? Have you not suspected that Mrs. Seymour was the Mary Calvert, who, years ago, gave her hand to one, while her heart belonged to Ira Herndon? Her story is soon told. She had respected her husband, and had struggled hard to conquer her love for one whom it were a sin to think of now. In a measure she succeeded, and when, four years after her marriage, she stood by the open grave of her husband, she was a sincere mourner, for now she was alone in the world, her father having been dead some time. He had died insolvent, and when her husband's estate was settled, it was found that there was just enough property left to support herself and son comfortably.

A few years after, she chanced to be traveling through

the western part of the state, and curiosity led her to the village where she knew Squire Herndon resided. She was pleased with the romantic situation of the place, and learning that the neat, white cottage among the mountains was for sale, she purchased it, and soon after removed thither. This, then, was the history of the woman whose frame shook with so much emotion at the mention of Ira Herndon.

CHAPTER IX.

FATHER AND CHILD.

NIGHT had settled around the old red house among the mountains, where Alice was listening eagerly, while Aunt Polly recounted the incidents we have already related. Suddenly a shadow darkened the casement, through which the moon was pouring a flood of silvery light. A heavy footfall echoed on the little piazza, and in a moment Ira Herndon stood within the room, transfixed with surprise at the beautiful vision which Aunt Polly presented to him, saying, " This is Alice, your daughter. I have loved her as my own ; but take her,—she is yours."

Something of Alice's old timidity returned, and she was half inclined to spring through the open door, but when she ventured at length to lift her eyes to the face of the tall, fine looking man before her, a thrill of joy and pride ran through her heart, and twining her soft, white arms around the stranger's neck, she murmured,

"Am I, indeed, your daughter,—and may I call you father?"

"God bless you, Alice, my child, my daughter," was the answer, as Ira folded his newly found treasure to his bosom. At that moment Uncle Amos entered, and saw at a glance how matters stood. Tear after tear rolled down his sun-burnt cheek, as taking the hard hand of his faithful old wife, he said, "Yes, Polly, she will love him and go with him, and we shall be left alone in our old age."

Alice released herself from her father's embrace, and going up to the weeping old man, fondly caressed him, saying, "I will always love you, and call you father, too, for a kind, devoted parent you have been to me for fifteen years, when I knew no other."

"Nor need you ever be separated," said Mr. Herndon, "if you will go with Alice. I have wealth enough for us all, and will gladly share it with you."

To this generous offer Mr. and Mrs. Carey made no reply, and Ira continued: "I have to-day told my father all, and I regret I did not do so years ago."

"What did he say?" asked Aunt Polly, quickly.

"He said not a word, save that he wished he had known it before," answered Mr. Herndon. "He seems quite ill, and I am fearful his days are numbered."

At a late hour that night Mr. Herndon took leave of his daughter, promising to introduce her to her grand-father as soon as possible.

CHAPTER X.

THE OLD MAN'S DEATH-BED.

HIGH up in one of the lofty chambers of the Herndon mansion, an old man lay dying. What mattered it now, that the bedstead on which he lay was of the costliest mahogany, or the sheets of the finest linen! Death was there, waiting eagerly for his expected victim. Memory was busily at work, and far back through a long era of by-gone years, arose a dark catalogue of sin, which made the sick man shudder as he tossed from side to side in his feverish delirium. "Away, away," he would shout, with maniacal frenzy. "I did not turn you all from my door. I only told my servants to do it. And you, starving, weeping women, I only did what thousands have done when I sold your all, and imprisoned your husbands for debt. Away! I say. Don't taunt me with it now." Then his manner would soften, and he would call out, "But stay,—is it money you want? Take it ;—take all I've got, and let that atone for the past."

At this juncture Ira entered the room, on his return from visiting his daughter. He was greatly alarmed at the change in his father, but learning that a physician had been sent for, he sat down, and endeavored to soothe his father's excitement. He succeeded, and when the physician arrived, he found his patient sleeping quietly. From this sleep, however, he soon awoke, fully restored to consciousness.

Turning to his son, he said, "Ira, did n't you tell me she was your child ? "

Mr. Herndon answered in the affirmative, and the old

man continued: "I would see her ere I die. Send for her quickly, for the morning will not find me here."

Ira arose to do his father's bidding, when he added, "And, Ira, I must make my will; send for the proper persons, will you?"

Ira saw that his father's orders were executed, and then returned to his bedside to await the coming of Alice. She was aroused from a sound sleep, and told that her grandfather was dying, and would see her. Hurriedly dressing herself, she was soon on her way to the village. As she entered her grandfather's house, she looked around her in amazement at the splendor which surrounded her.

As she advanced into the sick-room, Squire Herndon fixed his dark, bright eye upon her, and said, "Alice, they tell me you are my grand-daughter; I would I had known it before; but come nearer to me now, and let me bless you."

Alice knelt by the bedside of the white-haired man, whose hand was laid amid her silken curls, as he uttered a blessing upon the fair young girl. When she arose, he said to his son, "Now I must make my will. Call in the lawyer."

The words caught Alice's ear, and involuntarily she sprang back to her grandfather, and kissing his feverish brow, said, "Dear grandpa, I wish I could tell you something,—could ask you something."

"What is it, my child?" asked her grandfather. "Let me know your request, and it shall be granted."

Alice blushed deeply, for she felt that her father's eye was upon her, but she unhesitatingly said, "You have seen Frank, grandfather,—you know him?"

"Yes, yes," said the squire. "I know him and like him, too. I understand you, Alice; I will do right."

Alice again kissed him, and then quitted the apartment, in which, for the next half hour, was heard the scratchings of the lawyer's pen, and the faint tones of the dying one, as he dictated his will.

CHAPTER XI.

THE RECOGNITION.

SOFTLY from the rosy east came the glorious king of day, shedding light and warmth over hill and dale, river and streamlet, tree and shrub. In the same room where he had passed away, Squire Herndon lay in a long, eternal sleep. The servants held their breath, and whispered as they trod softly through the darkened rooms, as if fearful of disturbing the deep slumbers of the dead.

The villagers met together, and their voices were subdued, as they said, one to the other, "Squire Herndon is dead." Yes, Squire Herndon was dead, and little children paused in their play as the solemn peal of the village bell rang out on the clear autumn air, wakening the echoes of the tall blue mountains, and dying away down the bright green valley. The knell was repeated again and again, and then came the strokes, louder, faster, and the children counted until they were tired, for seventy-five years had the old man numbered. At length the sounds ceased, and the children went on with their noisy sports, forgetful that death was among them.

In the Herndon mansion many whispered consultations were held, as to how the body should be arranged for burial. It was finally decided to send for Mrs. Seymour.

"She is tasty and genteel," said one, "and knows how such things should be done."

Mrs. Seymour did not refuse, for she felt it her duty to go; and yet she would much rather have braved the storm of battle than enter that house. She, however, bade the messenger return, saying she would soon follow. When alone with her thoughts, she for an instant wavered. How could she go? How again stand face to face with the only man she ever loved? Yet she did go, trusting that nineteen years had so changed her that she would not be recognized.

Under her directions, everything about the house was done so quietly, that there was nothing to grate on the ear of him who sat alone in the large, silent parlor. He intuitively felt that some kindred spirit was at work there, and calling Alice to him, he asked "who the lady was that seemed to be superintending affairs so well."

"Mrs. Seymour," answered Alice.

"Mrs. Seymour," repeated her father, as if dreamily trying to recall some past event.

"Yes, Mrs. Seymour," said Alice. "She is Frank's mother, and a widow."

In an adjoining room, Mrs. Seymour, with a beating heart, listened to the tones of that voice which she had never hoped to hear again. Earnestly did she wish to see the face of one whose very voice could affect her so powerfully. Her wish was gratified, for at that moment Alice opened the door, and Mrs. Seymour's eyes fell upon the features of him whose remembrance she had so long cherished. She was somewhat disappointed, for the tropical suns of fifteen years had embrowned his once white forehead, and a few gray hairs mingled with the dark locks which lay around his brow.

Alice was surprised at the wild, passionate embrace

which Mrs. Seymour gave her, as leading her to the window, she looked wistfully in her face, and said, "My dear Alice, tenfold more my child than ever."

Alarmed at the increased paleness of her friend, Alice started forward, and said, "You are sick, faint, Mrs. Seymour. Let me call Mr. Herndon,—I mean my father."

But Mrs. Seymour was not faint, and she endeavored to prevent Alice from calling her father, but in vain. Alice called him, and he came. His daughter stood in front of Mrs. Seymour, whose cheeks glowed and whose eyes sparkled with the intensity of her feelings, as she met the searching glance of Ira Herndon.

He recognized her,—knew, as if by instinct, that he again beheld Mary Calvert; but the fever of youth no longer burned in his veins, so he did nothing foolish. He merely grasped her hand, exclaiming, "Mary—Mary Calvert,—Mrs. Seymour! God be praised, we have met again!"

CHAPTER XII.

THE FUNERAL.

Two days passed. The third came, and again over hill and valley floated a funeral knell. Groups of villagers moved with slow and measured tread toward the late residence of Squire Herndon. Forth from many a mountain cottage and many a village dwelling came the inhabitants, old and young, rich and poor, to attend the funeral.

On a marble-topped table stood the rich, mahogany coffin, in which lay the remains of one who for many years had excited the admiration, envy, jealousy, and hatred of the people, many of whom now trod those spacious halls for the first time in their lives. Near the coffin sat Ira. At him the villagers gazed anxiously, but their eyes soon moved on until they rested upon the fair Alice, who had been so suddenly transformed from the humble mountain girl into the wealthy heiress.

Uncle Amos and Aunt Polly were there, too. Ira had kindly and thoughtfully invited them to take seats with himself and daughter, as mourners for the deceased. Aunt Polly appeared arrayed in a dress of costly black silk, and shawl of the same texture. They were the gift of Ira, and for fear of being disputed, we will not tell how many times the good lady managed to move so that the rustle of her garments might be heard by her neighbors, who remarked, that "Aunt Polly seemed a plaguy sight more stuck up than Alice;" and yet the benevolent matron looked down complacently upon them, thinking how kind and amiable she was, not to feel above them!

At last the funeral services were over. Down one street and up another moved the long line of carriages and people on foot, to the grave-yard, where was an open grave, into which the body was lowered, "earth to earth, ashes to ashes, dust to dust."

As the company were leaving the church-yard, Alice suddenly found herself by the side of Frank. She had seen him but once before since her grandfather's death, and then she had won from him a promise that after the funeral he would return with her to what henceforth would be her home. She now reminded him of his promise, at the same time introducing him to her father, whom she observed closely, to see what impression Frank would make. It was favorable, for no one could look at Frank and dislike him. Rather unwillingly he consented to accompany them home. He could not imagine what Alice wanted of him, but was not long kept in doubt.

The will of Squire Herndon was soon produced and read. The old man had intended to bequeath most of his property to his son, but this Ira would not suffer. He had more than he knew what to do with, already, he said, and greatly preferred that his father should give it all to Alice, or divide it between her and Frank, as he saw proper. Accordingly, after bestowing twenty-five thousand dollars in charitable purposes, the remainder of his property, amounting to a hundred and fifty thousand dollars, was equally divided between Frank and Alice, Ira being appointed their guardian.

Frank at first declined the wealth so unexpectedly placed before him, but Alice and her father finally overruled him, the latter saying, playfully, " You may as well take as a gift from the grandfather what you would probably sometime receive with the grand-daughter." So Frank was finally persuaded; but he bore his fortune meekly, and when next he returned to college, no one would have suspected that he was the heir of seventy-five thousand dollars.

———◆———

CHAPTER XIII.

"ALL'S WELL THAT ENDS WELL."

NOT long after Frank returned to college, Alice, also, was sent to Troy, N. Y., to complete her education. Soon after she left, her father invited Mr. and Mrs. Carey to share with him his house, but they had good sense enough to know that they would be far happier in their own mountain home, so Ira settled upon them an annuity for the remainder of their lives.

When the warm sun of an early spring had melted the ice from the brooks and the snow from off the hillside, there was a wedding at the little white cottage. Parson Landon again officiated, and Ira Herndon was the bridegroom, but the bride this time was our friend, Mrs. Seymour, whose face, always handsome, seemed suddenly renovated with a youthful bloom and loveliness. Aunt Polly, too, was present, and declared that the ceremony gave her more satisfaction than did the one which took place seventeen years before, beneath her own roof. After the wedding, Mrs. Seymour, now Mrs. Herndon, removed to her husband's home in the village. The villagers hailed her presence among them as a new era, in which they could hope occasionally to visit at the " great house," as they were in the habit of calling Squire Herndon's former residence.

We now pass rapidly over a period of little more than three years, during which time Frank was graduated, with honor, of course, and returning home, commenced the study of law. We next open the scene on a bright evening in October, in which the little village at the foot of the mountain was in a state of great excitement. This excitement was not manifest in the streets, but in-doors, band-boxes were turned inside out, drawers upside down, as daughter and mother tried the effect of caps, ribbons, flowers, &c.

The cause of all the commotion was this: It was the bridal night of Alice Herndon, at whose request nearly all the villagers were invited to be present. At eight o'clock she descended to the crowded parlors, and in a few moments the words were spoken which transformed her from Alice Herndon into Alice Seymour.

But little more remains to be said. Alice and Frank resided at home, with their parents, who had gained the respect and love of the villagers by their many unostentatious acts of kindness and real benevolence. And now, lest some curious reader should travel to New England for the purpose of discovering whether this story really be true, we will say that the events here narrated occurred so long ago that there is probably nothing left save the cellar and well to mark the spot where once stood "the old red house among the mountains."

Glen's Creek.

CHAPTER I.

REMINISCENCES.

O'ER Lake Erie's dark, deep waters,—across Ohio's broad, rich lands, and still onward, among the graceful forest trees, gushing springs, and fertile plains of Kentucky, rests in quiet beauty, the shady hillside, bright green valley, and dancing waterbrook, known as Glen's Creek. No stately spire or glittering dome point out the spot to the passing traveler, but under the shadow of the lofty trees, stands a large brick edifice, which has been consecrated to the worship of God. There, each Sabbath, together congregate the old and young, the lofty and the lowly, bond and free, and the incense which from that altar ascends to heaven is not the less pure, because in that secluded spot the tones of the Sabbath bell never yet were heard. Not far from the old brick church are numerous, time stained grave-stones, speaking to the living of the pale dead ones, who side by side lie sleeping, unmindful of the wintry storm or summer's fervid heat.

A little farther down the hill, and near the apple tree, whose apples *never* get ripe, stands a low white building, —the school house of Glen's Creek. There, for several years, "Yankee schoolmasters," one after another, have tried by turns the effect of moral suasion, hickory sticks,

18

and leathern straps on the girls and boys who there assemble, some intent upon mastering the mysteries of the Latin reader, and others thinking wistfully of the miniature mill-dam and fish-pond in the brook at the foot of the hill, or of the play-house under the maple tree, where the earthens are each day washed in the little "tin bucket," which serves the treble purpose of dinner-pail, wash-bowl, and drinking-cup.

But not with Glen's Creek as it now is has our story aught to do, although few have been the changes since, in the times long gone, the Indian warrior sought shelter from the sultry August sun, 'neath the boughs of the shady buckeye or towering honey locust, which so thickly stud the hillside of Glen's Creek. Then, as now, the first spring violet blossomed there, and the earliest crocus grew near the stream whose waters sang as mournfully to the dusky maiden of the forest, as they since have to the fair daughter of the pale-face.

The incidents about to be narrated are believed to have taken place near the commencement of the nineteenth century, when the country of Kentucky, from Lexington to Louisville, was one entire forest, and when, instead of the planter's handsome dwelling, now so common, there was only the rude log hut surrounded, perhaps, by a few acres of half cleared land. Brave, indeed, must have been the heart of the hardy yeoman, who, forsaking the home of his fathers, went forth into the wilds of Kentucky, and there, amid dangers innumerable, laid the foundation of the many handsome towns which now dot the surface of that fair state. Woman, too, timid, shrinking woman, was there, and in moments of the most appalling danger the daring courage she displayed equaled that shown by her husband, father and brother. Often on the still midnight air rang out the fearful war-cry, speaking of torture and death to the inmates of the rude dwelling, whose flames, rising high over the tree tops, warned some other lonely settler that the enemy was upon his track.

But spite of all dangers and difficulties, the tide of emigration poured steadily in upon Kentucky, until where once the Indian hunter and wild beast held undisputed sway, there may now be seen fertile gardens and cultivated fields, handsome towns and flourishing cities.

CHAPTER II.

DEACON WILDER.

BRIGHTLY looked forth the stars on one February night, while the pale moon, yet in its first quarter, hung in the western sky, illuminating as far as was possible the little settlement of P——, Virginia. In a large square building, the house of Deacon Wilder, there was a prayer meeting, consisting mostly of members from "the first families in Virginia."

In this meeting Deacon Wilder took a prominent part, although there was an unusually mournful cadence in the tones of his voice; and twice during the reading of the psalm was he obliged to stop for the purpose of wiping from his eyes two large tear-drops, which seemed sadly out of place on the broad, good-humored face of the deacon. Other eyes there were, too, on whose long lashes the heavy moisture glistened, and whose faces told of some sad event, which either had happened or was about to happen. The cause of all this sorrow was this: Ere the night for the weekly prayer meeting again came, Dea con Wilder and his family, who were universally liked, would be far on the road toward a home in the dense forests of Kentucky. In that old-fashioned kitchen were many who had come long, weary miles for the sake of again shaking the deacon's hand, and again telling his gentle wife how surely their hearts would go with her to her home in the far west.

The meeting proceeded decently and in order, as meetings should, until near its close, when Deacon Wilder, for the last time, lifted up his voice in prayer with the loved friends and neighbors he was leaving. At this point, the grief of the little company burst forth unrestrainedly. The white portion of the audience gave vent to their feelings in tears and half smothered sobs, while the blacks, of whom there was a goodly number present, manifested their sorrow by groans and loud lamentations.

Among these was an old negro named Cato, who, together with his wife Dillah, had formerly belonged to Deacon Wilder's father, but on his death they had passed into the possession of the oldest son, Capt. Wilder, who lived within a stone's throw of his brother. Old Cato was decidedly a Methodist in practice, and when in the course of his prayer Deacon Wilder mentioned that in all human probability he should never on earth meet them again, old Cato, who was looked upon as a pillar by his colored brethren, forgetting in the intensity of his feelings the exact form of words which he wanted, fervently ejaculated, "Thank the Lord!" after which Dillah, his wife, uttered a hearty "Amen!"

This mistake in the choice of words was a slight setback to the deacon, who was feeling, perhaps, a trifle gratified at seeing himself so generally regretted. But Cato and Dillah were a well-meaning couple, and their mistake passed unnoticed, save by the young people, who

smiled a little mischievously. The meeting continued un·
til a late hour, and the hands of the long Dutch clock
pointed the hour of midnight, ere the windows of Deacon
Wilder's dwelling were darkened, and its inmates were
dreaming, may be, of a home where good-bys and partings
were unknown.

Next morning, long before the sun had dallied with the
east until over its gray check the blushes of daylight were
stealing, the deacon's family were astir. Fires were lighted
in the fire-place, candles were lighted in the candlesticks,
and breakfast was swallowed in a space of time altogether
too short for the credulity of modern dyspeptics. Then
commenced the exciting process of " pulling down " and
" packing up." Bedsteads were knocked endwise, bed-
clothes were thrown all ways, crockery was smashed, and
things generally were put where there was no possible
danger of their being found again for one twelve-month.
Deacon Wilder scolded, his wife Sally scolded, old Cato
and Dillah, who had come over to superintend matters,
scolded, the other negroes ran against each other and
every way, literally doing nothing except " 'clarin' they's
fit to drap, they's so tired," while George, the deacon's
oldest son, looked on, quietly whistling " Yankee Doodle."

In the midst of all this hubbub, little Charlie, a bright,
beautiful, but delicate boy of nine summers, crept away
to the foot of the garden, and there, on a large stone under a tall sugar maple, his face buried in his hands, he
wept bitterly. Poor Charlie! he was taking his first lesson in home-sickness, even before his childhood's home
had disappeared from view. He had always been opposed
to emigrating to Kentucky, which, in his mind, was all
" dark, dark woods," where each member of the family
would be tomahawked by the Indians every day, at least,
if not oftener.

But Charlie's tears were unavailing,— the old homestead was sold, the preparations were nearly completed, and in a few hours he would bid good-by to the places he loved so well. "I shall never sit under this tree again," said the weeping boy, "never again play in the dear old brook; and when I die there, I shall be afraid to lie alone in the dark woods, and there will .be none but our folks to cry for me, either."

A soft footstep sounded near, two little arms were wound round Charlie's neck, and a childish voice whispered, "Oh, Charlie, Charlie, *I* will cry when I hear you are dead, and if you will send for me before you die, I will surely come."

It was Ella, his cousin. She was a year his junior, and since his earliest remembrance she had been the object of his deepest affection. Together they had played in the forest shade, together in the garden had they made their flower beds, and together had they mourned over torn dresses, lost mittens, bumped heads, nettle stings, and so forth. It is not altogether improbable that Charlie's grief arose partly from the fact that Ella must be left behind. He had always been delicate, and had frequently talked to Ella of dying, so that she readily believed him when he told her he should die in Kentucky; she believed, too, that she should see him again ere he died. Did she believe aright? The story will tell you, but I shall not.

CHAPTER III.

CATO AND DILLAH.

EVERYTHING was in readiness except the little wagon which was to convey the best looking-glass, the stuffed rocking chair, Mrs. Wilder, and Charlie. On an old stump near the gate sat Aunt Dillah, industriously wiping the tears from her dusky cheeks, and ever and anon exclaiming, "'Pears like I could bar it better, if I was gwine with them."

This remark was overheard by her master, Capt. Wilder. He had frequently heard Cato express the same wish, and thought it quite natural, too, inasmuch as Jake, their only child, was to accompany the deacon. For a moment the captain stood irresolute. We will not say what thoughts passed through his mind, but after a time he turned away and went in quest of his brother. There was a short consultation, and then Capt. Wilder, returning to Dillah, laid his hand on her shoulder, and said, " Aunt Dillah, would it please you and Cato to go to Kentucky, and be killed by the Indians along with Jake ? "

" Lord bless you, marster, that it would," said Dillah, rolling up her eyes till only the whites were visible.

" Very well, you can go," was Capt. Wilder's reply.

By this time old Cato and Jake had gathered near, and the " Lord bless you's" which they poured in upon the captain sent him into the house, out of sight and hearing. But Dillah had no time to lose. Her goods and chattels must be picked up, and old Cato's Sunday shirt must be wrung out of the rinsing water, Dillah declaring, " she could kind o'shake it out and dry it on the road ! " While putting up her things, the old creature frequently lamented the unfortunate fact, that the new gown given her last Christmas by " old Miss," was not made, " for," said she, "I shall want to look toppin' and smart-like amongst the folks in Kentuck."

"Ain't no folks thar," said Jake ; but as often as he repeated this assertion, Aunt Dillah answered, "Now and then one, I reckon, 'less why should marster tote the whole on us out thar."

"For the Injuns to eat, I s'pose," answered Jake, and then he went through with a short rehearsal of what his mother would say, and how she would yell, when one of the natives got her in his grip. Little Ella wept passionately when she learned that Dillah, too, was going, but when Charlie, stealing up to her, said, " she will take care of me," her tears were dried, and her last words to Dillah were, " Be kind to Charlie till he dies."

Sweet Ella, it would seem that a foreshadowing of the future had fallen around her, for when at last Charlie's farewell kiss was warm upon her cheek, her voice was cheerful, as she said, " You will send for me and I shall surely come." Could she have known how long and wearisome were the miles, how dark and lonely was the wood, and how full of danger was the road which lay between herself and Charlie's future home, she might not have been so sure that they would meet again.

One after another the wagons belonging to Deacon Wilder passed down the narrow road, and were lost to view in the deep forest which stretched away to the west as far as the eye could reach. Here for a short time we will leave them, while we introduce to our readers another family, whose fortunes are closely interwoven with our first party.

CHAPTER IV.

THE GORTONS.

FIVE years prior to the emigration of Deacon Wilder, Mr. Gorton, a former neighbor, had, with his family, removed to Kentucky, and found a home near Lexington. Around his fireside in Virginia once had gathered three young children, Robert, Madeline and Marian. Robert, the eldest, was not Mr. Gorton's son, but the child of a sister, Mrs. Hunting, who on her death-bed had bequeathed her only boy to the care of her brother. Madeline, when three years of age, was one day missed from her father's house. Long and protracted search was made, which resulted, at length, in the discovery of a part of the child's dress near a spot where lay a pool of blood, and the mutilated remains of what was probably once the merry, laughing Madeline. As only a few of the bones and a small part of the flesh was left, it was readily supposed that the wolves, of which there were many at that time in the woods, had done the bloody deed. Amid many tears the remains were gathered up, placed in a little coffin, and buried beneath the aged oak, under which they were found. Years passed on, and the lost Madeline ceased to be spoken of save by her parents, who could never forget.

Marian, the youngest and now the only remaining daughter of Mr. Gorton, was, at the time of her father's emigration, fourteen years of age. She was a fair, handsome girl, and already toward her George Wilder, who was four years her senior, had turned his eyes, as toward the star which was to illuminate his future horizon. But she went from him, and thenceforth his heart yearned for the woods and hills of Kentucky, and it was partly through his influence that his father had finally determined to re-move thither. Thus, while Charlie, creeping to the far end of the wagon, wept as he thought of home and Ella, George was anticipating a joyous meeting with the beautiful Marian, and forming plans for the future, just as thousands have done since and will do again.

CHAPTER V.

THE NEW HOME.

It is not our intention to follow our travelers through the various stages of their long, tiresome journey, but we will with them hasten on to the close of a mild spring afternoon, when the whole company, wearied and spiritless, drew up in front of a large, newly built log house, in the rear of which were three smaller ones. These last were for the accommodation of the negroes, who were soon scattering in every direction, in order to ascertain, as soon as possible, all the conveniences and inconveniences of their new home. It took Aunt Dillah but a short time to make up her mind that "Kentuck was an ugly-looking, out-of-the-way place, the whole on't; that she wished to gracious she's back in old Virginny;" and lastly, that "she never should have come, no how, if marster hadn't of 'sisted and 'sisted, till 'twasn't in natur to 'fuse."

This assertion Aunt Dillah repeated so frequently, that she at length came to believe it herself. The old creature had no idea that she was not the main prop of her master's household, and we ourselves are inclined to think that Mrs. Wilder, unaided by Dillah's strong arm, ready tact, and encouraging words, could not well have borne the hardships and privations attending that home in the wilderness. Weary and heart-sick, she stepped from the little wagon, while an expression of sadness passed over her face as her eye wandered over the surrounding country, where tract after tract of thick woodland stretched on and still onward, to the verge of the most distant horizon.

Dillah, better than any one else, understood how to cheer her mistress, and within an hour after their arrival, a crackling fire was blazing in the fire-place, while the old round iron tea-kettle, or rather its contents, were hissing and moaning, and telling, as plainly as tea-kettle could tell, of coming good cheer. At length the venison steaks and Dillah's short-cake, smoking hot, were placed upon the old square table, and the group which shared that first supper at Glen's Creek, were, with the exception of Charlie, comparatively contented. He, poor child, missed the scenes of his early home, and more than all, he missed his playmate, Ella.

Long after the hour of midnight went by, he stood by his little low window near the head of his bed, gazing up at the hosts of shining stars, and wondering if they were looking upon his dear old home, even as they looked down upon him, homesick and lonely, afar in the wilderness of Kentucky.

CHAPTER VI.

ORIANNA.

WEEKS passed on, and within and without Deacon Wilder's door were signs of life and civilization. Trees were cut down, gardens were made, corn and vegetables were planted, and still no trace of an Indian had been seen, although Jake had frequently expressed a wish to get a shot at the "varmin," as he called them. Still, he felt that it would be unwise to be caught out alone at any very great distance from his master's dwelling.

This feeling was shared by all of Deacon Wilder's household, except Charlie, who frequently went forth alone into the forest shade, and rambled over the hills where grew the rich wild strawberry and the fair summer flowers, and where, too, roamed the red man; for the Indian was there, jealously watching each movement of his white brother, and waiting for some provocation to strike a deadly blow. But Charlie knew it not, and fearlessly each day he plunged deeper and deeper into the depths of the woods, taking some stately tree or blighted stump as a way-mark by which to trace his homeward road, when the shadows began to grow long and dark.

Although he knew it not, Charlie had a protector, who each day, in the shady woods and wild gullies of Glen's Creek, awaited his coming. Stealthily would she follow his footsteps, and when on the velvety turf he laid him down to rest, she would watch near him, lest harm should befall the young sleeper. It was Orianna, the only and darling child of Owanno, the chieftain whose wigwam was three miles west of Glen's Creek, near a spot called Grassy Spring.

Orianna had first been attracted toward Charlie by seeing him weep, one day, and from a few words which he involuntarily let fall, she learned that his heart was not with the scenes wherein he dwelt, but was far away toward the "rising sun." Orianna's heart was full of kindly sympathy, and from the time when she first saw Charlie weeping in the forest, she made a vow to the Great Spirit that she would love and protect the child of the "pale-face." The vow thus made by the simple Indian maiden was never broken, but through weal and woe it was faithfully kept.

It was a long time ere Orianna ventured to introduce herself to her new friend; but when she did so, she was delighted to find that he neither expressed fear of her, nor surprise at her personal appearance. From that time they were inseparable, although Orianna exacted from Charlie a promise not to mention her at home, and also resisted his entreaties that she would accompany him thither. In reply to all his arguments, she would say, mournfully, " No, Charlie, no, the pale-face is the enemy of my people, although Orianna never can think they are enemies to her; and sometimes I have wished,— it was wicked I know, and the Great Spirit was angry,— but I have wished that I, too, was of the fair-haired and white-browed ones."

In Charlie's home there was much wonder as to what took him so regularly to the woods, but he withstood their questioning and kept his secret safely. In the wigwam, too, where Orianna dwelt, there was some grumbling at her frequent absences, but the old chieftain Owanno and his wife Narretta loved their child too well to prohibit her rambling when and where she pleased. This old couple were far on the journey of life, when Orianna came as a sunbeam of gladness to their lone cabin, and thenceforth they doted upon her as the miser doats upon his shining gold.

She was a tall, graceful creature of nineteen or twenty summers, and her life would have been one of unbounded happiness, had it not been for one circumstance. Near her father's wigwam lived the young chief Wahlaga, who, to a most ferocious nature, added a face horridly disfigured by the many fights in which he had been foremost. A part of his nose was gone, and one eye entirely so ; yet to this man had Owanno determined to wed his beautiful daughter, who looked upon Wahlaga with perfect disgust, and resolved, that sooner than marry him, she would perish in the deep waters of the Kentucky, which lay not many miles away.

CHAPTER VII.

MARIAN.

The deacon and his family had now been residents at Glen's Creek nearly three months. Already was the leafy month of June verging into sultry July, when George Wilder at length found time to carry out a plan long before formed. It was to visit Marian, and if he found her all which as a child she had promised to be, he would win her for himself.

Soon after the early sun had touched the hill tops as with a blaze of fire, George mounted his favorite steed, and taking Jake with him for a companion, turned into the woods and took the lonely road to Lexington. Leav ing them for a moment, we will press on and see Marian's home.

It was a large, double log building, over which the flowering honeysuckle and dark green hop-vine had been trained until they formed an effectual screen. The yard in front was large, and much taste had been displayed in the arrangement of the flowers and shrubs which were scattered through it. Several large forest trees had been left standing, and at one end of the yard, under a clump of honey-locusts, a limpid stream of water, now nearly dry, went dancing over the large flat limestones which lay at the bottom. In the rear of the house was the garden, which was very large, and contained several bordered walks, grassy plats, and handsome flower-beds, besides vegetables of all descriptions. At the end of the garden, and under the shadows of the woods, was a little summer-house, over which a wild grape-vine had been taught to twine its tendrils.

In this summer-house, on the morning of which we are speaking, was a beautiful young girl, Marian Gorton. We have not described her, neither do we intend to, for she was not as beautiful as heroines of stories usually are; but, reader, we will venture that she was as handsome as any person you have ever seen, for people were handsomer in those days than they are now,— at least our grand-parents tell us so. Neither have we told her age, although we are sure that we have somewhere said enough on that point to have you know, by a little calculation, that Marian was now eighteen.

This morning, as she sits in the summer-house, her brow is resting on her hand, and a shadow is resting on her brow. Had Marian cause for sorrow? None, except that her cousin Robert, who had recently returned from England, had that morning offered her his hand and been partially refused. Yet why should Marian refuse him, whom many a proud lady in the courtly halls of England would not refuse? Did she remember one who, years ago, in the green old woods of Virginia, awakened within her childish heart a feeling, which, though it might have slumbered since, was still there in all its freshness? Yes, she did remember him, although she struggled hard to conquer each feeling that was interwoven with a thought of him. Nearly three months he had been within twenty miles of her, and yet no word or message had been received, and Marian's heart swelled with resentment toward the young man, whose fleet steed even then could scarce keep pace with his master's eager wishes to press onward.

From her earliest childhood she had looked upon Robert as a brother, and now that he was offered as a husband, her heart rebelled, although pride occasionally whispered, "Do it,—marry him,—then see what George Wilder will say;" but Marian had too much good sense long to listen to the promptings of pride, and the shadow on her face is occasioned by a fear that she had remembered so long and so faithfully only to find herself uncared for and forgotten.

Meantime, the sound of horses' feet near her father's house had brought to the fence half a dozen negroes and half as many dogs, all ready in their own way to welcome the new comers. After giving his horse in charge of the negroes, George proceeded to the house, where he was cordially received by Mrs. Gorton, who could scarcely recognize the school-boy George, in the tall, fine looking young man before her. Almost his first inquiry was for Marian. Mrs. Gorton did not know where she was, but old Sukey, who had known George in Virginia, now hobbled in, and after a few tears, and a great many

"Lor' bless you's," and inquiries about "old Virginny," she managed to tell him that Marian was in the garden, and that she would call her; but George prevented her, saying he would go himself.

Most of my readers have doubtless either witnessed or experienced meetings similar to that which took place between George and Marian, so I shall not describe it, but shall leave it for the imagination, which will probably do it better justice than can my pen, which comes very near the *point* of being used up. We will only say, that when at twelve o'clock Mr. Gorton and Robert returned from a ride, George and Marian were still in the summer-house, unmindful of the sun which looked in upon them as if to tell them of his onward course. But then, the question that morning asked and answered, was of great importance, so 'twas no wonder that they were alike deaf and blind to the little darkies, who on tip-toe crept behind the summer-house, eager to know "what the strange gentleman could be saying to Miss Marian, which made her look so speckled and roasted like." These same hopefuls, when at dinner time they were sent for their young mistress, commenced a general hunt, which finally terminated in the popping of their woolly heads into the summer-house door, exclaiming between breaths, "Oh, Miss Marian, here you is. We've looked for you every whar! Come to your dinner." On their way to the house they encountered old Sukey, who called out, "Ho, Mas' George, —'specs mebby you found Miss Marry-'em," at the same time shaking her sides at her own wit.

Mr. Gorton received his young friend with great cordiality, but there was a cool haughtiness in the reception which Robert at first gave his old playmate. He suspected the nature of George's visit, nor did Marian's bright, joyous face tend in the least to allay his suspicions. But not long could he cherish feelings of resentment toward one whom he liked so well as he had George Wilder. In the course of an hour his reserve wore off, and unless George should chance to see this story,—which is doubtful,—he will probably never know how bitter were the feelings which his presence for a few moments stirred in the heart of Robert Hunting. Before George returned home, he asked Marian of her father, and also won from her a promise that, ere the frosts of winter came, her home should be with him, and by his own fireside

---

CHAPTER VIII.

ROBERT AND ORIANNA.

THERE was much talk and excitement in Deacon Wilder's family, when it was known that in a little more than three months' time a young maiden would come among them, who would be at once daughter, sister and mistress. From Jake, the negroes had received most of their information, and verily George himself would scarcely have recognized Marian in the description given of her by his servant. So many beauties and excellences were attributed to her, that the negroes were all on the *qui vive* to see this paragon.

Charlie, too, was delighted, and when next day he as usual met Orianna in the woods, he led her to a mossy bank, and then communicated to her the glad tidings. When he repeated to her the name of his future sister-in-law, he was greatly surprised at seeing Orianna start quickly to her feet, while a wild light flashed from her large black eye. Soon reseating himself, she said, calmly, "What is it, Charlie?" What is the name of the white lady?"

"Marian,—Marian Gorton," repeated Charlie. "Do you not think it a pretty name?"

Orianna did not answer, but sat with her small, delicate hands pressed tightly over her forehead. For a moment Charlie looked at her in wonder; then taking both her hands in his, he said, gently, "Don't feel so, Orianna. I shall love you just as well, even if I do have a sister Marian."

Orianna's only answer was, "Say her name again, Charlie."

He did so, and then Orianna repeated, "Marian,—Marian,—what is it? Oh, what is it? Marian;—it sounds to Orianna like music heard years and years ago."

"Perhaps it was a dream," suggested Charlie.

"It must have been," answered Orianna, "but a pleasant dream, fair as the young moon or the summer flowers. But tell me more, Charlie."

"I will do so," said he, "but I am afraid you will forget your lesson."

He had been in the habit of taking to the woods some one of his reading books, and in this way he had unconsciously awakened in Orianna a desire for learning. For some time past a part of each day had been spent in teaching her the alphabet. It was an interesting sight, that dark, handsome girl, and the fair, pale boy,—he in the capacity of a patient teacher, and she the ambitious scholar.

On the afternoon of the day of which we are speaking, they were, as usual, employed in their daily occupation. The excitement of the occasion heightened the rich glow on Orianna's cheek, while the wreath of white wild flow ers, which Charlie had woven and placed among her shining black hair, gave her the appearance of some dark queen of the forest. The lesson was nearly completed, and Charlie was overjoyed to find that his pupil knew every letter, both great and small, when they were startled by the sound of a footstep, and in a moment Robert Hunting, who had accompanied George Wilder home from Lexington, stood before them.

Swiftly as a deer Orianna bounded away, while Charlie, in evident confusion, attempted to secrete his book, and Robert burst into a loud laugh, saying, "Well done, Charlie! So you've turned schoolmaster, and chosen a novel pupil, upon my word. But who is she? If she be a native, she is handsomer far than half the white girls!"

"She is Orianna," said Charlie, "the daughter of a chieftain, and I love her, too.

"Nobility, hey?" said Robert laughing. "Better yet. But what made her run so? Did she think I was the evil one? Can't you call her back?"

"She won't come," answered Charlie, "she don't like you, and I can't make her."

"So you have been saying a word in my favor, have you?" said Robert, a little sarcastically. "Greatly obliged to you, Master Charlie. But I prefer doing my own pleading."

"I didn't mean *you*," said Charlie, a little indignantly. "She don't know that there is such a thing as you. I meant all the white folks."

"Oh, you did," answered Robert, looking wistfully in the direction where Orianna had disappeared.

At that moment there was the report of a rifle, and a ball passed between him and Charlie and lodged in a tree a few feet distant.

"Soho," exclaimed Robert, "was n't content with sending an arrow at my heart, but must hurl a bullet at my head."

Charlie was confounded. He never for a moment doubted that Orianna had sent the ball, and a fearful distrust of her filled his heart. A week went by, and still he neglected to take his accustomed walk, although he noticed that Robert went daily in his stead.

At length one morning Robert came to him and said, "Orianna bade me tell you that each day, 'neath the buckeye tree, she's watched for you in vain."

Charlie's eyes opened wide with astonishment, as he exclaimed, "Orianna? Where have you seen Orianna?"

"Where should I see her, pray, but in the woods?" answered Robert. "We have spent the last five days together, there, and I have taken your place as teacher."

Here we may as well explain what the reader is doubtless anxious to know. The bullet which passed between Robert and Charlie was not sent by the hand of Orianna, but by the vicious Wahlaga, whose curiosity had been roused as to what led Orianna so frequently to the woods. On that day he had followed and discovered her, just at the moment when Robert appeared before her. The jealous savage, thinking that he looked upon his rival, made ready his gun, when Orianna, suddenly coming upon him, threw aside his arm, thus changing the course of the ball, while at the same time, she led the excited Indian away, and at length succeeded in convincing him that never before had she seen Robert, nor did she even know who he was.

The next morning Orianna was overjoyed to learn that Wahlaga was about leaving home, to be absent an indefinite length of time. Her happiness, however, was soon clouded by some expressions which he let fall, and from

which she gathered that her father had promised to give
her in marriage as soon as he should return. "It shall
never be; no, never," said the determined girl, as, immediately after his departure, she took the narrow foot-
path to the woods of Glen's Creek.

Throughout all the morning she waited in vain for Charlie, although she several times saw Robert at a distance,
and felt sure that he was looking for her. She knew that
she had saved his life, and this created in her a desire to
see him again. Accordingly, when that afternoon they
once more came suddenly face to face, she did not run,
but eagerly asked after her young companion. Robert
knew well how to play his part, and in a few moments
Orianna's shyness had vanished, and she was answering,
with ready obedience, all the questions asked her by the
handsome stranger. Ere they parted, Robert had learned
that to her he owed his life, and as a token of his gratitude he placed upon her slender finger a plain gold ring.
He did not ask her to meet him again, next day, but he
well knew she would, for she, who knew no evil, thought
no evil.

As Robert had said, he took Charlie's place as teacher;
but, ah me! the lessons thus taught and received were
of a far different nature from the alphabet in Charlie's
picture-book. Many a time, ere that week went by, the
simple Indian girl, in the solitude of night, knelt by the
streamlet which ran by her father's door, and prayed the
Great Spirit to forgive her for the love which she bore
the white man, the enemy of her people;—and he?—why
he scarce knew himself what his thoughts and intentions
were. He looked upon Orianna as a simple-minded, innocent child; and while he took peculiar delight in studying her character, he resolved that neither in word nor

deed would he harm the gentle girl who each day came so timidly to his side.

Day after day was his stay at Glen's Creek protracted, and yet he would not acknowledge that he was even interested in her within whose heart a passion had been awakened, never more to slumber. The day on which he spoke to Charlie of Orianna, was the last which he would spend at Glen's Creek, and as he did not wish to be alone when he bade her adieu, he asked Charlie to accompany him. Oh, how bright was the smile with which the maiden greeted them at first, and how full of despair was the expression of her face when told by Robert that he must leave her. Not a word did she speak, but closely to her heart she pressed the little Charlie, as if fearful lest he, too, should go.

"Farewell, Orianna," said Robert. "When the nuts are brown upon the trees, look for me, for I shall come again."

A moment more, and he was gone,—gone with poor Orianna's heart, and left her nothing in return. Covering her face with her hands, she wept so long and bitterly, that Charlie at last wound his arms around her neck, and wept, too, although he knew not for what. This token of sympathy aroused her, and after a moment she said, "Leave me now, Charlie; Orianna would be alone." He arose to obey, when she added, "Don't tell them,— don't tell *him* what you have seen."

He promised secrecy, and Orianna was left alone. The forest was dark with the shadows of coming night ere she arose, and then the heart which she bore back to the wigwam by Grassy Spring was sadder than any she had ever before carried across the threshold of her home. The next day Charlie noticed a certain listlessness about his pupil, which he had never observed before; and though her eye wandered over the printed page, her thoughts were evidently away. At last a happy thought struck him, and drawing closely to her, he whispered, "I think *Robert* will be pleased if you learn to read."

He had touched the right chord,—no other incentive was needed,—and from that day her improvement was as rapid as the most ambitious teacher could wish. Frequently she would ask Charlie concerning Marian, requesting him to repeat her name; then she would fall into a fit of musing, saying, "When heard I that name? and where was it?—oh, where?"

Yes, Orianna, *Where was it?*

CHAPTER IX.

THE BRIDAL.

SWIFTLY and on noiseless wing sped on old father Time, and they who thought the summer would never pass, were surprised when o'er the wooded hills the breath of autumn came, bearing the yellow leaf—the first white hair in nature's sunny locks. The golden harvests were gathered in, and through the forest "the sound of dropping nuts was heard," showing that

> "The melancholy days had come,
> The saddest of the year."

It was the last day of October, and over the fading earth the autumnal sun was shedding its rays as brightly as in the early summer. The long shadows, stretching far to the eastward, betokened the approach of night, and when at last the sun sank to its western home, the full moon poured a flood of soft, pale light over the scene, and looking in at a half opened window, shone upon a beautiful young girl, who, with the love-light in her dark blue eye, and woman's holy trust in her heart, was listening, or seeming to listen, while the words were said which made her the wife of George Wilder.

Scarce was the ceremony completed, when the light from the window was obscured, a shadow fell darkly upon Robert, and a voice, clear and musical, uttered words which curdled the blood of the fair bride, and made more than one heart stand still with fear. They were, "*The Indians, the Indians!*—they are coming in less than an hour!"

The next moment a tall and graceful figure appeared in the doorway, and laying its hand on Robert's shoulder, exclaimed, "It is *your* life they seek, but Orianna will save you!"

Then away glided the maiden, so noiselessly that but for the tidings she brought, the party would almost have doubted that she had been there. For a time the company were mute with surprise, and involuntarily George clasped closely to his side his Marian, as if to shield her from the coming danger. At length, Mr. Gorton asked Robert for an explanation of what the stranger had said.

Robert replied, "Two days since, I was hunting in the woods not far from the house, when a rustling noise behind some bushes attracted my attention. Without stopping to think, I leveled my gun and fired, when behold! up sprang an Indian girl, and bounded away so swiftly that to overtake her and apologize was impossible. This I suppose to be the reason why my life is sought."

His supposition was correct, and for the benefit of the reader we will explain how Orianna became possessed of

the secret. The night before, when returning to her father's wigwam, she was startled by the sound of many
voices within. Curiosity prompted her to listen, and she
thus learned that the Indians who lived east of Lexington
had been insulted by a white man, who had fired at one
of their squaws. From the description of the aggressor,
she knew it to be Robert, and with fast beating heart she
listened to the plan of attacking Mr. Gorton's dwelling
on the night of the wedding.

Ovanno heard them to the end, and then, to Orianna's
great delight, he refused to join them, saying he was now
too old to contend with the pale-face, unless himself or
family were molested. The old chief would not acknowledge how much this decision was owing to the influence
of his gentle daughter. He knew she liked the whites,
and he knew, too, another thing,—but 'tis not time for
that yet.

Orianna had now something to do. A life dearer far
than her own was to be saved, and Marian, too,—whose
very name had a power to thrill each nerve of that noble
Indian girl,—she was in danger.

The next day Charlie waited in vain for his pupil, for
she was away on her mission of love, and the stern
features of many an Indian relaxed as he welcomed to
his cabin the chieftain's daughter. Ere the sun set she
fully understood their plan of attack, and then, unmindful of the twenty-five miles traversed since the dawn of
day, she hied her back to Lexington, to raise its inhabitants, and as we have seen, to apprise the bridal party
of their danger.

Not a moment was to be lost, and while they were consulting as to their best means of safety, the Indian girl
again stood among them, saying, "Let me advise you.
It is not the town they wish to attack,—they will hardly

do that,—it is *this* house,—it is *you*," laying her hand convulsively on Robert's arm. "But there is yet time to escape; flee to the town, and leave me here—"

"To be killed!" said Robert.

"To be killed!" she repeated, scornfully. "In all Kentucky there lives not the red man who dares touch a hair of Orianna's head."

Her proposition seemed feasible enough, and after a little hesitation it was resolved to adopt it. The negroes had already done so, for at the first alarm they had taken to their heels, and were by this time half way to Lexington. Thither the whites, with the exception of Robert, soon followed. He resolutely refused to go, saying, in answer to his friends' entreaties, "No, never will I desert a helpless female. You remove the ladies to a place of safety, and then with others return to my aid."

So they were left alone, the white man and the Indian. Together, side by side, they watched the coming of the foe. At Orianna's direction the doors had been barricaded, while the lights were left burning in order to deceive the Indians into a belief that the inmates still were there. A half hour went by, and then, in tones which sent the blood in icy streams through Robert's veins, Orianna whispered, "They come! Do you see them? Look!"

He did look, and by the light of the moon he discerned the outlines of many dusky forms, moving stealthily through the woods in the direction of the house. The garden fence was passed, and then onward, slowly but surely, they came. So intent was Robert in watching their movements, that he noted not the band of armed men who, in an opposite direction, were advancing to the rescue; neither did he observe in time to prevent it the lightning spring with which Orianna bounded through the window, and went forth to meet the enemy, who, mistaking her for some one else, uttered a yell of savage exultation and pressed on more fiercely. Loud and deafening was the war-cry which echoed through the woods, and louder still was the shout of defiance which rent the air, as the whites came suddenly face to face with the astonished Indians.

It was Orianna's intention, when she leaped from the window, to reach the leader of the savages, and by telling him the truth of the matter as she had heard it from Robert, she hoped to dissuade him from his murderous design. But her interference was not needed, for the savages were surprised and intimidated by the unexpected resistance, and in the fear and confusion of the moment they greatly magnified the number of their assailants. Accordingly, after a few random shots, they precipitately fled, leaving Orianna alone with those whose lives she had saved.

Almost caressingly Robert wound his arm about her slight form, as he said, "Twice have you saved my life. Now, name your reward, and if money—"

There was bitterness in the tone with which Orianna interrupted him, saying, "Money! Orianna never works for money. All she asks is that you let her go, for the path is long which she must tread ere the sun's rising."

"To-night! You will not leave us to-night!" said Robert.

"Urge me not," answered Orianna, "for by the wigwam door at Grassy Spring Narretta waits, and wonders why I linger."

Remonstrance was useless, for even while Robert was speaking, she moved away, and the echo of her footfall was scarcely heard, so rapid and cat-like was the tread with which she disappeared in the darkness of the woods. Robert looked thoughtfully after her for a time, and then, with something very like a half smothered sigh, he turned away. Could that sigh, faint as it was, have fallen on the ear of the lone Indian girl, she would have felt fully re-paid for her toil, but now a weight of sorrow lay upon her young heart, crushing each flower of gladness, even as she, with impatient tread, crushed beneath her feet the yellow leaves of autumn.

CHAPTER X.

ORIANNA'S FAITH.

LONG had the old square table, with its cloth of snowy whiteness and its load of eatables, waited the coming of the bridal party. Many times had Mrs. Wilder stood in the doorway, and strained her eyes to catch a sight of the expected company, and more than many times had old Dillah declared "that the corn cake which riz so nice would be fell as flat as a pewer platter, if they didn't come along."

At length, from the top of a large old maple, in whose boughs several young Africans were safely ensconced, there came the joyful cry of, "There, they's comin'. That's the new miss with the tail of her dress floppin' round the horses' heels. Jimminy! ain't she a tall one!" and the youngsters dropped to the ground, and perched themselves, some on the fence and others on the gate, with eyes and mouth open to whatever might happen.

In the doorway Mrs. Wilder received the bride, and

the ready tears gushed forth as for the first time in her life she folded to her heart a daughter. From his stool in the corner, Charlie came, and throwing his arms around Marian's neck, he said, "I know I shall love you, for you look so much like Orianna!"

Old Dillah, who was pressing forward to offer her congratulations, was so much surprised that she forgot the bow and fine speech which, for more than a week, she had been practicing. Her command of language, however, did not wholly desert her, for she said, somewhat warmly, " Clar for 't, Master Charles, young miss won't feel much sot up to be told she favors a black Injun."

George, too, was evidently piqued at having his bride likened to an Indian, but Robert came to Charlie's relief, saying, " that he had often noticed how wholly unlike an Indian were the features of Orianna, and that were her skin a few shades lighter, she would be far more beautiful than many pale-cheeked belles, with their golden curls and snowy brows."

The conversation now turned upon Orianna, and the strong affection which existed between her and Charlie, whom Robert teased unmercifully about his " dark-eyed ladye love."

Charlie bore it manfully, and ere the evening was spent, he had promised to take Marian with him when next he visited his Indian friend. This promise he fulfilled, and the meeting between the two girls was perfectly simple and natural. Both were prepared to like each other, and both looked curiously, one at the other, although Marian at last became uneasy at the deep, earnest gaze which those full, black eyes bent upon her, while their owner occasionally whispered, " Marian, Marian."

Visions of sorcery and witchcraft passed before her mind, and still, turn which way she would, she felt that the dark girl's eyes were fixed upon her with a strangely fascinating look.   But fear not, young Marian, for though she strokes your silken curls, and caressingly touches your soft cheek, the forest maiden will do you no harm.   At length Marian's timidity gave way, and when she arose to go, she did not refuse her hand to Orianna, who for a time kept it between her own, as if admiring its whiteness; then suddenly throwing it from her, she said, " Oh, why can't Orianna be white and handsome, too ! "

"You are handsome," answered Marian.   "Only two evenings since I heard Robert Hunting say that you were far more beautiful than half the white girls."

"Who takes my name in vain ? " said a musical voice, as Robert himself appeared before them, and laid his hand gently upon Orianna's glossy hair.

If Marian had any doubts of her beauty before, they were now dispelled by the rich color which mounted to her olive cheek, and the joy which danced in her large eye.   Yet 'twas not Robert's presence alone which so delighted Orianna.   A ray of hope had entered her heart. " He thought her beautiful, and perhaps—perhaps—"

Ah, Orianna, think not that Robert Hunting will ever wed an Indian, for Robert is no Rolfe, and you no Pocahontas !

As if divining and giving words to her thoughts, Robert, while seating himself between the two girls, and placing an arm around each, said, playfully, " Hang it all, Orianna, why were you not white ! "

"Don't, Bob," whispered Marian, who with woman's quick perception half suspected the nature of Orianna's feelings for one whose life she twice had saved.

"Don't what, my little Puritan ? " asked Robert.

"Don't raise hopes which you *know* can never be realized," answered Marian.

Robert was silent for a while, and then said, "I reckon my orthodox cousin is right;" then turning to Orianna, he asked how her reading progressed.

Charlie answered for her, saying that she could read in words of one syllable as well as any one, and that she knew a great deal besides! Robert was about testing her powers of scholarship, when they were joined by George Wilder, before whom Orianna absolutely refused to open her mouth, and in a few moments she arose and left them, saying, "I shall come again, to-morrow."

That night, by the wigwam fire Narretta was listening to her daughter's account of the "white dove," as she called Marian. Suddenly a light seemed to dawn on Orianna's mind, and clasping her hands together, she said, "Mother, do you remember when I was sick, many, many moons ago?"

"Yes, child," answered Narretta, and Orianna continued: "I slept a long time, I know, but when I woke, I remember that you, or some one else, said, "She is getting white; it will never do." Then I looked at my hands, and they were almost as fair as Marian's, but you washed me with something, and I was dark again. Tell me, mother, was I turning white?"

"*Turning white!* No, child," said Narretta; " now shut up and get to bed."

Orianna obeyed, but she could not sleep, and about midnight she stole out at the door, and going to the spring, for more than half an hour she bathed her face and hands, hoping to wash off the offensive color. But all her efforts were vain, and then on the withered leaves she knelt, and prayed to the white man's God,—the God who, Charlie had said, could do everything. "Make Orianna white, make her white," were the only words she uttered, but around her heart there gathered confidence that her prayer would be answered, and impatiently she waited for the morrow's light.

"Mother, am I white?" aroused Narretta from her slumbers, just as the first sunlight fell across the floor.

"White! No; blacker than ever," was the gruff answer, and Orianna's faith in "Charlie's God" was shaken.

CHAPTER XI.

PREPARATIONS FOR A JOURNEY.

O'er the forest dark and lonely,
   Death's broad wing is brooding now
While each day the shadow deepens
   Over Charlie's fevered brow.

CHARLIE'S health, which had always been delicate, seemed much impaired by the Kentucky air, but with the return of winter, there came the hacking cough and darting pain, and Orianna already foresaw the time when, with a flood of bitter tears, she would lay her darling in the grave. The meetings in the woods were given up, and if Orianna saw her pet at all, it was in his home, where she at length became a regular visitor, and where Marian daily taught her as Charlie had before done. Many were the lessons learned in the sick-room where Charlie lay, fading day by day, and many were the talks which he had with his Indian friend concerning the God whose power she questioned. But from the time when she was able herself to read in Charlie's bible, the light of truth slowly broke over her darkened mind.

From the commencement of Charlie's illness, he looked

upon death as sure, and his young heart went back to his playmate, Ella, with earnest longings, which vented themselves in pleadings that some one would go for her,—would bring her to him and let him look upon her once more ere he died. 'Twas in vain that his mother tried to convince him of the impossibility of such a thing. He would only answer, "I shall not know her in heaven, unless I see her again, for I have almost forgotten how she looked."

*   *   *   *   *   *

Winter was gone, and Charlie, no longer able to sit up, lay each day in his bed, talking of heaven and Ella, whom he now scarcely hoped to see again. One afternoon Orianna lingered longer than usual, in low, earnest conversation with the sufferer. Charlie listened eagerly to what she was saying, while his eye sparkled and his fading cheek glowed as with the infusion of new life. As she was about leaving she whispered, softly, "Never fear though the time be long, I will surely bring her."

Yes, Orianna had resolved to go alone through the wilderness to Virginia, and bring to the dying boy the little Ella. Filled with this idea, she hastened home; but list,—whose voice is it, that on the threshold of her father's door makes her quake with fear? Ah, Orianna kens full well that 'tis Wahlaga! He has returned to claim his bride, and instantly visions of the pale, dying Charlie, the far off Ella, and of one, too, whose name she scarcely dared breathe, rose before her, as in mute agony she leaned against the door.

But her thoughts soon resolved themselves into one fixed determination—"I will never marry him;" and then with a firm step she entered the cabin. Wahlaga

must have guessed her feelings, for he greeted her mood-
ily, and immediately left her with her parents. To her
father, she instantly confided her plan of going for Ella,
and as she had expected, he sternly forbade it, saying she
should stay and marry Wahlaga.

Owanno was surprised at the decided manner with
which Orianna replied, " Never, father, never. I will
die in the deep river first."

At this juncture Wahlaga entered, and the discussion
grew warmer and more earnest. Words more angry the
chieftain spoke to his daughter than ever before he had
done. Suddenly his manner softened, and concerning her
going for Ella, he said, " If you marry Wahlaga, you can
go; otherwise you cannot, unless you run away."

"And if she does that," fiercely continued Wahlaga,
" I swear by the Great Spirit, I'll never rest until I've
shed the blood of every pale-face in that nest—sick whi-
ning boy and all."

Like one benumbed by some great and sudden calam-
ity, Orianna stood speechless, until her father asked,
" Will you go?"

Then, rousing herself, she said, " I cannot answer now;
wait till to-morrow." Then forth from the cabin she went,
and onward through the fast deepening twilight she fled,
until through an opening in the trees she espied the light
which gleamed from Charlie's sick-room. Softly approaching the window, she looked in and saw a sight
which stopped for a moment the tumultuous beatings of
her heart, and wrung from her a shriek of anguish. Supported by pillows lay Charlie, panting for breath, while
slowly from his white lips issued drops of blood, which
Marian gently wiped away, while the rest of the family were
doing what they could to restore him. When Orianna's
loud cry of agony echoed through the room, Charlie

slowly unclosed his eyes, and in an instant the Indian girl was beside him, exclaiming, wildly, "Charlie, Charlie, do not die. I'll marry him, I'll go for her, I'll do anything."

The astonished family at length succeeded in pacifying her, by telling her that Charlie had, in a fit of coughing, ruptured a blood vessel, but that there was no immediate danger if she would keep quiet. Quickly the great agony of her heart was hushed, and silently she stood by the bedside; nor did they who looked on her calm face once dream of the tornado within, or how like daggers were the words of Charlie, who, in his disturbed sleep, occasionally murmured, "Ella,—oh, Ella,—has Orianna gone?—she said she would."

Suddenly turning to Marian, Orianna, with a pressure of the hand almost crushing, said, "Tell me what to do?" and from the little cot, Charlie, all unconsciously answered, "Go for Ella."

"I will," said Orianna, and ere Marian had recovered from her astonishment, she was gone. When alone in the forest, she at first resolved to start directly for Virginia, but the remembrance of Wahlaga's threat prevented her, and then again in the stilly night the heroic girl knelt and asked of Charlie's God what she should do.

Owanno was surprised when, at a late hour that night, Orianna returned, and expressed her willingness to marry Wahlaga, on condition that she should first go for Ella, and that he should not follow her.

"What proof have we that you will return?" asked Wahlaga, who was present.

Orianna's lip curled haughtily, as she answered, "Orianna never yet broke her word."

"The tomahawk and death to those you love, if you

fail of coming," continued the savage, and "Be it so," was the reply.

Old Narretta with streaming eyes would fain have interposed a word for her beloved child, but aught from her would have been unavailing. So on the poor girl's head which drooped heavily upon her lap, she laid her hard, withered hands, and her tears fell soothingly on the troubled heart of one who stood in so much need of sympathy.

With the coming of daylight Orianna departed. Narretta accompanied her a short distance, and learned from her how much more than her life she loved the white man, and that were it not for this, not half so terrible would be her marriage with Wahlaga.

"I would help you if I could," said Narretta, " but I cannot, though each night I will ask the Great Spirit to take care of you."

So they parted, Narretta to return to her lone cabin, and Orianna to pursue her way, she scarce knew whither. For many days they missed her in the sick-room, where all but Charlie wondered why she tarried, and he finally succeeded in convincing them that she had really gone for Ella, though at what a fearful sacrifice he knew not.

CHAPTER XII.

ELLA.

THE town of P—— is almost exactly east of Glen's Creek, and by keeping constantly in that direction, Orianna had but little difficulty in finding her way. In twelve days' time she accomplished her journey, stopping for food and lodging at the numerous wigwams which lay on her road.

It was near the middle of the afternoon when, at last, she entered the woods on the borders of which lay the settlement of P——. Wearied with her day's toil, she sought a resting-place beneath the same old oak where, seventeen years before, Mr. Gorton had laid his little Madeline; and the same large, rough stone which he had placed there to mark the spot, and which had since fallen down, now served her for a seat. But Orianna knew it not, nor ever dreamed that often had Robert and Marian stood there, the one listening tearfully, while the other told her all he could remember of the sister who, in childish playfulness, he had often called his little wife.

It was now near the first of April, and already had the forest trees put forth many a dark green leaflet, while the song birds gaily caroled of the coming summer; but Orianna did not hear them. Sadly her heart went back to her home, and what there awaited her. Weary and worn, it is not strange that for a time she yielded to the despair which had gathered about her heart. Covering her face with her hands, she wept bitterly, nor until twice repeated did she hear the words, "What makes you cry so?" uttered in the soft tones of childhood.

Looking up, she saw before her a little girl, her deep blue eyes filled with wonder and her tiny hands filled with the wild flowers of spring.

Something whispered to Orianna that it was Ella, and brushing away her tears, she answered, "Orianna is tired, for she has come a long way."

"What have you come for?" asked the child.

"Charlie sent me. Do you know Charlie?" and Orianna looked earnestly at the little girl, whose blue eyes opened wider, and whose tiny hands dropped the flower·

ets, as she answered, "Charlie, my cousin Charlie? Have you come from him? What word did he send me?"

"Walk with me and I will tell you," said Orianna, rising and taking by the hand the unresisting child, who, with the ready instinct of childhood, could discriminate between a friend and foe.

For more than an hour they walked rapidly on, Ella, in her eagerness to hear from Charlie, never once thinking how fast the distance between herself and her home was increasing; nor had she a thought of her companion's intention, until Orianna, suddenly lifting her in her arms, said, "I promised Charlie I would bring you, and for that have I come."

Then a cry of fear burst from Ella, who struggled vainly to escape from the arms which gently, but tightly, held her. "Let me go, oh, please let me go," she cried, as Orianna's walk quickened into a run; but Orianna only replied, "I told Charlie I would bring you, and I promise you shall not be hurt."

"Mother, oh, mother, who will tell my mother?" asked Ella.

"I will send some one to her in the morning," answered Orianna; and then in order to soothe the excited child, she commenced narrating anecdotes of Charlie and the place to which they were going.

Finding it impossible to escape, Ella by degrees grew calm, and as the night closed in, she fell asleep in the arms of Orianna, who, with almost superhuman efforts, sped on until a wigwam was reached. There for a short time she rested, and won from a young Indian a promise that he would next morning acquaint Capt. Wilder of the whereabouts of his child. Fearing pursuit, she could not be prevailed upon to stay all night, but started forward, still keeping in her arms the little Ella, who at last slept as soundly as ever she had done in her soft bed at home.

The night was far spent when Orianna finally stopped beneath the shelter of a large, overhanging rock. The movement aroused Ella, who instantly comprehending where she was, again plead earnestly that she might go home. Orianna soon convinced her that to return alone was impossible, and then painted the meeting between herself and Charlie so glowingly, that though her eyes were full of tears, her voice was more cheerful, as she asked, " And will you surely bring me back ? "

" As yonder stars fade in the rising sun, so surely shall you go home," said Orianna. Then spreading in her lap the blanket which, with ready forethought, she had brought from home, she bade Ella lie down and sleep.

" And will you keep the bad Indians off ? " asked Ella, looking shudderingly around at the dark woods.

" No one will harm you while I am here," was Orianna's reply, and with the trusting faith of childhood Ella was soon fast asleep, while Orianna carefully watched her slumbers.

Once during her night vigils she was startled by the distant cry of some wild beast, but it came not near, and the morning found them both unharmed. Dividing with her little charge the corn bread and cold venison which had been procured at the wigwam, Orianna again set forward, leading Ella by the hand, and beguiling the hours in every possible way. The next night they passed in a wigwam, where dusky faces bent curiously above the " pale flower" as she slept, and where, next morning, in addition to the bountiful supply of corn-cake and venison, a bunch of spring violets was presented to Ella by an Indian boy, who had gathered them expressly for the " white pappoose," as he called her.

Blest season of childhood, which gathers around it so many who are ready to smooth the rough places and pluck the sharp thorns which lie so thickly scattered on life's pathway! It was Ella's talisman; for more than one tall Indian, on learning her history from Orianna, cheer-fully lent a helping hand, and on his brawny shoulders carried her from the sun's rising to its going down.

With Ella for a companion, Orianna proceeded but slowly, and nearly three weeks were spent ere familiar way-marks told her that they were nearing Lexington. "In less than two days we shall be there," she said to Ella, as at the close of one day they drew near that town.

Lighter grew Ella's footsteps, and brighter was her eye, while darker and deeper grew the shadows around poor Orianna. She was right in her calculations, for on the afternoon of the second day they struck into the narrow footpath which led to Deacon Wilder's house, and which she and Charlie oft had trodden.

Here for a time we will leave them, while in another chapter we will read what has taken place since we in the wilderness have been roaming.

———◆———

CHAPTER XIII.

THE DEATH-BED.

ANXIOUSLY as the sun was going down, did Mrs. Wilder watch from her window for the return of her daughter, and as the gray twilight deepened into night, and still she came not, the whole household was alarmed, and every house in the settlement was visited, to learn, if possible, some tidings of the wanderer. Some remembered having seen her enter the woods soon after dinner, but farther than that none could tell; and the loud, shrill cry of "Lost! lost! A child lost in the woods!" echoed on the evening air, and brought from a distance many who joined in the unsuccessful search, which lasted all night. Morning came, and Mrs. Wilder, pale and distracted with grief, ran hither and thither, calling loudly for her lost darling.

Three hours of the sun's daily journey was accomplished, when a young Indian was seen to emerge from the woods, and rapidly approach the house of Capt. Wilder, where he communicated all he knew concerning Orianna, and ended his narrative by saying, "It will be useless to follow her."

But Capt. Wilder did not think so, and instantly mounting his horse, he started in pursuit; but the path he took was entirely different from the one chosen by Orianna, and at night-fall he returned home, weary and discouraged. For some time he had been contemplating a visit to his brother, and he now resolved to do so, hoping by this means to fall in with the fugitives. Mrs. Wilder warmly approved the plan, but made him promise that if no good news were heard of Ella, he would instantly return.

Taking with him two negroes, he started on his journey, but no trace of Orianna did he discover, and he reached Glen's Creek before she had accomplished half the distance. Assured by his brother's family of Ella's perfect safety with the Indian girl, he grew calm, although he impatiently waited their coming.

Meantime, little Charlie had grown worse, until at last he ceased to speak of Ella, although he confidently expected to see her, and requested that his bed might be moved to a position from which he could discern the path which led up from the woods. There for many days he watched, and then turning sadly away, he said, "Mother, now take me back. Ella will come, but I shall be dead."

From that time he grew worse, and the afternoon on which we left Orianna and Ella in the woods was the last he ever saw on earth. Gathered around the dying boy were weeping friends, who knew that the mild spring sun which so gently kissed his cold, pale brow, would never rise again for him. Kind words he had spoken to all, and then in a faint whisper, he said, "Tell Ella ——;" but the sentence was unfinished, for Ella stood before him, while the look of joy that lighted up his face told how dear to him was the little girl around whose neck his arms twined so lovingly.

And now a darker face, but not less loving heart, approached, and whispered softly, "Charlie, do you know me?"

"Orianna," was the answer, as on her lips a kiss was pressed.

Then the arms unclasped from Ella's neck, over the blue eyes the heavy eyelids closed, and Charlie had gone home. With a bitter wail of sorrow Orianna bent for a moment over the marble form, for which she had sacrificed so much, and then, from among those who fain would have detained her, she went, nor paused for a moment, until the wigwam of her father was reached.

In the doorway she found Narretta, whose first exclamation was, "Have you heard? Have they told you? The Great Spirit has answered my prayer!" and then to her daughter she unfolded a tale which we, too, will narrate to our readers.

It will be remembered that on the day when Orianna left home for Virginia, Narretta accompanied her a short distance, and learned from her the story of her love for

Robert. To tnat story there was another,—an unob-served listener,—Wahlaga, who from that hour resolved to take the life of his pale rival, but his designs were foiled by a summons from the invisible world, which he could not disobey.

A week after Orianna's departure, he was taken ill of a disease contracted at the Indian camp, where he had spent the winter. All the skill of the "medicine man" could not save him, and on the fifth day he died, cursing, with his last breath, his hated rival.

When it was known at Deacon Wilder's that death had been at Grassy Spring, words of kindly sympathy were sent there for the sake of the noble Orianna; and for her sake, perhaps, Owanno's feelings softened toward the inhabitants of Glen's Creek. It is impossible to describe Orianna's feelings on learning that the dreadful Wahlaga was dead, really dead, and would trouble her no more. Her whole being seemed changed, and the slumber which that night stole o'er her was sweeter far and more refreshing, than for many weary days had visited her.

At Glen's Creek that same night Capt. Wilder, with his darling Ella pressed to his bosom, was listening, while between her tears for little Charlie, she told him of the many virtues of her Indian companion, urging him to send for her mother, that she, too, might know and love Orianna. But Ella's strength was exhausted long before her theme, and when, as her voice ceased, her father looked down upon her, she was far in the depths of dreamland.

CHAPTER XIV.

THE DENOUEMENT.

As if to mock the anguish of those who were about to lay their last-born in the earth, the day of Charlie's funeral was bright and beautiful, as the spring days often are 'neath the warm Kentucky sun. Sweetly the wild flowers were blooming, and merrily sang the summer birds, as underneath a maple tree, a tree which stands there yet, they dug that little grave,— the first grave at Glen's Creek. Mr. and Mrs. Gorton, Robert, and several others from Lexington had come to shed the sympathizing tear with the bereaved ones, but besides the nearest relatives, there was not so sincere a mourner as she who, apart from the rest, looked silently on, while into the earth they lowered the cold, dead Charlie.

Long after the mourners had returned to their desolate home, she lingered, and on the little mound deplored in piteous tones her loss, saying, "Oh, woe is me, now Charlie has crossed the great river, and left Orianna all alone. Who will love me now, as he did?"

"Many, many," answered Robert Hunting, who purposely had returned, and been an eye and ear witness of Orianna's grief. "Yes, many will love you," he continued, seating himself by her, and drawing her closely to him. Then in the bewildered girl's ear he softly whispered, "I am not worthy of you, Orianna, but I love you, and I know, too, on what condition you went to Virginia, and that had Wahlaga lived, he had sworn to murder me and marry you."

For this information he was indebted to Narretta, who, three days before Wahlaga's illness, overhearing him unfold his plan of revenge to Owanno, went to the door of Deacon Wilder's house, and asking for Robert, led him to the woods, and there communicated to him what he has just told Orianna. Robert did not ask Orianna to be his wife; and perhaps 'twas well that he did not, for the confession which he did make, added to the excitement of Wahlaga's and Charlie's death, was too much for a frame already weakened by the hardships attending that journey to and from Virginia. The next morning found her burning with fever and raving with delirium. Owanno, too, was smitten by the same disease which had consigned Wahlaga to an early grave.

With anxious heart Narretta hurried from one sufferer to the other, and the first Indian that looked in at the door, was urged to go immediately to Deacon Wilder's and ask some one to come to her. Robert and Marian instantly obeyed the summons, but human skill could not save Owanno. In three days after the commencement of his illness, it was said of him that he had gone to the fair hunting grounds, while the despairing howl of the assembled Indians mingled with the mournful wail of the widowed Narretta and the feeble moans of Orianna, who incessantly cried, "Bury me under the maple tree with Charlie, where we sat when he told me,—where he told me,——" but what he told her she never said.

At Marian's request, Mrs. Gorton had remained for some time at Glen's Creek, and one day, not long after Owanno's burial, she accompanied her daughter to see Orianna, who, though very weak, was still much better. They found her asleep, but Narretta arose to receive them. As Mrs. Gorton's eye fell upon her, an undefined remembrance of something past and gone rose before her, and at last, taking the old Indian woman's hand, she said, "Narretta, have I never met you before?"

"Plenty times," was the laconic answer; and after a moment's pause, Mrs. Gorton, continued: "I remember, now, eighteen or twenty years ago your wigwam was near my home in Virginia, and you one morning came to me, saying you were going away toward the setting sun."

"White woman remembers wonderful," said old Narretta.

"I might not remember so well," answered Mrs. Gorton, "but you loved my little Madeline, and about the time you went away she died."

Something out of doors attracted Narretta's attention, and she abruptly turned away. For more than an hour she was gone, and when she returned she was muttering to herself, "Yes, I'll do it. I shall do it."

"Do what?" asked Marian, a little alarmed at Narretta's excited manner.

But Narretta made her no answer, and going up to Mrs. Gorton, said rapidly, "Madeline did not die! Narretta loved her, loved all children, but the Great Spirit gave her no pappooses of her own, and when she went away she stole her. She took her, and under the tree she left a part of her clothing and the smashed carcass of a young fawn, to make the white woman think the wolves had eaten her up."

Here she stopped, and Mrs Gorton, grasping the wasted hand of Orianna, turned to Narretta and said, "Tell me, tell me truly, if this be Madeline, my long lost daughter!"

"It is," answered Narretta. "You know she was never as fair as the other one," pointing to Marian, "and with a wash of roots which I made, she grew still blacker."

She might have added, also, that constant exposure to the weather had rendered still darker Orianna's complexion, which was naturally a rich brunette. But whatever else she might have said, was prevented by Mrs. Gorton, who fell in a death-like swoon at her feet. The shock was too great, to know that in the gentle Orianna, whose noble conduct had won the love of so many hearts, she beheld her long wept-for daughter Madeline.

Upon Marian and Orianna the knowledge that they were sisters operated differently, according to their different temperaments. With a cry of joy Marian threw her arms around Orianna's neck, who, when made to comprehend the reality, burst into tears, saying, "I thought I should be white, sometime,—I almost knew I should."

By this time Mrs. Gorton had recovered from her fainting fit, and clasping her newly found daughter to her bosom, thanked the God who so unexpectedly had restored her. The next day the news reached Lexington, bringing thence Robert, who, in the intensity of his joy, seemed hardly sane. At a glance he foresaw the future. Orianna, for so he would always call her, should go to school for five years, and at the end of that time, images of a noble, beautiful bride, rose before him, as he hurriedly traversed the road to Grassy Spring. Their interview we shall not describe, for no one witnessed it, though Marian impatiently remarked, "that it took Bob much longer to tell what he had to say than it did George when he first came to Lexington." But then Marian had forgotten, as who will not forget, or pretend to.

Old Narretta was the only one who seemed not to share the general joy. She looked upon Orianna as lost to her forever, and heard the plan of sending her to school with unfeigned sorrow. Still, she made no objections to whatever Mr. and Mrs. Gorton chose to do with their child; and when Orianna was well enough, she gave her consent that she should be removed to her father's house, where every possible indulgence was lavished upon her by her parents, in order to attach her to them and their mode of life.

There was now no tie to bind Narretta to Grassy Spring, and yielding to Orianna's entreaties, she accompanied her to Lexington, occupying a cabin which Mr. Gorton built for her on the edge of the wood at the foot of the garden. Here, many times a day, she saw her child, who was now Robert's daily pupil. But Robert found it more difficult to tame his Indian girl than he had at first anticipated. On one subject, that of dress, she for a time seemed incorrigible. Occasionally she would assume the style worn by Marian, but soon casting it off, she would don her old costume, in which she felt and looked most at home. But one day the Indian dress mysteriously disappeared. More than a week Orianna sought for it in vain; then, with a flood of tears, she yielded the point, and wore whatever her friends thought proper. Her complexion, too, with which great pains was taken, gradually grew fair, until all trace of the walnut stain disappeared.

In October she was placed in the best school of which Philadelphia could then boast. She was always shy and timid, but her gentle manners and sweet disposition, to say nothing of the romance connected with her history, made her a general favorite with her companions, while the eagerness with which she sought for knowledge, rendered her equally a favorite with her teachers. In speaking of this once, to her mother, who was visiting her, she said, "When dear Charlie died, I thought there was no one eft to love me, but now it seems that every body loves me."

Here we will say a word concerning little Ella, who, two days after Charlie's funeral, and before Orianna's parentage was known, had gone home with her father to

Virginia. Almost constantly sne talked of Orianna, and on learning that she was Marian's sister, her delight was unbounded. When intelligence was received that she had been placed at school in Philadelphia, Capt. Wilder, yielding to Ella's importunities, consented to send her there, also. Ella had not taken into consideration how greatly changed her Indian friend must necessarily be, and when, on reaching Philadelphia, a beautiful young lady entered the room, neatly and fashionably attired, she could scarcely believe that it was her companion of the forest.

At Orianna's request they became room-mates, and it was difficult to tell which was more child-like, the tall maiden of twenty-one, or the curly-haired girl of nine.

Five years seems a long, long time, but to Orianna it soon glided away, and then she left school, a much better scholar than now is often graduated at our most fashionable seminaries. During her stay in Philadelphia, she had become greatly attached to the city, and Robert, whose wealth would admit of his living where he pleased, purchased a handsome dwelling, fitting it up according to his own taste, which was rather luxurious.

Six years from the night of Marian's bridal, there was another wedding at the house of Mr. Gorton, and Orianna, now a beautiful woman of twenty-six, was the bride. George and Marian both were present, together with a lisping Charlie, and a dark-eyed baby " Orianna," who made most wondrous efforts to grasp the long diamond earrings which hung from its auntie's ears, for, Indian-like, Orianna's passion for jewelry was strong and well developed.

Old Narretta, too, was there, but the lovely young creature whose head so fondly lay upon her lap, asking her blessing, was unseen, for Narretta was now stone blind. Already in her superstitious imagination warnings had come from the spirit world, bidding her prepare to meet Owanno. Gladly would Orianna have taken her to her Philadelphia home, but she answered, "No, I will die and be buried in the woods;" and the first letter which went from Mrs. Gorton to her daughter, told that Narretta was at rest.

On the first anniversary of Orianna's wedding day, Robert, still madly in love with his handsome wife, wished to give her a pleasant surprise. Accordingly, besides the numerous other costly presents which he brought her, he presented her with a large square box, saying that its contents were for her.

On opening it, Orianna saw disclosed to view the old Indian dress, whose loss she years before had wept. Bright as the sunlight of her happy home were the tears which glittered in her large black eyes, as, glancing at the rich heavy silk which now composed her dress, she said, "Oh, Bob, how could you?" and "Bob" answered, "How could I what?"

The Gable-Roofed House at Snowdon.

"Now, Mary," said my Great-Aunt Sally, as o'er the title of this tale her golden spectacles for a moment peered, "Now Mary, what could possess you to choose such a subject? Seems as though you had no knack in getting up a taking title. Why don't you ever write about 'The Murdered Sisters,' or 'Lover's Revenge,' or some such thrilling themes?" and Aunt Sally settled herself for her afternoon nap, in the large, stuffed easy chair, before the grate of glowing Lehigh, greatly lamenting the incapacity of her niece for "getting up taking titles."

Dear Aunt Sally, who, since my earliest remembrance, has worn the same sweet, placid smile, the same neatly fashioned caps, and carried the same large tortoise shell snuff-box! Could I not, if I would, weave a story of her now so quietly passing into the winter of life!

And now her heavy breathings show that I and my story have ceased to trouble her, while Malta, the pet kitten, snugly nestled in its mistress' lap, purrs out her contentment, occasionally lifting her velvet paw toward the nose which bows and nods so threateningly above her. Darkly across the floor fall the shadows of the locust trees, whose long branches make mournful music as they sweep against the loosened shutter. On the almost de serted sidewalk is heard the patter of the September rain, and in the delicious quiet of a still, smoky, rainy afternoon, commences the first chapter in the life of one, who, in the somber old church at Snowdon, was christened Josephine Clayton.

------◆------

CHAPTER I.

JOSEPHINE.

THE house which Uncle Isaac Clayton, the shoemaker of Snowdon, called his, was an old brown, gable-roofed building, containing wide fire-places, huge ovens, ash-pits of corresponding magnitude, and low rooms, where the bare rafters looked menacingly down, strikingly suggestive of bumped heads, especially to those who, being above the medium height, carried their heads too high. Then there were the little narrow windows, so far from the floor, that every time a wagon was heard, the six red-backed, splint-bottomed chairs were brought into requisition by Uncle Isaac's six white-haired boys, all eager to know "who's goin' by!"

It was in the same room which contained these six red-backed chairs, that Josephine first opened her eyes on the light of a fair September morning, and, in the same room, too, the six white-haired boys, on tip-toe, stole up to the bed to see the novelty, for never before had a daughter graced Uncle Isaac's domestic circle.

"She makes up just such faces and looks just as ugly as Jim did when he was a baby," said Frank, the oldest of the boys; and with a whistle which he meant should be very indifferent, he walked away, followed by all his brothers save Jimmy, who lingered longer to look at the stranger, who so unceremoniously had usurped his rights and privileges as the youngest. Though cradled in the lap of poverty, a more restless and ambitious being has seldom sprung into existence than was she, whose soft cheek and tiny fingers Jimmy so lovingly caressed. Yes, Jimmy, love her now, lavish upon her all the affection of your noble heart, for the time will come when she, a haughty, beautiful woman, will turn her back on you, ashamed to own that once beneath the old gable-roof she called you brother.

Over Josephine's early days we will not linger, or stop to tell how both early and late Uncle Isaac's pegs and long waxed-ends flew, to meet the increased demands for money which the new comer made, nor how Jimmy, in order that his sister might have the bright pink dress, which so well became her rosy cheeks and silken curls, went, with generous self-denial, without the new Sunday coat, wearing the old patched one, until it was hard to tell which piece belonged to the original article.

It was no ordinary love which Jimmy Clayton bore his only sister; and as she grew older and he saw her passion for dress, he carefully hoarded every penny which he earned, and then when she least expected it, poured his treasure into her lap, thus, with mistaken kindness, gratifying a fondness for dress far above her means. Though possessing less of it than most small villages, Snowdon had its *ton*, its *upper set*, who, while they commented upon the marvelous beauty of Josephine, still passed her by as one not of their number. This was exceedingly mortifying to her pride, and when at the school which she attended, Mabel Howland, the lawyer's child, spoke sneeringly of " the poor shoemaker's daughter," her spirit was fully roused, and she resolved to leave no means untried until *money* was within her reach. Accordingly, when sixteen years of age, she was willingly apprenticed to a milliner in the city, with the understanding that at the end of six months she should return home for a short visit. Many articles which were absolutely necessary for the coming winter, did Mrs. Clayton deny herself, that a decent outfit might be procured for the thankless girl, who, without a tear, left the humble home she so much despised.

But, in spite of her faults, she left behind her loving hearts, which many long days missed her bright, handsome face and bounding footstep. Darker than ever seemed the dark old kitchen at Snowdon, while the cricket 'neath the large flat stones which served as a hearth, mournfully chirped, "she's gone," as on the first evening after her departure Mr. and Mrs. Clayton and Jimmy gathered around the frugal board. The other five boys, now grown to manhood, were away, three of them being respectable farmers, and the other two mechanics.

Jimmy had always been a home boy, and he remained with his mother, learning his father's trade, and working in the little shop which had been built in the rear of the house. In his childhood he had thirsted for more knowledge than could be obtained by a yearly attendance of five months at the district school of Snowdon, but, taught by his father to believe that education was only for the rich, he hushed the desire he had once had for something noble and high, and patiently, day by day, he toiled uncomplainingly in the shop, thinking himself sufficiently rewarded by the smile of approbation with which his mother *always* greeted him, and the few words of kindness which his sister *occasionally* gave him. But in that close, smoky shop was the germ of a great mind. The scholar and statesman was there, who one day would stand forth among the great men of the land.

But not with Jimmy must we tarry. Our story leads to the noisy city, where already had Josephine's uncommon beauty been the subject of remark, drawing to Mrs. Lamport's shop many who were attracted thither by the hope of seeing the beautiful apprentice girl, who was frequently sent to wait upon them. "What a pity that she should be a milliner," had more than once been whispered in her hearing, and ere three months of her apprenticeship had expired, she was devising schemes by which to rise to the level for which she believed nature intended her; and fortune, or rather ill fortune, seemed to favor her wishes.

Among the millionaires of the city was a Mr. Hubbell, who, with a gouty foot, restless mind, and nervous, sickly daughter of eighteen, managed to kill time by playing chess, reading politics, giving dinner parties, humoring his daughter, visiting every fashionable watering place, cursing the waiters, and finding fault generally. Not always, however, had Mr. Hubbell possessed so peculiar a disposition. Late in life his quiet bachelor habits had been broken by a young, joyous creature, on whom he doted with an almost idolatrous love; but the same sun which first shone on him, a happy father, left him at its setting, a stricken, desolate mourner. Anna, his cherished girl-wife, had left him forever. He had not thought she *could* die, and when they told him she was dying, with the shriek of a madman he caught her in his arms, as if he would contend with the king of terrors for the prize he was bearing away. She died, and from the quiet, easy husband, Enos Hubbell became a fault-finding, fretful, disconsolate widower.

His daughter Anna had, in her childhood, been subject

to severe and protracted fits of sickness, and now, at eighteen, she was a pale, delicate, kind-hearted girl, though rather peculiar in her likes and dislikes, for upon whatever object her affections chanced to fasten, she clung to it with a tenacity which nothing could weaken. For one thing in particular she was famous. She was always discovering people whom she thought "far below their position in life." These she generally took under her special notice, and as might be expected, usually succeeded in making them both discontented and unhappy.

Josephine had been in Mrs. Lamport's employment nearly three months, when she was one morning sent to wait upon Miss Hubbell, who came on some trifling errand. Something in the face and appearance of the apprentice girl deeply interested Anna, who felt sure that for once she discriminated rightly,—that she had at last found one really worthy of being her protege,—in short, Josephine was discovered! Many were the visits made to Mrs. Lamport's, until the intimacy between Anna and Josephine became a subject of gossip among the shop girls, each of whom, according to her own pretensions for beauty, was jealous of her handsome rival.

Anna Hubbell's nature was largely spiced with romance, and she had long sighed for a companion near her age, who would be the confidant of all her thoughts and feelings, and in Josephine Clayton, she fancied she had at last found the desired friend. She believed, too, it would be an act of kindness to lend her a helping hand, for Josephine had often insinuated that reverse of fortune, alone, had placed her where she was. To her father Anna first communicated her plan, seizing her opportunity when he was not only free from gout, but had also just beaten her at chess three times out of four. First she descanted on Josephine's extreme beauty and natural refinement of manner; next she spoke of the misfortune which had obliged her to become a milliner, and finished her argument by telling how lonely she herself was, when obliged by ill health to remain in the house for weeks.

Mr. Hubbell heard her through, and then striking the ashes from his cigar, said, "Why don't you come to the point at once, and say you want this girl to pet, flatter, and make a fool of you generally?"

"And if I do," answered Anna, "you have no objections, have you?" And Anna wound her arms around her father's neck, until a twinge of the gout suddenly returning, he threw her half way across the room, exclaiming, "For pity's sake and the old Harry, lug in a wash woman for all of me, if you wish to!"

So the matter was settled, and in the course of an hour a note was dispatched to Josephine, bidding her come that evening, if possible, as her friend had something pleasant to communicate. Just as the street lamps were lighted, Josephine ascended the marble steps of Mr. Hubbell's stately dwelling, and in a moment was in Anna's room, where she soon learned why she was sent for. So unexpected was the proposal, that for a time she was mute with surprise, and then on her knees she thanked Anna Hubbell for the great good she was doing her.

The bells of the city were tolling the hour of nine ere Josephine returned to her pleasant room at Mrs. Lamport's, which now looked poor and humble, compared with the elegant home she was soon to have. When Mrs. Lamport was informed of the plan, she refused to release Josephine until the term of her apprenticeship should have expired, alleging, as one reason, that Josephine might sometime find her trade of great service to her. Accordingly, though much against her will, Jose phine was obliged to remain until the end of the six months; but she resolved not to go home, and about the time when she would be expected, she wrote to her parents, telling them of her future prospects, and saying that, as Miss Hubbell wished for her immediately, she should be obliged to forego her expected visit.

Owing to some mistake, this letter did not reach its destination, and Jimmy, all impatient to see his beloved sister, started for the city on purpose to accompany her home. Going to Mrs. Lamport's, he was told that "Josephine had gone out shopping." "Gone to buy some presents for mother, I presume," thought he, as he retraced his steps through the crowded streets. Coming to a jeweler's shop, he concluded to step in, as he had long contemplated the purchase of a watch. At the further end of the store were seated two young ladies, surrounded by jewelry, from which they were making selections. As Jimmy entered the door, one of the young ladies glanced at him; their eyes met, and involuntarily Jimmy started forward, half exclaiming, "Josephine!" but the lady's lip curled scornfully, and a dark frown lowered on her brow as she turned quickly away. Jimmy was puzzled, and glancing, for the first time, at the young girl's dress, he thought, "Of course 't isn't Josephine; what a blunder I should have made!"

Just then the clerk asked him to step into an adjoining room, where they would show him the kind of watches he wished for. As he was passing the two ladies, the one whose face he had not seen looked up at him. He would have thought no more of this occurrence, had he not overheard her say to her companion, "Why, Josephine, that young man looks enough like you to be your brother."

The reply, too, he distinctly heard, uttered in Josephine's well remembered voice: "Oh fie, Miss Hubbell pray, don't take that clownish clod-pole to be *my* brother!"

Jimmy instantly turned toward the speaker, but with her companion she was leaving the shop. Mechanically declining to purchase anything, he also left, and, going to the hotel, called for a room, where, locking himself in, he burst into a flood of tears. "Josephine, his sister Josephine, was ashamed to own him,—had denied him!" For half an hour he wept bitterly; then over him a reäction stole, and rising up, he rapidly paced the room, saying, "*Ashamed of me!*—she shall see the day when she will be glad that I am her brother." Then in that little room was a resolution made, and a course of life marked out which made for America a son of whom she has since been proud.

That evening Jimmy met his sister at Mrs. Lamport's, but not as in the olden time. A change had come over him, which even Josephine noticed, although she scarcely regretted it. He offered no remonstrance when told that she would not accompany him home; but, after bidding her good-by, he turned back, and with a scarcely steady voice, said, "When I return home, and mother, your mother, weeps because you do not come, shall I tell her that you sent no word of love?"

"Why, Jim," said Josephine, "what a strange mood you are in to-night! Of course, I send my love to all of them. Have n't I told you so? If I have n't, it was because I forgot it."

"One of us, at least, will not forget you so easily," answered Jimmy, but he told not what fresh cause he had for remembrance.

CHAPTER II.

A PEEP AT THE GABLE-ROOFED HOUSE AT SNOWDON.

NEVER was floor scoured whiter than was the floor in the long, dark kitchen at Snowdon, on the day when Mrs Clayton, with a mother's joy, said, "Josephine is coming to-night." Everything within told of recent renovation and fixing up, and the large square room, whose four bare walls had echoed back the first shrill cry of Uncle Isaac's seven children, now looked really neat and pretty, with its bright rag carpet, its polished brass andirons, and its six flag-bottomed chairs, for the old red-backs had long since been removed to the kitchen, their place being supplied by six yellow chairs, which now in turn gave up their long standing right to flag-bottoms of a more modern date.

The two boys who lived nearest came home, the one bringing several pounds of coffee, while the other brought the snow-white sugar loaf, which was only to be used in Josephine's cup, for "Josephine was coming home." Yes, "Josephine was coming home," and Uncle Isaac finished work full three hours earlier, in order that he might have ample time to remove the heavy beard, don the clean linen, and assume the blue, Sunday coat with the brass buttons.

In one corner of the old rickety barn, a turkey, the only turkey Isaac Clayton owned, had long been fattening, and now in the oven was roasting, for "Josephine was coming home;" and as the sun drew nearer and nearer to the western horizon, Mrs. Clayton's step grew lighter, while the smile on her face grew brighter and more exultant. Again was the white counterpane on the best bed smoothed, and the large round pillows gently patted, for Josephine's soft, fair cheek would ere long nestle there. Alas! poor, fond, but disappointed mother! The Josephine, so anxiously waited for, slept that night on finer linen and softer couch than could be found, I ween, 'neath the gable-roofed house at Snowdon.

Now the sun has set behind a pile of purple clouds, and there is darkness in the nooks and corners of the house at Snowdon. The maple fire in the large square room is crackling and laughing and blazing, and casting on the somber walls fantastic shadows, which chase each other, " chassee, cross over, and then cross back," while to the dancing flames Uncle Isaac adds still another stick, for it is a raw March night, and Josephine will be cold. Upon the time-worn bridge which crosses Snowdon creek is heard the sound of wheels; and the crack of the driver's whip, together with the tramp of many feet, shows that the stage is coming at last. But what! Why does not the driver stop at the little board gate which stands so invitingly open? Is he going to let Josephine dismount in the muddy street?

Before these queries are satisfactorily solved, the stage rattles on, and only Jimmy stands among them, beset by inquiries for Josephine.

" Wait until I get to the fire and I will tell you," said he, as he blew his red fingers; but Mrs. Clayton could not wait, and leading him toward the house, she said, " Tell me, is Josephine sick ? "

" Perfectly well, I believe," he answered, and then, when seated before the cheerful blaze, he told them why he was alone; but of the insult he had received he said nothing. That was a secret, which he kept to himself, brooding over it until its venom ate into his inmost soul.

It was a sad group which gathered around the supper

table that night; and, as over the dishes she had prepared with so much care Jimmy saw his mother's tears fall, his heart swelled with resentment, and he longed to tell her how unworthy was the selfish girl who scorned her own brother, but he did not, though he resolved, by an increased kindness of manner, to compensate his honored mother for the love which Josephine refused to give. Noble Jimmy! In this world there are choice spirits like yours, but their name is *not* legion!

Next morning the two older boys returned to their employment, while Mr. Clayton sold to Mabel Howland, who had long coveted them, the fairy-like slippers, which for two weeks he had kept for his daughter; and amid a rain of tears Mrs. Clayton put away in the drawer the lamb's-wool stockings which she had knit for Josephine, weaving in with each thread the golden fibers of a mother's undying love. After his daily work was done, Jimmy stole up to the little green trunk under the gable-roof where lay the pile of bright half dollars he had hoarded for Josephine. Counting out half, he threw them into his mother's lap, and with the remainder repaired to the Snowdor bookstore, exchanging them for their value in books. The old desire for learning had returned, and early and late was each leisure moment improved. His parents offered no opposition, but approved his plan of reciting two hours each day to Mr. Allen, the clergyman, who became much interested in the young student. "Excelsior" was Jimmy's motto, and his teacher became surprised at the rapid improvement and the magnitude of the mind committed to his care. Ere long, Jimmy's fame as a scholar became known throughout the village, attracting toward him many who had never before noticed the humble boy, except, perhaps, to remark his fine face and figure. Now, however, they came thronging about him, offering books and advice in large quantities. But Jimmy respectfully declined their attentions, for Mr. Allen's library, to which he had free access, contained whatever books he needed, and his good sense, together with Mr. Allen's experience, furnished all the advice necessary. At one time Mr. Allen hoped that the brilliant talents, which he knew his young friend possessed, would be devoted to the ministry; but Jimmy's taste and disposition turned toward the bar, and as Judge Howland was in want of a clerk, Mr. Clayton was induced to give up the services of his son, who now bent all his energies upon the study of law, and the course of instruction which Mr. Allen had marked out for him. Leaving him to pursue his onward path to greatness, we will return to Josephine, who for some time has been the *bosom friend* and companion of Anna Hubbell.

CHAPTER III.

LOCUST GROVE.

ABOUT fifty miles west of the city, at the foot of a bright sheet of water, lies the small village of Lockland, consisting of one broad, handsome street, and two narrow ones, diverging at right angles. The quiet which forever reigns in this secluded spot, seemed not unlike the deep hush of a Sabbath morning. In the center of the village stand the two dry goods stores, where kind-hearted clerks, in consideration of its being *you*, measured off calico at a shilling per yard, which *positively* cost fifteen cents, and silks for a dollar, which could n't be bought in the city for less than a dollar and a quarter.

Directly opposite these sacrificing stores stands the hotel, on whose creaking old sign is written in flaming letters, "Temperance House," although the village gossips, particularly the woman who lives next door, have frequently hinted, confidentially of course, that the word "temperance" was all humbug. Side by side with the hotel stands the old brick church, the only church in Lockland.

A little out of the village, and on an eminence which overlooks it, is a handsome, white cottage, which, from the number of locust trees around it, had long been known as "Locust Grove." This cottage was the property of Mrs. Wilson, Anna Hubbell's grandmother, and thither, each summer, Anna repaired, in hopes of coaxing to her pale cheeks the hue of the roses which grew in such profusion around the doors, windows, and porticos of her grandmother's dwelling.

Across the way was another, a large building, elegant in structure and imposing in appearance. It was owned by Gen. Granby, who had retired from public life, and was living upon the interest of his money. These two families were on terms of intimacy with but few of the villagers, and consequently were called proud and haughty by those who had nothing to do except to canvass affairs at Locust Grove and Elmwood Lodge, as Gen. Granby's residence was termed.

One morning in early June, the little village suddenly found itself in a state of fermentation, occasioned by Mrs. Wilson's traveling carriage, which passed up Main street, and from the windows of which looked forth, not only the plain, delicate features of Anna Hubbell, but also another, a most beautiful face. Such eyes, such curls, and more than all, so dazzling a complexion, had seldom been seen in Lockland, and the villagers were all eager to know who the

22

stranger could be, and why Anna Hubbell had brought her there. Did she not fear her influence over George Granby, to whom, for a long time, she was known to have been engaged, and who, with his sister Delphine, had been traveling in Europe, and was now daily expected home? Still more was the gossip increased when, that afternoon, Lockland's back parlors and sitting rooms were vacated by their inmates, who from behind half-raised curtains and half-closed shutters, peeped out, while with long black skirts and leghorn hats, Anna Hubbell and her companion galloped leisurely through the village and down upon the lake shore. But not upon Anna did an eye rest. All were fixed upon the lady at her side, whose red lips curled in scorn at the same curiosity of which she had often been guilty in the gable-roofed house in far off Snowdon.

That night, in Anna's dressing-room, Josephine was weeping, and to Anna's repeated inquiries as to the cause of her tears, she at last answered, "It is foolish, but I cannot help it. In the city all knew I was your *hired* companion; but here, in the country,—oh, need they know?"

"I appreciate your feelings," said Anna, "but rest assured that no one shall know you are not fully my equal. Grandmother, indeed, knows your real position, but if I request it, she will be silent."

So the terrible secret that Josephine was *poor*, and a dependent, was kept from the villagers, who marveled at her great beauty and the richness of her attire, for all her wages were expended in *dress*. Not one penny ever found its way to Snowdon, where it would have been joyfully received, not because they were in actual want of it, but because it came from Josephine.

Mrs. Granby, who was an amiable and lady-like woman, treated Josephine with great cordiality, frequently expressing a wish that her daughter, Delphine, would return, as it would be so pleasant for her to have two companions so near. Josephine had no objections to seeing George Granby, whose many excellences Anna each day lauded to the skies, but she greatly dreaded the return of Miss Granby. Six years before, when but a child, she remembered that Mabel Howland had one day brought to school a cousin, Dell Granby, two or three years her senior, and whose place of residence she felt sure was at Lockland. Always fearing that her humble parentage might be discovered, she trembled lest Dell Granby should recognize her, or that in some way her real position should become known.

"I shall soon know the worst," thought she, as one afternoon, about three weeks after her arrival at Lockland, she saw a handsome carriage drive up in front of Gen. Granby's residence. From it sprang a gentleman, who was quickly followed by a young lady of remarkably elegant appearance. After embracing Mrs. Granby, who came out to meet her, she turned toward the window, where Josephine was sitting, and thinking it was Anna, playfully threw a kiss from the tips of her snowy, jeweled fingers; then she instantly disappeared in the long hall, followed by the gentleman.

"That must be Dell Granby," thought Josephine; "but if that is her brother, he is not one-half as fine looking as Anna has described him to be; but then she is in love, and of course no judge."

Just then, Anna, who had been sleeping, awoke. On hearing of Delphine's arrival, her cheeks alternately flushed and grew pale, as she nervously ordered her waiting maid to dress her becomingly, preserving at the same time the utmost simplicity. When her toilet was completed, she asked Josephine's opinion. Both were standing before the mirror, and as Josephine noticed the con trast between herself, dressed as usual, and Anna, arrayed in the most becoming manner, the thought for the first time entered her mind, that if possible she would supplant her benefactress in George Granby's affections.

At that moment a servant entered, bearing a tiny note. Anna hastily read it, and then throwing herself on the sofa, burst into tears. Josephine ordered the servant girl to leave the room, and then, while Anna's face was buried in her hands, she picked up the note, and in a lady's delicate handwriting, read:

"DEAR ANNA—I know you will be provoked; I was, but I have recovered my equanimity now. George, the naughty boy, has not come home. He is going to remain for two years in a German university. I am the bearer of many letters and presents for you, which you must come for. Hugh M'Gregor accompanied me home. You remember I wrote you about him. We met in Paris, since which time he has clung to me like a brother, and I don't know whether to like him or not. He is rich and well educated, but terribly awkward. It would make you laugh to see him trying to play the agreeable to the ladies; and then,—shall I tell you the dreadful thing? he wears a *wig*, and is *ten* years older than I am! Now, you know if I liked him *very much*, all this would make no difference, for I would marry anything but a cobbler, if I loved him, and he were intelligent.

"By the way, mamma tells me there is a handsome young lady with you, but whether in the capacity of seamstress or companion, I have not found time to ask Pray, come over, *sans ceremonie.*

"Yours, as ever,   DELL."

The cause of Anna's grief can be explained in a few words. Two years before, when only sixteen, she had been betrothed to George Granby, whom she ardently loved, fearing, at the same time, that her affection was but half returned. Their engagement had been a sort of family arrangement, in which George tacitly acquiesced, for Anna was not indifferent to him, although she possessed but few attractions which could fascinate a fashionable young man of twenty-two. Still, he had never seen one whom he liked better, and as Anna was extremely young, he hoped that during the five years which were to elapse before their marriage, she would be greatly improved.

The last year he had spent in Europe, whither his sister, a girl of superior endowments, had accompanied him. He wrote frequently to Anna, his letters being more like a brother's than a lover's. Still she prized them highly, and had looked forward joyfully to his return. But now he was not coming, and as she threw herself upon the sofa, she thought, with some reason, "I know he does not love me."

Josephine, too, was disappointed. If George came not, her plan could not well be carried out. But not long did she dwell upon this. The words "seamstress," and "companion," troubled her, and awoke within her heart a hatred for Delphine Granby, as undying as it was unfounded. Soon, however, her thoughts took another channel. This M'Gregor, was *he* not worth winning; suppose he was awkward, he was rich! and Josephine smiled exultingly, as, glancing in the mirror, she smoothed her luxuriant curls, and said, "the shoemaker's daughter will yet out-shine them all"

CHAPTER IV

DELPHINE AND M'GREGOR.

IN Mrs. Wilson's parlors Josephine first met the two persons who were so greatly to influence her after life. It was the day following their arrival, and Anna had invited them to tea. Pleading a headache, Josephine did not make her appearance until evening, thinking her charms would be greatly enhanced by candle light.

With all the dignity of a queen she swept into the room, and Anna herself was surprised at the ease with which she returned the salutations of M'Gregor and Delphine. Seating herself upon a low ottoman, she for a time seemed unconscious of M'Gregor's presence, but fixed her eyes curiously upon Delphine, who, she concluded, was the most polished, lady-like person she had ever seen. Envy, too, crept in, and mingled with her admiration, for though she knew Miss Granby was not as beautiful as herself, there was still a nobleness, an elegance of appearance about her, which would readily distinguish her from a thousand.

At length it was Delphine's turn to look, and her bright hazel eyes fastened upon Josephine, whose face turned scarlet, for she fancied that the hated words, "milliner," "shoemaker," "gable-roof," were stamped upon her brow as legibly as "seamstress," "companion," were written in the tiny note. Delphine was puzzled at Josephine's confusion, but soon forgetting it, she complied with Anna's request, and seated herself at the piano.

"Do you play, Miss Clayton?" asked M'Gregor.

"No, sir," was the reply.

" Nor sing ? " he returned.

" Certainly not," Josephine answered somewhat haughtily. "If I could sing I should play, of course. They
usually go together."

M'Gregor was taken aback. He was perfectly bewildered with Josephine's beauty, although her cool reserve
had slightly disconcerted him; and as he was nothing of a
lady's man, he had tried hard to think of something to
say to her, and now that he said it, 'twas not the thing.
Josephine, however, had scanned him from head to foot,
wig and all, and with Delphine's assertion, "he is rich,"
still ringing in her ears, she had secretly concluded that
he would do, in spite of his awkwardness. Fearing lest
he should question her on other points than music, she
did not wait for him to broach another subject, but did it
herself, by asking about his European tour.

Once during the evening she heard Delphine telling
Anna that on her return home she had stopped for a day
and a night with her cousin Mabel, at Snowdon. In an
instant her brow became crimson; but her fears were
groundless, for not a word was spoken of the "gable-
roof," and her heart was beginning to beat at its usual
rate, when Delphine added, " By the way, Anna, I must
tell you that at Snowdon I saw my *beau ideal*."

"Indeed," said Anna, and M'Gregor continued: " Oh,
yes, and she has done nothing since but talk of the handsome student, who is still in his minority."

"What is his name ? " asked Anna.

"Clayton, I believe," answered M'Gregor, and then
turning to Josephine, he said, " A relative of yours, perhaps! You remind me of him."

"I am not aware of his being so, for I have no relations in Snowdon!" was Josephine's unhesitating answer; and in the first part of the assertion, she spoke

the truth, for at Jimmy's request, a knowledge of his studies had been kept from her, and she did not believe that Jimmy, her homespun brother, could possibly inter- est the elegant Miss Granby.

But all doubt on the subject was removed, when, as Delphine was about to depart, she remarked, "There is something, too, so romantic about this young Clayton. His father, as I am told, is a poor shoemaker at Snowdon, and his son, until recently, has worked with him at his trade. Just think of it, a learned shoemaker. Of course he will be a great man;" and she ran gaily down the steps followed by M'Gregor, horribly jealous of Jimmy Clayton, two-thirds in love with Josephine Clayton, and never suspecting the relationship between them.

That night Josephine bitterly repented her falsehood, for if Delphine Granby could be interested in Jimmy, knowing his poverty, she really would not scorn his sis- ter; but 'twas too late to retract, and though she knew that, sooner or later, her lie would be known, she resolved to put a bold face upon the matter and make the best of it. She had never spoken of Snowdon as being the residence of her parents, consequently Anna had no suspicion that the student whom Delphine extolled so highly was in any way connected with her protege.

It would make our story too long to enumerate the many ways in which Josephine sought to enslave M'Gregor, who for three weeks lingered at Lockland, vacillating between Delphine and herself. Josephine fascinated him, but there was about her something which bade him beware; and he never would have thought seriously of her, had not Delphine kindly but firmly refused the hand he offered her, her mother mean- time wondering what she could object to, for if he was not quite as polished as some, he was rich, well educated, and amiable to a fault, or as one of the villagers said, "wonderful clever." But it was this very cleverness which Delphine disliked. Had M'Gregor possessed more intellect, more energy and decision of character, she might ——, but no, she had seen Jimmy Clayton, and though she would not own it, either to herself or to M'Gregor, the remembrance of his high, classical brow, bright, intelligent eye, and sad, handsome face, influenced her decision.

After M'Gregor's first mortification was over, he turned to Josephine, and in the sunshine of her smiles soon forgot that Delphine had said, "I can never love you;" but, other than by actions, he did not commit himself, and when he left Lockland, he was not pledged to Josephine, who for several days kept her bed, troubling in every possible way poor Mrs. Wilson, who wondered at her grand-daughter's fancy in choosing such a companion, as much as Aunt Sally wondered at my choice of a subject.

CHAPTER V.

JIMMY.

THICK and fast from the heavy laden clouds the fringed snow-flakes had fallen the livelong day, covering sidewalk and street, doorstep and roof, with one thick vail of whiteness. As the night closed in, the feathered flakes ceased to fall, while in the western sky the December sun left a few red beams, the promise of a fair to-morrow. In Mr. Hubbell's parlor the astral lamp was lighted, and

O*

coals were heaped in the glowing grate, whose bright blaze rendered still more brilliant the flowers of the costly Brussels. Curtains of rich damask shaded the windows, and around the marble center-table were seated our fair friends, Josephine, Anna, and Delphine, the last of whom had recently come to spend the winter in the city.

Josephine seemed nervously anxious, starting up at every sound, and then blushing as she resumed her former attitude. The cause of her restlessness was, that she was hourly expecting Mr. M'Gregor, her affianced husband! Two weeks before she left Lockland he had visited her, and ere his return she had promised to be his wife, regretting, meantime, the fatality which left George Granby across the Atlantic until she was given to another. "If I could only see him," thought she, "only have an opportunity to judge of his merits and my chance of success;" but it could not be. The ocean lay between them; so she engaged herself to M'Gregor, with many assurances of affection, of the sincerity of which our readers can judge as well as ourselves.

As yet Delphine had no thought that her "beau ideal" was aught to Josephine, although Anna knew it all. Compelled by necessity, Josephine had, with many tears and protestations of grief, confessed her falsehood, and Anna not only forgave her, but weakly took her again to her confidence, thinking her sufficiently punished by the sorrow she professed to have felt on account of her sin.

M'Gregor had written that he should probably be in the city that night, and each moment they were expecting him. At length the sound of a footstep was heard on the threshold, the door-bell echoed through the hall, Delphine and Anna exchanged smiles, while Josephine half rose from her seat, and as the parlor door opened the six eyes of the three girls fell upon—M'Gregor? no, not M'Gregor, but Jimmy Clayton! He had come to the city on business for Judge Howland, and had been commissioned by Mabel to carry a letter to her cousin Delphine, besides her love, which of course could not be sent in a letter!

Delphine arose to meet him, but not on her did his eye rest. It wandered on until it fell upon Josephine, to whom Delphine immediately introduced him. A little sarcastically he answered, "Thank you, Miss Granby, but I hardly need an introduction to my own sister!"

"Your sister!" repeated Delphine. "Impossible!" And she glanced quickly at Josephine, who seeing no escape sprang forward, overwhelming Jimmy with caresses and questions concerning Snowdon and its inhabitants, taking care to inquire after the *rich* and those whom Delphine had probably heard of, though she herself had never exchanged over a dozen words with them.

After a time Jimmy gave Delphine her letter, which she received with a smile and a glance of her eyes which made his blood tingle, and when Anna asked him if it were not unpleasant traveling, he answered, "Quite well, I thank you!"

By this time Josephine's old coldness had returned. She was afraid M'Gregor might come, and, although she was not now ashamed to own her brother, she feared the result. Jimmy soon arose to go, but Anna insisted upon his remaining all night. This plan Delphine warmly seconded, and Jimmy began to waver. He looked at his sister, one word from whom would have decided the matter, but that word was not spoken, and Jimmy departed, saying he would call again on the morrow.

Scarcely had the door closed after him when Delphine looked sternly and inquiringly at Josephine, who, in the most theatrical manner, fell upon her knees, sobbing out the confession of her falsehood, and finishing by saying, "Do not betray me to M'Gregor, will you?"

"M'Gregor!" repeated Delphine scornfully, "You wrong him if you suppose he would love you less for your poverty."

"'Tis not that, 'tis not that," said Josephine, and Delphine continued: "But he would despise you for scorning your own parents, and refusing to own a brother of whom you should be proud."

"But you will not betray me?" persisted Josephine. "Promise that you will not, and a falsehood shall never again sully my lips."

"Of course I shall not tell M'Gregor," answered Delphine, "but it will be long ere I can again respect you." Here Anna interposed a word for her friend, saying that "Delphine had never known what it was to contend with poverty, and have the cold finger of scorn pointed at her——"

"And if I had," interrupted Delphine, "I should not revenge myself by pointing *my* finger at my parents and brother."

There now ensued an embarrassed silence, and, as it was past the hour for M'Gregor to arrive, Josephine repaired to her room, gratified to think that if her sin had found her out, M'Gregor had not.

The next day M'Gregor did not come, but Jimmy did, and as he was about to leave, he asked Josephine to accompany him home, saying his mother would be delighted to see her. Delphine waited for Josephine's answer, that she could not go, as she was expecting a *friend*, and then said, "Suppose, Mr. Clayton, you take me as a substitute."

"You!" exclaimed Anna. "You go to Snowdon!"

"Yes; why not," answered Delphine. "Mabel is anxious to see me, and the sleighing is fine."

Accordingly, next morning, Jimmy's sleigh stood before Mr. Hubbell's door, and Delphine, warmly wrapped in furs and merinos, tripped down the steps, and was soon seated by Jimmy, whose polite attentions during the ride only increased the estimation in which she held him.

The same day that Delphine left the city, M'Gregor came, overjoyed to meet his beautiful Josephine, whom, with strange infatuation, he sincerely loved. That evening, as they sat alone in the parlor, Josephine, fearing that in some way he might discover the falsehood, determined to tell him herself. In the smoothest manner possible, she told her story, saying that her parents *now* lived in Snowdon, but intimated that they had not always resided there. Jimmy was then mentioned, and acknowledged to be her brother, although she said that he had been long in Judge Howland's office ere she knew of it.

M'Gregor heard her through, and then drawing her more closely toward him, assured her that he did not love her less for being poor, for he had never supposed her rich, and ended by proposing to accompany her to Snowdon. The proposal was made in such a way that Josephine could not refuse, but she determined not to go, for though M'Gregor might love her with poverty in the distance, she fancied that a sight of the "old gable-roof" and "shoemaker's shop" would at once drive him from her. The next day was fixed upon for the journey, but when the morning came, Josephine did not appear at the breakfast table, sending word that she was suffering from an attack of the influenza! Snowdon of course was given up, and M'Gregor paced the long parlors, inquiring every ten minutes for Josephine, who knew enough not to be convalescent *too soon*, and all day long did penance by keeping her bed and drinking herb tea.

-------◆-------

CHAPTER VI.

SNOWDON.

WITH unbounded delight Mabel welcomed her cousin Delphine, but she whispered, " Now Dell, I know well enough that nothing but the agreeable escort of James Clayton could have brought you to this stupid place in the winter."

Delphine's only answer was a deeper glow on her cheek, which she declared was owing to the chill night air, and Mabel said no more on the subject until they retired for the night. Then, in the privacy of the dressing room and before a cheerful fire, she teased and tortured her cousin concerning her evident preference for the young student, saying, " I know he is noble and generous, and father thinks him a gem of rare talents, but after all—"

" After all what ? " asked Delphine, suspending for a moment the operation of brushing her silken hair.

" Why he is of a very *low* family," answered Mabel, and Delphine continued: " Why low ? Is there anything bad or disreputable about them ? "

" Oh, no," said Mabel. " I don't suppose there is a more honest, upright man in town than cobbler Clayton, but they are dreadfully poor, or, as mother says, shiftless. Why, Dell, one glance at the old gable-roof, and one whiff of the leather smell, constantly around it, would spoil all romance connected with the handsome son."

"Pshaw!" was Delphine's only reply, and there the conversation ended; nor was it resumed again until two or three days after, when Delphine announced her intention of calling on Mrs. Clayton!

"Call on Mrs. Clayton?" exclaimed Mabel, who was listlessly turning over the leaves of her music book, and occasionally striking the keys of her piano. "Call on Mrs. Clayton? You cannot be in earnest."

"I am," answered Delphine, and Mabel continued: "Pray don't ask me to accompany you."

"You need not be alarmed on that score, as I greatly prefer going alone," was Delphine's answer, as she left the room.

In a few moments she was on her way to the "gable-roof," which really looked poor enough; for, as Mrs. Howland had expressed it, Uncle Isaac was rather "shiftless," and though he now had only himself and wife to care for, he was worth but little more than when, in years gone by, seven hungry children clustered around his fireside. His wife, who was greatly his superior, was a paragon of neatness, and made the most of what little she had. On this afternoon, with clean cap and gingham apron, she sat knitting, so wholly absorbed in her thoughts of Josephine, that, though thrice repeated, she heard not the timid knock of Delphine, nor was she aware of her presence until the lady stood before her. Then, in some confusion, she arose, but Delphine immediately introduced herself, apologizing for her call, by saying that she thought Mrs. Clayton might be glad to hear from Josephine. Eagerly then her hand was grasped, and for the next hour Mrs. Clayton listened breathlessly, while Delphine recounted everything concerning Josephine which she thought would interest her mother. As she saw how many times the gingham apron was brought into requisition, to wipe away the tears of maternal love, she felt indignant toward the heartless girl who could thus spurn her home and fireside, because they lay beneath a gable-roof.

Swiftly the time flew on, and though upon the polished stove the highly polished tea-kettle boiled and boiled, and then boiled over, Mrs. Clayton heard it not; and though token after token that daylight was departing fell around them, still Delphine sat there, gazing at the high, placid brow and clear, hazel eyes of her new acquaintance, and tracing therein a likeness to Jimmy, who at last suddenly opened the door, astonished beyond measure when he found who was his mother's companion. At his unexpected appearance, Mrs. Clayton started up, exclaiming, "Bless me, it's past tea time! How I forgot myself!" while Delphine, casting a rueful glance at the little narrow window, said, "Dear me, how dark it is! What shall I do?"

"Stay to tea," answered Mrs. Clayton, "and then Jimmy will see you home. He'd just as lief, I know!"

For an instant Jimmy's and Delphine's eyes met, and the next moment a velvet cloak and rich hood were lying on the little lounge, while Delphine, demurely seating herself in the corner, thought, "How funny! I wonder what Mabel will say. Perhaps she'll think I came here on purpose to see him; but I didn't."

By this time tea was ready, and though the table lacked the transparent china, silver forks, and delicate napkins, to which Delphine had always been accustomed, she has frequently declared that never was tea so hot, bread so white, butter so sweet, or honey so delicious, as were they that night in Isaac Clayton's sitting room. After supper, Jimmy, inasmuch as his mother had offered his services, felt in duty bound to conduct Miss Delphine home, and all the misgivings which she had felt as to what Mabel would say, were put to flight by that delightful moonlight walk.

"I declare, Dell," was Mabel's first exclamation, "you are actually reversing the order of things, and paying your addresses to young Clayton, instead of waiting for him to pay them to you."

"And shows her sense, too," said Judge Howland, who was present, "for James, who looks upon her as far above him, would never presume to address her first. But, Mab," he continued, "you had better have an eye on her, for, in case Dell does not secure him, I intend him for my own son-in-law."

"Oh, capital!" said Mabel, clapping her hands, "won't that be nice? He can attend to all of Uncle Isaac's lawsuits, and, in return, Uncle Isaac can make all our shoes."

"But I am in earnest," said Judge Howland, seriously. "You will never do better."

"How absurd," said Mabel. "Why, he is six months younger than I am."

"Six months be hanged," answered the judge. "Why, there's your mother, five years my senior, though I believe she *owns* to only one!"

"Mr. Howland, how can you talk so?" said the highly scandalized lady, who, with fair, round face, clear, blue eyes, and white, sound teeth, really looked five years the junior of her portly spouse, and probably was.

Had Jimmy been questioned concerning his feelings for Delphine Granby, he might have pointed to some bright star, which, while it hovered round and over his pathway, was still too far distant for him ever to hope to reach it. And yet, no matter how big the law book was which he opened, or how intently over its printed leaves he pored, one face, one form, and one voice ever came between him and his studies; and once, in making out a bond, he wrote, instead of "Know all men by these presents, &c," "Know *Delphine Granby*, &c.," nor was he aware of his mistake, until, with the best natured twinkle in the world, Judge Howland pointed it out, saying, "Not so bad, after all; for if a woman knows it, all the world stand a fair chance of knowing it, too."

Poor Jimmy! How he blushed, and stammered, and apologized, apologized, stammered, and blushed, while the judge good humoredly said, "Never mind; Dell is a girl of the right stamp, and if you play your cards right, 'tis not *her* fault if you do not win her."

CHAPTER VII.

THE NEW HOUSE.

CHRISTMAS came and went during Delphine's stay at Snowdon, and a few days after it, she went to visit Mrs. Clayton, who with eager joy told her that Christmas morning she had received from the city a hundred dollar bill, enclosed in an envelope, on which was simply written, "Do with it as you see fit." A deep flush mounted to Delphine's brow as she quietly remarked, "You must have some unknown friend in the city."

"Oh, no," said Mrs. Clayton, "it was Josephine of course; she is a dear good girl, and then she speaks about it so modestly."

"What does she say?" quickly asked Delphine, and Mrs Clayton replied, "I immediately wrote to her, thank ing her for the money, and saying I hoped she did not rob herself. To-day I got her answer, in which she merely alluded to the subject by saying that whatever she gave me I must enjoy without thinking she was denying herself."

"She is worse than I supposed," thought Delphine, but she said nothing, while Mrs. Clayton continued: "It has come in the right time, too, and is just what we need."

Then she proceeded to tell Delphine how for years they had tried to lay by enough to build a house, which would cost about one thousand dollars. "We have already nine hundred, and with this one hundred we shall venture to commence."

Here the conversation ceased, and Delphine, soon after, returned home. Many were the consultations which she afterwards held with Mrs. Clayton concerning the construction of the new house, a plan of which she and Jimmy at length proposed drawing. This took a deal of time, and frequently kept them together for hours; but at length the plan was completed, and Delphine returned to the city, leaving Snowdon all a blank to Jimmy, who, solitary and alone, pursued his studies.

In the spring the house was commenced, and early in autumn there stood in the corner of Isaac Clayton's garden, a small, handsome cottage, contrasting strangely with the brown old gable-roof, which in a rage shook off a few shingles and clapboards, as at Jimmy's suggestion a poor widow, with three children to feed and nothing to feed them with, was placed in it, rent free. One act of charity made way for another, for the woman thus assisted took from the poor house, where she had been for more than a year, her blind old mother, who gladly exchanged the cold charities of a pauper's home, for a seat by her daughter's fireside

Alas! within the fairest flower is found the sharpest thorn.   Scarcely had three months passed since Isaac Clayton and his wife had taken possession of their new home, when over their quiet dwelling the dark pall of death was unfurled, covering with its shadow the wife, who, for more than thirty years, had walked faithfully and lovingly by the side of her husband.   Fever, which took the typhoid form, settled upon her, and when the physician who attended her was questioned concerning the probable result, he shook his head mournfully to the group of six young men, who, with filial affection, had gathered around their mother's sick-bed.

And where all this time was Josephine?   Why came she not to soothe her mother's last great agony, and administer consolation to those who, stern of heart and strong of nerve, still in the hour of affliction bent like a broken reed?   Yes, where was she?   This question Mrs. Clayton often asked, for at the commencement of her illness a letter had been dispatched, to which no answer had been received, and at last Jimmy was sent to bring her home.   Judge Howland kindly offered his covered sleigh and horses, and as Jimmy was driving from the yard, Mabel, who knew that Delphine was in the city, requested him if convenient to bring her cousin back with him, saying that Kate Lawrence, a mutual friend and school-mate of theirs, was then visiting her, and wished to see Delphine.

Jimmy drove nearly all night, and at dawn of day the spires and roofs of the city were discernible in the distance.   Impatiently he waited at a hotel, until an hour when he thought Mr. Hubbell's family would be astir. Then going to the house, he nervously rang the door bell His call was answered by a servant girl.

"Is Miss Clayton at home?" he asked.

"She is," was the answer.

"I must see her, instantly," said he.

The girl eyed him curiously, and replied, "What name shall I give her? 'cause, unless it's something extraordinary, she won't see you. It's her wedding day."

Jimmy handed her his card, and then in the parlor sat down to await her coming. In an upper room Josephine was seated, together with Anna and Delphine, who unwillingly had consented to be present at the wedding, and had twice nearly broken her promise not to acquaint M'Gregor with the nature of her he was taking to his bosom. As Josephine glanced at the card which the servant girl gave her, she exclaimed, "What can Jim want in the city at this time?"

"Oh, is James Clayton here?" asked Delphine. "How fortunate?"

Josephine's manner changed, as she said faintly, "Yes, 'tis fortunate, for now he can see me married. But I wonder what he wants."

"Go down and see," answered Delphine, and Anna added, "Or ask him up here to see Dell;" to which Josephine rejoined, "Delphine can go down with me—I wish she would."

Acting on the impulse of the moment, Delphine accompanied Josephine to the parlor. But the sight of Jimmy's pale, sad face alarmed her, and she instantly asked, "What is the matter? Is any one dead?"

He soon told all, and then repeated to Delphine Mabel's request that she, too, should accompany him to Snowdon. Without once thinking it possible that his sister could refuse, he asked how soon she would be ready. Bursting into tears, which arose more from the dilemma in which she was placed than from actual grief, Josephine wrung her hands, saying, "Oh, I cannot go, I cannot. To-night is my bridal night. The guests are all invited, and I cannot go. Mother will not die. I know she will not. She must live, and to-morrow I will surely come."

Jimmy was confounded, but ere he had time to open his mouth, another had stepped in to plead his cause. "Josephine Clayton," she said, more sternly than ever before she had spoken to her—"I have long known that you had no heart, but I did not suppose you so perfectly callous as not to go when your dying mother bids you come. I would leave all the bridegrooms in the world to go to mine. Go, or I shall blush that I, too, am a woman!"

Angrily Josephine turned upon her, saying, "Who are you that presumes to question my conduct? I shall go, or not, just as I choose, and on this occasion I choose not to go."

"Is that your decision?" asked Jimmy.

"It is, for how can I go?" she answered. "Mother cannot expect it of me."

"Then I will go without you," said Delphine, who, besides being pleased at again meeting Kate Lawrence, whom she so much esteemed, was also glad of an excuse not to see Josephine married.

Jimmy, though pleased at having her for a companion, would still gladly have exchanged her for his sister;—for how could he go home without her? how tell his dying mother, when she asked for Josephine, that she had not come? When they were alone, almost convulsively he threw his arms around his sister's neck, beseeching her to go; but she only gave him tear for tear, for she could weep, while her invariable answer was, "I cannot, oh, I cannot."

At length his tears ceased, and Delphine reëntered the parlor in time to see him, with blanched face, quivering lips, and flashing eye, seize Josephine's arm, as he said, "For more than two years you have not been at home. Twice have I come for you. Once you spurned me, and denied that I was your brother, and this, the second time, when I come from mother's death-bed, you still refuse to go. Far be it from me to curse you, for gladly would I shield you from harm, but from this hour I feel that you are cursed! You and yours! Blight will fall upon everything connected with you, and remember, *when next I come, you will surely go!*"

Long, long did these words haunt Josephine, and in the years of bitterness which came, she had reason to remember them but too well. Weary and sad was that ride to Snowdon; but with Delphine for a companion, and her encouraging words sounding in his ear, Jimmy grew more strong and hopeful, though his mother's face was constantly before him. Delphine knew that it would take more time to leave her at her uncle's, so with kind consideration she requested him to drive immediately to his father's.

Supported in the arms of her eldest son, Mrs. Clayton lay in a death-like stupor, from which she occasionally roused to ask if Josephine had come. Upon the old stone bridge there was again heard the sound of horses' feet, and a smile of joy broke over her face, as some one whispered, "They are coming."

Instantly Isaac Clayton and his sons went forth to meet the travelers, but the face they met was strange to them all, save Uncle Isaac, who quickly asked for Josephine. 'She is to be married to-night, and deemed that a sufficient excuse for not coming," said Jimmy, stamping on the ground, by way of adding emphasis to his words.

With a bitter groan Uncle Isaac staggered backward,

and would have fallen, but for the timely assistance of Frank. "Who, oh, who can tell her!" said he.

There was silence for an instant, when Delphine said, "I will tell her, if you wish it."

Then, with the stricken group, she entered the room, where the first words which met her ear were, "Josephine and Jimmy, I have blessed them all but you. Now come to me, while there is time."

Side by side they advanced to her bedside. With a wild, searching look at Delphine, she said, "You are not Josephine. Where is she? Shall I not see her?"

"In heaven, *perhaps*, you may," answered Frank, "but in this world you never will."

Those who were present will long remember the shriek which echoed through the room, as Mrs. Clayton exclaimed, "She is not dead! Tell me, is Josephine dead?"

Delphine's soft white hand was placed on the brow already wet with the moisture of death, and she gently whispered, "It is her bridal night, and she could not come."

For a time Mrs. Clayton seemed paralyzed. Then raising her head, she beckoned for Jimmy to come near her. He did so, and taking his and Delphine's hand in hers, she said, "May God in heaven be with and take care of you both, and bless you, even as you have been a blessing to me, my dear, my precious boy, my Jimmy. And you, Delphine, my child, my children." There was a moment's pause, and then, as if the departing spirit had summoned all its energies for one great effort, she let go the hand of Jimmy and Delphine, clasped her own together, and raising them high over her head, started up erect, exclaiming, "Will God forgive my Josephine for all she's made me suffer." Then, with one long, low, des pairing cry, she fell back upon the pillow, and naught was left of Josephine Clayton's mother, save the tenement which once enshrined the soul.

CHAPTER VIII.

MRS. M'GREGOR.

THE marriage ceremony was ended, and Josephine Clayton, now Mrs. M'Gregor, was receiving the congratulations of her friends. First among them came Anna, but the gentleman who accompanied her was a stranger, and Josephine was greatly surprised at hearing him introduced as Mr. Granby, Delphine's brother. He had returned from Europe sooner than he expected. On reaching home, and learning that his sister was in the city, he hastened thither, reaching Mr. Hubbell's just in time to witness the ceremony. Thoughts of him, as we well know, had occupied many of Josephine's waking dreams, and now when she at last saw him, the knowledge that she was not free to try upon him her powers of art, only rendered him doubly attractive.

In personal appearance and manners he was as unlike M'Gregor as was Josephine unlike Anna; and once during the evening, as he and Josephine were standing side by side near the center-table, they overheard a remark not intended for their ears. It was, "How much better the bride looks with Mr. Granby than she does with that awkward M'Gregor!" To which the person addressed replied, "Yes; and M'Gregor seems far better suited for

P

plain Miss Hubbell! See! they are standing together there by the window."

Instantly George Granby's and Josephine's eyes met, and then glanced across the room to the spot where M'Gregor was making most desperate efforts to play the agreeable to Anna Hubbell, who was smiling, and bowing, and twirling her fan. Again their eyes met, and this time a scarcely perceptible smile curled the corner of Josephine's mouth, while George Granby, offering her his arm, conducted her back to her husband, and taking Anna, led her to the music-room, where some one was playing the piano. But Josephine's eyes and thoughts followed him.

As we well know, she had not married M'Gregor for love, but because he was rich, and she knew that riches would procure for her the position in society she so greatly coveted. Insensibly she began to contrast her husband with George Granby, and ere long she was blaming the former for having hastened their marriage. This was an uncommon mood, surely, for a young bride to be in, but Josephine was an uncommon bride, and by the time the last guest was gone, and they were alone, she might safely be said to be in a fit of the sulks, whilst poor M'Gregor, distressed beyond measure, strove to ascertain the cause of her apparent melancholy. She saw the necessity of making some explanation, so she told him, for the first time, of her mother's illness, alleging that as the cause of her sadness.

"Why did you not tell me before?" said M'Gregor. "I would, of course, have postponed our marriage for a few days."

"Would to heaven I had!" said Josephine, with more meaning in her words than M'Gregor gave her credit for.

The next morning, at an early hour, a gay livery stood

before Mr. Hubbell's door, and M'Gregor, helping in his young bride, and taking a seat beside her, was driven off in the direction of Snowdon. It was a delightful morning, and under almost any other circumstances Josephine would have enjoyed the ride. Now, however, she chose to find fault with all her husband's assiduous attentions and politeness, saying, at last, ill-naturedly, "Do, M'Gregor, stop your fussing. I am doing well enough, and will let you know if I am uncomfortable."

He complied with her request, as who would not, thinking she had changed her tone and manner very soon. About three o'clock they reached Snowdon, and by the side of her pale, dead mother, the ice about Josephine's heart gave way, and in the most extravagant terms she bewailed her loss. Uncle Isaac, overjoyed at again beholding his daughter, and deceived by her loud show of grief, wound his arm about her, blessing her, and calling her his precious child. The next day they buried Mrs. Clayton, and the day following, Josephine returned to the city, in spite of her father's entreaties that she would stay a while longer with him. Promising to return in the spring, she bade him good-by, and when again in the city, she, to all appearance, soon forgot that death had been so near her.

Frequently she met George Granby, but the influence she had hoped to gain over him was partially prevented by the presence of Delphine, who, together with Mabel Howland and Kate Lawrence, had come to the city to pass the winter, her father, at her earnest request, having removed there for the season.

M'Gregor took a house opposite Mr. Hubbell's, and commenced housekeeping in great style. Nothing could exceed the elegance of his establishment; and Josephine, who managed to keep the house filled with a set of fashionable young men, seemed at last perfectly happy, though her husband was far from being so. True, he had the best furnished house and the handsomest wife in the city, but he found too late that beauty alone is not the only requisite in a wife; and before the winter was over he would have hailed the disfiguring small pox as a blessing, had it succeeded in keeping from his house the set of young men so frequently found there.

M'Gregor was not naturally jealous, but when, night after night, on his return from business, he found his wife so engrossed with company as to be wholly incapable of paying him any attention, he grew uneasy, and once ventured to remonstrate with her; but she merely laughed him in the face, telling him that whatever he could say would be of no avail — that he could n't expect one so young and gay as she to settle down into the humdrum Mrs. M'Gregor—that it would be time enough to do that when she wore a wig or colored her hair.

George Granby at first only called occasionally, but on such occasions Josephine did her best, acting the agreeable hostess so admirably that, insensibly, George became attracted toward her, and ere Delphine was aware of it, he was a regular visitor at the house of M'Gregor, who never objected to him; for, unlike the others who came there, George treated him with the utmost deference, always seeming pleased to see him present.

One evening the three were together, and conversing about ill-assorted marriages. Josephine, as one who ought to know, discoursed eloquently on the matter, and descanted so feelingly on the wretchedness resulting from such unions, that two large tears actually dropped from her eyes, and fell upon her worsted work. M'Gregor would have given anything to have known if his wife considered their marriage an unfortunate one, but he wisely kept silent, and

Josephine continued: "Whenever I see a person for whom I feel an uncommon interest, about to unite himself with one every way unsuited to him, my heart aches for him, and I long to warn him of his danger."

"Why not do so, then?" said George.

"Would my advice be kindly received?" asked Josephine, at the same time giving him a searching look.

He understood her, but made no reply, and when the conversation changed, somehow or other it turned upon Anna, who, Josephine said, was a kind-hearted girl, but it was such a pity she hadn't more character,—more life.

"But do you not think she has improved in the last respect?" asked George.

Josephine faintly admitted that she had, but in the next breath she spoke of her as possessing very little, if any intellect, and lamented her utter incapacity to fill the sphere for which she was intended. George Granby needed not that she should tell him all this, for he feared as much, though he had never once thought of breaking his engagement with her. He had returned from Europe intending to make her his wife, and hoping to find her greatly improved. And she was improved, both in personal appearance and manners. Constant intercourse with Delphine had been of great benefit to her, and when George came home, he was pleased to see how much she had brightened up. Her health, too, had greatly improved, and as she always dressed with the utmost taste, she more than once had been called quite pretty, though at all parties where Delphine, Kate Lawrence, Mabel, and Mrs. M'Gregor were present, she was entirely overlooked, or pointed out to strangers as the young lady who was engaged to the polished Mr. Granby.

We have not yet described Kate Lawrence, and we cannot do so better than to say, that to a style of beauty fully equal to Josephine, she added a proportionate kind-heartedness and intelligence. She was just the one whom Delphine would have selected for her brother, had he not been engaged to Anna Hubbell. Now, however, she never harbored such a thought, and she assiduously strove to assimilate Anna more to her brother's taste, always speaking encouragingly to her, and kindly of her.

George had as yet never directly asked Delphine's opinion of Anna, but the morning following his conversation with Josephine, he sought an interview with his sister, abruptly asking her if she sincerely thought that Anna Hubbell would make him happy as his wife.

Delphine was taken by surprise. She had that morning accidentally discovered that Kate Lawrence had a secret liking for her brother, and she was just wishing it might be—wishing it could be—when George startled her with his question.

"Why, George," said she, "what could have put that idea into your head? Have Kate's bright eyes dimmed the luster of poor Anna's charms?"

"No, no; I am not thinking of Kate," said he, somewhat impatiently; "but tell me, honestly, your opinion."

And Delphine did tell him her opinion. She spoke of Anna's gentleness and kindness of heart, admitting that on many points she was rather weak and inefficient. "But," said she, "you are engaged to her, you have promised to marry her, and my brother will surely keep his word." Here a loud call from Mabel that Delphine should join her in the parlor, put an end to the conversation.

Meantime, Mr. M'Gregor was about to commit a sad blunder. Thinking George to be his sincere friend, as indeed he was, and knowing the great influence which he possessed over Josephine, he resolved upon asking him to use that influence in dissuading her from receiving the visits of so many gentlemen. Accordingly, the next time George called, M'Gregor took the opportunity, when they were for a few moments alone in the drawing-room. After stammering awhile, he broached the subject, and with much difficulty succeeded in making George understand what he wanted.

"Silly old fool," said Josephine, who in an adjoining room had overheard every word. "He is meaner than I thought him to be;" and then she listened, while George respectfully declined any interference with M'Gregor's family matters.

"Your wife has sufficient discretion," said he, "to prevent her doing anything wrong; besides, I should be working against myself, for I come here as frequently as any one."

This was true; and as Josephine at that moment joined them, M'Gregor said no more on the subject, but soon after recollecting some business which he had down street, he left them alone. For an hour they conversed on different topics, and then Josephine, demurely folding her hands, said, "When are you going to begin to lecture me? I believe you have been requested to do so, have you not?"

George blushed scarlet, and while he admitted the fact, he disclaimed all intention of doing so; then, in the tones of a deeply injured woman, Josephine detailed her grievances, saying that each day she saw more and more her mistake, and that though she did not exactly regret her marriage, she yet many times wished she had not been quite so hasty. George Granby was perfectly intoxicated with her beauty, while the tones of her voice and the glance of her eye thrilled every nerve. Snatching her hand to his lips, he exclaimed, "Josephine, Josephine! why did you not wait a little longer?"   Then, as if regretting what he had said, he hastily rose, and saying that he had another engagment, bade her good night, and hurried away, almost cursing himself for the words and manner which he had used toward a married woman.

The engagement of which he had spoken was with Anna Hubbell, and going to her father's, he asked to see her.   She had long been expecting him, but was not prepared for the vehemence with which he insisted upon her naming an early day for their marriage.

"Why such haste?" asked Anna.

"Ask me no questions," said he, "but if you would save me from evil, become my wife, and that soon."

In an instant Anna thought of Kate, and looking him fully in the face, she said, "Answer me truthfully, George, do you love Kate Lawrence?"

"No, no," said he, "it would not be sinful to love her —she is free; but that other one—"

Anna knew that he was in the habit of frequenting M'Gregor's house, and suddenly a light flashed upon her mind, and she said, "It cannot be Josephine, my friend Josephine."

"Your friend!" he answered, bitterly; "call her not your friend, she does not deserve it.   But you have guessed right; I blindly put myself in the way of temptation, seeing no danger, and believing there was none."

The color receded from Anna's cheeks, and when George looked at her for an answer, he was surprised at the changed expression of her face.   Something between a sob and a groan came from her white lips, but he succeeded in soothing her, and ere he left the house he had gained her consent that the marriage should take place in one week from that day, and that he might speak to her father.

Mr. Hubbell was in the library. On learning the nature of George's errand, he gave vent to a few impatient "umphs" and "pshaws," but ended by giving his consent, on condition that Anna remained with him a year after her marriage.

Scarcely had the street door closed upon George, ere Anna was told that her father wished to see her. "Well, now, what's the mighty hurry?" were his first words, as she entered his room, but anything further was prevented by the sight of her unusually white face and swollen eyes. "Why, Anna, child," said he, "what's the matter? Don't you love George? Don't you want to married?"

"Yes, yes, father," said she, "but don't ask me anything more, for I am very unhappy;" and bursting into tears, she sat down on a stool at her father's feet, and laying her face in his lap, sobbed until wholly exhausted, and then fell asleep, while Mr. Hubbard gently stroked her soft, brown hair, wondering what ailed her, and if his Anna cried so a week before they were married.

The remembrance of his own darling wife caused two tears to drop from his eyes and fall upon Anna's face. This roused her, and rising up, she said, "Forget my foolishness, father. To-morrow I shall be myself again." Then bidding him good-night, she repaired to her own room. For several days she had been suffering with a severe pain in the head, and when she awoke next morning, it had increased so rapidly that she could scarcely rise from her pillow without fainting. Her father, instantly alarmed, sent for a physician, who expressed a ear that her disease might terminate in brain fever. On learning of her friend's illness, Delphine immediately hastened to her. During the afternoon a servant girl entered the sick-room, saying that Mrs. M'Gregor was in the parlor, and wished to see Miss Hubbell.

"I cannot see her," said Anna; then calling Delphine to her, she said, "Will you stay with me while I am sick?"

"Certainly, if you wish it," was the answer, and Anna continued, "And, Dell, if I should get crazy, and Josephine comes again, you won't let her in, will you?"

Delphine promised that she would not, wondering what could have produced this change in Anna, in regard to Josephine. Next day Anna was much worse, and, as had been feared, she grew delirious. Constantly she talked of Josephine, who, she said, "had stolen away the only heart she ever coveted." Delphine was greatly puzzled, and when that night she for a few moments returned home, she mentioned the circumstance to George, who, with his usual frankness, immediately told her all. Delphine heard him through, and then repeated to him all which she knew concerning Josephine's character for intrigue and deceit, blaming herself for not having warned him before. The scales dropped from George's eyes · Josephine's power over him was gone, and he saw her in her real character. The next day, at his earnest request, he was allowed to enter Anna's room; but she did not know him, though her eyes, intensely bright with the fire of delirium, glared wildly upon him as she motioned him away. Approaching, and bending over her, he said, "Anna, don't you know me? I am George, and next Thursday will be our bridal day."

For a moment she was silent, and then with a satisfied smile she answered, "Yes, that's it; that's what I've tried so hard to remember and couldn't." Then as the physician entered the room, she said to him, "Next Thursday is to be my bridal day, and you will come, for it will be a novel sight. Everybody will cry but George, and I, the bride, will be in my coffin."

Poor Anna! Her words proved true, for the sunlight of Wednesday morning fell upon her gray-haired, stricken father, weeping over his dead, and the next day at the same hour at which the wedding was to have taken place, the black hearse stood before Mr. Hubbell's door. In it a narrow coffin was placed, and then, followed by a long train of carriages, it proceeded slowly toward the home of the dead, while each note of the tolling bell fell like a crushing weight on the heart of Mr. Hubbell, as by the side of her, long since laid to rest, he buried his only child.

CHAPTER IX.

CHANGES.

TEN years have passed away, since we followed poor Anna Hubbell to her early grave. With the lapse of time many changes have come to those who have kept with us in the early chapters of this story. Jimmy Clayton, long since admitted to the bar, is now a lawyer of some celebrity in one of our western cities. For six happy years he has called Delphine Granby his wife, and in his luxurious home a little boy four years old watches each night for his father's coming, while the year old baby, Anna, crows out her welcome, and Delphine, beautiful as ever, offers her still blooming cheek for her husband's usual greeting, and then playfully assists the little Anna in her attempts to reach her father's arms. Truly, Jimmy's was a happy lot. Blest with rare talents, abundant wealth, and influential friends, he was fast approaching that post of honor, which he has since filled, and of which we will not speak, lest we be too personal.

But on his bright horizon one dark cloud heavily lowered. He could not forget that Josephine, his once beautiful sister Josephine, was now an object of reproach and dark suspicion. Step by step she had gone on in her career of folly, until M'Gregor, stung to madness by the sense of wrong done him, turned from his home and sought elsewhere a more agreeable resting place. At first he frequented the more fashionable saloons, then the gaming room, until at last it was rumored that more than once at midnight he had been seen emerging from some low, underground grocery, and with unsteady step wending his way homeward, where as usual Josephine was engaged with her visitors; and her half intoxicated husband, without entering the parlor, would repair to his sleeping room, and in heavy slumbers wear off ere morning the effect of his night's debauch. In this way he became habitually intemperate, ere Josephine dreamed of his danger.

One night she was entertaining a select few of her friends. The wine, the song, and the joke flowed freely, and the mirth of the company was at its height, when the door bell rang furiously, and in a moment four men entered the drawing-room, bringing with them Mr. M'Gregor, in a state of perfect insensibility. Laying him upon a sofa, they touched their hats respectfully to the ladies and left.

With a shriek of horror and anger Josephine went off into violent hysterics, wishing herself dead, and declaring her intentions of taking immediate steps for becoming so, unless some one interfered and freed her from the drunken brute. One by one the friends departed, leaving her alone with her husband, whose stupor had passed away

and. was succeeded by a fit of such silly, maudlin fondness, that Josephine in disgust fled from his presence.

From this time matters rapidly grew worse. Still, as
ong as Josephine was surrounded by the appliances of
wealth, her old admirers hovered around her; but when
everything was gone, when she and her husband were
houseless, homeless beggars, they left her, and she would
have been destitute, indeed, had it not been for her eldest
brother, Frank, who did for her what he could, remem-
bering, though, that in her palmy days of wealth she had
treated him and his with the utmost contempt. Her second brother, John, was in one of the southern states.
The next one, Archie, was across the ocean. Jimmy, too,
was away at the west, and for the two between Archie
and Jimmy, graves had been dug in the frozen earth just
three years from the day of their mother's death. It was
well for Uncle Isaac that he, too, was sleeping by the side
of his wife, ere he heard the word dishonor coupled
with his daughter's name.

For a time after their downfall, M'Gregor seemed trying to retrieve his character. He became sober, and la-
bored hard to support himself and wife, but alas! she
whose gentle words and winsome ways should have led
her erring husband back to virtue, spoke to him harshly,
coldly, continually upbraiding him for having brought her
into such poverty. At length, in a fit of desperation, he
left her, swearing that she might starve for aught more
he should do for her. For a time she supported herself
by sewing, but sickness came upon her, and then she was
needy indeed.

Once, in her hour of destitution, George Granby, now
the happy husband of Kate Lawrence, found her out, and
entering her cold, comfortless room, offered her sympathy
and aid; but with her olden pride she coldly rejected

both, saying she was doing well enough, though even then she had not a mouthful of food, nor the means of buying it. George guessed as much, and when after his departure she found upon the little pine table by the window a golden eagle, she clutched it eagerly, and purchased with it the first morsel she had eaten in twenty-four hours.

*   *   *   *   *   *

In a snug, cozy parlor in the city of C——, are seated our old friends, Jimmy Clayton and Delphine. The latter is engaged upon a piece of needle-work, while the former in brocade dressing gown and embroidered slippers, is looking over an evening paper, occasionally reading a paragraph aloud to his wife. At last throwing aside the paper he said, "I have been thinking of Josephine all day. It is a long time since I heard from her, and I greatly fear she is not doing very well."

"Do you believe her to be in actual want?" asked Delphine.

"I don't know," was the answer. "From her letters one would not suppose so, but she is so proud and independent, that you can hardly judge. Frank, too, has left Snowdon, and there is now no one left to look after her."

There was a rap at the door, and a servant entered, saying, "The evening mail is in, and I brought you this from the post-office," at the same time presenting a letter to Mr. Clayton, who instantly recognized the hand writing of Josephine. Nervously breaking the seal, he hurriedly read the blurred and blotted page. Jimmy had not wept since the day when the coffin lid closed upon nis mother, but now his tears fell fast over his sister's letter. It was as follows·

"Jimmy, dear Jimmy, my darling brother Jimmy. Have you still any affection for me, your wretched sister, who remembers well that once, proudly exultant in her own good fortune, she denied you, and that more than once she turned in scorn from the dear ones in the old Snowdon home? You cursed me once, Jimmy, or rather said that I was accursed. Do you remember it? It was the same day that made me a wife and our blessed mother an angel. They ring in my ears yet, those dreadful words, and they have been carried out with a tenfold vengeance. I am cursed, I and mine, but my punishment seems greater than I can bear; and now, Jimmy, by the memory of our mother, who died without one word of love from me,—by the memory of our gray-haired father, —and by our two brothers, whose graves I never saw, and for whom I never shed a tear,—by the memory of all these dead ones, come to me or I shall die.

"Patiently I worked on, until wasting sickness came, and since then I have suffered all the poor can ever suffer. Frank is gone; and from those I once knew in this city, I dare not seek for aid. Perhaps you, too, have heard that I was faithless to my husband, but of that sin God knows that I am innocent. The firelight by which I am writing this is going out, and I must stop. I know not where M'Gregor is, but I do not blame him for leaving me. And now Jimmy, won't you come, and quickly too? Oh, Jimmy, my brother Jimmy, come, come.".

*   *   *   *   *   *

It was a chill, dreary night. Angry clouds darkened the evening sky, and the cold December wind swept furiously through the almost deserted streets, causing each child of poverty to draw more closely to him his tattered garment, which but poorly sheltered him from the blasts of winter. In a cheerless room in the third story of a crazy old building, a young woman was hovering over a handful of coals, baking the thin corn-cake which was to serve for both supper and breakfast. Everything within the room denoted the extreme destitution of its occupant, whose pale, pinched features told plainly that she had drained the cup of poverty to its very dregs. As she stooped to remove the corn-cake, large tears fell upon the dying embers, and she murmured, "He will not come, and I shall die alone."

Upon the rickety stairway there was the sound of footsteps, and the gruff voice of the woman, who occupied the second floor, was heard saying, "Right ahead, first door you come to. Yes, that's the one; now be careful, and not fall through the broken stair;" and in another moment Jimmy Clayton stood within the room, which for many months had been his sister's only home.

There was a long, low cry of mingled shame and joy, and then Josephine was fainting in her brother's arms. From the old broken pitcher upon the table Jimmy took some water, and bathed her face and neck until she recovered. Then was she obliged to reassure him of her identity, ere he could believe that in the wreck before him, he beheld his once beautiful sister Josephine.

He took immediate measures to have her removed to a more comfortable room, and then with both his hands tightly clasped in hers, she told him her sad history since the day of her husband's desertion. She did not blame M'Gregor for leaving her, but said that were he only restored to her again, she would, if possible, atone for the past; for, said she, "until he left me, I did not know that I loved him."

Jimmy heard her story, and then for a time was silent. On his way to the city he had stopped at Snowdon, at the home where his father and mother had died, and which now belonged to him. He had intended to place Josephine in it, but the time for which it was rented would not expire until the following May. At first he thought to take his sister to his western home, but this he knew would be pleasant neither to her nor his wife. The old "gable-roof" was still standing, and as there seemed no alternative, he ordered it to be decently fitted up as a temporary asylum for his sister. When at last he spoke, he told her all this, and then with a peculiar look, he said, "Will you go?"

"Gladly, oh, most gladly," said she. "There, rather than elsewhere."

The lumbering stage coach had long since given place to the iron horse, which accomplished the distance to Snowdon in little more than an hour. Accordingly, the evening following the incidents just narrated, Jimmy Clayton and his sister took the night train for Snowdon. The cars had but just rolled out from the depot, when a tall, thick set man, with his face completely enveloped in his overcoat and cap, entered and took a seat directly in front of our friends. For a moment his eye rested upon Josephine, causing her involuntarily to start forward, but instantly resuming her seat, she soon forgot the stranger, in anxiously watching for the first sight of Snowdon. It was soon reached, and in ten minutes time the door of the old gable-roof swung open, and Delphine, whom Jimmy had left at Judge Howland's, appeared to welcome the travelers. On the hearth of the old fashioned sitting-room, a cheerful fire was blazing. Before it stood the neatly spread tea-table, and scattered about the room were various things, which Delphine had procured for Josephine's comfort.

Sinking into the first chair, Josephine burst into a fit of weeping, saying, "I did not expect this; I do not deserve it." Then growing calm, she turned to Jimmy and said, "Do you know that eleven years ago to-night our angel mother died, and eleven years ago this morning, you uttered the prophetic words, "when next I come, you will surely go?"

She would have added more, but the outside door slowly opened, and the stranger of the cars stood before them, saying, "Eleven years ago to-night, I took to my bosom a beautiful bride, and I thought I was supremely blessed. Since then, we have both suffered much, but it only makes our reünion on this, the anniversary of our bridal night, more happy."

Drawing from his head the old slouched cap, the features of Hugh M'Gregor stood revealed to his astonished listeners. With a wild shriek Josephine threw herself into his arms, while he kissed her forehead and lips, saying, "Josephine, my poor, dear Josephine. We shall be happy together now."

After a time he briefly related the story of his wanderings, saying, that immediately after separating from his wife he resolved upon an entire reformation, and the better to do this, he determined to leave the city, so fraught with temptation and painful reminiscences. Going west, he finally located in a small country village, engaging himself in the capacity of a teacher, which situation he had ever since retained.

"I never forgot you, Josephine," said he, "though at first my heart was full of bitterness toward you; but with improved health came a more healthful tone of mind, and in the past I saw much for which to blame myself. At last, my desire to hear something from you was so great, that I visited the city where your brother resides. I went to his house, but on the threshold my step was arrested by the sound of your name. James was speaking of you. Soon a servant entered, bringing your letter. I listened while he read it aloud, and wept bitterly at the recital of your sufferings. I knew he would come to you, and determined to follow him, though I knew not whether my presence would be welcome or not. I was at the door of that desolate room when you met. I was listening when you spoke kindly, affectionately of me. I heard of your proposed removal to Snowdon, and made my plans accordingly. Now here I am, and it is at Josephine's option whether I go away or stay."

He stayed, and faithfully kept was the marriage vow that night renewed in the "Gable-roofed House at Snowdon."

THE END.